Also by Debbie Burns

Summer by the River

RESCUE ME
A New Leash on Love
Sit, Stay, Love
My Forever Home
Love at First Bark
Head Over Paws

TO BE LOVED BY YOU

BY YOU

🐾 A RESCUE ME NOVEL 🐾

DEBBIE BURNS

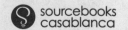
sourcebooks
casablanca

Published by Sourcebooks Casablanca, an imprint of Sourcebooks
P.O. Box 4410, Naperville, Illinois 60567-4410
(630) 961-3900
sourcebooks.com

Printed and bound in Canada.
MBP 10 9 8 7 6 5 4 3 2 1

For Wendy, Bree, and Ciara,
My sisters in spirit, I trust you know why better than I can say

Chapter 1

Ava Graham pulled into the High Grove Animal Shelter a solid six minutes ahead of schedule and snagged one of the last open parking spots. With the wild morning she'd had, the handful of extra minutes was a gift. An hour ago, making it here at all—let alone on time, let alone early—had seemed next to impossible despite the promise she'd made to her sister, Olivia. Considering this afternoon's dog wash was one of the few things Ava had been looking forward to all week, she was pleased on many levels.

Ava's eleven o'clock Saturday-morning real-estate closing had gone from bad to worse when her high-profile clients had come up with a handful of nitpicky items on their final walk-through.

While waiting on hold for the front-desk assistant to reschedule the closing for Monday, Ava fished out the first three wrapped chocolates she could reach at the bottom of her purse. Finding them to be one chocolate caramel, one dark chocolate, and one milk chocolate, she smiled. Too much repetition wasn't as enjoyable as a variety. Most everyone had their vices; Ava's was chocolate—sweets in general, but chocolate always topped her list of stress-relieving indulgences.

As the assistant clicked her tongue while combing their agency's packed schedule and the sound rolled over Ava's Jeep's speakers, she glanced discreetly at the silver van immediately to her left. The passenger seat closest to her was empty, but the driver was still inside. Like her, he was on the phone. She could hear the faint, muffled voice of a woman through his speakers.

A movement through the van's middle window caught her attention. Where she'd expected to spy a kid or two, her gaze landed on a dog, a big, adorable black-and-tan one. The window was too tinted for her to be confident of the breed, but the animal was watching her attentively, head tilted thirty degrees, as its handsome owner stared off into the narrow strip of trees between the parking lot and street.

A touch guiltily, Ava popped the dark chocolate piece into her mouth. *You aren't thirteen and bingeing in your closet*, she reminded herself. Grabbing a bite of food when she'd be occupied the next several hours was nothing to be embarrassed about. Like it or not, in the wake of her short-lived marriage, the resulting sale of the condo she'd adored, and moving into her sister's one-bedroom apartment until she had a better sense of what she wanted to do next, Ava had been feeling particularly uprooted, and this had her feeling not so far removed from the teenager who'd hidden in closets and school bathrooms to binge on brownies, cupcakes, and candy bars when the world was too much to handle.

Thankfully, two things had kept her afloat these last few months—her rekindled relationship with her sister and her decision to enroll in a yoga-teacher-training program. When Ava was on her yoga mat, everything made sense.

When the assistant let out a sigh, Ava tensed, hoping for good news. "Looks like we can squeeze your clients in at eleven thirty."

"Thank heavens." Ava let her head fall back against the headrest.

When the meeting time was booked, she hung up and settled back in her seat, popping the milk chocolate piece into her mouth and promising herself a nice, healthy dinner later tonight. While her clients hadn't gotten the keys to their dream house this morning, they were getting a two-night stay at the Ritz, and most of their demands had been met. It was a good enough way to go into the second half of her Saturday.

Before heading inside, Ava savored a few seconds of silence while attempting to work some of the tension from her shoulders. Just as she was opening the driver's-side door, a new text popped up from her sister.

> *Spotted you pulling in. The dogs will be here soon. Glad you're joining! Left a bag of clothes behind the counter. Find me out back when you're done with Tess.*

Leaving her door ajar, Ava responded by filling one entire line with alternating soap and dog emojis before dropping her phone in her purse. She was unwrapping the last chocolate—the milk chocolate caramel—and was about to pop it into her mouth when the big dog she'd been admiring rushed right up to her, planting his front paws on her doorjamb and pressing in to greet her.

Ava jumped reflexively before looking into the most endearing brown eyes mere inches away. He must've gotten out on the other side of the van while she'd been on her call. He was a big dog, no question, maybe eighty or ninety pounds, and he took up most of the open doorway of her Jeep, so much so, she could feel his breath on her face. His mouth gaped open in a playful grin, his ears perked forward but folded at the tips, and his tail was wagging. His expression, at once playful and pleading, was priceless, and his long, silky black and brown fur invited her to bury her hands in it. Whatever assortment of breeds he was, it was a big-dog mix that blended together into a ball of perfection. "Seriously, could you be any cuter?"

"Rolo! Down, buddy." The guy had gotten out as well and

was jogging over. Reaching them, he locked his hand around the dog's collar, gently pulling him down from Ava's doorjamb, causing the dog to let out what could only be described as a disappointed grunt. "Sorry!" the guy added, his tone sincere. "He's never run up to someone's car like this before. Ever."

Ava grinned at the connection between the dog's name and the chocolate caramel in her hand even before the dog was out of the way and she was able to get a good look at his owner. "It's okay. Rolo, huh?" Dang, the dog and owner were a well-matched pair. The guy was even cuter head-on, a grounded, classical kind of handsome with dark, wavy hair, broad shoulders, and a short beard. And those eyes—hazel green and piercing. They were more effective at filling her with a spurt of energy than a double shot of espresso. "Well, it was fated, I'm sure." She lifted the chocolate in her hand for him to see. "It's a Dove, not a Rolo, but it's still chocolate caramel." To the dog, Ava added, "I'm sorry, buddy, if it wasn't chocolate, it'd be all yours."

The guy raised an eyebrow. "How about that? There's some synchronicity for you."

Synchronicity. Ava had heard her yoga teacher say something similar more than once in yoga-teacher training. *"Pay attention to life's little synchronicities. They're like road signs on a trip with no map."*

Still looking at her, the dog whined and wagged his tail. Ava reached out and let him sniff her hand, his cold, wet nose tickling her knuckles. "That's for sure," she replied.

She was about to ask the guy's name when her phone rang out from inside her purse, its tone somehow considerably more jarring than normal and cutting right through the pleasant vibe hanging in the air.

The guy stepped back a foot, and his easygoing smile vanished.

"Hey, I'll let you take that. Sorry again." With a glance at his dog, he clapped his hand once against the side of his thigh. "Rolo, come."

He headed off in the direction of the shelter before Ava had time to reply. *That's it? Didn't we just have a little moment there?*

Rolo obeyed his owner but glanced back longingly as they crossed the parking lot, causing Ava's disappointment to settle in deeper. She fished out her phone from her purse to see that her agency had called with a potential lead that she wasn't about to take on right now. Her schedule was already packed to the brim.

Popping the chocolate into her mouth, she watched in her rear-view mirror as the two neared the shelter's front entrance, the dog trotting confidently at the man's side without a leash. After they headed in, Ava closed her eyes and rolled her neck in a few slow circles, wondering what exactly had her feeling so unexpectedly disappointed.

No dating until you're in your own place, remember? And even if his dog is adorable, he's most likely married with kids.

After a handful of calming breaths that helped wash away the lingering buzz of her chaotic morning and a quick teeth check, she chugged some water and hopped out.

The door to the shelter popped open as she was crossing the parking lot, and Tess, the shelter's lead trainer, stepped into view, a wide smile on her face. "Thanks for squeezing me in first. With as many dogs as we'll be washing this afternoon, I doubt you'll want to stick around long afterward."

"I bet you're right." Ava followed Tess into the building. It was awash with commotion and crowded with a slew of potential adopters talking to staff, watching the cats in the kitty play area, and browsing in the gift shop.

On the far side of the room, Ava spotted the guy again and immediately reminded herself she wasn't noticing guys on the other side of the room—or anywhere else, for that matter. He was listening attentively to Patrick, the quirky staff member who'd be coordinating today's large-scale dog wash, no doubt better than anyone else here could. Rolo was five feet away, standing on his back legs, front paws resting on the back counter, as he sniffed the shelter's resident senior cat, who was curled up contentedly and ignoring the giant canine checking her out.

"No doubt all this chaos makes it obvious why I'm proposing we do your class after hours." Tess motioned around the room as she led them to the only open adoption desk.

"No kidding. I'm sure the quieter it is, the better chance we'll have of getting the dogs to relax." Truth be told, in her two hundred hours of yoga-teacher training, Ava hadn't learned a single thing about introducing dogs to yoga.

"I can't tell you how pumped I am to offer this class." Tess's excitement was evident on her face and in her tone as she took a seat on the opposite side of the desk. "I figured we'd offer the first one as a pop-up class before we list the series on the website. I'm sure you know we have a loyal following who'll bring their dogs back to visit any chance they get, but I can't tell you how many requests I get for yoga with dogs. You're still good for starting this Tuesday?"

"Yep. I went ahead and blocked off Tuesday nights in my calendar for the next two months. I've found if I'm not proactive, I spend all my waking hours with my clients touring houses and at closings and such."

"That's like me and dogs. My fiancé asked me the other day if I dream in barks and whines instead of English."

Ava laughed. Having heard about Tess's skill with dogs, she could almost imagine that.

Over the next fifteen minutes, they decided on the flow of the trial class and came up with a list of poses to try. Tess would be announcing the class to the High Grove Heroes Facebook group, a group whose seasoned canine alums would hopefully be comfortable enough here to relax next to their owners. Ava decided she'd start the class with a few simple poses for the new yogis while the dogs—hopefully—hung out on their owners' mats. During the second half, Ava and Tess would help the yogis assist their canine counterparts in some beneficial poses for them.

As they were wrapping up, the drone of oversize vehicles nearly drowned them out. Through the wide front windows, Ava spotted three full-sized cargo vans and one small moving truck pulling into the parking lot. Brakes squeaking, they headed toward the back parking lot.

"Looks like it's go time," Tess said, standing up.

"It's hitting home how many dogs you guys are taking in with this rescue. That's a genuine convoy out there."

"No kidding. Between the new kennels and the two revamped trailers out back, we'll be doubling our numbers of dogs. Another twenty or so are going to be fostered by staff and volunteers. The rest will be moving through to other shelters. The plan was to expand slowly, but then this came up, and you know how it goes. On the bright side, considering the dogs' breeds, we expect they'll move right on out of here after they get out of quarantine."

Ava was having a hard time wrapping her head around how anyone could've kept upward of three hundred dogs on their property, even a for-profit venture. Growing up on her grandparents' farm, she'd found it difficult to divide her attention between the two or three dogs that were always around. "I can imagine goldendoodles and labradoodles getting snatched up fast. And what's the other breed, Maltipoos?"

"Yep. If Ewoks had dogs, they'd be Maltipoos, no question."

Ava giggled. "I can't wait to see what they look like. Speaking of which, I'd better get moving. I still need to change. I got hung up at a signing and didn't have time to run home."

Tess promised to meet her out back, and Ava headed to the counter for the bag her sister had left before locking herself in the nearest bathroom. She sifted through the tote to find pink jogging shorts, a sleeveless orange exercise tank, and flower-power flip-flops and let out a groan. *This is what I get for not having time to run home first*.

Begrudgingly, she stripped down and slipped into clothes that were markedly tighter on her than Olivia's clothes used to be. "I'm going to look like a walking sherbet cone. And an over-stuffed one at that."

She reminded herself that it wasn't as if she were here to impress anyone, and her thoughts immediately flashed to Rolo's owner, whom she'd lost track of while talking to Tess. *You have no one to impress, Ava. No one*.

As she stashed her purse, phone, and the tote bag in one of the empty lockers in the shelter's break room, it occurred to her how familiar she was becoming with this place. She wasn't an official volunteer, but today's dog wash would be the third project she'd be helping with in the last few months.

"You really need to make this volunteering thing official," Olivia had said last night, and Ava couldn't deny the wisdom in it. Her hesitation was her packed real-estate schedule and hope-fully expanding yoga classes. She'd been known to create time in her schedule that wasn't there, but even she had her limits.

She headed through the kennels, pausing to pet a few dogs who were pleading for attention. Her insides melted at the look an adult pit bull with silver-blue fur and matching eyes gave her. The sweet thing licked the flat of her palm and wagged her nubbin tail. Heart melting, Ava sidestepped into the break room where she knew a jar of treats was stashed and snuck a couple paw-print-shaped treats to the happy dog before heading outside through the rear exit. "Sweet girl, I hope you're snatched up quicker than those newly renovated condos in the West End."

Shielding her eyes from the bright midday sun as she stepped outside, Ava looked around at all the people and stations that had been set up.

Patrick, the newly promoted operations manager with an uncanny ability to retain facts and figures that would make him an MVP at any trivia night, was holding two orange traffic batons tucked under one arm and was over by the vehicles that had pulled in, talking to the drivers. He was dressed in a red polo and his typical cargo pants that had as many pockets as Ava had shoes.

Elsewhere, several of the staff were setting up what would soon be various washing stations.

"Hey, I was just coming to check on you. I see you found the clothes."

Ava turned to spy Olivia heading her way, her long, red hair aglow in the midday light. Ava's own mop was as black as coal and hardly faded in the sun. This and their eye colors, Ava's blue and Olivia's hazel, were the first differences strangers typically commented on when they found out they were sisters. They'd both gotten their mom's fine features and their dad's height. Beyond the surface, their differences expanded exponentially. In their teen years, their differences had driven them apart, but in the last year or so, they'd found their way back to each other again.

Noticing the playful grin on her sister's face, Ava pursed her lips. "Yeah, and I want to be grateful you helped me out, I really do, but I look like I'm about to teach an eighties retro aerobics class."

Wearing an old T-shirt and cutoff jean shorts that were fitting for a dog wash, Olivia stifled a laugh as she gave her sister a once-over. "You'd need a sweatband and a pair of pastel tennis shoes for that. Besides, just like I knew you would, you look cute. Though why am I not surprised you wear my clothes better than I do?"

"Why am I surprised that you wear these clothes? *Together*."

Olivia's suppressed laughter became hearty. "I can't say I've worn them together, but you're olive-skinned and can get away with it. I'm pale and freckled. You look great...and you fill that shirt out so much better than me." She rolled her eyes good-naturedly. "You don't burn, *and* you have bigger boobs. Not fair."

Ava waved her off. "Says the exotic redhead." She was about to ask where she'd be stationed when Olivia took her by the elbow.

"Come on. We're over there toward the back."

"To what part of today's chaotic venture have we been assigned?" She scanned the busy lot in the direction her sister was leading them.

"Washing station three, at least that's what Patrick labeled it."

"So, prepare to get soaked?"

"Better that than being at the shaving station for the dogs who are really knotted, if you ask me. Gabe's stationed with us, but he might get pulled away if any of the dogs are in rough shape."

"I can understand that, but for the dogs' sakes, I hope there aren't any." Gabe was Olivia's boyfriend of the last several months. He and his business partner, Yun, were the shelter's main two vets who were in the process of relocating their practice to the property next door to the shelter.

"Oh, and Jeremy's with us." There was something in the tone of her voice—a forced sort of casual that Ava picked up on instantly.

"Who's Jeremy?" Her flip-flops thwacked against the bottom

of her feet as they crossed the asphalt. Her heart sank and leaped at the same time as they neared the far edge of the lot where Gabe was standing underneath the shade of a towering tree. A few feet away was Rolo, still off leash, sniffing a row of buckets and sponges, and not far behind him was Rolo's owner.

So, this wasn't the last she was going to see of him. Not even close. She swallowed back an unexpected wave of nervousness the size of which she'd not experienced since early middle school.

"He's Gabe's friend, if you want the short of it," her sister was saying. "The long version is he's related somehow to Dr. Washington, the vet whose practice Gabe took over last year."

Please say he's single. Wait, no, scratch that. You're not dating right now, remember? Make that married.

Ava stopped in her tracks before they got too close, dropping her voice. "Hey, tell me the truth. This isn't a setup, is it?"

Olivia made a face before sweeping her hand in a dramatic circle. "You've got me. Credit where credit is due. It wasn't easy, locating a puppy mill to bust up and all that."

A half snort escaped in response to her sister's reply. "Sorry. I don't know what I was thinking. Wait, actually, I do. I was talking to Mom this morning, and she started the conversation with how she's hoping you'll introduce me to 'one of that nice vet's friends.'" She made air quotes at the last bit.

"Ava," Olivia said as they started walking again, "if I ever feel called to set you up without getting your permission first, I can tell you with one hundred percent certainty, I'm not going to breathe a word of it to Mom until *after* the fact."

"Touché." As they neared, Ava made eye contact with the guy again—with Jeremy—and the way her body responded, she might as well have swallowed a fish. It wasn't just his looks. Something about him called to her, something calm and inviting, like a book with a tempting cover to pull off a shelf and peruse while sitting in a quiet corner.

Only right now she wasn't perusing.

To breathe easy again, she had to remind herself she was the Graham sister who'd gotten her first boyfriend at twelve and hadn't had a dull year since that wasn't of her choosing. She was more than capable of navigating an afternoon dog wash in the company of this man without him distracting her from the big, hairy, audacious goal she'd set for herself upon moving into her sister's place post-divorce: figuring out where she'd gotten off track with her life and getting back on.

Chapter 2

SOME PEOPLE NOTICED CARS, OTHERS, SUNSETS AND BIRDS. JEREMY Washington, on the other hand, picked up on irony the same as Rolo picked up burrs in the woods. Here he was, a seasoned counselor for at-risk teens and creator of a burgeoning nonprofit dedicated to promoting their rebalance after trauma, yet, in the face of a slight change of routine, he was no better than an uprooted tree.

He wondered if it would come across as rude to move to a different washing station. Ideally, one where Olivia's sister wasn't in his line of sight.

After attaching drain hoses to the two mobile bathtubs, he dried one hand on the back of his cargo shorts, then slipped it into his pocket. His fingers locked around the two bronze coins he kept with him day and night, one marking his first month of drug and alcohol-free sobriety, his most painfully earned milestone, the other marking the eight years since that he'd been sober.

With as many service projects as his program kids had completed for High Grove the last few years, Jeremy was used to keeping his eye on a handful of teens when he was here, so it was no surprise it felt like he was forgetting something as they finished prepping their washing station. Still, he knew better than to pretend this was what had him fisting his coins and silently reciting the serenity prayer. Nope. It was Ava. He might as well be honest with himself.

He couldn't believe he hadn't made the connection sooner. As often as Gabe talked about Olivia, he'd mentioned her sister by name at least a handful of times. If he'd said her occupation, too, Jeremy couldn't remember, but he certainly hadn't connected the dots.

For months, while walking his dog, Jeremy had glanced at Ava's real-estate ad on a bus stop bench near his Lafayette Square home and had never once managed to remain one hundred percent unaffected by it. Black hair, blue eyes, a remarkable smile, that body. If he had a type, it was Ava Graham.

The thing was, Jeremy had worked hard over the last several years not to have a type. Like a grandfather clock with its multitude of parts intricately working together, his cram-packed life worked better that way.

Attentive as ever, Rolo was on his feet from where he'd spread out under the shade of a big oak a few minutes ago to watch the commotion, content to stay put so long as Jeremy was in his line of sight. Even amidst all the chaos, Rolo didn't miss a trick when it came to his owner. Over their five years together, the dog had connected Jeremy's coin fiddling with a greater sense of internal distress. He pressed against Jeremy's leg and whined until Jeremy bent down to offer him a reassuring pat. "Hey, buddy, it's all good."

Rolo circled back and leaned his opposite side against Jeremy's leg, studying all the commotion behind the shelter, his mouth gaping open. He then flicked his tail and looked up at Jeremy, his brown eyes focused and attentive as he watched for his next cue.

Jeremy had no idea what had made Rolo run over to check Ava out in the parking lot earlier. He himself hadn't recognized her until her phone rang; then he'd taken off with the skill of an old recluse who'd completely lost touch with his manners.

"Do you think he's thirsty?" Ava asked from a few feet away, having overheard him reassuring his dog.

Somehow understanding she was talking about him, Rolo trotted over to where she was dropping big sponges into the three suds-filled buckets to which she'd added a hypoallergenic dog shampoo and then filled them with water. He whined and shoved his head under her free hand in hopes of a petting.

Ava dropped the last sponge into the final sudsy bucket and sank onto her heels, fisting Rolo's wide jowls in both hands before giving him a hearty scratch. Clearly, she was a fan of big dogs who had no boundaries. When Olivia had officially introduced them earlier, Ava had guessed half of Rolo's breed, long-haired German shepherd, but had incorrectly put it to Rottweiler contributing to his bulky frame and black and brown fur rather than the half Bernese mountain dog that he was. "You're so cute, you'll melt me into a puddle, I swear. Those ears—the way they stand straight and fold over at the tips—it's almost too much cuteness in one package."

Jeremy chuckled at her enthusiasm, and she glanced his way just as he was doing his best not to notice how squatting brought out the definition in those never-ending thighs of hers. In person, her eyes weren't an ordinary blue; they were the sky blue of early summer. Looking into them made his lungs constrict.

Turning away, he fiddled with the hose connection to have something to do as they waited for their first dog. Why did it suddenly feel as if an afternoon of working so closely with her was going to tempt disaster just as strongly as an open bottle of Jack on his most stressful days?

While he wasn't the volatile mess he'd once been, he knew what he could handle, and Ava Graham didn't fit into that category. Eight years ago, he'd walked away from a short-lived and destructive marriage to a fellow addict and alcoholic after getting the wake-up call of his life. Since then, he'd managed to get sober, agonizing as it had been, and had gradually assembled a life that not only worked for him, but also was one that he fully believed was his calling.

He reminded himself he'd proved capable of doing hard things. An afternoon of dog washing with Ava Graham wasn't going to be his undoing.

"I'm sure there's an extra water bowl or two inside…or a hundred, more likely," she added. "I can run in and grab one if you'd like."

It occurred to him that he hadn't answered her about whether he thought Rolo was thirsty. *You dolt*. "Thanks, but no need. There's a dog fountain on the hill by the play areas. I can run him up there while you grab our first dog, assuming we're ready to get started."

Ava patted Rolo on the top of the head and stood, totally unaware of the roller coaster of emotions she was awakening in Jeremy. She glanced over at the small team of people unloading the crates from the truck and vans. "Sounds good to me."

Luck would have it that it was down to just the two of them for the moment. As the crated dogs had begun being unloaded, Gabe had been called off to look at one who'd drawn the concern of one of the drivers. When the crated dog had been hauled inside, Jeremy hoped it wasn't anything serious and selfishly wondered if his friend would be back anytime soon. Then Olivia had jogged inside to grab a pile of towels, leaving Jeremy alone with Ava and reaching for his coins.

As Ava headed across the lot, he called his dog. "Come on, Rolo. Let's grab you a drink." Rolo obligingly followed him up the shaded hillside away from the small crowd in the parking lot. The normally bustling play and training areas were empty for the afternoon since all available staff and volunteers were focused on the dog wash.

Proving not to be overly thirsty, Rolo still lapped up a couple licks of fresh water before returning his attention to the commotion below. That was life with Rolo; so long as Jeremy was fine, Rolo was fine. The irony that Jeremy was making a career of teaching people how to be the healthiest versions of themselves yet was the owner of a heavily codependent mutt was one of the finer ones in his life.

"It's only ghosts, boy, that's all. Once I get my shit together, it's going to be like any other day here, except there's going to be a few hundred dogs moving through."

He'd brought along a tie-out cable to use if he had to, but he was betting on his dog settling down once things got moving. Rolo wasn't jealous of other dogs, and he didn't mind how they passed their days, so long as he was within eyesight of Jeremy.

Jeremy patted Rolo heartily before heading back down the hillside, appreciating the hollow thump of his hand against Rolo's chest. At the edge of the lot, he pointed to the strip of grass alongside the tree where Rolo had been lying earlier. "Lie down, Rolo."

With a whine that dragged out like a protest, Rolo sank next to the tree in doggy slow motion.

"Good boy." Jeremy headed back to the washing station as Ava returned empty-handed from the other side of the lot.

"Patrick's bringing our first one over in a minute. I think he wants to make sure we've got 'the plan' down." She had beautiful teeth when she smiled and a great mouth. Inviting lips.

Jeremy flexed his fingers to keep from reaching back into his pocket for the comfort of his coins. "Sounds like Patrick. How well do you know him?"

Ava shrugged. "Enough to know he's both brilliant and quirky."

"That's him, all right. Just making sure you didn't need a heads-up about not having to remember every detail the way he does."

"I doubt I could if I tried." That smile again. "So, how long have you volunteered here? My sister said you're related to Dr. Washington."

"Yeah, he's my uncle. He introduced me to this place when I was a teenager. I've been doing service projects here with my program kids the last few years, but I helped with the occasional fundraiser before that." He nodded toward his dog, who was getting comfortable again, watching them and thumping his tail in a slow, relaxed motion that gave Jeremy hope he'd stay put for a while. "And I adopted him from here five years ago."

"No wonder he's so comfortable here."

He raised an eyebrow. "You wouldn't have said that when I first got him. To put it lightly, he was a mess. Twenty-four seven. It took a couple years for him to really calm down, no matter where we were."

Ava's hand clamped over her chest, and her mouth turned down in a frown. "That's sad. I hate when animals have a rough go of it."

"Agreed, though you'd hardly know it now with him." He cocked his head. "Unless you leave him alone. Then he's a mess all over again."

"Aww. I'm guessing you have to kennel him when you leave then?"

"I used to, but not anymore. Getting him in is a feat, and he cries for hours. Mostly I try not to leave him alone." He was about to mention Rolo's well-worn plush cat toy that traveled with him between the house and van most days but stopped himself. "My landlords are usually home, but they're out of town this weekend, or I wouldn't have dragged him to this."

As if knowing he was the center of their attention, Rolo plopped his head onto the ground, thumped his tail faster, and whined.

"I'm not even kidding when I say he's the cutest dog I've ever seen." When she made eye contact with Jeremy, her smile faltered for half a second before she turned away. "Here comes Patrick, and look at that dog. That's one of the Maltipoos, I'm guessing?"

He eyed the short-legged ball of curly, golden fluff Patrick was encouraging without much luck to walk alongside him. "I can't say I know my doodles and poos well enough to answer that."

She laughed again, soft and easy. There was a small, faded scar on her collarbone that looked like a sideways check mark. Everyone had scars, visible or not, but Jeremy wanted to know what had caused that one. "Me, either, but Tess said if Ewoks had pets, they'd be Maltipoos, and I have to say, I'm seeing it with that one."

Jeremy chuckled as Patrick gave up attempts to urge the dog along and picked it up. "Me, too, now that you mention it. And I guess one thing that can be said about all these hypoallergenic breeds is that no one here should be sneezing today."

"Actually, that's a misnomer," Patrick said as he walked up, overhearing them. "No dogs are one hundred percent hypoallergenic. Though you're correct these breeds with their nonshedding coats have less dander. But I anticipate that with the sludge that'll be washing off them, anyone here suffering from seasonal allergies will need a dose of diphenhydramine tonight."

Only Patrick. God love him. "Good point."

As Patrick placed the dog on the ground, Ava must've spotted the filthy condition of the dog's coat at the same time Jeremy did, because she let out a gasp. The poor dog was trembling, and its tail was tightly tucked against its hind end.

Ava sank down and held out her hand, but the dog scooted back as far as it was able. "You poor thing. I knew this was going to be rough. Who could let a dog get so dirty?"

"Two breeders with two hundred and ninety-six dogs in their care," Patrick answered matter-of-factly. "None of the ones we've handled so far have had much, if any, socialization. We don't have enough harnesses, so be mindful not to let them slip the leash."

When the dog had zero interest in approaching Ava, she stood, and Patrick passed her the leash. Olivia made it back with an armful of towels, her lower lip curled downward at sight of the dog as well.

Patrick surveyed their station, which consisted of the two elevated tubs that were portable dog bathing and grooming stations—something Jeremy hadn't known existed before today—a cart with several bottles of hypoallergenic shampoo and extra sponges, a hose with a soft spray tip, and the buckets of sudsy water. "Looks like you've got everything on my checklist. The focus this afternoon should be to give the dogs a quick wash to get the bulk of the dirt off. The ones who stay at High Grove will get baths again when they come out of quarantine, and I suspect the rest will get baths wherever they end up."

"As grungy as this one is, they'll need a series of them, I'm guessing," Ava said.

Instead of responding, Patrick said, "I believe you've been told your group is wash station three." As far as Jeremy had seen, Patrick had never been one for chitchat. "From here, if your dogs are matted, you'll need to take them to station five for the mats to be shaved off. Heavily matted dogs will need to be shaved before they're washed. We have two professional groomers working in there to do just that." He pointed to the mobile grooming van parked on the far end of the lot. "If their mats are minor or they have no mats, you'll take them to station seven over by the vans and the truck."

"What's at station seven?" Jeremy and Ava asked at the same

time, something that most likely threw Jeremy off more than Ava, considering the way it suddenly took all his effort to focus his attention on the conversation at hand.

Except for Patrick's unruly hair pointing in all directions, Jeremy could almost picture him organizing a battalion in the hours before battle. "It's where the bathed dogs will go to have numbered tags attached to their collars for assignment to our shelter, another shelter, or foster care. The dogs will get fed and walked before being recrated, but that will happen after you turn them over. Here at station three, you'll check your dogs for mats, rinse them of sludge, suds, wash, and dry them. Questions?"

Jeremy did the math. "So, with two-hundred and ninety-six dogs and four washing stations, you're anticipating seventy-some dogs will be washed at each station?" It didn't sound feasible, not even close.

Patrick's answering nod showed a confidence Jeremy wasn't buying into yet. "Seventy-four, in fact. We have thirteen more volunteers helping today than we did at our Dog Days of Summer dog wash last year, and that was for the public, so it wasn't as tightly run as this. A hundred and eighty-three dogs were washed here that afternoon—our standing record."

"Wow, that's a lot of dogs." Olivia's tone carried a touch of disbelief.

"We went through six bottles of hypoallergenic shampoo that afternoon, but I'm anticipating double that today as dirty as this lot is."

Ava's eyes grew round as she shot a glance at her sister, making Jeremy wonder if Olivia had given her any idea as to the scale of this event.

"With four washing stations and four to six people in each station, working diligently, I anticipate each station will be able to wash six dogs every twenty minutes."

"Six dogs every twenty minutes," Olivia repeated.

The dog on the opposite end of Ava's leash seemed to tuck her tail even tighter as she whined.

"Olivia, you know our dog-bathing protocol. I'll let you go over it with them, but I'll be in the vicinity if you need me."

As Patrick took off across the lot, Ava let out a breath. "When in Rome, as they say."

One thing was for sure; they were about to be busy enough that no matter how much Ava was unknowingly throwing him off-balance, Jeremy wasn't going to have a spare second to step away to clear his head if needed. He'd be white-knuckling it just the same as most of the kids on entry into his program.

Chapter 3

IT SEEMED AS IF THERE MIGHT BE A SMALL SPOT ON THE BACK OF AVA'S shorts that was still dry. Everywhere else, she was a saturated mess of suds and soiled water. How many showers did it take to wash away this many layers of wet dog on one's skin?

"Hey, Olivia," she said loud enough for her sister to hear over the spray of the hose. Gabe had returned three dogs ago—or was it four? Ava was losing count. At that point, Olivia had declared she and Gabe would grab a dog and take advantage of the second tub, leaving Ava to work with Jeremy, which was somehow both completely fine and not fine at all.

"Yeah?" Olivia said over her shoulder.

"Just making it clear I get first dibs on the shower…whenever that happens to be." A few months ago, she'd moved in with her sister in Olivia's one-bedroom, one-bathroom apartment. She hadn't anticipated staying long. As a full-time real estate agent, she really didn't have an excuse for not having found a place. She knew when all the best homes for the value popped up on the market for sale or for rent. The problem was, Ava might as well be in a canoe smack-dab in the middle of the lake with a varied and inviting shoreline in all directions. She had no idea which way to start paddling when it came to where she might want to live.

"And how is that fair?" Olivia dragged the back of her hand across a muddy smear on her cheek, both dulling and widening it. Fortunately, Olivia was enjoying her time with her extended-stay houseguest, at least when it wasn't boiling down to who was getting the first chance at a shower. That water heater of hers had seen better days—better decades, possibly.

"It's fair because this morning you included the words 'a few' when you asked me to help with this dog wash."

Olivia grinned. "To be fair, I was in my own delusional bubble when it came to the scale of this."

Gabe quit spraying the hose to wink at his girlfriend. "You can always come home with me and shower at my place."

Ava wondered if Jeremy was also suddenly warring with awkward images of Gabe and Olivia in the shower. A sideways glimpse showed his expression was as unreadable as it had been the last time she'd stolen an intimate glance, focused as he was on the dog in front of them.

The current victim of an unwanted bath was a gangly, almost full-grown labradoodle, whose hair was both long and tightly curled. It hung in dripping-wet springs close to his body.

Perhaps sensing Ava's attention had been pulled off him, the dog attempted to shake dry, showering Jeremy and Ava in more suds. They both reached for his tethers at the same, and one of Jeremy's hands locked over hers, giving Ava just enough sense of what it would feel like to have her hand secured in his and sending a wash of unexpected comfort over her.

Really now. You're washing dogs, not holding hands on a romantic stroll.

Regardless of what Ava told herself, her body wasn't listening. The occasional brushing of skin, the deeper baritone of Jeremy's muttered declarations as they worked together, passing sponges, rags, and the hose, and the soft whiffs of his scent that she could catch when they were close were better than chocolates of any flavor. For a reason she'd never have expected upon coming here today, Ava found herself much more okay with the vast number of dogs needing baths than she'd have guessed. As far as she was concerned, this event could stretch on into the night.

The dog's exasperated whines at being bathed and constrained caught Rolo's attention. After a good stretch, he sauntered over and gave the dog a half-interested sniff before pausing by Ava. He licked a few drops of water off her knee before settling down on the pavement a foot or so behind her.

"I'm still wrapping my head around how chill he is with other dogs." An hour into this and Ava had realized that Jeremy wasn't much for conversation. She could, however, get him to talk about his dog who mostly had been dozing under the tree since the bathing had begun.

"That's Rolo for you. For the most part, dogs are no more interesting to him than parked cars. Cats are a different story though." Jeremy's light smile drew her attention to his mouth again. It was that cropped beard, accenting his lips without over-powering his face. She stared a second too long, wondering what he looked like without it, and blood warmed her cheeks. Ava was almost as good at picking up on strong jawlines as she was a well-built foundation in an overly crowded open house, and the jawline underneath Jeremy's beard was anything but lacking. Above that, a hairline scar snaked through his left eyebrow, and more than once she needed to resist the urge to brush her fingertips across it.

Just then, the labradoodle managed to shake a large, sudsy drop right into her eye. Jeremy must have noticed because he passed Ava the hand towel hanging over the far side of the tub without saying a thing. Taking it, she dabbed until her eye no longer stung. "Thanks."

"How is it you two look like such a well-oiled machine?" Olivia asked as she handed over their shared hose. Without needing to clarify it, Ava and Jeremy had fallen into a pattern of alternating who did the sponging and who did the rinsing, switching with each new dog. Clearly, Olivia had noticed. "Is there a Dog Bathing 101 that I missed? God love him, if Gabe steps on my toes one more time, I'm heading inside to find a pair of rubber boots."

Overhearing, Gabe gave her a mock-affronted look. "I am sorry about that, but it seems to me your toes have been finding their way under my shoes." With a wink, he added, "But I promise to give them a good rubdown later."

Ava wrinkled her nose. "We can pass on the toe-rubbing visuals, please."

Jeremy chuckled heartily, which made Ava's heart sing. *Dogs, Ava, you're here to wash dogs, not to crush on a High Grove volunteer.* Seventy-four dogs to be exact. "What number is this?" She'd gone back to helping wash the labradoodle's back end while the dog kept yanking his legs as far from her as possible.

"Nine, I think, though at this stage in the game, maybe it's better not to keep count."

"Spoiler alert. Pizzas are coming soon," Gabe said. He and Olivia were washing a similarly aged labradoodle, making Ava wonder if it was from the same litter. "I overheard when I was inside."

"Oh, yay." Olivia clamped a wet hand over her stomach. "I was starting to seriously regret not packing snacks. I'm hungry enough to eat half of one myself."

"I could take on the other half." Aside from the chocolate, Ava hadn't had a bite of food since the toast she'd had with her coffee hours ago. "I can't imagine caring for this many dogs on a daily basis."

"Me either," Jeremy agreed.

Gabe tilted his head in response. "I suspect these guys received little beyond food and water. Their muscle tone is nothing to write home about, but I've seen worse."

"Did you ever hear what tipped animal control off?" Jeremy asked. The dogs had been confiscated from two breeders, sisters who'd lived in the middle of nowhere a few hours outside of the city.

"Yeah, they were caught at night on camera outside one of the shelters where they were dumping some of the dogs who didn't sell. They'd been doing it on and off for a while, not parking within range to catch their plates, until one day they did."

"I guess the saving grace is that they were taking them to shelters and not dumping them." Ava stepped closer to Jeremy as she got ready to rinse off the dog's suds.

Spying the hose, the labradoodle fought against his constraints again, and Jeremy's arm smashed against her boob. "Sorry."

"You're fine." As Ava pressed down the nozzle, she berated herself for not coming up with something more intelligent than "You're fine" to a boob smash. Perhaps certain apologies didn't require a response, particularly ones involving soaked-through shirts and boobs.

While Jeremy was wet, too, he wasn't as wet as her. The places where his T-shirt had gotten soaked clung to him as he moved, highlighting an athletic core. The writing on his dark-gray shirt drew her attention as much as the body underneath it. *There's no wrong direction to reach your center* had been screen-printed in what looked like handwriting on the front. The shirt had been washed its share of times, enough that the lettering had hairline cracks throughout.

Both genuinely curious and also wanting to fill the silence that suddenly felt awkward, Ava plunged ahead with a change of topic. "You know, I feel like I've been living and breathing yoga every spare second the last few months, and I have to say, I love your shirt. I've never heard it put quite like that before."

He stopped working for a second and looked at her, his hazel eyes reflecting a piercing green in a patch of sunlight shining through the leaves. "Yoga, huh?"

"Yeah, I finished a teacher-training program a little while ago, and I'm picking up classes."

"I'm not being partial when I say she's a great teacher," Olivia called over her shoulder as her dog began to do something while being rinsed that looked an awful lot like bucking. As Gabe attempted to corral it, she added, "She's teaching a class here Tuesday night. Gabe and I are coming and bringing our dogs. You should give it a try. As well behaved as Rolo is, he'd rock it."

With the dog under control, Gabe raised an eyebrow at Jeremy and directed a single nod toward his girlfriend. "What she said."

Letting go of the sponge, Jeremy stepped back a foot and grabbed a towel to dry the suds along his hands and arms. "You teach yoga?"

"Yeah, but I have to work around my day job, which is selling houses." Something about him seemed less grounded than he'd been a minute ago. "Why? Are you a yogi?"

With a shake of his head, Jeremy shoved one hand into his cargo shorts. Still practically at their feet, Rolo lifted his head and watched his owner, thumping his tail attentively. Ava wondered if Jeremy was fiddling with his keys and if Rolo had connected keys with a time to leave.

"I've not tried it," he said after a delay long enough to make her wonder if he was going to answer. "But I've been wanting to introduce it to my kids."

Kids. *Poop*. When he hadn't been wearing a ring—or had a tan line to show he'd removed one for today's event—the longer they'd worked together, the more she'd begun hoping he was single.

As she picked up the hose, she remembered him mentioning

something earlier about program kids. She'd meant to ask more but had gotten distracted in the chaos. "How old are they?" He was talking about introducing them to yoga; it was a fair question.

"Ah, let's see; the youngest right now is twelve, but that's atypical. My oldest is nineteen."

Considering he couldn't be a day older than thirty-five on the far end, it seemed safe to assume he was talking about the program kids again. "What is it you do?"

"Olivia didn't introduce you two properly, did she?" Gabe asked over his shoulder before his dog started the bucking thing again. "Whoa, boy, whoa."

Olivia flicked a handful of soap bubbles Gabe's way. "It's been a bit chaotic if you didn't notice."

Ava was taken off guard when their labradoodle spotted the hose in her hand and attempted the bucking thing as well, rocking the tub underneath him as he did.

Jeremy stepped in fast and held the protesting thing down by the tethers attached to his collar. "Easy, guy."

In the chaos, a coin from Jeremy's pocket rolled across the pavement. Catching the movement out of the corner of her eye, Ava rested the hose on the tub and stepped over Rolo to retrieve it. Her fingers froze just shy of touching it. On its bronze face was a large number one inside a triangle with *Unity, Service, Recovery* surrounding it. Even before spotting the word "month" under the one, she recognized that it was a sobriety coin. Growing up, she'd had an uncle in AA who'd kept a few in his pocket too.

Feeling as if she was trespassing in personal business, she picked up the coin and found it still warm to the touch. Stepping over Rolo again, she offered it Jeremy's way when the labradoodle was calm enough again for him to take it.

"Thanks." He slipped it back into his pocket without explanation. "To answer your question, I run a nonprofit for at-risk teens. I usually bring a group of them with me here. For liability purposes, they weren't able to help out today."

"Don't downplay it, man," Gabe said. "You landed a big grant and started a nonprofit from scratch. It's getting a crapload of publicity too."

Jeremy raised an eyebrow slightly as he glanced over at his friend. "Thank you."

"Good for you," Ava said. "I for one knew my share of kids growing up who could've benefited from such a program. Honestly, I'm sure I would've been one of them."

He huffed lightly. "You'd be surprised how many people say that."

She wanted to ask more, but the other awareness had her mind racing.

One month sober. The inflated rush she'd experienced upon realizing Jeremy's "kids" weren't biological—leaving the door open for him being potentially available—receded a bit. She applauded anyone for recognizing themselves to be in the throes of addiction and finding the courage to face it head on. Still, one month into sobriety—that was one rough road to travel.

You're doing it again. It was a habit she'd been working to break, internally debating the long-term success of potential relationships with near-perfect strangers. *You're washing dogs together, not going to dinner.*

As Jeremy continued to hold the labradoodle, Ava began rinsing the unhappy dog from the hind end first, allowing him to get accustomed to the feel of the water. "I don't know anything about your kids aside from the general universality of teens, but I can only imagine yoga being good for them. That is, if they're open to the experience."

Jeremy twisted sideways as the dog shook. "Their being open

to it has been my hesitation. That, and not knowing any yoga teachers who'd come out to the center."

Sobriety coin or no, Ava could feel the charm creeping into her smile. In the short time they'd been working alongside each other, she could list as many reasons as she had fingers not to pursue this crazy attraction to him, but there was no denying how much she wanted to give herself permission to do so. She didn't have to go far down the rabbit hole, but she could peek in, at least.

And that wasn't even taking into account his remarkable dog. She wanted to wrap her arms around Rolo and not let go. "Well, now that you do, I guess the question is, what would you like to do about it?"

Chapter 4

WHAT WAS HE GOING TO DO ABOUT IT? THE THOUGHT STUCK around long after they'd left the conversation behind. Considering how hyperaware he was proving to be of Ava's presence nearby, the safest thing to do was nothing. While they were at the center, his kids had the rec room in which to shake off excess energy. When they needed to calm down, they could retreat to the contemplation room or go outside to work in the garden.

The problem was, none of that helped them after they headed home. No doubt, this was why his go-to mentor for the program had been encouraging him to work meditation and yoga into their group-therapy time. He didn't doubt she was right, but he was best off looking for someone else—no matter how often she kept telling him to trust what the universe was sending his way.

The fact was, he had zero doubt Ava would be his undoing if he let her into his world. And he'd worked so damn hard to get to where he was.

His stomach comfortably full of pizza, Jeremy stretched back on the grass, propping himself up on his elbows. Rolo settled next to him with a grunt that seemed to declare he'd been hoping for another few bites of crust before Jeremy finished eating.

At best guess, they'd reached the halfway point with the dogs, and it was nearing four o'clock. Good thing he didn't have plans tonight. *Good thing you never have plans on a Saturday night*.

"When I was a kid and my fingers got wrinkled like this," Olivia said, "I used to worry they'd stay this way forever." She was sitting on the grass next to Gabe and had twisted to use him as a backrest.

"I'm wondering when you were ever around this much water for your fingers to get this wrinkled." Ava was walking back from taking their plates to the recycling bin, her flip-flops wet enough to squeak as she walked. "It's not like we ever passed our summer days lying around anything bigger than a kiddie pool."

Olivia pursed her lips. "You have a point. Then from baths, I guess. And we played in the creek, remember? Then there was high-school swim team."

Ava pointed a finger her way playfully. "I forgot you liked high school enough to participate in sports."

Jeremy was about to ask where they'd gone to high school when Olivia made a face. "Says the girl voted prettiest, best smile, and what was the last one? Most likely to succeed?"

Ava's gaze flicked Jeremy's direction for a split second. "That doesn't mean I enjoyed it."

Olivia opened her mouth, then shut it with a light shake of her head, heightening Jeremy's curiosity. All afternoon, they'd seemed as close as sisters could be, but there was an energy in the air now that hinted of a past that wasn't quite settled.

Still standing, Ava raised her arms overhead and stretched. "If I sit down, I don't think I'll summon the energy to get back up."

Forcing himself to look anywhere but at her, Jeremy reminded himself that chemistry wasn't necessarily compatibility. He spotted Patrick walking their way, rolling a flatbed cart with an extra-large crate on top. "If you're ready to get going again, I'm game."

"How goes it, Patrick?" Gabe asked as he neared.

"It's going as I anticipated. We're a hundred and sixty-two dogs in and one hundred and thirty-four more to go. For those who can stay through the end, we have frozen custards from Ted Drewes in eight varieties being delivered at seven thirty."

"Nice. Who can turn down Ted Drewes?" Ava said.

Patrick's forehead knit together as he set the crate on the ground near the washing tubs. "I suspect people with egg allergies and those on a sugar-free diet."

Jeremy pressed his lips into a flat line to keep from breaking into a smile. Patrick had proven not to be one for rhetorical questions, but even with people who knew this, asking them could be a hard habit to break.

Ava's eyes had widened just a touch, but she seemed nothing but earnest. "True."

Patrick gave the group an abrupt thumbs-up. "You four are doing well, you two in particular." He nodded at Jeremy and Ava. "Station three has the record of most dogs washed before lunch, with you two being three ahead of Gabe and Olivia."

"I didn't realize anyone was keeping count," Gabe muttered.

"Have you not checked out my spreadsheet? As a group, you're two dogs ahead of station one, and five above station two, so you've earned bathing these little guys." He stepped to the side and opened the crate door.

"Puppies!" Ava and Olivia sounded as if they'd just won the lottery.

Jeremy stood and wiped the back of his shorts, chuckling at the girls' enthusiasm. He could see an entwined mess of ginger-colored fur inside the crate. A closely knit jumble of puppies was sleeping, but two were awake and hiding out in the back.

"Yes, puppies," Patrick answered. "I estimate this litter of goldendoodles to be between nine to ten weeks old."

"I couldn't think of a better after-lunch pick-me-up, Patrick." Ava grinned.

Patrick paused, not seeming quite sure how to respond for a second or two. "Megan is bringing over a portable play yard so they can get some energy out while you're bathing their littermates. And I would give them the opportunity to go to the bathroom before you place them in the tubs."

"Good idea," Jeremy said.

As Patrick took off, Jeremy headed over to check out the puppies with Rolo trailing closely after him, no doubt hoping he was heading back over to the pizza boxes still on the snack and drink table. Rolo lost his cool when it came to pizza crusts.

Ava and Olivia were squatting in front of the crate door and cooing. Gabe caught Jeremy's eye and winked. "You'd think they hadn't just washed more than a dozen dogs under the age of one."

"Oh, don't be a spoilsport!" Olivia stood up with a chunky puppy in her hands. "Though fair warning, this guy doesn't smell so great."

Gabe warded her off by putting his hands out flat in front of him. "I think I'll hold off on snuggles until after their baths."

"More snuggles for me then." Olivia headed for the strip of grass as Megan, the director, came out the back door of the shelter carrying the collapsed play yard by a handle strap.

"It turns out one of the vans was full of a *lot* of little ones, so you'll be needing this play yard for a while. I'm guessing we'll be able to move a bit faster, too, judging by their smaller size."

"Well, no complaints here if they're this cute." Ava was cradling one of the puppies as well. "Though Olivia wasn't kidding about the smell."

"Poor things are overdue for their first bath, that's for sure."

Jeremy followed Megan to the grass and helped set up the play yard. Rolo walked along the circular pen as it was unfolded and snapped into place, sniffing the lingering scents from the last time it was used.

"Thanks for giving us your whole afternoon, Jeremy," Megan said. "Does it feel odd without your kids here?"

"It did at first. They'd have loved helping out today, though I understand why they couldn't. Honestly, them not being here has me thinking about fostering a few of these guys for you, assuming you still need foster help."

Her face brightened. "We're bulging at the seams with all of these guys we're taking on. If you're serious, you can have your pick, for sure."

After Jeremy promised he would, Megan headed off to take play yards to the other washing stations.

After all five puppies were inside, they stuck together like they'd been Velcroed. They took in their new surroundings with wide eyes, sniffing the ground and squatting to use the bathroom in a way that made it seem like they were taking turns. When a bucket was dumped at the neighboring wash station, the resounding splash had them scattering to the far side of the pen.

Rolo, who'd been hanging nearby, was looking back and forth between the people and puppies as if trying to determine what the fuss was about. He barked a baritone woof, making them scatter again.

Jeremy chuckled. "They're cute, that's for sure." They were a mass of awkwardly long legs, slim bodies, dark-brown noses and eyes, and a sea of dirty fur of varying shades of ginger and blond. "I bet this is quite a shock for them, isolated as they've been."

Ava clicked her tongue. "Thankfully, they're young. They'll adjust quickly, don't you think?" When Jeremy agreed, she brushed her fingertips against his arm. "How about you pick one to start with?"

"Sure." Anyone else could've touched him like that and not sent heat racing through his veins. He scooped up the nearest puppy to find that she immediately went limp and stayed frozen until the first spray of water connected with her feet. As Ava moved the hose higher, the terrified thing whimpered and cried and turned into a wiggly, hard-to-hold ball in his hands. "Something tells me none of these guys were offered baths until they were headed to meet a potential buyer."

"I'm betting you're right." After handing the shared hose off to Olivia when she was finished, Ava eyed the puppy skeptically. "She's pretty wriggly. Want to keep your hold of her, and I'll wash her?"

Jeremy agreed, but as she stepped in close again and he was no more immune than he'd been before the pizza break, he racked his brain for a scrap of the advice he was always passing out to his program kids. *Breathe, yeah, that's one.*

He focused on the puppy's slight body underneath her soaked, sudsy cream-colored fur. The unhappy animal continually picked up her feet like she was in a high-legged dance. "She looks like one of those trick horses, picking her feet up like that."

"She does." Ava laughed. "It's probably a good thing I'm absolutely not in the market for a dog." She used her shoulder to wipe at a mess of suds on her cheek. "This little girl is almost too cute to be real."

"Why no dogs?" Maybe talking would help divert his attention from the way the small bubbles of soap were clinging to the delicate bones of her wrists like a bracelet.

She shrugged sheepishly. "Technically I'm homeless right now and shacking up with my sister. Her one-bedroom apartment has all it can handle with Morgan—her dog—my cat, Cleo, and us."

"That makes sense."

"Hey, we're ready for the hose whenever," she called to her sister. To Jeremy, she added, "It's both a plus and minus of being a real estate agent. I think I know every fabulous nook and cranny this city has to offer in terms of great places to live. I was crazy about my condo in Kirkwood. It was right on Kirkwood Road and no more than a few hundred yards from a Kaldi's Coffee. It wasn't until recently that I realized my daily coffee purchases rivaled my monthly car payment."

He laughed. "I'm sure if I counted my morning trips to my corner coffee shop down the street from me in Lafayette Square, I'd be in the same boat."

"You're in Lafayette Square?" When he nodded, she added, "That's one of my favorite city neighborhoods."

"Oh yeah? Well, you'll hear no complaints about it from me. It's been a great place to live and work."

"I bet. Had I realized I'd be selling my condo a little over a year after I bought it, I would've made different decisions all around." She waved a hand dismissively and, after her sister passed her the hose, she began to rinse off the squirming puppy. Jeremy couldn't help but notice how naturally they began to move around each other again, like today was a dress rehearsal after a string of practices. "One of them would've been not getting married in the first place, but that's the gift of hindsight, right?"

His gaze went automatically to her ring finger. Catching the direction of his gaze, she added, "I'm recently divorced."

"He's a total prick, FYI," Olivia said, making it clear she and Gabe were following along with their conversation. She stopped washing their puppy and shook her head exasperatedly. "Like seriously, the biggest ever."

Ava smiled softly. "I love that you have my back, Sis." To Jeremy, she gave a one-shoulder shrug. "The marriage was a mistake on my part. The way it fell apart proved it—and proved I was best off with it ending when it did."

"Yeah, you were." Olivia flicked a hand dismissively. "His loss, no question."

Then Ava exhaled, her shoulders dropping an inch or two.

"My sweet sister will never forgive him, and I don't blame her. My ex stood me up on our first anniversary, and shortly after, he sent a text saying he wanted a divorce."

"Ouch. That's rough."

Olivia tsked loud enough to be heard over the spray of the hose. "Isn't it? I blocked him on social media after that."

"It was inconsiderate, no question. So was immediately shacking up with a woman he works with—someone he's known even longer than me." Ava looked at Jeremy again and shrugged. "Turns out, our marriage was the catalyst they needed to realize they wanted to be together."

In Jeremy's line of work, he could typically find words for just about anything, but for some reason, the best he could do was take the hose and offer her the towel to wrap up the puppy. As soon as he let go of the unhappy thing, the puppy shook wildly, showering them with a fresh spray of water.

He wiped his face as dry as he could with a cleanish-looking spot on the back of his arm and forced himself to start talking, trusting the words would make sense. "These things—when they happen—for the most part we end up being thankful for them later."

Ava met his gaze, her eyes blue and bright enough to shorten his inhale. "Thanks, and honestly, for the most part, I already am."

After Gabe took a short call from the project manager who was remodeling the building next door for his and Yun's new veterinary center, talk turned to the upcoming grand opening.

By the time the dogs were bathed, numbered, fed, and either transferred to the foster families and representatives of other shelters who began arriving in late afternoon or were set up in one of the shelter's available kennels inside the building or in the two new temporary trailers, everyone's energy was all but drained.

"Normally when I'm this tired and dirty, I soak in a warm

bath," Olivia said, "but I may well break out into hives the next time I even hear that word."

Everyone laughed, including a few of the volunteers within earshot.

Gabe pulled his phone from his back pocket. "You've got to give it to Patrick. He was dead-on about the time. We finished up a little before seven forty-five."

After washing up in the bathroom, Jeremy stuck around to have some custard, refusing to admit it had little to do with the custard and everything to do with a bit more time with Ava. Over the course of the day, he'd gone from seeing her as the woman behind the photo on the bench to a real person who was as kind and personable as she was stunning. At the refreshment table, he lifted aside the brown paper bag of dry ice at the top of the box and picked a cup at random.

"What'd you pick?" Ava asked, joining him. Now that the work was done, the groups were beginning to mingle with one another, but she didn't appear any more eager to part ways with him than he did with her.

He flipped it over to read the bottom. "Muddy Mississippi. You ever tried it?"

"Multiple times. Great pick. And trust me, I know. I have a thing for sugar." She closed a hand over her lower belly, making him wonder if she appreciated her goddess-like figure. "I bet I've tried every flavor they have at least once."

"What'd you pick?"

"The Dottie. A personal favorite. It's got mint, chocolate, and macadamia nuts."

While they headed over to two empty chairs, Rolo lingered by the refreshment table in hopes of a handout. Spotting him, Megan stepped over and dug through the box until she found what she was looking for.

"I meant to give you this," she said, walking over to Ava and Jeremy as Rolo followed at her heels, as if sensing he was about to score. "He was so great today, I ordered him a plain vanilla, so long as that's okay with you."

"Yeah, sure. He'll love you forever."

Megan peeled off the lid and placed it on the ground at Rolo's feet. As soon as Megan's hand was out of the way, he went to town licking the semisoft custard inside the cup. Like a pro, he locked the cup between his front paws and sank to the ground, stretching out against both Jeremy and Ava.

"Someone's day has been made," Ava said. "And how sweet; he's actually lying on my toes."

"He's big on physical connection. No matter what room I'm in, the second I sit or lie down, there he is right beside me—or on me. If he were fifty pounds smaller, he'd make a great lap dog."

While the worn-out group of dog washers began to eat, Megan finished thanking everyone for their hard work, and Patrick wrapped up with a few stats of his own, including announcing that Jeremy and Ava had held on to their lead of most dogs bathed and offering everyone at station three a ten-dollar gift card to spend in the shelter's gift shop.

Ava raised her paper cup of custard to toast against his own. "Well done, partner."

Jeremy grinned. "I couldn't have done it without you."

"I think I'll use mine on those homemade tuna-and-catnip croutons. My kitty loves them."

"Oh yeah? In good conscience, with as long as Rolo's been here today, I can't leave without taking home a bag of the sweet-potato-and-salmon bites that he goes crazy for."

As Patrick continued talking, Ava bent down and gave Rolo an appreciative pat. When Patrick's laundry list of stats no one else in the world would think to share seemed to be nearing an end,

Ava offered her cup of custard in Jeremy's direction. "Wanna try?" she whispered.

Dipping his spoon into her cup was a different sort of intimacy than accidentally brushing against each other as they washed the dogs, but he found himself doing it anyway. In six and a half hours, she'd broken down some of his barriers faster than he'd like to think possible. "It's good." He offered her his, which had turned out to be blended with peanut butter, chocolate chips, and pieces of sugar cone.

She started to wave him off but changed her mind. "I know what it tastes like, but it's really good."

He did his best to focus on anything but her mouth as she took the bite.

"So," she said, smiling at him when Patrick finished talking, "you should come Tuesday night. If you're free." She nodded toward Rolo who now had the rapidly disintegrating cup sideways and was trying to get every last lick. "My sister was right, I'll bet. He'll be the best-behaved dog in the group."

Jeremy huffed lightly. "You know, with all the commotion today, he may have come across better behaved than he typically is, but maybe we'll give it a shot. What time again?"

"Seven thirty. And it's okay if he's a little naughty."

Crap. Really? This flirting thing was flaying him open. He yearned to reach for the solace of his coins but flexed his fingers instead. "I have a group session that ends at seven. I think we can probably make it."

"Yay."

As close as they were sitting, he could pick up on the warmth radiating between their outer thighs. "Heck, it'll probably be good for both of us."

"I have zero doubt it will be. Yoga's like that. It'd be good for your kids, too, if you decide you want give it a try."

He cleared his throat. Imaging Ava at his place on a regular basis, his body was equal parts yes and no. "How about we get through Tuesday and see how that shakes out?"

"Sure." Her smile was slow and inviting. "I'm good with that."

Having licked up every last lick of his own, Rolo raised onto his haunches and panted, staring at their cups. Moving hers out of reach, Ava gave him a hearty scratch on the jowl. "You sweet boy, custard is one of those things that's only good in small doses. Too much, and you'd get yourself sick."

Ava's simple declaration stirred up a fresh slew of doubt. Jeremy had once been the king of not knowing when to leave well enough alone. He'd like to think he wasn't that person anymore, but he knew how challenging it was to truly leave the darkest parts of oneself behind. What reason he had for the spark of hope that, with her, he wouldn't want to spiral down that path again, he didn't know, but he'd be lying to deny it was there, hiding under the blanket of fear. Maybe growing a bit too.

Chapter 5

THE HANDLES OF AVA'S REUSABLE GROCERY BAGS DUG INTO HER palms as she headed up the split staircase to her sister's top-floor apartment Sunday night. She was already regretting all the impulse buys she'd added to the cart as she'd passed by inviting displays, starving and exhausted from another whirlwind Sunday at work. It was nearly 8:00 p.m., and she'd been going nonstop since ten this morning, holding two open houses practically back-to-back on opposite sides of town before spending the rest of the afternoon showing a new-to-town couple a string of condos, all of which they'd shown little interest in. When she'd not found five minutes to break for lunch, she'd broken into the last survival pack of omega-3 trail mix she kept in her Jeep.

By the time she reached the top-floor apartment, her fingers were going numb, and she was more than ready to kick off her heels. Days like this, she wistfully imagined wearing yoga pants and being barefoot as she taught a string of flow and restorative classes instead of being immersed in the never-ending chaos of the real-estate market. *Some day*.

Half expecting her sister to still be at Gabe's new house, Ava shifted the heavy bags into one hand and pressed the code on the keypad, unlocking the door. Morgan, her sister's lanky German shorthaired pointer, rushed up, wagging his tail and shoving his nose in through the top of the bags. "Hey, Morgs." Ava gently shooed him out of the bag. Raising her voice, she called, "I'm here!"

"Long day that was. Hungry?" Her sister's voice floated out from down the hall in the kitchen.

"Starving." Ava sniffed the air and kicked her sling-back pumps into the corner by the door. "Is that marinara? You're a saint, making dinner."

"It is, with eggplant and red pepper. I've been craving it all week."

"Smells heavenly." Before heading to the kitchen of the long, narrow apartment, she paused in the living room to scratch Cleo along the side of her cheek. The cream-colored cat she'd adopted a few months ago had turned out to be the most laid-back and chill cat Ava had ever been around. Cleo wanted nothing more than a window in the sun to watch birds and a lap to curl into in the evenings. Currently, she was curled on the wide windowsill, dozing in a fading patch of evening sunlight, and she began to purr loudly at Ava's touch.

"How was your day?" Olivia poked her head around the corner. "Open houses go well? Anyone wowed enough to submit contracts?"

"They were well attended. No contracts yet, but I'm sure they'll be coming in. They're both good finds in this market."

Olivia eyed Ava's bags as Ava followed her into the kitchen. "Let me guess, you didn't find time for lunch?"

"You know me, nuts on the run. I swung by the store to refill my stash and proceeded to negate any good I'm doing eating nuts by splurging on junk food."

Olivia dipped a spoon into the saucepan and blew on a heaping spoonful of chunky sauce as Ava began to unpack her bags. Morgan, who was still zeroed in on the groceries, had a counter-height view with his long legs. He sniffed the air, wagged his tail, and gave Ava a hopeful stare.

"Yes, you little doggy vacuum, I remembered you, too, while I was buying cat food." To her sister, she asked, "Want him to have this chew now or wait till later?"

"He's already been fed. Go for it."

Ava fished the specialty dog bone out of the bottom of one bag and asked him to sit while she tore it open. Morgan obliged but sank barely enough onto his haunches to be acceptable. As soon as the treat was unwrapped and she was lowering it in his direction, he swiped it from her hand and took off for the shag rug in the living room.

"Ugh. He lurched again. I don't know how you get him to be so still and patient."

"I've practiced with him more. He knows I'll wait him out." Finished blowing on the sauce, Olivia offered the spoon Ava's way. "What do you think? Too much garlic?"

Ava's taste buds watered as the rich, savory sauce washed over her tongue. "Mmm. It's perfect. How long till it's done? My stomach has been threatening to eat itself the last hour."

"All I need to do is cook the pasta. I put the water on when you came in."

"You're the best, really. If I lived alone, it would be a microwave dinner night, no question." While unloading her groceries onto the only narrow strip of open counter, it was clear Ava's sugar cravings were getting the best of her. Her stash of healthy items was overshadowed by dark-chocolate-covered almonds, two pints of ice cream, chocolate milk, double-chocolate brownie mix, gummy bears, and peanut butter cookies.

Olivia made a face. "You're the only person I know who wouldn't get sick just eyeing that much sugar."

Ava slumped. "You'd think by now I'd have learned moderation when it comes to sweets, as long as I've been struggling with this."

Her sister squeezed her shoulder affectionately before heading to the undersized cupboard for a box of pasta. "You know what they say, the first step is recognizing the addiction."

A memory flashed of jogging over for the coin that had fallen out of Jeremy's pocket and discovering it was a sobriety coin, and disappointment crept in all over again.

But that chemistry! On her end, at least. She'd thought butterflies like that had gone away with her teen years. Exhausting as the dog washing yesterday had been, the hours had sped by, and it had been dark when they'd walked to their cars together. As if realizing they were parting ways, Rolo had whined and rubbed against her before jumping in through the open side door of Jeremy's van. "So, I guess we'll see you Tuesday night," Jeremy had said, making her heart want to sing, and not only because at least one of the dogs in class was sure to be well behaved.

In answer to her sister, she said, "Don't you think it depends on the power the addiction has over you?"

Olivia gave her a sharp look that was layered with concern. "You aren't purging again, are you?"

"No. I haven't since I called you that time. Thanks to the abundance of cognitive behavioral therapy sessions that you pushed me to take." Ava had been nineteen then and carrying around the shame of hightailing it out of her hometown after a boy and not looking back, on top of all the reasons that had made her so desperate to leave. As much as she didn't want to admit it, she'd gotten control of her unhealthy coping mechanism, but she'd never really wanted to lift the lid to inspect all the reasons she'd started bingeing and purging at sixteen in the first place. That handful of late-teen years was the last thing she wanted to think about.

She opened the packed-full freezer and began to shift things around to make space for the ice cream. "Besides, I wasn't talking about me, not really."

Olivia checked the lidded pot for the second time in a few minutes to see if it was amply boiling. "What am I missing?"

With apprehension threatening to lock up her words, Ava closed her eyes a second or two. This was her sister. The one person she told everything to. "Jeremy—what do you know about him?"

Olivia's hazel eyes went round in surprise.

"And please don't make any more out of this than necessary."

"I'm not. I kind of thought maybe... I just wouldn't have guessed you two would hit it off, you know, given your dating history the last several years." Her cheeks reddened when Ava paused in her rearranging of the freezer to give her a look, and she added, "I mean, think about it. He's so outdoorsy...and he drives a minivan. Wes went fifty shades of white when he spotted a bug, and he drove a Beemer. And he was pretty typical of your type, that I'd seen, anyway."

After Ava tucked the two cartons, one rocky road and one mint chocolate chip, into the spot she'd created, she was pleased when the freezer door shut and sealed. "His fear of bugs was irrational, wasn't it?"

"I was afraid Gramps would find out and call him out on it. Nobody can make a guy feel like less of a man than Gramps, if you ask me. But Jeremy, he's great—really great. I think maybe a little scarred, but Gabe isn't big on airing other people's dirty laundry."

Scarred? He'd had such a calm exterior, aside from the coin, that Ava wouldn't have had a clue. "So yesterday definitely *wasn't* a setup?"

Her sister blinked a little too hard and checked the water in the pot again. This time the water had reached a rolling boil, and she left the lid off.

"I knew it," Ava said into her silence.

Olivia's shoulders dropped. "Truth? When I heard he was going to be there yesterday, I had this weird feeling you needed to come too. I know I'm always asking you if you want to go with me, but this was different. I wanted you to meet him—even though my rational mind kept insisting there wasn't a chance you two would be interested in each other. And then those vibes yesterday—wow! This intuition thing has merit."

"I'm not entirely sure those vibes were two-sided." After opening the container of chocolate-covered almonds, Ava grabbed a small handful and headed for the window overlooking the side yard at the far end of the galley kitchen. She planted herself on the stool and popped an almond in her mouth, resting her feet on the highest bar. From where she sat, she could see a robin, half-covered by leaves, quietly sitting on a nest in a sprawling oak tree. She debated pointing it out to Olivia but decided not to. Something about the moment felt private and intimate, and she didn't want to frighten the bird away.

"Oh, they were. Jeremy's well contained, I'll give him that, but they were *electric*. Even Gabe picked up on it."

Butterflies fluttered up her middle, and Ava swallowed them down. "So, what do you know about him?"

Olivia shrugged as she dumped in the noodles. "Honestly, I hardly know him. He's at the shelter sometimes when I am, but until yesterday it's been while doing service projects with his program kids."

"Do you by chance know anything about him being a recovering alcoholic?"

"No, why?"

"Because a sobriety coin fell out of his pocket. I saw it happen and handed it back to him."

Olivia pursed her lips for a second. "Gabe mentioned once that he thinks Jeremy's so dedicated to his kids because he had an exceptionally rough start in life. He didn't say how; I'm not sure if he even knows. My guess is that he heard something from Dr. Washington at one point or another."

Ava stretched to reach her purse on the counter and fished out her phone. Ignoring the two new texts from existing clients—she deserved twenty minutes to herself on a Sunday night—she typed in "Washington Therapy Center." She'd first clicked on the website last night after she'd gotten home and couldn't stop thinking about him.

"Did you by chance happen to notice the year on the coin?" Olivia asked.

Ava looked up from her phone to meet her sister's gaze. "One month."

"Yikes. But that isn't definitive, you know. He could have a whole slew of coins. Or it might've belonged to one of his program kids. Who knows?"

"I hear you, thus the question a moment ago."

Jeremy's site was clean and uncluttered with good graphics and sharp, clear images. On the *About the Program* page were images of kids, some close-ups, others action shots. Even before she'd realized one of the action shots had been taken at High Grove, Ava had suspected the photos were of real kids. They appeared to be from all walks of life, and most seemed happy.

Even though it felt like she was snooping, she clicked on the *About Jeremy* page and skimmed his bio for the second time but kept getting distracted by his photo. The picture had been taken outside in the shade but was close enough that she could make out the deep line of green in his hazel eyes. The hairline scar that ran across the top of his left eyebrow that had drawn her attention yesterday was visible in the photo as well. Yesterday, Ava had resisted the urge to brush a fingertip across it. Hearing that he'd had a rough past made her fingertip itch even more to experience it against her skin.

She scrolled down a bit more until she reached a few photos of Rolo with taglines that talked of him being a therapy dog who hung out in sessions, helping to reduce stress levels. In one, Rolo was looking up at the camera, his head cocked slightly sideways, and his ears perked forward. "*Oh, that dog.*"

"He's cute, isn't he?"

Glancing up, Ava realized her sister thought she was talking about Morgan, who'd finished inhaling the chew that was supposed to last the better part of an hour and was now planted directly underneath the groceries still needing to be put away. "He is, but I meant this dog." She held out her phone.

"Aww. Those eyes of his. They'll melt you straight through. Did Jeremy tell you what breed he is, by chance?"

Picking up on the affection in his owner's tone, Morgan popped his head off the floor and pricked his ears, watching her curiously. Her sister had adopted him only a few months ago, but there was no doubt about it. Olivia was Morgan's person.

"Yeah, he DNA tested him a few years ago. He's part long-haired German shepherd and part Bernese mountain dog with a little bit of something that was too diluted to pick up."

"No wonder he's so dang cute." Olivia gave her a pointed look. "I don't suppose Rolo's picture was the only one you were looking at, by chance?"

With a guilty flush, Ava scrolled up and turned the phone toward her sister again.

"Mmm. Look at *those* eyes."

Ava knew her sister was just being supportive. In the throes of her blossoming relationship with Gabe, Chris Hemsworth could walk naked in front of her, and Olivia wouldn't notice. Well, maybe she'd notice a little. "He does have great eyes. I kept feeling like he was cutting through all my layers and really seeing me. Only maybe that's because he's a degreed therapist, and it's a trick he does with everybody."

"I doubt it, not with vibes like you two had."

"You said he isn't my type, and I hear you, but I keep thinking it's the other way around. He's dedicated his life to helping at-risk teens. I sell pretty houses for a living."

Olivia stopped stirring to point the slotted pasta spoon at Ava. "I swear, you're harder on yourself than anyone I know. That coat drive you organized last fall was ginormous. And you pay it forward by making a donation with every property you close, which you started doing when you didn't have a dollar to spare. Besides, you don't have to run a nonprofit to corner the market on being a good person."

Ava closed out of the website and slid her phone back into her purse. "Thanks. I think my insecurities are still stirred up from this last year, is all." She nodded toward the junk food on the counter. "In case you hadn't noticed."

Olivia opened her mouth to speak but held it.

"I know," Ava added. "No one can make you feel anything without your permission."

"That." Olivia pointed the spoon her direction again. "If you want my advice… He's attending Tuesday night. I may not know him well, but I *have* attended your yoga classes. He won't be able to walk away from it without an Ava crush if he doesn't have one already. After that, just see where it goes. And take it slow. Guard your heart, and all that fun stuff. Blah, blah, blah."

Ava crunched another chocolaty almond as she envisioned herself attempting to teach eagle pose to an eclectic group of people while their dogs milled around. *While* Jeremy was watching her.

She glanced out the window in time to see another robin bringing a mouthful of food to the one in the nest, and an unexpected wave of wistfulness swept over her. That's how it was supposed to be, partners supporting partners, working toward a common goal. Only there was something about being human that made it so much more complicated.

Chapter 6

AFTER THE LAST PARENT AND TEEN HEADED OUT, JEREMY LOCKED THE center's front door and glanced at the clock. Seven sixteen. If he left right now and didn't hit any traffic, at best, he'd be pulling in right under the wire.

Even though he'd promised otherwise, a half-dozen reasons to skip Ava's class floated through his head. He'd made it almost seventy-two hours since he'd last seen her. No doubt, the safest thing to do would be to put Saturday behind him completely. He could text Gabe to pass along his regrets.

Don't be a douche. You committed to this, man.

He walked down the hall of the 2,300-square-foot space he rented that encompassed the main floor of the house and into the small kitchen at the back, Rolo trailing after him. An ancient rectangular wooden table that seated ten took up most of the open space. It had been left behind by the salon that had operated out of here before he'd taken over the lease. Jeremy's guess was that the kitchen had been used as a break room back then.

He poured a glass of water and pulled out his phone, finding he didn't need to scroll far to find Gabe's name in his texts. It was sandwiched between texts from his mom—who he was in no hurry to answer—and an auto-generated text from the women's shelter his last group of program kids had done a supply drive for.

Saving his mom's texts for later, he pulled up Gabe's.

You're doing this thing with me tonight, right?

As Rolo lapped up water from his bowl on the floor in the corner, Jeremy hammered out a response.

> Sorry, man. Got caught up here and going to miss. Give
> Ava my regrets.

His finger hovered over Send. *Give Ava my regrets*. Ava, who'd been in half his thoughts since Saturday. Ava, who he'd made a commitment to. He must have let out a long breath because Rolo stopped lapping up water and stared his way intently before letting out a single sharp bark. "You wouldn't look so eager if you knew what it is I'm turning down."

Rolo trotted over and whined, pressing against him.

"It's dog yoga. Actually, I think they're calling it doga, which makes the whole thing a step closer to all-out ridiculous. Ass in the air, head on the ground sort of thing."

Rolo stared up at him, ears perked and mouth gaping open.

"Yeah, I know. That's pretty much the way you stretch out from every nap."

Rolo wagged his tail expectantly.

With a light shake of his head, Jeremy backspaced through the existing text and typed out a new one before sending it. "You win. We'll give it a try."

> On my way. Pushing it on time though.

"Come on then. We're gonna have to hurry if we're going to make it." He jogged up the back stairs to his apartment. He'd begun leasing the 800-square-foot studio apartment on the back side of the top floor when it became available last year, cutting his commute to work to mere seconds and officially becoming neighbors with his landlords, two of the coolest eighty-year-olds he'd ever met.

He changed into jogging pants and a T-shirt—leaving his pockets empty of his coins and feeling naked without them—and grabbed his wallet and keys in the time it took Rolo to finish circling into a cozy ball in the center of Jeremy's bed. "We're not staying long enough for you to get comfortable, bud."

Rolo hopped down and trailed after him without complaint. Jeremy's phone dinged with a new text from Gabe as he was opening the side van door for Rolo to hop in.

No problem. Setting up a mat for you.

He'd forgotten about needing a mat.

The highway proved clear, and he met green light after green light on the side streets, so Jeremy pulled into the High Grove parking lot no more than a minute or two late.

It wasn't until he spotted Ava's blue Jeep among the handful of cars in the lot that his palms began to sweat. The closest open spot was the one sandwiched between it and Gabe's truck. Remembering how he'd wanted to do so much more than shake her hand when they'd parted ways Saturday evening, he pulled into the spot. He turned off the ignition, but his body didn't budge.

What was he doing here? Yoga wasn't his thing, and Ava Graham wasn't someone who he needed to move to a metaphorical Safe Senders list. By taking a class of hers, he'd be doing just that.

As much work as he'd done—and as deep an understanding of PTSD as he'd gained through his master's in clinical psychology—his father's voice still resounded through his head, telling him what a dumb shit he was, taking a yoga class. Jeremy's neck muscles tensed reflexively, bracing for the too-familiar smack on the side of his head that had most often been just forceful enough to be an attempt at humiliation and not abuse—most often but not always. Sometimes his old man had hit to hurt. "No son of my mine is pussy enough to have tears to shed." How old had Jeremy been the first time his dad had said that? Young enough to wonder if cats cried and dogs didn't. Young enough to get smacked even harder a second time for asking it aloud.

He was lying to himself to hope Ava would be anything less than a mistake for him—not after the way his body had been stirred by her. History had shown what a bad idea it was to give in to desires as deeply rooted as this one. As much drinking and experimenting with drugs as he'd done as a teen, it was possible, likely even, he'd have gone down the rabbit hole of addiction on his own even without his destructive relationship with his ex to sweep him there.

Jeremy's life so far had been like a series of building-block towers, most had been shoddy ones that toppled in a mess of chaos. His current tower of blocks seemed to have stronger footing than anything before it. He didn't need to bring in something—or someone—that would no doubt stir him up and throw in a measure of instability.

Receptive of his energy as always, Rolo whined.

When he needed to be backing up the van and heading out, instead, he was unbuckling his seat belt. "Come on, boy, let's do this. We're not doing anyone any good sitting here."

—⁓—

Although she'd promised herself otherwise, the quiet half-hour slot Ava had penciled in before tonight's yoga class had been sucked away by one client emergency after another, most of which she handled from her phone while in her Jeep in High Grove's parking lot. Her new clients in Olivette had declared they couldn't possibly be ready for tomorrow morning's photo shoot—an appointment that had been scheduled for over a week and was an integral step in their house going live on Friday.

As soon as she worked a small miracle to squeeze an early photo shoot Thursday into her photographer's overly packed schedule and was putting away her phone for the rest of the evening, another fire needed to be put out. The large, multigenerational family she'd be taking to see six different properties tomorrow texted with the urgent request that she call two of the property owners to ask if they'd remove their cats from the premises for the showings since their seventy-nine-year-old mother-in-law would be coming along and was terrified of them.

Ava hadn't held much hope in this being well received but had placed the calls anyway, confirming that both owners would only be willing to remove their cats on a second showing, not a first. By the time she'd broken this news to her clients, she'd been left with so little time to change into her yoga clothes before helping Tess get ready for class that she wouldn't be a bit surprised if someone pointed out she'd put something on inside out.

Tess's exclamation of how all available spots in this trial class had filled up within ten minutes of her posting it didn't ease Ava's mounting nerves. Nor did the fact that most of the participating dogs had a similar energy to ones about to be unleashed at a dog park. *Oh well.* Ava was focusing on people. It would be up to Tess to help with the dogs.

Thanks to some creative rearranging on the far side of the main floor near the gift shop, they'd made space for three rows with four attendees each and their dogs. As she appraised the room, it seemed they'd created sufficient room that the dogs weren't on top of one another. Most of them were, however, prancing back and forth at the far reach of their leashes and whining or barking at neighboring dogs, ignoring their owners attempts to corral them, while a handful of calm dogs were hanging out by their owners even after their leashes had been taken off.

As it neared go time, Ava took in the small crowd that included her sister and Gabe in the front row. Gabe's senior-aged golden retriever, Samson, was proving to be one of the most chill of the group; he was leashless as usual and falling into a doze on the mat next to Gabe. Morgan, on the other hand, was still on leash and prancing back and forth at the far reach of it in hopes of getting closer to the kenneled cats on display in the back of the room. Thankfully, Tess had had the foresight to shut Trina, the shelter's resident free-roaming cat, in the back room for the next hour or the yoga class would likely turn into pandemonium.

The empty mat next to Gabe made Ava's pulse flutter in anticipation. Not only was Jeremy going to be here, but he'd also be nearly front and center. Goose bumps popped up on her arms and the back of her neck at the thought.

"Are the dogs a bit more hyper than you expected?" she whispered to Tess. "Morgs looks like he's about to run a race."

Tess smiled good-naturedly. "You know, he does, but I expected a chaotic first class. It's going to be all about the treats to keep them in line until they get the hang of what we're doing."

After turning on the gentle flow playlist she'd created, Ava nodded toward the basket of clip-on pouches filled with treats Tess was getting ready to pass out. "Then let's hope those are tried and true."

"They are, trust me. One of our volunteers dropped them off when she found out we were doing this. Just watch. Once they get a taste, these dogs'll be doing pretzel twists for them."

"A few deep back and leg stretches will be a success in my book."

Tess pointed a finger in agreement. "I suspect there's going to be a steep learning curve this first class. Next time, it'll be easier."

Next time. Ava hoped this went well enough there'd be such a thing.

Envisioning a calm washing over her she didn't quite feel, Ava settled onto her mat on the small stage amid a small sea of battery-operated candles that she'd swapped out for the real-flame ones she used when there were no dogs running around. Once the class started, Ava would be the only one on High Grove's small stage. She'd prefer to be on the floor with her class, but there wasn't space for that here.

Soon, the ceiling lights were turned off, leaving nothing but the fading sunlight flowing in through the windows. To open the class, Tess ran through a short list of instructions.

"Should I keep his leash on?" one of the women in back asked when Tess was finished. Her dog seemed to have settled down fairly well after a rambunctious first few minutes, giving Ava hope the others would follow suit.

"While ultimately we'd like them all to be off leash, that's probably not a good idea while there's so much energy in the room," Tess answered before turning the class over to Ava.

Looks like it's go time, Ava thought. She was seated on her mat and had her hands folded in her lap. "Hello, everyone. It's an honor to be here. We'll start tonight by settling into our bodies and hope our four-legged friends begin to relax into the experience as well." With a pointed look at Samson, who was now stretched out on his side and snoring softly, she added, "Those who aren't already, that is."

As soft laughter died down, Ava led the group into easy pose and closed her eyes. As she did, the last bit of nervousness disappeared. This yoga thing, *this* was what she was meant to do.

"We'll start tonight by connecting to our breath. Imagine your breath flowing in through your nostrils, down to the base of your spine, and into your limbs."

She breathed through the next minute as the room began to go quiet, savoring the calm washing over her and soaking in the melodic tune playing over the portable speaker. She was about to continue her settling-in guidance when something warm and wet swept straight over her mouth and the tip of her nose. Her eyes flew open to spy Rolo pressing. Narrowly avoiding a second inundating lick, she ducked sideways, dragging a hand over her mouth and working hard to suppress a laugh that might distract the class.

Jeremy stood frozen at the edge of the spare mat Gabe had laid out for him, looking as horrified as he was attractive. She smiled his way as he mouthed that he was sorry.

Ava scratched Rolo behind the ear as the big, fluffy dog sank onto his haunches beside her, oblivious to the candles underneath him. His mouth gaping open in a big, easy grin, he checked out his surroundings from the vantage point of the stage, his long black fur glistening in the soft light and tickling her arm, his tail sweeping a few more of the tea-light candles out of place.

Most everyone aside from Jeremy and her were oblivious to the disruption, and some of the dogs seemed to be settling down. In the front row, Morgan had spotted a robin on the brick windowsill out front and had stretched out in full pointing mode, tail erect and front paw tucked. Beside him, Olivia was oblivious to his cues, her eyes closed as she relaxed into easy pose, the leash loose in her hands. Next to her, Gabe seemed to be attempting to work his face into relaxed submission while Samson dozed contentedly next to him. Sweet Gabe. Ava had no doubt that man would one day be her brother-in-law, and she had no complaints about it either.

Tess worked her way over to Jeremy and offered him one of the treat bags before heading to the back to help an older woman with her timid-looking spaniel who seemed to want nothing more than to head for the door.

Jeremy settled onto the floor and crossed his legs. Rolo hopped off the stage and trotted over, planting himself smack-dab in front of his owner rather than on the mat until Jeremy cajoled him with a treat to sink down alongside him.

After allowing space for another breath or two, Ava guided the group through a series of warm-up poses for the humans. As the stretching progressed, all dogs aside from the dozing Samson seemed to notice their owners were up to something unusual. A few pranced around their owners, wanting to be a part of their game. By the time Ava had everyone tucked into child's pose, body in a ball and head down, a few of the dogs were dropping into play bows and wagging their tails as if they were being enticed into a game of hide-and-seek.

When Jeremy tucked into the pose, Rolo planted both front paws on Jeremy's shoulder and sniffed around his neck and ears until Ava could see Jeremy's toned obliques shaking in laughter. The sight blanketed her in simple joy that reminded her of when she was a kid, making mud pies along the bank of the creek on a warm summer day.

Really, wasn't this what life was about?

From there, she led the group into downward dog. "Palms flat on the floor, feet planted firmly on the mat, we'll rise up, stretching our hips up and back." When one woman's terrier went wild barking, the energy in the room ramped up again. "This isn't a traditional class," she reminded them when the laughter died down, "so don't feel obligated to hold your poses with the same focus you might normally. Tonight is for you to bond with your dogs and get them used to hanging out with you on the mat."

"And," Tess added, "seeing that their excitement levels are picking up, this might be a good time to treat them again—once your hands are free, that is. And remember to offer these babies reassuring snuggles between poses."

"What if your baby's asleep and hogging most of the mat?" Gabe muttered, his arms stretched out to accommodate Samson as he did his downward dog.

"I would savor him exactly as he is." Ava's tone must've piqued Rolo's interest again because he bounded up onto the stage, circling her and wagging his tail. He even dipped into a play bow and barked. After holding her pose another few seconds, Ava guided everyone onto their mats again.

"It's occurring to me I should've leashed him for this part." Jeremy's easy smile made her heart sing.

"Not on my account. I'll take all of this dog I can get." Ava pulled Rolo into a hug as he settled down next to her, his tail thumping. "I planned to do this next pose, bird dog pose, in honor of my sister's dog even before I spotted him doing the pose a little while ago."

For the benefit of the members in the group who didn't know him, Ava pointed him out. After the bird flew off, Morgan had sunk onto his haunches as close to Olivia as he could get, as if he wasn't entirely sold on this new experience. "If he does it again, I'll point it out, though we may need that bird to fly back first."

Ava guided everyone onto their hands and knees and demonstrated the pose, savoring the stretch in her limbs and lower back after a day in heels. It introduced a bit of a challenge working around Rolo, but one she soaked right up.

"Imagine lengthening the back of your neck before tucking your chin into your chest. This is a great pose for helping to alleviate lower back pain, and one you'll want in your yoga arsenal."

After switching the group to their opposite hand and leg, Ava got a hunch the bird was back when Morgan launched straight into his own version of the pose again as he stared out the front window, as still as a statue.

"See why they call it bird dog pose?"

A glance in Jeremy's direction that resulted in direct eye contact got her pulse racing in an entirely different way. She could perfectly recall the intimacy with which she'd studied his face as they sat close to each other Saturday night, eating their servings of Ted Drewes. Surely, he'd felt it too. Hadn't he?

Now here he was, participating in class, and his dog had been without a doubt happy to see her again.

She thought back to the day her divorce became final. She'd spent the afternoon mapping out a plan for the rest of this year that was chock-full of things like plenty of time on the mat and loads of fun with her sister. Dating hadn't made it into the plan. If it had, a man of few words who ran a therapy center for at-risk teens and who at best guess was working through a crippling addiction wouldn't have been the profile she'd have dreamed up. At this stage in her life, she never would have imagined a man of that description might warm her heart and heat her blood.

But it was like her grandma said: even the best-made plans were sometimes worth ditching.

Or, at the very least, modifying.

As if he couldn't agree more, Rolo flipped over onto his back and wriggled his way almost directly underneath her, his feet pressing against her playfully and his tongue flailing.

And if that man also happened to come with this remarkable dog, well, that was one hundred percent okay with her.

Chapter 7

"THE NUMBER-ONE TIP HERE IS NOT TO FORCE ANYTHING. BEFORE you know it, this time with you on the mat will be the reward," Tess was saying. "You won't even need treats."

Coming in, Jeremy had had his doubts, having assumed this would be like teaching a group of dogs a few cute tricks, but he could see how it wasn't the same thing. He was always doling out affection to Rolo—patting, scratching, and petting him, letting him sleep on his bed, and giving him choice scraps after meals. He'd never, however, given his dog an intentionally soothing rubdown reminiscent of a doggy massage. And he certainly hadn't imagined doing so in a room full of practical strangers. Thus, the unexpected wave of vulnerability he was experiencing. At moments like this, it was too easy to envision his father watching over his shoulder, a calculating smirk on his face, ready to dole out a blow as soon as Jeremy's guard was down.

"Starting at the ears," Tess was saying, "rubbing in a circular motion, work your way down your dog's neck and shoulders." After a minute or two, she added, "Next, with the flat of your hand, apply smooth, gentle pressure along the sides of the spine, moving downward from the top of the head to the base of the tail."

At first, judging by the questioning glances Rolo shot his way, his easygoing dog seemed to be waiting for the punch line. By the time Jeremy had worked his way to the dog's hips, Rolo was relaxing and leaning into it. He even made a little grunt that seemed to say "Oh, right there" as Jeremy worked out a tight spot.

While Tess roamed the floor, assisting with the more anxious dogs and spending most of her time with an overstimulated Chihuahua in the second row, Ava was two mats over, planted in front of Morgan. She was acting as a barrier to help entice the now leashless dog into staying on the mat when the kenneled cats and occasional wild birds proved such tempting distractions. On the mat between him and Rolo, Gabe's senior golden retriever had woken and was soaking up the massage and grunting appreciatively with every stroke, making those around him chuckle.

As Jeremy reached the tip of Rolo's spine, Rolo sank onto the mat like his legs were made of warm butter and then rolled onto his side, half lifting one front leg and thumping his tail eagerly.

Noticing it, Ava gave Jeremy a nod of approval. "His timing is perfect. We're hoping to get them onto their backs next."

"Rolling over is one thing he's good at. Back when he was surrendered, he did it when anyone gave him attention. That's how he got his name. Though I think this right here is all about relaxation."

Earlier, as she moved between poses, Ava had reminded him of water and a gentle wind blended into one. She had the grace of a dancer and the voice of a sultry temptress, and the cropped pants and thin-strapped tank that fit like a layer of skin stirred up the sort of thoughts he hadn't had in a long time. It had taken considerable effort to stay focused on her instructions.

From what he'd seen so far, he had no doubt his kids would benefit from a yoga class with her. The challenge would be enticing them to give it a genuine shot. *Assuming you're dumb enough to ask her when you know what kind of mistake it would be long-term.*

By the time the dogs were on their feet again for standing leg stretches after being cajoled onto their backs for a belly massage and front and back leg stretches, a few of the kittens in the kennels at the back of the room had woken from their naps and were starting to play. Catching sight of this proved enough to be Morgan's undoing. He dashed over, barking and planting his front paws against one of the kennels. A couple other dogs were following suit when Rolo dashed off as well. "Hey, Rolo! Come here, bud." In all the times they'd been here, Rolo had never done anything aside from give the kenneled cats a good sniffing.

Instead of joining in, Rolo sandwiched himself between Morgan and the cats, barking his loudest, most baritone bark and backing Morgan and the other dogs away from the frightened kittens, who were dashing for hiding spots inside the big kennel.

"Well, look at that," Tess exclaimed over the barking as they rushed to corral the dogs. "I bet it's the mountain dog in him. They have a giant protective streak."

"I bet so, though I didn't realize his protective streak extended to cats, though considering his favorite stuffed animal is a cat, maybe it shouldn't be a surprise."

After they herded the dogs across the room, Olivia decided to slip the leash back on Morgan for the final five or ten minutes of class, and Ava caught Jeremy by surprise by sinking down to the floor in front of his mat. After giving Rolo a little scratch, she began rubbing downward along the length of his legs the way Tess had demonstrated on the Chihuahua.

"You're going to have to add 'cat protector' to that bio of his on your website," Ava said, her teeth shining white in the fading light pouring in through the front windows. Jeremy's surprise over her comment must've been visible because she added with a shrug, "I wanted to read more about your program. You're modest about it, but you're doing amazing things for those kids."

In the dim light, the blue of her eyes was a deep sapphire. Damn, if she didn't do it for him. *You need to say something, you idiot.* "Thanks. I appreciate it. And this has been great, by the way. I can see why they say it's therapeutic."

She raised an eyebrow enticingly as she stretched Rolo's front right leg and held his extended paw for a few beats. Rather than attempting to pull away, Rolo seemed transfixed. "Enough to offer it to your kids? I'd be happy to give your group a free trial class, especially if this guy can hang out during it."

"I'd pay you." It slipped out as an objection to her no-cost offer, not as a definitive yes, but he had a hunch it wasn't how it came across.

She raised an eyebrow. "How about if your program kids like it enough you want me back, we work out a deal then?"

After she gently lowered his leg, Rolo lurched forward, ready to douse her with a few licks. This time, she saw it coming and turned away. Undeterred, Rolo licked her ear until she draped her arms around him and buried her face in his thick fur. "This dog, really. He's too cute. I'll take him in the rain, in the dark, on a train. In a box, with a fox. Here and there and everywhere—I forget how it goes," she said with a laugh.

Was she paraphrasing *Green Eggs and Ham*? The unexpected-ness of it made him laugh louder than he should've, and a few heads turned their way.

"That reminds me," he said quietly after Tess gave everyone the next set of instructions. "Sorry about that assault of his at the start of class. That was full-on, wasn't it?"

"Yep, not filtered at all," Ava whispered as Rolo settled back onto his haunches and she began to massage down the length of his left front leg. "I'd say he owes me dinner for that much tongue action, but I'm not sure it works like that in dog world."

Jeremy smiled. "I'm not sure it does either."

They made eye contact again and that sapphire blue stabbed at him. "Then how about we split it down the middle?"

"Dinner?" Was Ava asking him out? The conversation couldn't have turned that fast, could it have?

She shrugged like this was the sort of conversation she had every day. Come to think of it, she was a real estate agent. Maybe grabbing a meal with someone you hardly knew between looking at houses was as natural as swinging by the gas station. "I'd like to hear more about your kids. It'll help me decide which poses to plan on."

"Yeah, okay. Tonight?" He racked his brain in search of an excuse but couldn't think of anything strong enough with which to object.

"Sure. Works for me." She stretched Rolo's leg forward, gently extending it to full reach and cupping his paw in her hands. His mouth gaped open, and he grunted again. "I think we may have found his new favorite activity."

This is you not bringing her into your life any deeper than you can handle? Great job. "Seems like it."

She gently lowered Rolo's paw to the floor and rubbed his ear. "Don't worry, Rolo. We'll go someplace you'll like too."

Up in Chicago one January in undergrad, he and a few buddies had participated in the polar plunge into Lake Michigan. Even wildly drunk as he'd been, he'd stood out on a frozen patch of ice before jumping in, knowing he didn't have a change of clothes and the long walk back to the car would take everything he had and maybe more, but doing it anyway. Now here he was, going to dinner with Ava, who was stirring up so much of what he'd done his best to bury under a mountain of distraction the last several years, and he didn't even have his coins with him. Discomfort lodged in his chest and stomach. Somewhere in the recesses, the child he used to be sat tense, waiting for the blow that would no doubt be coming when he least expected it. And he was going to jump anyway.

Chapter 8

AN INVITING WARMTH RADIATED OFF THE REDBRICK WALL BEHIND her. Ava scooted closer even though it meant closing the distance between her and Jeremy and possibly making him even more on edge. The fact was she was on the verge of having to run back to the car in hopes of finding something warmer than the airy, loose wrap she'd draped over her tank after class. She'd not imagined a nine o'clock patio-side dinner when she packed her clothes this morning, and the clothes she'd worn to work today were no warmer.

She and Jeremy had been fortunate enough to land an open table on the quieter side of SqWires's patio in Lafayette Square, though the music, a muted rock blend, boomed softly through the windows, just loud enough to drone out the conversations of other patio-side diners. A string of lights zigzagged the length of the patio overhead, and a single candle flickered in the center of the table. She suspected Jeremy was picking up on the intimacy as well, because he was sitting with his back straight and his hands on his thighs like he might need to stand up at any second.

He seemed like someone who was holding a thousand things in, and she wanted to know them all. Until such a time came that he trusted her, lighter conversation would have to do. Fortunately, she'd mastered such a thing over countless client lunches. She glanced across the wide plaza to the street where they'd parked. "I may not know you well, but I still don't quite peg you as a driver of a minivan."

His eyebrows lifted a little in surprise. "I can't say I'd peg myself as a driver of a minivan, either, but it works."

That voice of his... Even if the rest of him was tense, it was smooth and steady. She could envision lying in a bed next to him and closing her fingertips over the side of his throat to hear it resonating as he spoke. Realizing where her train of thought had gone, she blinked. *Focus, Ava.* "How so?"

"Before I bought it, parents needed to drive the kids to our Saturday outings. I had a truck at the time. It came in handy for hauling wood and tools, but a lot of the kids missed out when they didn't have transportation. So, last year I traded it in for the van. I ended up buying a flatbed trailer to haul supplies when we need to."

"Makes sense."

Rolo had planted himself against the wall of the building smack-dab between them and was watching the staff and other diners in a more subdued fashion than at the shelter. Jeremy had walked him in on a leash but had taken it off once they were seated. Ava resisted doling out another stream of affection his way since she'd already swung by the bathroom to wash her hands.

"So, your program," she said after one of the extra waitstaff topped off their water glasses and cooed at Rolo, promising their food wouldn't be long. "Was it something you started or took over?"

A bit of the tension seemed to be easing from Jeremy's shoulders. He brushed his thumb over a bead of condensation on the side of his glass, drawing her attention to his hand. "Started, but there are similar ones in other cities. One of the focuses in this field in recent years has been on how not to invalidate the coping skills these at-risk kids have but instead to help offer ways to develop healthier ones for their arsenal. You'll see, the kids come from all walks of life."

"Are they being treated for depression?"

"Depression and anxiety mostly. Some have even more challenging diagnoses. And they have a host of unhealthy coping mechanisms like eating disorders, drug and alcohol abuse, you name it. They can be hard to reach, but they're genuinely good kids."

"And you're able to reach them?"

He lowered his gaze. "Mostly."

But not always, his ensuing pause seemed to say. Ava remembered back to tenth grade at her rural high school when a girl she'd known since kindergarten had ended her life, leaving Ava to wish she'd stayed more connected to the childhood friend she'd played hopscotch with in first grade and slept next to at her first sleepover. "I can bet it's not easy, so I'm guessing it's rewarding."

The temperature had fallen into the mid- to low-sixties, and Jeremy wasn't wearing anything aside from the T-shirt he'd worn to class. Ava wanted to brush her fingers over the hairs along his wrist even as the defined muscles in his arm awakened her salivary glands.

"I can't think of anything I'd rather do," he answered.

She thought about the sobriety coin again and took a risk. "What drew you into it, if you don't mind me asking, working with kids facing such big challenges?"

He was quiet long enough that Ava thought he might not answer. "Addiction. And a rough start of my own."

Her lips pressed together, hoping he'd offer more but not wanting to push.

"I'm clean now," he added. "I have been for eight years."

Ava gathered her mass of thick hair in one hand, then let it fall away slowly. Eight years, not one month. *That's an entirely different story.* "That's commendable, and I think I have a small sense of the work it took. I had my own struggles to work through from my teen years, not drinking but purging. There were times when the road ahead was so daunting that staying on it seemed impossible."

Jeremy searched her face like he was seeing her for the first time after a decade of separation. "That isn't easy to come back from."

"I had help, thankfully. I sought it before things got too bad."

"A lot of people aren't able to do that. After seeing my dad's struggles, as often as I swore to myself when I was a kid that I'd never touch a drop, I was only twelve when I started drinking, maybe thirteen when I started experimenting with drugs." He sat back in his chair and gave a light shake of his head. "The truth of it is, even before I managed to get sober, I knew I wanted to be there for kids in a way no one was for me."

When a couple walked past after vacating a nearby table, Jeremy cleared his throat, and Ava sensed a curtain being drawn even before he spoke.

"So, what about you and yoga? Are you thinking of changing careers, or is it something you'll do on the side?"

She wanted to acknowledge his vulnerability, but he hadn't left her much of an opening, and she suspected that was intentional. She scratched at an eraser-sized crust of paint on the wrought-iron table, deciding whether to pursue it anyway. "Me and yoga," she said, cursing herself for chickening out. "I guess I'd love to teach full-time, but it's a challenge to make a good living that way. And the truth is, I've been doing pretty well in real estate—though I'm not always convinced it's worth the stress." She laughed it off even as she knew she'd never forget the all-too-familiar unspent adrenaline blended with fatigue that circled her body after a twelve-hour day of closings and showings and all the things in between. "The thing is, I never went to college, so it's not like I have a lot of options."

There was something in his face as he studied her; she could imagine his kids opening up for him in ways they wouldn't for just anyone. "I wouldn't let that stop you from doing something you feel called to do, yoga or otherwise."

"I keep telling myself that. I've made a promise that by the time the market slows down this fall, I'll cut my client load in half. This past year, I started catching myself not caring as much about getting the big listings and, even worse, forgetting little details about the properties I had on the market. Sometimes important ones even." She shrugged. "I eventually reached a point where the only time anything made sense was in yoga class. So, when my marriage proved to be as short-lived as a leap year, I dove into the teacher-training program. And I haven't regretted a single minute of it."

His compassionate look intensified. And that scar above his left eyebrow. Ava wanted to lean over and brush her lips against it. Actually, that was only where she wanted to start.

"After being in your class tonight, I have no doubt you're on the right path."

She wanted to downplay his comment—he'd only seen her do little more than a series of warm-up exercises—but words fled. The tiny hairs on her arms raised from more than the chill in the evening air.

Rolo lifted his head off his paws and thumped his tail, as if he were able to pick up on energy the same way he could catch new scents on the breeze.

The server, a younger guy in his twenties who exuded a confident charm, walked up with their appetizers. Ava had chosen the broiled goat cheese with wild mushrooms and flatbread, while Jeremy's pick had been the roasted wings and a Fitz's root beer.

The server nodded at the menus on the opposite side of the table, which they hadn't glanced at since ordering the appetizers.

"Just appetizers tonight, folks, or can I put in an order for something else?"

Jeremy glanced her way, and Ava picked up on the camaraderie in his gaze. "Up to you."

"How about checking back in a few minutes?" she asked.

"Of course."

As the server headed a few tables over, Rolo pushed up into a sitting position to sniff the food that had been delivered, his mouth gaping open in what looked like an eager grin.

"I'd like to say I never feed him from the table, but he's going to out me with all the begging he's about to do."

"Then maybe I should follow your lead on when to give in." Attempting to ignore Rolo's begging expression, which was even cuter than his normal ones, Ava scooted the plate of steaming-hot cheese in Jeremy's direction. "If you like cheese, you have to try this."

"Does anyone ever really not like cheese?" He grinned and took a piece of wedged flatbread, dipping it in cheese. "If so, I've not met them."

Ava dipped into the cheese with a nod. "Good point, but as far as cheese goes, this is amazeballs."

After taking a bite, he cocked an eyebrow. "Damn. You aren't kidding."

"Didn't you say you're only a couple blocks from here? I can't believe you haven't tried it."

"I get out to eat less than you might think."

Hello, he's a recovered alcoholic. SqWires isn't exactly low-key, especially inside. "Now that you say it, that makes sense."

His gaze was direct and unapologetic. "It isn't just the alcohol that's everywhere. I used to smoke. Sitting at a table, waiting for a meal to arrive, it can heighten the cravings."

"I can imagine that. My mom used to smoke before my sister

and I were born. She still fights cigarette cravings, and it's closing in on three decades for her." After another bite, she added, "I'm guessing you do a lot of cooking then?"

"More so back when I had my own place." There must have been something in her expression because he added, "Let me clarify that. My landlords own the space I operate the center out of. Edith and Eleanor. They've leased out the bottom floor for years—since back when the house was zoned both residential and commercial."

"What's the top floor then? Residential or commercial?"

"Residential. They still live upstairs, but five or six years ago, they had about eight hundred square feet divided off into a fully equipped apartment. Before I rented out the main floor, that apartment was rented to a professor at SLU. Last year, she moved to Scotland to teach at the University of Glasgow, and I moved in." An easy smile flashed across his face. "I don't have a single complaint about the commute to work, and my landlords love to cook and like company, so I end up over there for dinner quite a bit."

"That's cool."

"You'll meet them when you're there, no doubt. They're great."

He scooted the wing plate closer and offered her one. "Mmm. I'd say no, but that honey-and-mustard-sesame sauce they're brushed with makes doing so impossible." As she took one, their hands touched, sending an electric charge up Ava's arm, maybe his arm, too, based on the way he shifted in his chair.

She took a bite, savoring the flavors exploding over her tongue. "Sounds like you've got an amazing setup."

"I've got no complaints. The time and money I've saved has mostly gone into growing the center. I'd planned on buying my own place by now, but Edith and Eleanor are talking on and off about selling the house, and I'm hanging on to see how it plays out. It'd be nice to keep running the center out of there, and if I owned the place, there's a lot I'd do to it."

"Well, you can't go wrong buying property in Lafayette Square. Not with all this Victorian charm around here." She waved a hand toward the side of the restaurant. "Like these arched brick window frames. And the brick in general. Can you imagine the cost of building something so massive nowadays exclusively out of brick?"

Jeremy studied the restaurant that was formerly Western Wire Manufacturing and spanned a full city block. "It would be exorbitant, that's for sure."

"Since you live here, you probably know this, but I love that Lafayette Park's the oldest city park west of the Mississippi."

"I've heard that," he said, grinning. "I've also heard it said that we St. Louisans stoke our love of being first by adding 'west of the Mississippi' to a good majority of our 'first' claims."

She locked a hand over his wrist just long enough to realize she was doing it. "Not toasted ravioli, I hope. Please tell me we get real dibs on deep frying meat-filled pillows of dough?"

His laugh was infectious. "You're safe. I'm pretty sure that first was nationwide. Maybe even worldwide."

"Well, that's a relief. My disappointment over the ice cream cone not first being served at the 1904 World's Fair was disappointment enough."

The server returned before either of them had thought to look at the menu, and Rolo rose to all fours expectantly. "Anything tempting you?"

Um, a make-out session in Jeremy's van? Aloud, she turned to Jeremy and said, "Up to you."

After tossing out a few options, they agreed on splitting the pizza of the day.

"Anything else to drink?" the server asked, collecting the menus.

"Just water for me."

"I'm fine too." When the server walked away, Jeremy brushed the tips of his fingers over Ava's hand, sending a jolt of electricity all the way down into her toes. "Just so we're clear, I can handle people around me drinking without any problems, if you'd like to order something."

She nodded. "I was debating whether to order something and would have checked with you first, but it's nine o'clock on a Tuesday, and I have an early day tomorrow." After finishing another bite of cheese, she took the conversation in another direction. "Back to what you said earlier about not being able to think of anything you'd rather do, I've been thinking about that a lot lately—what I'd do if I could do anything I wanted."

"And do you have an answer?"

"I do, actually. I'd open my own yoga studio, one with a ton of windows and natural light, and I'd have my dad come up and do the windows."

Jeremy wiped his mouth after finishing another wing dipped into the spiced mustard sesame sauce. "Sounds like an obtainable dream to me. And what do you mean 'have your father do the windows'?"

"My dad's a stained-glass artist. He's great at it too."

"Really? That's impressive."

"Thanks, but probably not as impressive when you know how little a stained-glass artist in the Bootheel makes for a living."

"Sometimes it's all about location when it comes to being an artist."

"I hear you. When I was little, sometimes I'd go along on his jobs. Mostly he works in churches, repairing old windows and whatnot. I remember how I used to love sitting in a patch of sunlight that was streaming through the glass and feeling it warm my body. It was like magic, reflecting on my skin in an array of different colors." Thinking of it, that simple, contented joy she'd experienced fanned to life. "I had no idea what yoga was back then, but most of the time, it turns out I was sitting in easy pose. And sometimes I'd lie on my back with my arms spread out, palms up, which it turns out is another pose called savasana—the one at the end of class tonight. Before I started yoga, I don't think I'd connected with that sort of peace in years."

Jeremy wiped his hands before taking a drink of water. "That's cool. I hope you get to open that studio and your dad gets to do the windows."

"Thanks. Sometimes I think about all the money and time I lost in my last relationship and over the course of my marriage and get frustrated I didn't channel it elsewhere, but I've been thinking about what you said at High Grove the other day about how, when these things happen, we end up being thankful for them later, and you're right. I don't think I ever would've reconnected with my love for that stillness had I not gone through that unhappy phase, and that is what I found in yoga."

As he took in her words, Jeremy licked at a bit of seasoning on the tip of his thumb, and Ava nearly lost her train of thought.

He sat back in his chair. "I was married too," he said. "A long time ago. It's that way for me too. There are parts of the experience that still haunt me, but you're right. Without those not-so-great parts, I wouldn't have been spurred into seeking the career I sought."

Ava blinked, taking this in. Since that first meeting, she'd not imagined Jeremy as having been married before, though he was no doubt a handful of years older than her, so it shouldn't have come as such a surprise. "Do you mind if I ask how old you were?" It wasn't polite, but it poured out before she could stop herself. She wanted to know more than his age; she wanted the whole story. "Because I'm having a hard time digesting the long-time-ago part."

"I was twenty-one when I got married. Twenty-four when I left."

When he left. So, he was the one who walked away. As this sank in, Ava took another wing when he offered the plate again. Still planted between them, Rolo whined as if to remind them he was still waiting for his share.

"Dinner's coming, bud."

"So, that makes you thirty-two now?" she asked after doing the math in her head. "You said that bit before about being eight years sober," she added in explanation. She wondered where Jeremy's ex-wife was now and if she was thankful for the experience like he suggested, regardless of how painful their end had been.

"Yeah, right at it." After wiping his hands, he reached into his pocket and gave a light shake of his head.

She could sense his guard raising and figured the walls he'd built around himself in defense were likely very thick. "It's not the same thing, but it's been seven for me, and I can't say I ever feel one hundred percent past it, especially a few months ago when my life was imploding. I haven't purged and won't ever go there again, but the need to find solace in food, especially sugar, that's my struggle. I'm sharing this because I want you to know I sympathize with what you probably deal with on a daily basis, with sobriety and all."

"Thank you. Most of the time, I'm pretty convinced I'm winning."

"You certainly seem to be to me."

Ava hoped he'd offer more, but he did nothing other than raise an eyebrow. After a handful of seconds, he said, "Sugar addictions aren't easy to overcome either."

"And sweets are so accessible, anywhere at any time, and no one will be the wiser."

"Which do you struggle with more, chocolate or sugar?"

"Ahh, both, if you want the truth. That Ted Drewes was pretty killer. Kaldi's house-made vanilla lattes are a close second. But I'm not that picky. I can work my way through a package of Sprees faster than the average third grader when I'm really stressing."

Jeremy laughed and nodded toward his plate. "My downfall this side of sobriety tends to be wings, and usually with fries and a Fitz's root beer. A bit less accessible than Sprees, but no healthier. I had an addiction to Tic Tacs and sugar-free gum those first couple years after I quit smoking too."

"Oh, Tic Tacs, love 'em. I'm not one to chew gum though. I need to swallow for it to be satisfying." As soon as the words were out, Ava froze with a bite of flatbread mounded with cheese almost to her mouth. *Really, Ava?*

She scrambled to think of how to fill the silence as Jeremy ducked his head and cleared his throat, clearly suppressing a chuckle. "Moving on," she said, heat warming her cheeks. "Ah, let's see. What else would you never guess about me? Oh, I know. I can drive a combine. And I can consistently skip rocks six times; my record is eight."

"Impressive. And I don't why, but I can totally see you on a combine."

"Then you're about the only one." For some reason, this really touched her. "Oh, and when I was fourteen, I won a watermelon-seed-spitting contest at the county fair."

Jeremy laughed again, a deep, easy rolling laugh that sent a wave of happiness across her. "I knew your sister grew up on a farm, but this shows it really is in the details."

"Amen to that. It's the details that bring it all back for me. We spent our childhood smack-dab in the middle of nowhere. Fields of cotton and corn, stretching out into the ends of the earth." A soft sigh escaped as a wave of homesickness swept over her. "Though you know what they say about taking the girl out of the country and not vice versa. When I go home, the twang still slips out like a leaky faucet for days afterward."

"Like 'fordy' instead of forty?"

She pointed a finger his direction. "Guilty as charged."

"The twang runs deep in my family too. And I don't have the same excuse. I grew up less than fifteen minutes from the Arch."

"St. Louis is a melting pot of twangisms, among other things." She was about to ask where he'd grown up when he added, "So, what brought you to St. Louis?"

"A boy." She looked down and refolded her napkin. He was too darn practiced about leaving her the space to fill in the silence. "The summer after my senior year, I went away to be a camp counselor. When the job was over, I followed a boy I'd met there to St. Louis. I was the talk of my hometown forever."

"In a small town like that, I imagine so."

"It didn't work out, as you've no doubt guessed, but I stayed here anyway. Going home, that would've been facing a mountain of shame I wasn't ready to deal with."

"That was when you got into real estate?"

"First, I waited tables and took a few classes at the community college. It took a couple years before I got into real estate, but once I did, I never slowed down."

"And here you are."

She smiled. "Here I am. So, what about you?"

He wiped his hands on his napkin and sat back in his chair again. "Pretty much what you see is what you get."

"You don't like talking about yourself, do you?"

"I think I've grown accustomed to listening. Hazard of the trade and all."

"How about I give you a starter?" When he didn't object, Ava went with it. "My name's Jeremy Washington, I'm thirty-two years old. I run a program for at-risk kids, and I have a soft heart when it comes to rescue dogs." As if sensing a change in their energy, Rolo looked back and forth between them, then shoved his head under Ava's arm. Ava rested her temple against his forehead a few seconds before continuing. "I married who I thought was the girl of my dreams when I was twenty-one but didn't have things as together as I thought. After acquiring a host of addictions, I wizened up and quit them cold turkey and decided going it alone was the healthiest route for me." She paused. "Warm?"

"Warm enough."

"So, we divorced, and I went to school to be a—what are you, a therapist or social worker?"

"I'm a licensed clinical social worker, but yeah, I've crossed over more into therapy than social work the last few years."

Ava nodded. "Now I'm a social worker turned therapist whose cigarette cravings threaten to be my undoing some days, and about once a week, I give in and devour a meal of wings and fries, chickens be damned."

That laugh of his again. It was more rewarding than an entire carton of Ben & Jerry's.

"There you go," he said. "I told you quite a bit, didn't I?"

"Sort of, though on a trip from St. Louis to LA, that's nearly all Interstate 70 with a few pull-offs to fill the tank. Where's your colorful side roads, Jeremy? Like you said, it's all in the details."

A smile spread across his face as he shook his head. "The kids'll love you."

"Let's hope. I'm worried being around teenagers again might bring back those dreams where I'm walking into school without my pants. And please don't psychoanalyze that."

With an easy laugh, Jeremy agreed with her request.

She was finishing off another wedge of bread dipped in cheese when she spied their server walking over with their pizza. The sharp ache of hunger was already easing, and she'd adjusted to the temperature enough to want to stay out here with him all night.

She wanted to help break down those walls of his and get him talking. Even more so, she wanted to be a safe enough space for him that he'd let them down on his own. Like when she was a kid sitting in a ray of sunlight passing through stained glass, around him, she felt alive with all the color she'd been missing.

This connection between them wasn't something to ignore, no matter that it hadn't been in her plans — no matter that it was going to be harder for him to acknowledge it than it was her. Like Rolo, sitting between them patiently waiting for a bite to pass his way, Ava knew what she wanted, and she had time on her side.

Chapter 9

FIFTEEN MINUTES BEFORE HIS ALARM WAS SET TO GO OFF, JEREMY woke up in a still-dark room to Rolo at the far bedroom window, front paws planted on the windowsill, whining repeatedly as he stared outside, tail wagging. "What is it, bud?"

Rolo let out an exaggerated whine that stretched several beats, as if attempting to prove whatever raccoon or squirrel or creature had captured his attention was the most important thing on earth. Come to think of it, to Rolo, it likely was.

Jeremy rolled onto his back and dragged a hand over his face. He scratched the short beard he'd grown over winter, debating how soon to shave it off, something he always did when the weather grew warmer. He was groggy but uniquely energized for five fifteen in the morning. As much as he'd like to attribute the energy filling him to the new group of kids who were going to be starting this week, he knew there was more to it than that. Last night with Ava, he'd felt alive in a way he hadn't in years.

Before Saturday's dog-washing event had rolled around, he wouldn't have been able to imagine a thing he'd change, given a choice. He was sober, well paid, and doing what he loved. Being single suited him. He was thankful for every day.

Being with someone like Ava... Who was he kidding? He probably had better odds of swimming the English Channel than he did getting into a relationship with the likes of someone as remarkable as her without losing his shit—and he hadn't set foot in a body of water since the time his plastered self had jumped into Lake Michigan in winter.

Ready to get up, he swiped his phone off his nightstand and, after his eyes adjusted to the bright screen, turned his alarm off. He spotted several new texts in his support-group chat and clicked to find it filled with a slew of good mornings and well wishes for a new day as well as a Rumi quote he'd not heard in a long time.

"Come, come, whoever you are. Wanderer, worshipper, lover of leaving. It doesn't matter. Ours is not a caravan of despair. Come, even if you have broken your vows a thousand times. Come, yet again, come, come."

The quote brought his mother to mind and all the times she'd forgiven his father after declaring she was finished with him forever. He threw back the covers and dropped his phone back onto the nightstand, irritation threatening to pop in and dull the contented buzz lingering from last night.

Getting up, he headed over to Rolo, who still hadn't budged from the window. "What's got you riled up, bud?" Scratching the top of Rolo's head, he looked out in the direction his dog was staring.

In the silvery-gray predawn light, something small and dark was indeed walking across the yard. Jeremy waited for his eyes to adjust and was surprised to spy a cat rather than the raccoon who'd been leaving paw prints on the stone patio the last few weeks.

"Look at that, it's carrying something. Bet it's a mouse."

Rolo wagged his tail and whined again as the cat headed out of sight behind the carriage house at the back of the neighboring property.

"Why is it I think if you had your pick of another animal joining us, you'd choose a cat rather than a dog?" When Rolo wagged his tail hopefully, Jeremy added, "I hate to break it to you, but I'm not really a cat person."

With the yard empty again, Rolo trotted across the room and

hopped up onto the bed he seemed to believe he had uncondi- tional rights to and dug at the bedspread to plump it before curl- ing up in the center with a yawn.

"If someone pilots a 'Spoiled Dogs 101,' I'll send in your profile."

With an exaggerated yawn, Rolo closed his eyes. He knew Jeremy's morning routine took the better part of a half hour and wouldn't head for the front room until Jeremy was dressed, had had his first cup of coffee, meditated, and was ready to take him for a walk. On jogging days, Jeremy ventured out twice: first with Rolo for a walk, then alone. He'd tried jogging with Rolo a handful of times over the years, but after four or five blocks, Rolo would slow to a crawl, plant his feet, and—if Jeremy really pushed him—collapse to the ground refusing to budge like a toddler having a tantrum, though he'd walk for miles without complaint. It was Jeremy's best guess that Rolo found their walks second only to dinner.

After a so-so meditation during which he kept getting dis- tracted by images of Ava—from that body of hers to her smile and those eyes, as well as by some of the more surprising things she'd shared—Jeremy was slipping on his tennis shoes when Rolo hopped off the bed and trotted down the hall, tail wagging. "I think you sleep with one ear perked, don't you?"

Rolling thunderstorms had been forecast for later today, and as they stepped outside, Jeremy and Rolo both stopped moving to savor the promise of them in the air. Knowing the skies could open up unexpectedly this time of year, Jeremy stuck to the park and various blocks surrounding it.

As he headed inside through the park's north entrance, he thought of Ava asking if he knew about this being the oldest city park west of the Arch and the laughter that had led to. The truth was, he couldn't stop thinking about her. No doubt it had everything to do with the fact that he'd felt so alive both times they'd been together.

On the way out of the park, they intersected with a mom and two young kids who were walking a gangly-legged spaniel of some sort. The closer they got to one another, the more excited the spaniel became to greet Rolo.

"Hey, if your dog's good with other dogs, do you mind if they meet?" the woman asked. "We're trying to socialize her while she's young."

"Yeah, sure," Jeremy said. "He's friendly, but he's not super interested in other dogs, so he may not want to interact much. Unless your dog smells like a cat, that is."

Rolo had been walking alongside him off leash up to this point, but on the off chance that Rolo became too excited to listen, Jeremy snapped the leash back onto his collar before the two dogs were introduced.

"We have a cat," the girl said. While he was bad at guessing little kids' ages, Jeremy would put her at five or six. She was wearing a Minnie Mouse swimsuit top, a seen-better-days tutu over yellow leggings, and mismatched socks, so Jeremy had a feeling she'd dressed herself. "Maybe we all smell like cats."

"Well, if you do, Rolo certainly won't mind."

In a frantic attempt to get closer, the white and liver-brown spaniel pulled against the leash hard enough that her nails scraped on the concrete while the woman braced against her pull.

Rolo glanced up at Jeremy with a similar lack of excitement to his expression as he'd shown when Jeremy began adding green beans and carrots to his food as filler last year in hopes of helping him shed some weight before he entered his senior years and those few extra pounds of his expanded to several.

"How old's your dog?" he asked as the gangly spaniel lunged

in with an abundance of overzealous prancing and tail wags that Rolo endured without complaint but didn't reciprocate.

"Almost seven months," the mom said. "She's a bit over the top when it comes to other dogs. She's showing signs of settling down at home though."

"She's definitely energetic."

"Tell me about it. We think a playmate would help, but we're not ready to commit to a second dog permanently." With a look at her kids, who were giggling and consumed by the overzealous dog's antics, she dropped her voice. "My husband and I have been talking about fostering this summer while the kids are home and she's so young."

"Oh yeah, where from?"

"We're not sure yet. If you know a place, I'm all ears."

"I do, actually. Have you heard of the High Grove Animal Shelter in Webster? They're overflowing with dogs right now. Last I heard, they're looking for more foster families."

"Awesome. I'll give them a call." She patted her stomach, and Jeremy realized she had a third child on the way. "We bought her—Moxie—from my sister's neighbor before we were fully ready to commit to a dog, but here we are." In her excitement, Moxie was practically bouncing off all four paws at once.

"She seems like she'd be great with kids."

The woman rolled her eyes good-naturedly. "She loves the kids as much as they love her, so it gives her a lot of points when it comes to dealing with all this energy."

When Rolo sidestepped Moxie to sniff the kids' legs, hands, and feet, Moxie turned her attention to Jeremy and jumped to greet him. Jeremy sank onto his heels to give the excited dog some undivided attention.

As soon as he noticed, Rolo jealously beelined back to Jeremy. He barked once at the dog and dipped into a play bow, enticing her to play. The two dogs began to bark and wag their tails, with Moxie chasing Rolo in a circle and entwining their leashes. Jeremy let go of Rolo's leash as the kids laughed and clapped their hands.

By the time they untangled the dogs and went their separate ways, Rolo was panting heavily and walking with a slight prance to his step.

"Is that what you need? Another dog to really get you moving for a while?" Jeremy had been thinking about his conversation with Megan Saturday and debating whether to take a few foster dogs on for the benefit of his program kids, but suddenly it struck him that doing so might be exactly what Rolo needed too. As Megan had promised, it wouldn't take more than a phone call to set the process into motion. "You know what, Rolo? Maybe I'll take my own advice and make a trip to High Grove. Maybe I shouldn't be the only one of us whose world is getting shaken up a bit."

—–ᴡ–—

Jeremy climbed the metal steps to enter the second of the two High Grove trailers housing the bulk of the dogs from Saturday's puppy-mill confiscation. While AC window units cooled their interiors, he appreciated that several windows had been cracked in this trailer too. Thanks to the fresh air and the baths the dogs were given upon arrival, the smell inside, while anything but pleasant, wasn't unbearable.

He held the door open for Patrick, who was helping him choose dogs that would be good to foster, taking both Rolo and Jeremy's program kids into account.

Glancing around the cram-packed interior lined with kennels that appeared to be the aftermath of a game of Tetris, Jeremy was once again struck by the sheer numbers of dogs that had been confiscated.

Some of the dogs woke up and stretched at the presence of people in the trailer, and several of the younger ones began to whine and paw at the doors of their kennels. As in the other trailer, Jeremy noticed that the older dogs were less inclined to interact, as if they'd forgotten the possibilities offered by the outside world.

He paused in front of the kennel of one of the full-grown dogs, a resigned-looking thing who'd been shaved after coming in heavily matted. "How old is this one?" Jeremy couldn't imagine how it was possible after working with these dogs for less than a week, but Patrick had yet to even glance at the charts to answer Jeremy's questions.

Patrick looked up from the kennel of three young Maltipoos he'd been appraising to confirm who Jeremy was talking about. "She's between five and six was Gabe's estimation."

"Goldendoodle?" Even with a half-inch full-body shave, the dog's fur had a dense curl, and its unshaved paws revealed that its fur was a darker red when grown out.

Patrick nodded. "Yes, and she's had several litters, as evidenced by the swelling that was noticeable on her nipples during her exam."

How many is several? Jeremy hoped every one of these dogs would make it into a great home where they'd be loved and free to move about as they wished, but especially so with this one. Her big brown eyes, which were more visible than many of the adult doodles due to her clipped fur, carried the resigned look he'd witnessed in some of the harder-to-reach kids entering his program. "Have you gotten a feel for her temperament? It might be good to have a mature dog like her in the mix."

"Somewhat. She's one of eighty-six from Saturday's group I've worked with one-on-one, though only long enough for an initial personality assessment."

"Think she'll be okay around the kids?"

Rarely one for direct eye contact, Patrick stared off to the side, his brows slightly drawn. "I suspect so, yes. I walked her three blocks south of the shelter and back yesterday afternoon. With her, I encountered multiple birds, two squirrels, and one dog, a Lhasa apso. An elderly woman was walking him; she was wearing long sleeves, sunglasses, and an oversize sun hat." He nodded toward the crated goldendoodle. "She reacted most to the woman's floppy hat, but the reaction was nonaggressive, and she had almost no interest in the squirrels. She has considerable rehabilitation ahead of her, but I see no reason to advise you not to foster her."

Jeremy knelt in front of the goldendoodle's kennel and called to her, offering out the back of his hand. Her tail thumped, but she didn't budge from her curled position in the back. "I feel like it would be good for my kids to have a chance to bond with a dog like this, one who's got a long way to go."

"Would you like to see what Rolo thinks of her?"

"Sure." They'd left his dog in the care of Tess a few minutes ago, much to Rolo's chagrin. He was in the smaller of two fenced play areas with the litter of five goldendoodle puppies that Jeremy's group had washed Saturday. "And after her, how about that year-old labradoodle who was so anxious to get out of his cage in the other trailer? I know you said he'll be a handful, but it would be good for Rolo to have a role model when it comes to getting moving again. He is a bit thick in the middle."

Patrick offered him one of the leashes hanging by the door. "I noticed he was four or five pounds on the heavy side. I'll bring him up after Tess and I bring the puppies in."

"I like to think of him as a big-boned linebacker," Jeremy said, even though he knew not to take the comment personally. Still kneeling, he opened the kennel door and scooted back a foot.

He fished a few of the treats from his pocket and offered one the goldendoodle's way. She thumped her tail faster and licked nervously but didn't move as she looked at the two of them.

"I believe she'd be less intimidated if I'm not watching. I'll wait for you at the play area," Patrick said.

Once he stepped out and closed the door behind him, all crated eyes turned to Jeremy. "If I could get you all adopted, I would, but trust me, it's coming. You're going to get a second chance that's better than your first. By orders of magnitude."

As if drawn by the gentleness in his tone as much as the treat in his palm, the goldendoodle cautiously rose to her feet and crept forward, keeping more crouched than necessary for the height available.

"That a girl. How about some fresh air and a little fun? Actually, I can't promise Rolo is going to be much fun, but he won't give you a hard time, that's for sure."

Once she had stepped tentatively through the opening, Jeremy offered over the treats and clipped on the leash while she chomped them. Afterward, he let her sniff his hand and arm until she was satisfied, then he gently stroked her side, something she seemed to tolerate but not savor. Unlike Rolo's long, silky fur, hers was dense and curly but soft against Jeremy's fingertips. Underneath a thin layer of underdeveloped muscle, he could make out the definition of her ribs and her spine.

"I suspect at least a dozen of my kids are going to beg their parents to adopt you before this is over. Wherever you end up, I'll make sure it's with someone who'll let you sleep in their room and take you for walks every day from here on out. How about that?"

Also unlike Rolo, who typically watched him as he spoke as if attempting to discern what he was saying, she did nothing more than sniff his pocket until he offered another treat. She followed him to the door with little cajoling and surprised him by jumping the couple feet to the ground rather than attempting to clamber down the two metal stairs after him. She landed with a thump and shook herself off before looking around at her surroundings.

He led her along the back edge of the parking lot and up the wooded hillside. She clung to his side as if she weren't entirely confident some unforeseen enemy wouldn't lunge at her.

Rolo noticed them as they joined Patrick at the gate. He trotted over, hopping up to plant his front paws atop the gate, a look of what could only be described as abject betrayal on his face.

Not far behind him, four of the five puppies that Rolo was supposed to be interacting with romped in a tight huddle, tousling and rolling around in the mulch. The fifth puppy had trotted after him and was biting at his back legs as if they were chew toys.

Tess was inside the pen with them, ready to referee if needed. "I swear, this dog of yours has the personality of a toddler and a cranky old grandpa rolled into one. And I thought my fiancé's dog was a riot."

Jeremy cocked an eyebrow. "Eleanor swears Rolo's the Chewbacca to my Solo."

Tess laughed while Patrick gave Jeremy and Rolo a once-over, contemplating his comment. "Alden Ehrenreich or Harrison Ford?"

Jeremy cocked an eyebrow. "I've never asked, but I'm assuming Harrison Ford. I don't put much stock in her being versed in the newer movies."

Patrick nodded appreciatively. "I can see that, without the beard."

Jeremy was considering explaining that she'd meant it more figuratively when Tess took the conversation a different direction. "The important thing is it's obvious it's not in Rolo to so much as harm a fly, even if he is a bit of a curmudgeon." Tess sank onto her heels to interact with the brawling puppies. This got their attention. They pounced on her in unison, nipping and wagging their tails. With a sharp "No bite," she waggled the well-worn stuffed elephant in her hands in an attempt at redirection. "And you called it, by the way. He's been even less interested in playing with these guys than when you were here."

"I can't say that I'm surprised."

"After you disappeared from sight, he planted himself next to me and stared. Every time I made eye contact, he wagged his tail and looked in the direction you headed. No one can say dogs don't know how to communicate."

Jeremy chuckled. "That's for sure. When I don't give in and give him what he wants, sometimes I swear he thinks I'm a little dense and not getting his signals."

Tess paused to correct two of the puppies for biting. "Well," she said afterward, "if you're still interested in taking on one of these little guys, my suggestion is to take two of them. They'll share a crate and keep each other busy. Otherwise, you're going to have a *lot* of energy on your hands."

"That makes sense." Somehow, between the time he'd made the decision yesterday morning and now, the idea had grown from taking on a dog or two to three or four, depending on if he also took the high-energy labradoodle he'd be trying out with Rolo next.

Jeremy leaned over the top of the fence to gaze at the cream-colored ball of fluff alternately nipping at Rolo's heels and chasing his tail back and forth as he wagged it. "Seeing as Rolo isn't put out by them, I say let's do it. A part of me is tempted to forgo anything younger than six months, but the kids will love having a puppy or two around. So will Edith and Eleanor."

The timid goldendoodle clung close to Jeremy's side. She seemed more concerned with making sure nothing threatening was approaching from the direction of the shelter, including the volunteers shaking out mats behind the building, than wanting to interact with the dogs. Maybe Rolo was about to meet his match when it came to dogs not interested in other dogs.

"Just brace your kids. The puppies will likely be the first ones adopted." Tess stood back up when the puppies proved to be more interested in biting her clothes than the stuffed elephant. "But like Megan said, whether it's six weeks or six months, we're not going to list anything you take home as adoptable until you're ready for us to do so, not while your kids are benefitting from them."

"I appreciate that. Honestly, I won't be surprised if my kids end up applying to adopt most of what I foster."

Still looking a touch dejected at having found Jeremy with another dog, Rolo barked on the other side of the fence to get his attention. When Jeremy looked his way, he wagged his bushy black tail, ignoring the puppy chasing after it.

"How about we come in and join you, bud?" He reached over and gave his dog a pat.

Never one for wasting time, Patrick asked which of the puppies Jeremy wanted them to bring his way tomorrow.

Jeremy nodded at the puppy at Rolo's heels. "Him for sure; there's a connection to be had here even if Rolo doesn't recognize it yet. And how about that female we first bathed? I'm pretty sure that's her." He pointed to the lightest-coated puppy of the bunch who'd plopped onto the ground next to Tess, happily panting. "I remember her being the calmest of the bunch."

Tess scooped up two of the puppies closest to her in one swoop. "Sounds good. I'll get these guys put away while you introduce that sweet mama to him."

With Rolo still standing on his hind feet, blocking the gate, Jeremy waved him back. "Hey, down, buddy. I'm coming in."

Rolo reluctantly consented, releasing one paw, then the other, and fell to the ground with a thud. Sinking back on his haunches, he wagged his tail expectantly and let out an exaggerated whine that dragged on a bit comically.

As Tess approached with the two puppies in her arms, another two came chasing after her and biting her heels, and Rolo backed away from the gate. Patrick stepped inside and scooped the two puppies up, leaving the lone Rolo antagonizer for a second trip. Once Patrick and Tess were out, Jeremy cajoled the hesitant mama doodle inside with him.

As soon as he'd shut the gate, Rolo leaned against him, rubbing along the side of Jeremy's leg and panting happily.

Jeremy gave him a hearty pat after unhooking the golden-doodle's leash. She hung nearby, not seeming to want to interact but not ready to venture out into the play area either. Rolo gave her a thorough sniff which she didn't return. Following at Rolo's heels, the puppy began to whine and clung close enough to Rolo to be almost underfoot, likely having realized his littermates were suddenly nowhere to be found.

Jeremy watched the three of them standing close together, lost in their own experiences, with a smile on his face. He pulled out his phone and snapped a couple photos. After choosing one in which Rolo was looking at the camera with a "Really, now?" expression and both the mama doodle and puppy were in the shot, he sent it off to Ava. They'd exchanged numbers last night and a handful of texts this morning. When Jeremy texted her of his decision to foster, she'd been ecstatic, replying that she couldn't wait to meet them.

A glance at his recent text messages proved Jeremy had no shortage of longer-known confidants to text instead of her—from Gabe to Edith and Eleanor, and a dozen others. The fact was, none of them had been on his mind all morning. It was Ava he'd not been able to stop thinking of since they'd parted ways the other night. In more ways than one.

What do you think? Two of three chosen so far.

She texted back as the mama doodle was beginning to relax a little and sniff around in the mulch while Rolo had begun nudging the puppy along with the tip of his nose.

I was hoping you'd get a puppy! I'm overdo for a puppy fix. And that other one… What a sweetie! Are you bringing them home with you now?

Not till tomorrow. They've got another recheck with Gabe in the morning.

Can't wait to meet them! And your program kids. :)

His thumb froze over the phone screen as his limbs tensed. This was real. He was bringing this woman into his life. She'd be teaching a trial class tomorrow evening during his open session. If it went over well, then weekly, at least.

His body tensed as the vulnerability this introduced washed over him while fingers betrayed him with an easygoing response.

Looking forward to tomorrow evening. :)

Good luck with any additional canine picks.

After thanking her, he slipped his phone into his pocket. There was no pretending his pulse wasn't racing. This had his fingers itching to pull his phone back out and call the whole thing off.

Jeremy didn't exactly come from a line of people who had their shit together. Quite the opposite. So much so that even with as much work as he'd done to get healthy, he didn't have faith in ever pulling himself up by his bootstraps enough to be successful in a relationship. His messy three years with his ex had proven that. The few women he'd been with since hadn't been people he'd invested much of his self into. If something blossomed with Ava, that wouldn't be the case. Not with already feeling so invested like this right at the start.

And even knowing this, he wasn't canceling.

He looked back at the dogs to find that the mama doodle was rolling in the mulch, legs in the air. On the other hand, Rolo had stopped paying attention to the puppy and was staring at Jeremy sharply, ears perked. That dog of his could read him like they were members of the same pack.

"No worrying about me, bud." He forced an easy confidence into his voice he didn't entirely feel. "I'm fine. Right now, this is about figuring out which dogs you might have a chance in hell at bonding with."

Rolo lunged forward to press against him, panting softly and eyeing the mama doodle and puppy as if attempting to decipher what exactly today's visit to the shelter meant.

"Who says you can't teach an old dog new tricks?" When Rolo shoved his head under Jeremy's hand in an attempt to force a petting, he added, "You and me both, bud. You and me both."

Chapter 10

As Ava strolled along aisles of colorful toys in her go-to independent pet store, Chomps, excitement blossomed all the way down her limbs. Good thing she'd grabbed a full-size cart and not a petite one. When it came to shopping, buying things for others was as rewarding as buying things for herself. Apparently, this truth held true when it came to buying things for dogs too.

She'd woken up this morning with Jeremy's foster dogs on her mind. More accurately, she'd woken up with Jeremy on her mind, the same as he'd been the last two days. Now that she'd made it to Friday, she'd be seeing him again tonight for the yoga trial for his students.

Excited to connect with the sweet-tempered rescues she hadn't seen in nearly a week, her first thought had been to pick up a box or two of treats to bring with her tonight. That idea had quickly morphed into this. Instead of making a charity donation the way she typically did with a portion of her proceeds from Wednesday's closing, she was going on a small buying spree for Jeremy's foster dogs. *Way. More. Fun.*

Pulling out her phone, she texted Jeremy, downplaying her intentions a tad.

> Morning! Excited to meet your new four-legged arrivals tonight. Picking up a few goodies for them. Need anything from Chomps? Food? Bowls? Leashes?

While waiting for a response, she walked the aisles, loading the items that called to her most into the cart, like spiky squeaker balls, treat-hiding puzzles, ropes, chew toys, and plush toys that looked like squirrels, raccoons, and chickens. And what dog wouldn't want to play with a cozy teddy bear with a durable rope sewn to its paws? She wished she had more time to browse, but—no surprise—she was tight on time, so she loaded up quickly.

Her phone buzzed, and even though she was anticipating a quick response, her pulse raced to spy Jeremy's name on her screen.

> *That's nice of you! Anything you pick will be fine. I have the basics, thanks to Gabe. He set me up with extra bowls and food.*

After replying she was happy to do it and putting her phone away, Ava took a moment to be self-discerning. She was crushing on Jeremy, no question, but she trusted that no important boundaries were dropped by doing a good deed for the dogs he was fostering.

For the most part, Ava found people came across as either warm and fuzzy or cold and prickly. Having been slow to warm up to her, hesitant to laugh, and even, at first, slow to smile, Jeremy clearly leaned toward the cold and prickly side of things, with her at least.

Yet, she'd been lucky enough to catch glimpses of something much warmer underneath that exterior, something that promised to melt a part of her she hadn't even known needed unfreezing. She'd felt it most while experiencing his warm laugh the handful of times he'd really let it out. It was clear that he carried his share of scars, and letting people see his vulnerable side wasn't easy for him.

That's okay. I've got the patience and skill of Tim Robbins in

Shawshank Redemption. She'd get through that wall of his one way or another.

Her phone buzzed with a calendar reminder, alerting her that she had one hour before she was due to meet new clients at a property out in West County, and she still needed to swing by the office to verify a handful of items they'd inquired about in regard to some of the properties they'd be seeing today. After a quick count of her stash, Ava headed for the register, grabbing a handful of edible Nylabones on an end cap as she passed by.

The clerk eyed the contents of Ava's cart in surprise as she began scanning the first item. "How many dogs do you have?"

"Not a single one, actually. These are mostly donations for a group of foster dogs."

"Oh, how sweet." The girl stopped scanning and sifted through a pile of paper next to the register. Finding what she was after, she waved a rectangle of paper in Ava's direction. "A customer left an extra coupon a little bit ago and said to pass it along. Who better to give it to than someone who's doing a good deed? It's for ten percent off the total purchase."

Ava grinned. "Oh, thank you! I'm always so moved by people who pay it forward." She glanced at the register display and noticed that this month's donations were supporting the High Grove Animal Shelter. *What a small world.* When it came to making donations, Ava circled through a handful of her favorite organizations, and High Grove would've received a donation this time had she not chosen this shopping spree instead. "Not to complicate things, but that ten percent you're saving me, how about adding it back on at the end as a donation to High Grove?"

The girl laughed. "Absolutely!"

Three-hundred-and-twenty-five dollars later, Ava headed to her Jeep, the glow of a good deed spreading inside her. She itched to text Jeremy a spoiler picture of the stash but decided to wait.

A half-dozen times at dinner, she'd been inundated with an urge to lean over the table and brush her lips along his neck. And on that smooth dip of skin underneath his ear. And atop that spectacular mouth. She suspected Jeremy was the kind of attractive that would only increase as she managed to break through those barriers of his.

The opposite had been true in her marriage to Wes. Like an appealing room display at IKEA, he'd dressed well and had known how to walk the walk like many of her best-paying clients. It hadn't occurred to her until her pretty world begun tumbling apart as if it had been made out of cardboard on a stormy day that the life she'd built had been part of a big-picture end goal she'd been imagining for herself ever since she'd been a kid with a closet full of hand-me-down clothes.

Ava certainly wasn't that girl anymore, and if she was going to risk opening herself up to whatever this was turning out to be with Jeremy, she needed to trust herself that she was doing it for the right reasons. And like her grandpa was fond of saying, forcing a decision that hadn't made itself clear was no better than watching for the cotton to sprout before the seeds had sufficient time to germinate.

Driving away, she ran through a mental checklist of her day. Busy as it was undoubtedly going to get, she was determined not to get swept away in the chaos. Committed as she was at the onset, she still managed to get sucked into the vortex of intensity that went hand in hand with being a successful agent. After showing an older couple she was working with the five properties in West County and making second spur-of-the-moment appointments to swing back by the first two properties when they couldn't recall the "feel" of the kitchen, she then needed to run by her new listing in the Central West End to reset the lockbox after its owners became convinced the code had been compromised. Along the way, she fielded over a dozen calls.

It was nearing five o'clock when Ava realized she'd once again not managed to eat a single bite aside from a bag of trail mix and barely avoided a giant mess with three melted Kit Kat minis she'd stashed in the center console. Sadly, it had officially become the time of year that it was inadvisable to keep a stash of chocolate in her Jeep.

Knowing yoga on a full stomach was as unpleasant as on an empty one, she temporarily satiated her hunger with a piece of string cheese that she picked up at a gas station. *You could get an assistant*, she thought as she bit into the salty cheese and her mouth watered, hungry for more. If she picked up a few more properties each month, she'd hardly notice a drop in income.

That's not the solution and you know it.

The solution was doing less. Slowing down. Saying thank you, but no thank you.

Like always, her heart raced and her palms began to sweat at the thought. She'd sworn on a hundred bright, shiny moons outside her shared bedroom window over the years that as a grown-up, she'd be able to buy a dress in a department store that wasn't on sale and pay off a car years before it began to break down.

If those were the standards by which she measured success, then she'd made it. She could do that and more. But she didn't *feel* like a success. She felt like a compass at the North Pole spinning in all directions.

Finished with her string cheese, she entered Jeremy's address into her navigation system, hoping it was okay to arrive a little early. He'd given her the option of holding class inside or out in the backyard, and she wanted to get a feel for the place before setting up.

She'd listed enough properties in Lafayette Square over the years that she was familiar with his street, but it wasn't until she pulled in front of the house that she experienced a wave of déjà vu.

Considering the neighborhood, it wasn't a surprise that the house was beautiful, but it stood out from others on the block in that the lot immediately to the right was vacant and a wooden privacy fence joined the house and neighboring lot together.

Ava took in the unassuming sign staked in the ground on the left side of the wide front entry that read Washington Center. She'd noticed this place before, two, maybe three years ago as she was driving by. The sign had caught her eye, and she'd wondered what sort of business went on here. *Well, now you know.*

She parked in an open space along the side of the street two houses down and turned off the Jeep, taking a minute to collect herself. She twisted in her seat for another glance at the house, noting the unusual sensation it stirred in her.

The house was something to appreciate, all brick, a light brown that stood out in contrast to most of the redbrick homes in St. Louis, and unlike the signature flair of many Lafayette Square homes, the exterior had never been painted. It was a stately two-story topped by a third-floor mansard roof with quaint dormer windows, and it had an ornate cornice trim along the edge of the roof and elegant stone capping over the main windows.

Thick hostas circled an ornamental dogwood in the front landscaping, and off to the side, Ava spotted a tortoiseshell cat transfixed on something moving in the mulch. "Pretty kitty. Jeremy hasn't mentioned you."

Turning forward in her seat again, she fished out her phone and texted Jeremy.

> Hey, I'm a little early. Ready for me? I have a zillion emails to catch up on if you're not.

She closed her eyes and waited, breathing in and out until her phone buzzed a minute later.

Absolutely. Need my help carrying anything in?

Maybe later. Mind if I change first?

Sure thing.

Catching a glimpse of herself in the rearview mirror, she noticed the color on her cheeks and the light smile on her lips. "You know, you may not have an answer when it comes to anything else in your life, but I'm getting the feeling this is exactly where you're supposed to be right now."

Chapter 11

WHILE SEATED ON THE PATIO AT A WROUGHT-IRON TABLE underneath the wide pergola, Jeremy slipped his phone into his pocket and flattened his hands atop his thighs. "Looks like Ava's here a little early."

Across the table, Edith and Eleanor exchanged glances, making Jeremy suspect his tone carried an anxiousness he'd meant to suppress.

"We're in no hurry." Edith tugged on one side of her wide-brimmed gardener's hat that made her petite frame seem even slighter. "We'll wait here and watch the dogs while you show her around." She and Eleanor had been working in the flower beds and garden this afternoon and had stopped shortly after Jeremy finished with his last client for today, a graduate from his first group of program kids three years ago who had a standing monthly check-in.

"Yeah, if you don't mind." Jeremy took a swig of tea even though he wasn't thirsty. In the face of the vulnerability that went hand in hand with showing Ava his world, he wondered if it was too late to back out. "I won't keep you babysitting long."

Jeremy had been sitting out here with Edith and Eleanor the last twenty minutes, drinking tea and watching the foster dogs' antics. The dogs had arrived over the lunch hour and were enjoying their second stint in the backyard. No surprise, but the energetic labradoodle who'd been dying to get out of his cage yesterday when Jeremy was at the shelter had been going non-stop while the other three—the timid goldendoodle mama and the two ten-week-old puppies—were more hesitant when it came to checking out their surroundings. The labradoodle looked like a woolly deer with his long legs and shaggy cream-colored fur. So far, he was showing no signs of wearing down as he dashed about the yard, alternately pausing to sniff anything taller than a blade of grass and then barreling across the width of the double yard and back.

After chasing him the first five or ten minutes, Rolo had plopped down beside Jeremy, panting from the exertion. Whenever Jeremy looked Rolo's way, Rolo would glance deliberately toward the labradoodle with an expression on his face that seemed to say "I'm okay if the wild one leaves now." He'd not paid much attention to the others yet. Jeremy couldn't help but wonder when his dog would realize this home invasion had an extended stretch to it.

The tuckered-out puppies stirred as Jeremy headed across the patio. They'd been dozing off, curled together in a cool spot on the stone patio in the shade a few feet away. Eleanor, a fan of nearly every rock band that had formed in the '60s, was calling the sibling pair Simon and Garfunkel despite Jeremy reminding her that his program kids would get the final say when it came to names.

After being coaxed out of her crate, the mama doodle had sniffed around for a few minutes, urinated next to Edith's monarch bed—the small island of mostly milkweed plants flanking one side of the patio—then wedged herself underneath the most out of the way of two chaises. She'd been watching the commotion from there and hadn't budged since.

"I'm guessing she won't be giving you any trouble in the next few minutes." Jeremy knelt down to give her a quick pat as he passed by.

"She's like a snail, that one," Edith said. "If we give her the space to settle in, she'll come out of her shell when she's good and ready."

Showing zero dismay at abandoning his canine companions, Rolo trotted after him as Jeremy headed through the back of the house to the front. "Here goes nothing," he said under his breath before pulling open the front door.

The first thing he noticed was the big smile on Ava's face as she walked up the path—a smile that blasted away his mounting anxiety. "Hey there." There was an exuberance to her that called straight to his heart—and likely Rolo's too.

His dog bounded through the door opening before Jeremy realized he was going to do it. He dashed down the steps and circled around her, whining like he'd been starved of attention for months. With a laugh, Ava stopped to dole out a slew of affectionate pats before continuing up the stairs. "I missed you, too, sweet boy."

She had a large yoga bag slung over her shoulder and was wearing heels and a flowy skirt that stopped above the knee, drawing Jeremy's attention to something other than that smile of hers.

At the sight of those legs, Jeremy's pulse began to race all over again. Just shy of a week ago when they'd met at the dog washing, she'd been wearing jogging shorts, and he'd had to handle the enticement of the occasional bubbles of soap and beads of water running down her thighs and calves. He should be immune by now. Something about that skirt though.

Ava, on the other hand, was focused on the house. "Look at this place." She was taking in everything, even the tiled ceiling of the small portico at the top of the steps. "It was built in the 1870s or '80s, I'm guessing?"

"You're right on. Late '70s I think."

She murmured in appreciation. "They don't make houses like

this anymore, that's for sure. And that empty lot next door, it belongs with the house?"

"Yes and no. The house on it burned down in the late '90s—1990s I should say. An older woman who was friends with my landlords lived there and never had it rebuilt. Then she died unexpectedly, and her will was in probate for years. The lot belongs to her nephew now, but he's in Ohio, and my landlords have cared for the property since. Awhile back, they were granted permission to extend their privacy fence around it as well."

"That extra space is a blessing, I bet."

"It is. Wait till you see what my landlords have done with the backyard." Jeremy ran his thumb and fingertips along his jaw, scratching at his beard. "The kids shouldn't start arriving for another half hour or so. Want a quick tour before you change? The dogs are out back, and so are Edith and Eleanor."

"Sounds great," she said, stepping in with Rolo at her heels.

He shut the door behind them, and Rolo trotted a few steps deeper into the foyer but paused, waiting to see which direction they'd head. "I think I told you, the whole bottom floor is mine— the center's, actually. My apartment is upstairs to the back."

Ava clicked her tongue as she peered into the parlor room that was now used for group therapy. "Look at that wood paneling. I'm guessing it's original?"

"I would think so."

She looked from the walls to the thick crown molding and the ornate walnut banister. "There's so much intact millwork here. Impressive, especially for a house this old." She shook her head abruptly and smiled. "Sorry, I need to take off my agent hat. I've been showing property all day."

"I don't mind. It is a great house, and I make use of it too. I tend to start my kids' first group session with talk of the tornado that ripped through Lafayette Square in 1896. The park was destroyed, and a lot of homes were flattened or had their top floors ripped off. It's my segue into rebuilding after tragedy."

"I bet that's a powerful opening. I sold a house near here a few years ago that had its top floor rebuilt because of the tornado. Was this house damaged?"

"It wasn't in the direct path. Just windows and roof tiles for the most part."

She stepped into the parlor, taking in the circle of twelve mismatched chairs in the center of the room, brushing her fingers over the top of the closest one. "So, this is where the magic happens?"

The eclectic assortment of chairs and beanbags not only let the kids express themselves by their choice of where to sit, but also was meant to be less intimidating than a circle of uniform commercial folding chairs.

"You could say that. This circle is where most of the real progress is made, at least once they reach the point that they decide it's safe to start expressing some of what they've been bottling up."

The compassion in her gaze made Jeremy's lungs constrict for a second or two. "I don't doubt that one second," she said. "Twelve chairs, so eleven kids?" she asked, stroking Rolo's ear gently after he joined her.

"Ten kids per group max, and one assistant. I've been working with Maryville University the last few years, and I typically have one or two grad students a semester who need practicum hours. They participate in group sessions and tag along on most of our outings but are not in the kids' individual therapy sessions."

Ava rolled one ankle in a circle around the tip of her heel as she listened, inadvertently calling his attention to her legs again. "And how long did you say their program lasts? Six months?"

Forcing his gaze to stay locked on her face, he nodded. "That's how long their group sessions run, but many of the kids continue on with individual therapy after that. And a lot of them keep coming to open center time on Friday evenings too—so long as they abide by the rules."

She pursed her lips. "Any rules I should be aware of, since I'm teaching them tonight?"

He shrugged. "The basics, I guess. Respecting the self, respecting others, no sharing of other group members' stories, no smoking, drinking, or using drugs, and no dating. That sort of thing."

"Like ever?" Then, as if realizing the ambiguity in her question, she added, "The dating part, I mean. And each other? Or anyone?"

"Each other, but the full answer is a bit more complicated. While they're in the program, they aren't supposed to see one another outside of here. They're in a pretty vulnerable space, and it's about really doing the work. After they graduate, who they see is up to them. I started the open center nights to give them an opportunity to stay connected in a safe environment. The tricky part comes when graduates are dating other graduates and come to open center nights together."

She grinned. "Knowing teens and their hormones, I can imagine why."

He shook his head. "Let's say I learned the hard way that it's important to monitor the hall bathroom regardless of what kind of commitments they've made."

"Yikes." As he led her into the rec room on the opposite side of the foyer, she asked, "So tonight's kids will be from a hodge-podge of groups then?"

"A hodgepodge?" He smiled. "I can't remember the last time I've heard anyone use that word in a sentence, but yeah. Except I think most of the kids who started this week will be here."

She swept her hair to one side as she went from taking in the room to looking at him. "To be totally honest with you, I'm more nervous about teaching this class than any one yet."

"Don't be. Trust me when I tell you they're going to love you. You're genuine and friendly—" He stopped himself short of adding "and beautiful," even though he knew her appearance would be part of what pulled them in.

Clearing his throat, he turned his attention to the rec room, a favorite spot for the kids on open center nights because of the darts, pool, and ping-pong tables. From there, he gave her a quick peek in his office at the back of the main floor where he met with the kids individually.

As she appraised the leather sofa, his desk, and the various knickknacks, she raised an eyebrow. "It looks cozy in there, right down to the throw pillows and blankets. And that worn teddy bear seems pretty loved."

He grinned. "My kids have anointed it with its share of tears."

"That's sweet."

Next up was the kitchen. "Since the kitchen is hardly used, it's overdue for a remodel. I keep some healthy snacks stocked in the pantry and fridge for the kids to grab, and a couple times for our Saturday service projects, we've done some canning and baking in here with what comes out of the garden."

"You have a garden?"

"Edith and Eleanor do, but the kids and I help sometimes. We can head out back, and I'll show you."

Rolo had trotted to the fridge and was wagging the entire lower half of his body while giving Jeremy a pleading look.

"What does he want?" Ava laughed.

"Ah, I'm pretty sure he's reminding me it's time for a piece of string cheese. He always gets the last bite." In further explanation, he added, "When I eat with Edith and Eleanor, dinners are late."

"Well, he knows a good snack then. I just stopped at a gas station for the same thing."

"Oh yeah? Want another?"

She shrugged. "If I can give Rolo some."

"Sure." He grabbed two pieces and passed one to Ava. "I'm probably not doing myself any favors in the long term, giving in to him like this."

"He's a *great* dog; I hope you know that."

After disposing of the wrapper, Ava pulled off the first piece, a sizable bite, and offered it to Rolo, who inhaled it in the space of a second and was ready for more.

"He is, albeit a consistently hungry one."

As he led her outside to the back patio, he saw that, thanks to Edith's coaxing, the mama doodle had crawled halfway out from underneath the cover of the chaise. With their approach, she scooted backward until she was fully covered again.

"Aww, she's even sweeter in person," Ava said.

"Me?" Edith asked as they neared. With her childlike smile, petite frame, and oversize gardener's hat, she came across as more sincere than joking.

"Oh! Sorry, no, the dog." Ava's face reddened.

"She's messing with you." Jeremy grinned. "Ava, Edith. Edith, Ava." He then motioned to Eleanor who was still over at the table. "And Eleanor. Two of the coolest women you'll ever meet."

With that inviting grin, Ava shook Edith's hand first, then crossed over to the table to shake Eleanor's. The heavily panting labradoodle bounded over long enough to sniff Ava's feet and legs and for Rolo to utter a single, protective bark as if declaring Ava wasn't to be shared.

"It's so nice to meet you both and to tour your beautiful home. It's fantastic, inside and out." She paused to take in the well-landscaped double yards. "And that vacant lot still has an intact carriage house at the back of the lot. Impressive."

"We've not gotten around to making use of it," Eleanor said. "And it's our pleasure." Of the two of them, Eleanor was the slower to smile and hardly ever the one his kids went to when hoping for compliments. She was, however, a great source of reliable advice.

Edith joined them at the table after abandoning any further attempt to draw the mama doodle out of hiding. At just over five feet tall and less than a hundred pounds, Edith seemed as if a strong wind might blow her away, but she met Eleanor, who was tall and sinewy, pace for pace at yard work and everything else.

"Jeremy forgot to tell us what a pretty one you are, dear," Edith said out of the blue, "but then again, he's hardly one to be flowery, is he?"

Ava blinked as Jeremy shook his head.

"Never feel obligated to answer her rhetorical questions," Eleanor said, waving a hand dismissively. There was a directness about her that lingered from her career as one of the first openly gay women lawyers in the city.

Looking between them, Ava gave a little shrug in answer that Jeremy found endearing. He closed a hand over her shoulder before he realized he was going to do it.

"We used to take a yoga class at the Y. Years ago," Eleanor said. A sideways glance at Ava showed she was studying Eleanor's T-shirt, a boldly colored Judas Priest one. Now that Eleanor was retired, during the summer months, she was hardly seen out of one of her dozen or so sixties rock-band shirts.

"Oh, I remember that," Edith said. "Why'd we stop? It was when you got the knee replacement, wasn't it?"

"You're welcome to join tonight, if you'd like," Ava offered. "I have a few extra mats in my trunk if we need them." Ava scoped the yard a second time, then turned to Jeremy. "It's such a nice night; I'm all for holding class outside if you don't think the mosquitoes will be too bad. The big open patch of grass in front of that amazing garden would be perfect."

He shrugged. "The mosquitos haven't been bad this year, but we have citronella plants growing in the garden, and I have some tiki torches I can light."

After Edith and Eleanor finished debating how many years it had been since they'd attempted yoga, Eleanor took her up on the offer. "We'll give it a try, as long as you don't mind us serving a late dinner. Though one of you may need to help me get back to my feet when it's over." She gave Ava a direct look, making it clear the dinner invitation had been for her.

"Oh, I don't think—"

"Of course, you're invited. We love having guests for dinner. Jeremy can vouch for us on that." She left no space for rebuttal as she pointed to the basket on the table. "We're having fresh zucchini tonight. They're really coming in, as you can see."

"Have you had zucchini fritters?" Edith needed to tilt her head to address Ava, considering their height difference. "We make them every summer with the garden zucchini but haven't yet this year."

Ava clasped a hand over her stomach. "I've been known to eat an entire plateful of zucchini fritters. My grandparents have a big garden, and my grandma makes them all summer long."

"Ava's family owns a working farm down in the Bootheel," Jeremy offered as he struggled to process the fact that Ava would be coming upstairs. He always kept the kids and grad students on the main floor and out here. Upstairs was his private living space; downstairs was for business. This was too much, too fast, wasn't it? His body was equal parts yes and no.

Edith was oblivious to his inner turmoil. "Family-owned?"

When Ava nodded, she said, "Then we'll have a lot to talk about at dinner. Eleanor's from several generations of farmers in Arkansas."

"What do your kin grow down there?" Eleanor asked.

"Cotton mostly, but some corn and soy."

Eleanor nodded. "Mine too." Now eighty-one like Edith, she'd moved here to attend St. Louis University in her late teens and had never left. Her stories of childhood and her farming roots were starkly different from Edith's, who grew up practically in the shadow of Leeds Castle in an apartment above a family-owned souvenir shop. The two women had met here in St. Louis at a farmers market after Edith's American husband died in his fifties. A few years later, Eleanor had moved here to the home where Edith and her husband had raised their kids.

Suddenly, it occurred to Jeremy that in all his dinners with them, there'd been dozens of additional invited guests, but aside from his sponsor a handful of times, the guests had all been Edith's and Eleanor's connections.

Even the handful of dates he'd been on the last several years hadn't been with women he'd cared to bring deeper into his world. And while he realized he hadn't been ready to take any action of his own when it came to inviting Ava to join them for dinner, somehow, it seemed like exactly the right choice. Trust Edith and Eleanor to realize that before him.

As if sharing Jeremy's sentiments, when farm talk was put on hold so that Ava could get ready for class, Rolo trotted along after her, not even looking back to see if Jeremy was following. Maybe he was holding out hopes for another bite of string cheese, but maybe, like Jeremy, he was also picking up on the fact that Ava Graham seemed to fit right in here.

Chapter 12

When the kids began arriving, the occasional laugh or playful shout reached Ava's ears from the direction of the house as she set up for class. Even without her finishing touches, the backyard seemed to have been staged for the experience with its manicured flower beds, freshly mowed grass, citronella torches, and warm, glowing Edison bulbs strung underneath the wooden pergola. And that wasn't even taking into account the garden. It was still late spring for another few weeks, and the garden was flourishing well enough that Ava had no doubt even her green-thumbed grandma would be impressed.

Her butterflies began to subside as she unrolled her mat near the arched entrance to the garden and spread the mats Jeremy had purchased, all royal blue, on the grass in front of her. Behind those, she unrolled the three extra mats she'd had in her trunk. In front of each mat, she set battery-operated tea-light candles and then pulled up the cello-based playlist she'd selected to play over her portable speaker, believing her music choice to be mellow enough for yoga but not too "out there" that it might inadvertently get the kids laughing.

Around her own mat, she placed the last three candles, the speaker, and one of her favorite yoga books that she'd be sharing a quote from at the end of class. She'd given considerable thought to which poses to introduce tonight. There were tons of yoga poses that worked small miracles on the body, but to reap their benefits, the kids would need to let go of a good deal of inhibition and really settle into the moment. Otherwise, they might well end up on their mats knotted like pretzels and laughing uncontrollably. Tonight, her motto was "simple but effective."

A few minutes before class was scheduled to start, Jeremy stepped out of the house, a stream of teens trailing after him. Once he spotted her, Rolo bounded ahead of them, beelining to Ava for his second enthusiastic greeting of the night before trotting from one mat to the next, sniffing them and the candles. Rolo would be the only canine attending the class, and Ava suspected this wouldn't bother him.

Until the foster dogs had a better handle on potty training, they'd stay in the four oversize kennels the shelter had lent Jeremy whenever they couldn't be outside or closely watched inside. The goldendoodle puppies were sharing one and had enough space to do a bit of wrestling, and the mama doodle and leggy labradoodle had all the space they needed to both stand and stretch out in their separate ones. After unloading the Jeep, Ava and Jeremy had unpackaged a handful of toys, but as exhausted from the change of routine over the last several days as they likely were, all dogs including the labradoodle had curled up to doze before Ava headed outside.

"Ready for us?" Jeremy asked as the kids claimed their mats and he walked over to her. He'd changed out of the jeans and striped button-down shirt he'd been wearing when she got here into a black fitted T-shirt and exercise pants. Thanks to the angle of the late-evening sun and his black shirt, his hazel-green eyes stood out like a panther's.

Yes, please, she thought. "As ready as I'll ever be."

Jeremy's hand locked over the side of her arm for a second or two. "It's going to be great." She was still soaking up the comforting strength in his touch when he cleared his throat and turned to appraise the kids. "Turns out, my entire new group showed tonight, so I decided to cap the class with only them, hoping they'll bond a little more. Next week, it'll be fair game to anyone who's here."

"Sure. Sounds good to me." He was already talking about next week, and the class hadn't even started yet. *Please don't let me disappoint him.*

"There're more kids inside from other groups. And one of my grad students," he added with a secretive grin.

The kids were making themselves comfortable on the mats, and Ava wasn't surprised to spy that the back row had filled with the three teen boys who looked most like they didn't want to be here.

"Oh, and fair warning," Jeremy added, "to get a couple of these guys on board, I had to promise to participate. You saw my skills firsthand Tuesday, so you have a sense of how I'm about to look in front of this new group."

"You shouldn't say that. You looked great." After pausing awkwardly, she added, "Your form, I mean." *Get it together, girl.*

"How about we start with some introductions while we're waiting for Edith and Eleanor?" He waved the kids up. "Hey, all, how about we circle up and introduce ourselves?"

"If I leave this mat, somebody's gonna take it," one of the kids in the back called out, but he got up anyway.

They were a mixed bag, no question—varying sizes, races, and styles of dress. The only thing they seemed to have in common was that none of them seemed too excited to be here.

One girl, the second shortest of the bunch, who screamed old-school punk with her dyed-black hair swept forward on her face and dressed in all black, gave her a look like she'd been sipping on unsweetened kefir. "So, I guess you're Doc's girlfriend or something?"

Steeling herself, Ava dove in before Jeremy could respond. "I'm Ava Graham, Jeremy's friend, and I'm excited to be here."

"We're not," one of the tall boys coughed under his breath.

"Nolan." Jeremy's tone was somehow both gentle and repri-manding…and effective. Nolan mumbled an apology.

"You know, I get your reservation," Ava said. "At your age, I wouldn't have been excited to try yoga either. But it's done wonders for me, and I'm hoping you'll find the same thing."

"Doc said if we want to work with the dogs, we have to take yoga lessons and work in the garden pulling weeds and crap." It was the punkish girl again. Apparently, she was the voice of the group.

"That doesn't sound like a bad deal to me," Ava replied. "I love gardening." .

The last kid over, a straggler, was a striking girl who was plainly dressed, makeup free, and had long red hair that was a bit disheveled. Out of all of them, Ava felt a clear affinity toward her. Something more than the color of her hair reminded Ava of Olivia when she was younger—blissfully oblivious and without a care in the world about fitting in.

"Remember what I said Tuesday about how one of the best ways out of your head is to get into your body?" Jeremy asked. "Well, Ava's going to help you do that."

Um, no pressure. "Jeremy's right," she said more confidently than she felt. "In case you don't know, yoga's a five-thousand-year-old art form. And it was designed with the intent of quieting the mind by getting the mind to become aware of the body in a deeper way."

"You don't look like a yoga teacher." This comment came from the youngest-looking boy with shiny, dark hair and a slight build.

Ava tilted her head. "I didn't realize yoga teachers had a look."

Jeremy clapped his hands together as he looked over the group. "Before we scare her off entirely, how about names, everybody?

I'd like us to take turns introducing someone *else* in the group. I bet you can all tell Ava two or three interesting things we learned about each other in circle Tuesday afternoon." Projecting over a chorus of groans, he continued. "And let's keep away from anything personal that might've been shared. A good rule of thumb is if you'd mind it being shared on social media about yourself, don't share it about anyone else."

The groans and eye-rolling continued, but Jeremy wasn't deterred. He nodded at the punkish girl first. "How about you start us off, Hailey?"

Ava braced for Hailey to say something else semi-rude. To her surprise, after a beat or two, Hailey pointed to a tall boy with flawless brown skin and golden-brown eyes. "That's Nolan. Don't ask him if he plays basketball because it's a tall person stereotype, and it pisses him off." She planted her fists on her hips and looked at Jeremy. "If that doesn't count, I quit."

Jeremy smiled encouragingly. "That counts. What else do you remember?"

Witnessing his gentle but authoritative leadership, Ava wanted to hug him.

"I don't know, Doc. I guess I remember him saying something about being fifteen and not having a permit, but that he's still been driving his aunt to her chemo appointments for the last year."

"And I haven't gotten pulled over yet," Nolan added with a wink.

Ava felt a tug in her middle. Maybe underage driving was against the law, but it was also one of the most noble things she'd heard in a long time.

Encouraged, Hailey rolled back on her heels. "He likes oranges and string cheese, and he can peel an orange in one piece."

Nolan's eyebrows lifted. "You were paying attention, Half Pint."

The sour look reappeared on Hailey's face in a microsecond. "Don't call me Half Pint, Sasquatch."

"Aside from the fact that we all need to ask permission before we call anyone by a nickname they haven't called themselves, that was good, Hailey." Jeremy nodded at Nolan. "Your turn, Nolan."

"She can call me Sasquatch so long as I can call her Short Stack."

Ava was picking up on an underlying attraction between them that gave her a sense of all Jeremy had to manage in groups like this.

Nolan looked around the circle and pinched his lower lip between his thumb and forefinger. "Man, I'm glad I'm second because I was *not* paying attention in that circle half the time. Uh… Who do I remember anything about?" After a few seconds, he pointed at the redheaded girl with the far-off look to her. "What's your name again? Don't tell me. Rosebud or something."

"Lily," the shortest boy interjected with a snort.

"I knew it was a flower, didn't I?" Nolan shot off at him. "I guess she's got like a whole lot of stepbrothers and sisters in her house, but she's also an only child like me." He looked at Jeremy. "That's two things, right?"

"Let's count it as one," Jeremy said. "I have confidence in you, Nolan. What else can you share with Ava about Lily?"

Jeremy was great with the kids—calm and steady without being a pushover.

"Why do I think you set this up so you can quiz us?" Nolan asked.

Jeremy laughed. "It isn't a setup. Promise."

Nolan rolled his eyes without seeming genuinely frustrated. "Oh yeah, Lily's mom used to like to plant things before she stopped liking anything, and lilies were her favorite flower. Oh, and you said avocado rolls are your desert island food, didn't you?"

Lily looked at him in mild surprise. "They are."

Jeremy beamed. "Nice job, Nolan."

"Nolan and Lily, nice to meet you," Ava said, looking between them. "Lily, avocado rolls are *the best*. And Nolan, about the orange peeling, I can peel just about any fruit in one continuous piece. It's harder to do with potatoes."

She glanced at Jeremy when she finished talking, and there was something about the way he was looking at her—really looking at her—that made Ava's stomach drop into her toes.

Lily introduced Sammy, a solidly built girl with curly hair wearing a flannel shirt, well-worn jeans, and lime-green Converse shoes. Sammy owned a miniature schnauzer who was a chronic sneezer, liked to fly radio-controlled planes, and had six pairs of Converses.

Next, there was William, the shortest of the group, who seemed especially perceptive. He spoke four languages fluently, loved Mike and Ikes, and had a Guatemalan mom who'd come to the United States by marriage without knowing English but had since learned it and gotten a degree in auctioneering.

The others were Adam, who could juggle and ride a unicycle, and Christopher, the tallest and the former owner of a Mercedes he'd totaled after owning it seventeen days. Then it circled back to Hailey, who'd started off the introductions and who—to Ava's surprise—had a thing for soap operas, especially Hispanic tele-novelas, and liked bubble-gum ice cream.

"Growing up, bubble gum was my favorite flavor," Ava said, "but now it's anything Ben & Jerry's, with Americone Dream topping the list. So just a heads-up, all of you who give yoga a serious try will likely be treated to an ice-cream party at some point."

Adam grabbed his stomach. "I could eat me some Ben & Jerry's."

"Hey, no one did you, Doc." Hailey said, her hands shoved into her back pockets.

"'Cuz we all know him, you dweeb," Christopher scoffed. Ava had gotten the sense from his few side comments and the way he held himself—even before she'd heard the bit about him totaling a Mercedes seventeen days into owning it—that he was working through some anger issues.

"Remember the commitments we made Tuesday, Christopher?" Again, Jeremy's tone was assertive without being accusing.

The lanky teen dragged a hand through his light-blond hair, causing several fine ends to stick up like they'd been electrostatically charged. "Hailey."

"Thank you." Jeremy surprised Ava by turning to her and raising an eyebrow. "Want to go for it?"

Ava wiped the palms of her hands against the sides of her yoga pants at this display of trust. He'd certainly shared things with her he might not be ready to share with this group. "Um, let's see. Three things about Jeremy you all might not know…" She was tempted to add that she'd only known him a week, but she'd just witnessed a group of challenged teens rise to the occasion, sharing about peers they'd only met once. "Well, for starters, he did a polar plunge into Lake Michigan one January while in undergrad in Chicago." It was something he'd shared at the end of dinner the other night when he'd opened up and started talking a bit more about his life.

She ran her tongue along her top lip as the kids reacted with a chorus of varying exclamations, half claiming they wanted a chance at doing that, and others acting as if they couldn't believe it. "Ah, what else?" she continued. "He loves hot wings and has a soft spot for Fitz's root beer." *Time to go big or go home.* "And there's a groundedness to him that's different from anyone I've ever met."

She didn't look at him as she said it, but she could tell his feet shifted at the last sentence.

"Grounded?" Sammy said.

Ava shrugged. "Yeah, like a tree that doesn't get blown in a storm. Rooted."

"I can see that," Lily said, her voice a degree softer than the other kids.

"Is Adam grounded since he can ride a unicycle without falling down?" Nolan asked with a laugh.

"I think you're all on a journey to being grounded," Jeremy said. "And thank you, Ava. Well, there you have it, group. Less than two hours together, and not only do you know each other's names, you've already gotten to know some of what makes us unique…and connects us to one another, which I think can be easy to forget, especially in a world as virtual as the one you've been exposed to."

He noticed Edith and Eleanor walking out of the house at the same time Ava did. Eleanor was still rocking it in her Judas Priest shirt but had dated herself a little with the addition of a sweatband around her forehead and two more on her wrists. Edith, on the other hand, looked a little less fragile in the absence of her oversize gardener's hat, though her seersucker pants promised not to have much elasticity to them.

"Looks like it's go time," Jeremy said.

As the teens disbursed, half of them at a run to get back to the mat they'd already laid claim to, Rolo seemed to sense the change in energy. He trotted over from the corner of the garden where he'd been munching on the sparse, long blades of grass growing up between the bricks and shoved his head underneath Ava's hand.

"I'm hoping this means I'm going to have an assistant again." She bent down and draped him in a hug, soaking in the silky feel of his long black coat and appreciating the classic but mild dog smell he carried.

"Something tells me you will," Jeremy said. "He's becoming quite the Ava fan."

"Well, it's mutual, trust me." She smiled as she stood straight again. "And not that I had any doubts, but that was awesome. You're really good with the kids."

"Thanks."

As Edith and Eleanor made it to mats in the middle row, only one was left, front and center, which Ava and Jeremy seemed to notice at the same time. It seemed Ava was going to have an unobstructed view of Jeremy to unravel her focus this first class. Playing off her insecurities, she said with a laugh, "I guess no one wanted to be *that* kid tonight."

"Give 'em time," he said as he headed over to it. "I'm betting a few of 'em will be vying for that spot before it's all over."

Ava knelt to turn on her playlist, savoring the promise in his words. Maybe it was still undefined, but there was no denying this whole thing had a ring of permanence to it. And that was one hundred percent okay with her.

Chapter 13

AVA WAS GUIDING THE GROUP INTO SOMETHING CALLED SPHINX pose when Rolo popped up from the edge of her mat and trotted into the garden, offering Jeremy another uninterrupted view of her. This didn't help the fact that he was at war with himself, watching her for direction while doing his best not to be distracted by the beauty of her form as she guided them through the poses.

The hair he'd been longing to lose his hands in was pulled back in a low, loose ponytail that spilled over her shoulders. Her sleeveless light-blue tank with its interweaving back straps highlighted the fine muscles in her back and shoulders as she held the arched pose, her belly against the mat. Her legs were extended behind her, and her skintight leggings hugged the hips he'd been yearning to lock his hands around this last week. It didn't help that she'd planted herself in front of the garden entrance and was surrounded by a sea of flowering vines and plants, looking once more like a deity for his carnal desires.

He couldn't escape the feeling that being with Ava would be like taking a leap between high rises without a safety net below him. He carried a handful of physical scars from his father's abuse—on his brow, an arm, and a handful on his chest. They were scant in comparison to the emotional ones he'd done his best to leave behind but had ended up burying under a pile of distraction as he spent a career focused on other people's healing. If things were going to progress between them—something he suspected Ava wanted as much as some undeniable part of him did—he was going to have to come clean with his fears about what this would do to any relationship they aimed for. Yet, he couldn't imagine that going well. *"Hey, Ava, the thing is, I'm a little—a lot—terrified that a relationship with you will awaken the sleeping dragon of shadows I'll never be free of,"* was probably not something she was ready to deal with.

After the group worked their way up to standing on their mats again, he overheard Edith saying to Eleanor that she'd not felt a stretch that good in her lower back in twenty years. "Remember that one," she added. "I could do it in bed and not have to spend ten minutes picking myself up off the floor."

Jeremy chuckled quietly to himself as, at Ava's instruction, he folded in half at the waist with his legs straight underneath him, allowing his head to hang loose in front of his knees while cupping his calves. His quads and lower back immediately began to thank him. This yoga thing clearly had its merits.

Ava's smooth, strong voice and calm, steady presence no doubt helped the kids relax into the experience. They'd broken into laughter a few times as they moved through the poses, but she'd reined them back in fairly easily. She was guiding them into a lunge that was part of the warrior II pose when one of the boys in back let one rip. It was loud enough that most of the kids lost focus and began to laugh and fan their noses.

Ava didn't miss a beat. "The best warriors are never heard and certainly never smelt," she said and added, "Though that's a sign of release, too, I'll give you that."

A couple of the kids started tossing around one-liners about how they could beat each other in a game of release, while those nearest William fanned their noses.

Jeremy reminded them that they owed it to Ava to give her their best attempt at full attention. After taking a few seconds to collect themselves, the kids settled back into the pose, though a few shoulders continued to shake in laughter.

Having heard the commotion, Rolo burst out of the garden, tail wagging while he paused underneath the archway at the entrance. After a quick glance at Jeremy, he trotted over to check out a few of the kids before meandering back to Ava's mat and stretching out as she led everyone into a new pose. Jeremy had to hand it to his dog; Rolo was good at figuring out where he'd be the center of attention.

"Maybe he'll join us in a short savasana," she said with a glance at Jeremy. Moving over to share her mat, she guided the kids back onto theirs. Space hog that he was, Rolo rolled onto his back, his feet in the air as he wriggled back and forth, itching his spine. "Looks like he's ready," she added with a laugh.

"What's savasana?" Hailey asked, stretching out her legs and pointing her toes.

"It's one of the best poses in the world for feeling better if you're stressed, and it's how almost every yoga practice comes to a close." Ava paused to look over the class, and Jeremy could feel the energy in the air start to slow down. "Let's start to become aware of our breathing once again. Remember the mantra we talked about earlier: 'I breathe in, I breathe out.' That'll get you there."

Jeremy watched as the kids glanced around, no doubt wanting to make sure they weren't the only ones listening. From the middle row behind him, Jeremy heard Sammy mumble, "I breathe in, I breathe out" and smiled to himself. *This could really work.*

"Savasana is a pose of trust." Ava's tone was one of perfect calm. "We've built that with one another over the course of our practice tonight. We can settle into the pose and trust that we'll have this time not to be disturbed."

Ava patted the end of her mat to get Rolo out of the way after he stretched out.

Seeing that his dog was intent on outcompeting Ava for her mat space, Jeremy whistled. Rolo stood up with a grunt and trotted his way.

"Some say savasana is the easiest pose to perform and the most difficult to master. But when done right, the pose is a simple gift you can give yourself." She stretched out on her mat and lay back. "So, give yourself the gift of *this moment* and settle back onto your mats, stretch your legs out, and spread your arms at your sides, palms facing up. Your only job is to rest in this pose of relaxation."

As Rolo sprawled out alongside him, Jeremy closed his eyes. He could listen to Ava talk all night; that voice of hers was hypnotic. He wouldn't have guessed it to be likely, but he grew relaxed enough to experience the gradual rise and fall of his lungs and the slight buzz of energy in his hands and feet that he only noticed when his world was very still.

"Feel the weight of your body being supported by the ground." Ava sounded far away.

Jeremy focused his attention even more inward and experienced the weight of his calves, thighs, and back against the mat as the late-evening air brushed over his skin with just the right amount of coolness where it met beads of sweat that had risen to the surface. With his eyes closed, Jeremy sensed the warmth, soft sounds, and familiar smell of his dog beside him in a more heightened way, and a smile brushed his lips.

He wasn't sure how long had passed before Ava began bringing everyone back from their rest in a way that made it seem as if they had all night to gather their energy.

When Jeremy pushed up to a sitting position, she was already seated on her mat in easy pose, her legs folded and her back straight. Behind her, the sun was setting, and the sky was streaked with gold, orange, and red.

"I'm so thankful to each and every one of you for giving yoga a try tonight," she said.

A small chorus of thank-yous and a couple of yawns circled the group.

"Dude, I feel like I could sleep right here." Nolan stretched back on his mat again, looking more relaxed than Jeremy had ever seen him. Considering he'd been subject to considerable physical abuse from a heavy-handed father just as Jeremy had been, Jeremy appreciated the significance of his comment.

Ava ran her fingers absentmindedly through her ponytail and nodded at Nolan. "That means you did exactly what you were supposed to do in savasana. Many of us don't give our bodies the sleep they require. When we start really listening the way we learn to do in yoga, we'll hear them telling us what they need."

Jeremy was about to thank her when Sammy spoke up. "Maybe I'm backward then, because those couple minutes right there were the first time I didn't hear the voice in my head judging everything I do."

Ava smiled sympathetically. "I have one of those voices, too, and yoga is a great way to quiet it down."

"I have one too," Jeremy added.

Sammy looked at him, her eyes widening in surprise. "What does it tell you?"

"Different things at different times. Most recently it's been warning me that if I step out of my comfort zone, the footing I'm standing on won't be as solid."

"Is it *your* voice? Or someone else's?"

"That answer is pretty complicated," he said with a sympathetic smile. "We'll get to it in group sessions soon, but the voices in our heads are most often a form of self-protection, though not always a very helpful one."

"How come you have one, then, if you do all this?" Hailey asked.

Jeremy let out a breath. "Well, mine formed when I was a kid. My father beat me, and my mother spent half the time pretending she didn't see it and the other half attempting to convince me boys would be boys." It was more than he'd planned on saying in front of Ava, but this had morphed into a teaching moment that his kids could benefit from.

"Mine tells me I should take my aunt's car and keep driving until I get to a place where nobody knows me," Nolan said, fidgeting with a blade of grass, a forced playful look on his face despite the sincerity seeping into his tone.

"When I have these kinds of thoughts, ones that may not be in my best interest, I've found it's helpful to ask myself what I have to gain by listening to it, and what I have to lose," Jeremy said. "It might not make the thoughts stop coming, but it will help you deal with them better. Like I said, they don't always serve our best interest."

"How can you tell?" Sammy asked.

Jeremy nodded at Ava, who was watching attentively. "Well, that's what I'm hoping you'll find here. Getting quiet is certainly one way."

"Mine gets quiet when I eat chocolate," Edith said with a giggle.

After the kids' laughter died down, Jeremy gave Ava a nod to continue, and she leaned over to swipe a book from the grass at the side of her mat. "I mentioned earlier that I end every class with a quote from a book or article I've run across. I hope you'll find today's closing quote to be pretty apropos." She looked up at the kids after flipping to one of several marked pages. "I'm betting some of you have heard this one, but it never hurts to hear it again." Ava lifted up the book and waited until she had all the kids' attention. "'What lies behind us and what lies before us are tiny matters compared to what lies within us.'" She looked up and smiled at their murmurs of appreciation.

As the kids began to slip back on their socks and shoes, Jeremy took a minute to collect himself, taking in this unexpected synchronicity. He dragged his hand along Rolo's dense fur. His sponsor had said that quote to him a dozen times those first months he was sober and working to make it through another day.

When the kids began to ask about petting the dogs before their parents came, Jeremy gave Rolo one more pat and stood up. Frightening as it might be, there was no denying that he wanted to give this thing with Ava a shot. More than anything in a long time. And if he took the advice he dished out to his kids, he'd get out of his own way and give it a chance.

Chapter 14

It turned out the labradoodle liked chasing balls even more than he liked running. By the time the foster dogs were back in their kennels after a romp in the yard while the kids tossed around as many possible names as they did balls to the labradoodle, and the kids had all gone home with their parents, Jeremy had lost track of Ava and Rolo. She'd been in the kitchen when he last saw her, snipping tags off the remaining toys she'd brought.

Assuming she'd found her way upstairs with Edith and Eleanor, he jogged up the front staircase leading to their front door and rapped a few times. "Knock knock," he said, opening it to spy Edith setting the table for their late dinner. "Smells great. What is it, aside from zucchini fritters?"

Edith and Eleanor both loved to cook and alternated nights, and they had very different go-to recipes. Edith was a fan of traditional English dinners like Yorkshire pudding and shepherd's pie, especially in the winter months, while Eleanor was a bit more progressive in her cooking.

"Eleanor wanted to try those new veggie burgers everyone's raving about. The ones that taste like meat, though I can't fathom how they'll taste as good as the real thing."

"Oh yeah? I can tell a difference, but they're good."

"Tonight was lovely," she added. "Much like Ava."

"It was a good class," he said, and based on the second part of her comment, added, "I'm guessing she's not up here?"

"No, I thought she was downstairs with you."

"Nope." He walked to the front window and spotted her bright-blue Jeep still parked a few houses down. "She's probably out back then. I'll grab her and we'll be up in a few minutes."

As he jogged downstairs alone, it occurred to him that even his loyal dog had abandoned him to hang out with Ava. And Rolo was always underfoot. He headed out through the back, noticing how the labradoodle stirred from slumber as Jeremy walked through the room. It wasn't going to take much socialization for him to really start bonding with humans.

Outside, the horizon was still visible while the sky overhead had darkened to a cobalt blue, and the first few stars and planets were shining as the warmth of the afternoon dissipated, promising a cool evening ahead. As he crossed to the edge of the patio, a movement in the garden caught his eye.

Thanks to the streetlights out front, he could make out Ava in the thick of the vegetables near the green bean plants, her dark hair spilling over her bare shoulders. Jeremy's mouth went dry as he headed over. He spotted her slip-on sandals at the foot of the garden and realized she was still barefoot, filling him with surprise until he thought of her upbringing in the country.

He coughed once as he neared, more out of warning than need. Rolo bounded out of the garden, dashing over to greet him.

"Hey there." She met him at the entrance, a sheepish smile lighting her face. "You're probably wondering why I'm hanging out in your garden in the dark."

"Not at all, but feel free to share, if you'd like."

She laughed lightly. "This big garden got me thinking about my grandma. She likes to walk through hers at night. She swears you can hear the plants growing."

"And could you?" He scanned the garden until the image of the two of them tangled in sheets dissipated.

"No, but it made me a little homesick. I haven't been spending enough time with my grandparents—you know, while they're healthy and here and all that." Standing on the entry paver, she used her pointed toe to maneuver her sandals into position. As she slipped them on, she came unbalanced enough that, for a second, she grasped his arm to steady herself. Jeremy flexed his fingers to quiet the itch to lock his hand over the small of her back in return.

He wasn't ready to admit to her that, aside from his uncle, Jeremy's family hadn't been one to generate much, if any, nostalgia in him. "At least you're thinking that now while you can make a change," he said instead as she stepped onto the grass.

She nudged him with her elbow as they started crossing the yard. "Your kids were great. Terrific actually. You're amazing with them."

"Thanks, but you're the one who accomplished a small miracle tonight. After they relaxed a bit, they did so much better than I even had hoped."

"Well, I'm pretty sure this setting deserves half the credit." She waved a hand around the darkened yard, lit by the soft glow of lights above the pergola. "Oh! Before I forget, please tell me you have a key to that." She pointed at the old carriage house thirty feet from the garden.

"Edith and Eleanor do. Why?"

"When Rolo and I were in the garden, I'd almost swear I saw a cat slipping in through that broken window on the side. I guess it could've been a raccoon, but earlier I saw a cat out front. Regardless of what it is, if something's in there, I'd hate for it to get hurt by glass shards going in and out. I thought maybe you could prop open the door."

"Yeah, sure. I didn't realize a window was broken. I bet it was that storm midweek." He pulled out his phone and dialed Eleanor, who was a safer bet to have her phone with her than

Edith. When she answered on the third ring, he said, "Hey, how about tossing me the key to the carriage house?"

She agreed without asking questions, and Jeremy hung up. After having meandered off to sniff something, Rolo returned and walked alongside them as they headed toward the patio.

"How long did you say you've had him? Four years?"

"Ah, five now actually." Jeremy touched Ava's arm as they neared the patio. "Eleanor will toss it down."

The breeze was just strong enough that he caught the hint of vanilla and citrus wafting off her, leaving him with no doubt of the pleasure he'd find in tasting her skin. *Come off it, man.*

Overhead, the door to the small side balcony creaked open, and Eleanor peered out from the threshold. "Catch."

Jeremy caught the keys and sifted through them until he spotted the one marked for the vacant garage. "Ava spotted a broken windowpane in the garage next door. I'll see about getting someone out to repair it tomorrow."

"That's a shame. Those carriage house windows are original. Well, be up in about ten if you can."

Rolo kept close to Jeremy's heels this time as they headed back across the yard, and he could feel his dog's breath brushing against one hand.

"Do they eat so late every night?" Ava asked.

"I'd like to say no, but they keep the schedule of teens, right down to sleeping in late. Walking to a little grocery store near the park, working in the garden, and deciding what to make for dinner make up most of their day."

"They're cool...and, after seeing them on the mat tonight, I must say impressively agile for their age."

Jeremy agreed with her as they reached the single-door entrance facing into the yard. He needed to fiddle with the key to break through a thin layer of rust that had been building inside the lock.

"When do you think this was built?" she asked.

"I'm guessing with the house or right after it. Sometime in the late 1870s, back when horses got people where they needed to go."

"You know, these historic carriage houses are all the rage if you ever sell this lot. People are turning them into guest houses or studios."

"A neighbor down the street recently did that for her mother-in-law."

"That too."

When the lock gave, Jeremy glanced at Ava before opening the door. "Want to step back in case it was a raccoon?"

Jeremy turned the knob and cautiously pushed the door open. By now, his eyes had adjusted to the dark and enough street light poured in through the windows that it lit up patches of dim golden light across the part-concrete, part-dirt floor.

"Oh wow." After a few seconds when nothing seemed to stir, Ava stepped close to him again to peer inside, close enough that he felt the warmth radiating off the bare skin of her arm. "Exposed brick inside too. And are those the remains of old stalls?"

"They are." Her enthusiasm was infectious.

"This place would get snapped up in minutes if it went on the market. I can't believe the lot's sitting vacant." Her fingertips brushed his shoulder again, this time intentionally. "Not that having access to this property hasn't worked out great for you all."

"That it has." Jeremy cocked an eyebrow her direction. "So, how about it? Wanna leave the door open and walk away, or find out what you saw?"

"Find out, no question."

"I would've guessed that. Mind if I enter first, or is that too much machismo for you?"

Ava laughed and motioned him forward. "Chauvinism is what's dying out, not chivalry, I hope. Be my guest."

"Rolo, stay, buddy."

Rolo obeyed but whined as Ava stepped in behind Jeremy.

"Wow," she whispered, taking in the brick walls, windows, and rafters. A set of well-worn plywood shelves, mostly empty aside from a few old oil cans, pails, and boxes lined the wall with the broken window and glowed in the soft light.

Jeremy scanned the rafters and edges of the floor, looking for sign of an animal, but saw nothing. There were a few stacks of wood on the far wall, and he headed that way cautiously, suspecting something may be hiding behind it.

Halfway across, he stopped short and glanced at Ava in confirmation. He'd heard a meow, clear as day, but not the meow of an adult cat. It had been the frailer meow of a kitten.

Ava's face brightened, and she pointed toward a box on one side of the plywood shelving. "It came from inside there," she whispered.

Jeremy glanced at the door to make sure Rolo was staying put, but his dog was no longer in sight. Ava, who was closer to the box, tiptoed over, her hand loosely covering her mouth as if she were bracing for a shock.

She peered cautiously over the edge of the box and jumped when something inside hissed loudly. She backed up several feet. "I saw the mama cat in there, and she definitely has a litter. I could see them squirming around her."

In the quiet that followed, Jeremy could make out a series of soft meows. "Wow. Kittens, huh? And I'm guessing the mother's feral."

As if in proof, the mama cat jumped out of the box and landed light on her feet on the plywood nearby. Her back arched, the hair on her spine rose, and her tail stuck out behind her as she hissed again. She was hard to make out in the dark, but her coat seemed marbled brown and black, and she didn't look that far removed from being a kitten herself.

"She's a tortie. They're my favorite," Ava whispered.

"What's a tortie?"

"A cat with a tortoiseshell coat."

Now that Jeremy was looking at the shelving more closely, he could see a series of pawprints leading back and forth in the dust from the broken window to the box.

"What do we do?" Ava asked.

"Well, *not* looking more closely inside the box right now is a good idea, I'm betting. She's frightened and ready to defend her kittens."

"We're not going to hurt you, pretty girl." As soon as they'd backed up enough to be able to be clear of the door, Ava said, "Gabe! He'll tell us what to do. When it comes to feral cats, there's so much controversy that I don't know who's right."

Jeremy hardly noticed her pulling out her phone, distracted as he was by Rolo who was walking up from the side of the yard. He stopped five feet away, his head down and tail tucked the way he did when he'd done something Jeremy wouldn't approve of. Jeremy's knees nearly buckled as he realized a small animal was in Rolo's mouth. It took a few seconds to discern that it was a kitten—one that looked lifeless.

"Shit."

Ava whipped around and gasped. While Jeremy was debating what to do, Rolo continued forward, head down and tail tucked. In a posture of clear submission, he placed an impossibly small smoke-gray kitten gingerly at Jeremy's feet and licked it a few times.

Wanting to spare Ava the shock of staring at a dead kitten, Jeremy scooped it up to find that it stirred at his touch. It was weak but alive—and wet with dog slobber but zero marks from Rolo's teeth. "Good boy, Rolo, good boy!" Jeremy exhaled in relief as he turned to Ava. "It's responsive to the touch but not much."

"So, he just…found it?" Ava stepped in for a closer look.

"I'm guessing. He likes cats, and that wasn't predatory behavior just now."

"No, it definitely wasn't." She bent down and scratched Rolo with both hands. "What a good boy you are, Rolo!" Rolo's head lifted and his tail untucked at the praise.

"Do you think the mama cat moved them and forgot one, or do you think she intentionally left this one behind?"

"I don't think we can know for sure, and certainly not without seeing the condition of the others. Maybe he's a runt and not doing so hot, or maybe the mama can't count and forgot one when she was moving them to a new spot." He cupped both hands around the tiny kitten, certain it was missing the warmth of its siblings. Thankfully, it had been a warm day, not a chilly one, or the kitten might not have survived.

Using her phone's voice-to-text option, Ava asked her sister to have Gabe call ASAP. This late in the day, Gabe wouldn't still be working. Sure enough, in less than a minute, her phone rang.

"Thanks for calling," she said before diving in with what they'd found in the garage and the abandoned kitten. After listening as he talked for a bit, she said, "Okay, got it. We can do that." She fell quiet again, then added, "Yeah, sure. We're about to eat. We'll give it a half hour and see what she does."

After thanking him, she hung up and turned to Jeremy. "He'd like us to give the mama cat the benefit of the doubt and put the kitten back in the box with his littermates."

Jeremy glanced back through the doorway. The angry and frightened cat was nowhere in sight now. "I can do that."

"Wait." Ava closed her hand around his arm. "He suggested

wearing a thick jacket and using an oven mitt—and a hockey mask if we think the mama cat might lunge at us. Rabies is rare in cats but not impossible."

"Makes sense. I can run inside and grab them—sans the hockey mask."

"He said we could scare her off first, depending on how threatened she is and if she looks like she wants to attack."

"Okay, let me see what I can find. Here." He carefully transferred Ava the kitten, who stirred again in the process. "Be right back."

Jeremy took off toward the house as soon as the kitten was securely in her hands. One thing was for sure; this last week since he'd met Ava had been anything but monotonous.

Chapter 15

WHILE HELPING HERSELF TO ANOTHER MOUTHWATERING FRITTER, Ava suppressed the urge to get up from the table and head to the window facing the side yard. What if the mama cat carried the kitten away again and no one could find it?

That's not going to happen. Gabe said to give the mama some time to reaccept him, and that was what they needed to do.

Putting the kitten back with its littermates had proved easier than Ava had anticipated after donning the protective gear Jeremy had grabbed. She'd been the one to put the kitten in while he'd kept the mama away, and luckily, the upset cat had done nothing aside from hiss and arch her back.

As thoughts popped up again of adopting the entire group of warm bodies snuggled in the worn, musty box down in the carriage house, Ava reminded herself she had a wonderful cat at home—actually, at her sister's home. Remembering her currently homeless state was the validation she needed as to why a large-scale adoption wasn't in her best interest. It likely wasn't in the mama cat's best interest either. Adult feral cats often didn't fare well in homes. The kittens, on the other hand, could easily bond with people.

Forcing her attention back to her fellow diners, she nudged Jeremy with her elbow. "Here's a bit of trivia for you. It's from a feral cat organization whose newsletter I receive. What do you call a group of cats?"

After finishing a bite of his veggie burger, he said, "A herd?"

Edith held up a finger. "No, don't tell me, I know the answer.

It'll come, tomorrow maybe, as irritating as my recall has been lately, but it'll come."

"It's not a litter, is it?" Eleanor asked.

"That's of kittens," Ava said. Underneath the table, Rolo was stretched out on his side, his head draped across Ava's feet. "A group of cats has its own name, even if hardly anyone uses it."

"Oh! That last bit rang a bell." Tapping her bent-with-age pointer finger on the table, Edith began uttering names starting with *c* before abruptly pointing at Ava. "A clowder!"

"Bingo!" Ava high-fived her across the table, which made Edith chuckle with delight.

"Speaking of bingo, we haven't been to a bingo night all summer." Eleanor refilled her glass of water from the chilled quart-sized glass bottle in the center of the table.

Eleanor waved a hand dismissively. "Who needs bingo when we have Ava? What else have you got, dear?"

Ava considered this as she finished a bite of burger. "We could see who knows the most cat idioms. Or not…" She giggled after a sideways glance at Jeremy; he was shaking his head but smiling.

"Wouldn't that be the cat's pajamas?" Eleanor said, proving what Jeremy had said about her being quick on her feet.

"Now you've done it, Ava," Jeremy said. "Eleanor's the most competitive person I know. I see a contest coming."

"Don't you know it." Eleanor pulled out her phone. "I'm setting the timer for ten minutes. Whoever works the most cat idioms into the natural flow of the conversation in the next ten minutes wins."

"Is dinner always this exciting?" Ava whispered to Jeremy.

"Not when it's the three of us."

Suddenly, everyone fell quiet for the first time since dinner started. Ava could envision wheels turning in everyone's heads.

"What's the matter, Jeremy? Cat got your tongue?" Edith asked before sitting back in her chair and clapping her hands.

"Well played, Edith, though there's no reason to look like the cat who ate the canary."

Ava jumped in. "I hear it's going to rain cats and dogs tonight."

"Is it really going to rain, or are you making that up?" Jeremy asked.

She made a face. "I made it up. Does it still count?"

He dragged a hand over his chin. "I don't see why not, after all, there's more than one way to skin a cat."

All around the table, shoulders shook with laughter, and Ava sat back against her chair, wiping her eyes.

"Watch shedding those tears, dear, or you'll look like something—"

"The cat dragged in," everyone finished simultaneously.

When cat idioms were thoroughly exhausted, idioms continued to fly, from chewing the fat, under the weather, a dog in church, a piece of cake, and others until long after everyone lost count of who was winning.

"I say Eleanor wins," Ava said when they'd finished eating. As much fun as it had been, it was time to check on the kitten. "And Edith, you're a close second."

"How so?" Jeremy asked. The hint of a smile hadn't left his face since the idiom flying began, one that had Ava wanting to lock her arms around him as she savored the glow of joy flowing through her veins, telling her that this was exactly how life was supposed to be.

"Because Eleanor worked 'You can't pluck feathers off a bald chicken' into our conversation," she replied.

"I'll give you that." He chuckled.

Edith sat forward and flattened her hands on the table, a smile outing her mock-affronted look. "What about my 'squeezing blood out of a turnip'?"

"That was good, too, but not quite as unique," Ava assured her.

"And you didn't say it right." Jeremy's tone was gentle enough not to put even the most sensitive of people off. "The point is you *can't* squeeze blood out of a turnip."

Edith laughed, her thin shoulders shaking. "I got too excited with that one and spouted it out too fast." She patted Eleanor on the shoulder. "I'm proud of you. You're sharp as a tack, even at seventy-nine."

"And the last idiom flies." Jeremy stood and began to collect plates. Hearing him, Rolo clambered out from under the table. He paused beside it, his expression set in the most endearing of begs.

Edith waved Jeremy away from the dish clearing. "You have a clowder of cats to care for, or is it a kindle of kittens, since the kittens outnumber the cat? Whatever the answer, Eleanor and I will take care of this." To Ava, she said, "When are you here next, dear?"

Ava looked at Jeremy. "I teach again next Friday."

"I hope you'll plan on joining us for dinner again. I'll make you that cheese pudding we talked about."

Yoga, followed by another dinner like this. The promise of it was better than winning a coveted listing she and her fellow agents had been scrambling for. "If you don't mind." Jeremy was suddenly hard to read, but he wasn't exactly shooting daggers at Edith for her invitation either.

"It was a joy having you," Eleanor backed her up.

After thanking them again, Ava shrugged sheepishly at Jeremy, who winked as he picked a discarded bite of pretzel bun off his plate. After asking Rolo to sit, he placed it on the bridge of his nose. Rolo sat patiently until Jeremy gave him a nod, then the hunk of bread disappeared in a flash that was almost too quick for Ava to see.

"'Night, ladies. I'll text you a kitten update soon," Jeremy said as they headed for the door.

Ava trailed down the steps after Rolo, and Jeremy followed. "I wish we knew where he found it, to know for sure there aren't any more."

"Cat lover that he seems to be, I have no doubt he'd either have gone back, or he wouldn't have left the area in the first place. But let's give the yard another sweep to make sure."

As soon as they were through the back door, Rolo wasted no time beelining for the carriage house. Rather than leave the door ajar, potentially offering easy access to anything else that wanted in, Jeremy had opened the window with the broken pane for the mama to come and go. Rolo sniffed underneath the closed door; the sound amplified by the narrow opening at the bottom.

After a thorough sniffing, Rolo took off abruptly, his black and brown fur hardly visible in the darkness as he trotted straight for the far corner of the vacant yard. When he got there, he sniffed the grass and then turned to bark at Jeremy and Ava.

Ava braced herself for whatever was coming as they hurried after him. "I can't look." She locked her hand around Jeremy's wrist for a second or two as anticipation rocked her, and she found it harder to let go than she'd like to admit. This far from the house, it was clear how fully night had set in, and hundreds of stars were shining in the cloudless sky.

They closed off the last four or five steps in silence. Jeremy pulled out his phone and shone its flashlight into the grass, then sank onto the backs of his heels.

"Good boy, Rolo. Good boy." He turned off the flashlight and slipped his phone back into his pocket.

"Another kitten? Is it still alive?"

"Ava, it's not another kitten, it's *the* kitten."

Ava's top teeth dug hard into her bottom lip in anticipation. "Are you sure it's him? Want me to check the box to be sure?"

Jeremy stood, the kitten cupped in his hands, and nodded.

"Yeah, let's make sure, but it's all gray and seems smaller than the others."

"Darn it! But he's still moving?"

"He stirred again, but just barely."

Her heart sank. "Gabe said if she rejects it again, then it's likely failure to thrive. He said mother cats can sense it and stop feeding them."

As they neared the garage, kitten in tow and Rolo following closely, Ava pulled out her own phone to use as a flashlight. Turning the handle, she announced herself. "Mama kitty, I'm coming in to check your kittens." To Jeremy, she said, "I'll stay out of her way."

"Careful, Ava."

The dim starlight poured in through the many windows even without the brightness of a moon, swallowing up the artificial light of her phone so that it seemed insignificant. She kept talking, not paying attention to the words, as she crossed over to the box.

She held her breath as she peered over the top. Aside from the kittens who were mostly awake and snuggled together, the box was empty.

"The mama's gone, Jeremy," she whispered over her shoulder. "She must be out hunting."

Still cradling the kitten, Jeremy joined her in front of the box and peered inside. Even anxious as she was, Ava's skin tingled from the nearness of him.

"I can only make out four, and none of them are gray." This uninterrupted look at the kittens' home proved disheartening. Their would-be cozy bed was a hodgepodge of planting accessories: faded seed packets, an old bag of potting soil, well-worn gloves, and a hand shovel. Ava wished to set a blanket inside but knew the mother might move the litter if her nest was disturbed.

Instead, careful not to touch anything else, she cautiously pulled out the hand shovel and set it on the shelf a few feet from the box before heading out, Jeremy following closely behind.

Ava met Jeremy's gaze. "She took him back out." She proved unable to keep the plea from her tone. "She's not going to care for him. Maybe it's the natural course of things, but Jeremy, we've got to help him!"

"Of course." His gaze held hers with a confidence she'd not seen before. "Whatever we can do, we'll do."

"Thanks." She stepped in and gave him a half hug, avoiding the frail kitten cupped in his hands. "High Grove's closed for the night, but we can take care of him as well as Gabe. If you're up for keeping him warm, I'll make a run for kitten formula and a bottle. And I'll call Gabe again as I'm driving."

From the doorway, Rolo whined as if he knew what they were discussing.

"Go for it."

"And no electric heating pads, I know that much," Ava warned. "Warming bottles work, though, if you have one."

"Good to know. I'll keep the back door unlocked, and I'll be upstairs in my apartment."

"Okay. Call if you think of anything. My purse is inside. I need to grab it." She took off toward the house at a jog. She'd been raised on a farm and knew what it meant to make a fool's promise, but as she hurried across the lawn, she had no reservations against making one. If there was any possible way she could keep that kitten alive until morning, she'd find a way to do it.

Chapter 16

FATIGUE WAS PUSHING IN, THREATENING TO CLOUD JEREMY'S thoughts as he set the goldendoodle puppies down in the grass under the brilliant night sky. They stuck together like bookends without any books between them as they wandered a few feet into the grass, sniffing and stepping cautiously.

It was a little after one in the morning, and the night was alive with the sounds of early summer as an army of crickets and cicadas attempted to outcompete one another. The other two dogs were fast asleep, but he'd heard one of the puppies crying from all the way upstairs where he and Ava had been taking care of the kitten.

Stifling a yawn, Jeremy tried to recall his schedule for tomorrow but couldn't. As busy as his Friday had been, he'd forgotten to check at the end of it. He thought he remembered an early-morning Zoom call with his client case advisor but hoped it wasn't until next week. At ten thirty, his last group of program kids would be arriving for their final service project. They were headed back to High Grove to finish installing two benches near the fenced play areas that they'd been working on last month.

Regardless of his schedule, with the foster dogs here, he wouldn't be sleeping in past his usual five thirty for some time. After catching whatever sleep he could get once Ava left, he'd be relying on extra cups of coffee tomorrow, no doubt.

Standing under the glow of the stars, a wave of serenity washed over him, muting his fatigue. He'd been missing out the last few years, not accompanying Rolo into the yard at night for his final bathroom break of the day. Growing up in Cahokia, light pollution had been minimal, and gazing out at the night sky as he'd fallen asleep had been one of Jeremy's consistent sources of comfort. As busy as the last few years had been, he'd gotten into the habit of only taking time to appreciate the night sky when he was camping.

A few feet away, after investigating each blade of grass and getting distracted by every sound, the male puppy finally dipped his hind end to pee. "Good boy!" Jeremy sank onto his heels, praising him with a pat and offering one of the treats he'd brought with him. Even though the voting poll would stretch out another day, Jeremy was already thinking of him as Mortimer, a name Hailey had suggested earlier that really seemed to fit and all the kids had liked.

Seeing that the puppies were curious to explore, Jeremy opted not to rush them. While sniffing something buried in the grass, Mortimer sneezed loudly, startling his sister. She dashed over to Jeremy, tucking herself between his feet. Chuckling, he bent down and scratched her head before she took off to join her brother again.

Rolo, who had settled down on the brick pavement and was starting to doze, lumbered back to his feet and pressed in close. Jeremy wondered which his dog was hoping for more, a bit of praise or a treat of his own. Jeremy gave him a hearty scratch on the jowls. "You're dealing with a lot of change, aren't you, boy?"

Rolo licked Jeremy's chin, which Jeremy tolerated for several seconds before standing up and wiping his chin dry with his shoulder. "Thanks, but that's all I can handle. It's hard to forget where your mouth has been."

He glanced up at the light pouring out from the windows on the second floor. Ava had stayed inside with the kitten. When he stepped out, she'd been sitting cross-legged on the floor at the base of his couch, looking like a statue of an ancient earth goddess. The kitten had been on her lap, a towel and water bottle underneath his frail little body, and Ava had been yawning almost nonstop. He'd told her she could head home, and he'd see to the rest of the night's feedings, but it was clear she wasn't walking away from that kitten, no matter how tired she was.

After talking to Gabe a second time, she'd picked up a syringe at the store in addition to a bottle. When the kitten had shown zero interest in sucking, she'd been able to inject a few cc's of formula through the side of his mouth and had done so twice in the last few hours. Jeremy didn't think it was his imagination that the kitten seemed to be perking up a bit. He was more responsive to touch, and he'd even let out the frailest of meows.

Staring out toward the garden, Rolo grew stone-still and perked his ears forward. After a short pause, he took off at a trot, his tail relaxed enough that Jeremy assumed whatever he could smell or hear in the dark was neither a threat nor prey.

The cat. It was too dark to spot her tortoiseshell coat in the grass, but Jeremy suspected it was her even before he spotted the glow of her eyes. He thought about calling his dog back but decided Rolo knew what he was doing.

Jeremy walked deeper into the yard, moving far enough away from the light pouring out the windows that his night vision fully kicked in. Trailing as close to Jeremy's feet as possible, Mortimer whined until Jeremy scooped him up, then his sister when she began to whine as well.

Rolo approached the cat like he was greeting a familiar friend. Both their demeanors were calm enough that Jeremy was certain they'd met before, making him wonder how long the cat had been coming into the yard.

In addition to the supplies for the kitten, Ava had come back with two small bowls and an eight-pound bag of cat chow, an organic brand that claimed to be gentler on the earth than any other leading brand. "For the hardworking mama," she'd said. Jeremy didn't know enough about feral cats to know how readily they took to cat food when they were accustomed to hunting, but with any luck, a ready supply of food would help the mother cat provide for her other kittens.

A memory of Jeremy's own mother was stirred to the surface as he watched them. She had worked on her feet as a hairdresser for nine or ten hours a day to come home to a husband who was a consistent fixture on the couch between the jobs he somehow managed to secure but never keep. Most of his father's afternoons and evenings had been spent either drinking his way to a hangover or sleeping off one from booze bought with money they didn't have to spare.

As always, when thoughts led to his father, Jeremy shoved them away. He could handle ghosts but not demons.

Rolo's tail wagged as he and the cat sniffed noses, then Rolo sniffed along the length of her belly. To Jeremy's surprise, the cat walked right underneath Rolo and over to the edge of the garden toward the carriage house.

Jeremy wondered if she'd encountered the food-and-water-filled bowls they'd placed outside the carriage house not far from the open window. After observing the cat for several seconds, Rolo peed on a garden post, then trotted back across the yard.

"I'd love to know what you think about all this, bud. If only you could tell me." Rolo pressed against Jeremy's leg, soaking in the praise in his tone. "Come on, let's go tell Ava who you've made friends with."

He paused in front of the puppies' crate. They were beginning to tousle in his arms and gnaw at his hands. The other two dogs were likely to sleep through until morning, but these two weren't on the same schedule. "Just this time."

Pausing at the landing on top of the stairs, he shifted the female pup over one shoulder and opened his apartment door. He was about to announce that he'd not come back empty-handed but stopped himself. Ava had curled up on the floor with the kitten snuggled on the towel in front of her, and her eyes were closed.

When Rolo trotted over for a sniff of both Ava and the kitten, Ava didn't so much as stir. Jeremy's feet locked in place as he stared at her, her hair splayed on the floor, her feet bare, and her arm a pillow. If he'd ever been more stirred by such serene beauty in human form, he couldn't recall.

With her eyes closed, hiding that remarkable blue hue that kept him from noticing just about anything else, he took in the curves made by her lips and eyebrows, the straight line of her nose, and her long, smooth neck. When his gaze landed on the swell of her breasts, his internal reaction was a primal one and as effective as several swigs of coffee.

Forcing his gaze off her, he shut the door quietly behind him and headed to his bedroom. Once there, he set the puppies on the floor. The chubby-bellied, spindly-legged things immediately began to explore, while Jeremy searched around for Rolo's abandoned antler chews that often wound up getting kicked behind the door or under furniture.

As if Rolo knew what was at risk, he trotted over to his oversize dog bed on the floor that hardly got used and snatched up his well-worn stuffed animal cat, the one he'd carried around in his mouth so often its fluff was missing in the middle, and headed for the door.

Jeremy chuckled. "I hear you, bud. Some things you don't have to share."

As it turned out, one of the puppies located an antler first and dragged it out from underneath the edge of Jeremy's bed. "You had the advantage of that nose working for you."

Looking proud and guilty at the same time, Mortimer dragged it across the wooden floor right onto Rolo's bed, climbed on top, and began gnawing away.

Still watching from the doorway, Rolo looked from the puppy to Jeremy before heading back down the hall. Curious what was more interesting to Rolo than a puppy chewing his antler on top of his bed, Jeremy followed.

Rolo dropped the stuffed cat for a long drink from his bowl in the kitchen, then picked it up again and headed into the living room. He wasted no time stretching out underneath the coffee table near Ava, coming to rest with his nose less than a foot from the sleeping kitten.

"Who would've known?" Jeremy said.

Jeremy located a few more of Rolo's toys strewn across the apartment and headed back to his room to find that Millie—the name everyone seemed to like for her since it went so well with Mortimer—had joined her brother on Rolo's bed and was attempting to chew on the other end of the antler.

He dropped a second antler carefully between them, kicked off his shoes, and collapsed across his bed for a moment of rest. Sleep beckoned him almost instantly, but he pulled himself up from it. He first needed to contend with two un-potty-trained puppies roaming free in his bedroom, a kitten quite possibly on the brink of death in his living room, and a remarkable woman asleep on the living room floor.

Jeremy hadn't expected Ava to stay, but now that she was asleep, it didn't seem right waking her up and expecting her to safely drive home. They'd need to offer the frail kitten another few cc's of formula at 3:00 a.m. He opted for setting his alarm so he could doze a bit himself and wake her up then. *So, you're going to leave her on the floor to wake up with a crick in her neck?*

No, he couldn't do that. He kept a few spare blankets and a pillow in the hall closet for the occasional friend who came to visit. After grabbing them and setting them on the couch, he turned off the overhead light and, as quietly as possible, moved the coffee table out of the way.

Rolo lifted his head and pricked his ears, watching him. Realizing his loyal dog wouldn't want the kitten out of his sight, Jeremy moved the box they'd made into a cozy nest for the kitten to the floor nearby, then moved the kitten—towel and water bottle included—inside it. The tiny thing stirred as he did, enough that Jeremy was certain it was with more strength than he'd shown earlier. "Keep fighting, little guy."

As Jeremy was setting up the couch with the pillow and blanket, careful not to step on Ava in the process, the girl puppy came waddling down the hall, dragging the antler along with her.

"This place is a full-on circus tonight."

When he couldn't decide between waking Ava or lifting her to the couch, he gave a few seconds thought to flipping a coin. He told himself the decision to move her had more to do with giving her the opportunity for a longer stretch of undisturbed sleep than him wanting the experience of her in his arms—even though there'd be no forgetting the feel of her against him after he did.

She mumbled something in the darkened room as he lowered her to the couch, then turned to curl against the back of it. Jeremy gently extracted his arms from underneath her and stepped back, certain he'd be smelling that enticing scent of hers as he drifted off. He was attempting to rub the feel of her smooth skin from his palms as the puppy finished dragging the antler across the floor and settled down next to Jeremy's feet.

With Rolo determined to remain on guard duty, Jeremy hoisted the puppy into his arms, antler included, and headed back to his room. With exhaustion pressing in heavier now, maybe he'd be too tired to dream about Ava. Or anything at all. He put the puppy in the middle of his bed and did the same with her brother before flipping off the light and setting his alarm. An hour and a half were all he'd get before he needed to wake up and start the feeding process over again with the kitten.

"Tell me you'll be good for that long, you two, and you won't pee on the bed or gnaw holes through the comforter."

As if in answer, Mortimer stretched out, extending his hind legs behind him and locking his front paws around the antler, and went back to gnawing away at something he had zero chance of making a dent in.

"I'll take that as a yes," Jeremy said before the words were sucked up with a yawn. He stretched out across the bed, too tired to reach for a pillow, and fell asleep to the continuous chomping and horsing around of two determined young dogs.

Chapter 17

SOMETHING WET SWIPING ACROSS HER CHEEK DREW AVA OUT OF A deep sleep, that and the not-so-pleasant breath washing over her. She opened her eyes in a night-darkened room to find herself face-to-face with a massive dog.

Rolo, she realized as she began to orient herself again. "Hey, bud," she said, the words getting sucked up in a yawn. She'd dozed off while watching the kitten breathing in his sleep. She stiffened at once, terrified she'd crushed him in her sleep. She was sweeping the spot in front of her when Rolo walked a few feet away and whined.

Everything was coming back, except for her confusion over how she'd made it to the couch when the last thing she remembered was curling onto the floor, the kitten tucked safely in front of her.

Jeremy. Considering her head was lying on a pillow and she was covered by a blanket that hadn't been there before, there was no other explanation.

Had he woken her up, and she didn't remember? *Please don't say he lifted me.*

Realizing that Rolo was whining about a box on the floor, Ava sat up. Worries about being a well-padded deadweight fled in the face of something more important—the kitten.

Dear God, please let him be alive. Holding her breath, she got up and joined Rolo on the floor. She was reaching into the box, her top teeth digging into her lower lip, when a weak meow came from inside.

"Thank you, thank you, thank you!" she mumured.

Earlier this evening, the kitten hadn't been in shape to meow at all. He'd hardly been breathing. A handful of hours later, thanks to adequate warmth and a solid start at rebuilding essential hydration and nutrition, the kitten was crying out for more.

Ava reached in to brush the tips of her fingers over his tiny head. She could see his front paws flexing at her touch in the dark. "Sweet kitty, let me get you some more food."

She headed for the kitchen, stepping carefully. Aside from the dim glow from the streetlights coming in through the side-facing windows, Jeremy's apartment was dark.

Without turning on the light, Ava opened the fridge and took out the kitten formula. Standing at the counter, she filled the clean syringe with fifty cc's of formula, then wet a paper towel with warm water and wrapped it around the syringe in hopes of removing the chill.

The clock on the microwave showed it was almost three o'clock; Rolo had woken her up at the perfect time. Or, more aptly, the kitten had likely woken Rolo up as he'd gotten hungry.

While the serving of formula was warming, Ava tiptoed down the short hallway and peeked into Jeremy's room, assuming she'd find Jeremy. She paused in the doorway, her chest constricting.

In the moonlight, she could just make out Jeremy on his back atop the cover. He was sleeping diagonally across his wide bed. Despite the fact that he was a six-foot-tall adult man, something about watching him sleep touched her the same way the kitten did. She stood there for a string of seconds, appreciating the even rise and fall of his chest and wishing she were cuddled next to him, one hand on his stomach, soaking in the rhythm of his breath.

In the darkness, it seemed like a blanket was wadded up in the crook of his armpit, but then it moved, and Ava realized it was one of the foster dogs. Two of the foster dogs, more accurately— the goldendoodle puppies. One of the puppies, the boy judging by his darker coat, was awake and watching her, wagging his tail. It thumped against Jeremy's side just hard enough for the sound to carry.

In the dim light, Ava noticed the patch of smooth skin exposed below Jeremy's T-shirt and the thin trail of dark, curly hair above the elastic rim of the underwear peeking out from the top of his exercise pants. Her blood both warmed and pooled in a primal way, so much so that she could envision herself climbing on top of him and giving herself over to pleasure.

She was about to turn away when one of the puppies army crawled across the bed and began chewing on something that looked an awful lot like a phone. Ava tiptoed over and confirmed she was right. Right as she extracted Jeremy's phone from the puppy's mouth, its alarm went off. Startled, she clicked it off instantly and froze in place, humiliated by the prospect of being caught hovering over Jeremy while he was sleeping.

His eyes shot open, and Ava was about to launch into an explanation that hopefully wouldn't have her coming off like a stalker when they closed again. With a clearing of his throat, he turned onto his side, and his deep, even breathing resumed, not having woken up enough to notice her.

Oh, thank you, Lord!

She slid an antler that had been abandoned near the puppy into easy reach and tiptoed out, relaxing only after reaching the safety of the kitchen. Realizing his phone was still in her hand, she set it on the counter to deal with later.

Rolo, who'd been watching her from the edge of the living room, woofed once and trotted over to the kitten's box.

"I'm coming," Ava whispered and headed in with the syringe.

As gently as possible, she lifted the kitten out of the box, bringing one of the smaller towels along with it, and headed for the couch. Her heart warmed all over when the little guy meowed again.

She took her time working the syringe in through the side of his mouth, savoring his tiny perfection, from his still-toothless gums to his little paws to the still-rounded tips of his ears. This time, he was strong enough to struggle, clearly not liking the feel of a foreign object being inserted into his mouth. While fighting her, his eyes opened fully for the first time all night, something that Ava took to be another good sign. She'd noticed his stronger littermates had fully opened eyes as well, the ones who'd been awake, at least.

When Ava had told Gabe about the kittens' open eyes but still toothless gums, he'd guesstimated their age to be between two and three weeks old. He promised to swing by this morning to give all the kittens and their mama a once-over and figure out the best next steps for all of them.

"I'm a believer in positive thinking, Ava, but brace yourself," Gabe had said on the phone earlier as she drove to the store. "That mama didn't take a kitten away from her litter for nothing, not if she's still caring for the rest."

But just because an overworked, undernourished young mother couldn't care for him didn't mean it wasn't worth fighting for him.

Carefully, Ava squeezed out a drop or two of formula, making sure she didn't release so much that the kitten aspirated. When he swallowed, she felt the warm glow of success. His big, round eyes stayed open, almost hypnotic in the dark room. Before she inserted the syringe again, he meowed his loudest meow yet. Rolo pressed in over the top of her arm, sniffing the kitten without being too intrusive.

The experience reminded Ava of springtime on her

grandparents' farm and the calves born into their small herd of
Hereford cattle, the lamb or two born to an even smaller flock of
sheep, and, undoubtedly, the litter of kittens born to whichever
barn cat was around that year. Her grandma had cherished those
kittens as much as Ava and Olivia had. Ava had a dozen clear
memories of her grandma heading out to the barn to pick out a
kitten from the litter to cuddle on her lap while she watched a ball
game on the satellite TV.

"How come kittens are so much cuter than cats?" her sister
had asked one day as they hovered near Grams's recliner, swoon-
ing over the tabby kitten on their grandma's lap as it played with
the drawstring on her elastic-waisted pants.

"They're full of god dust, that's why." Grams had an answer
for everything. When both Ava and her sister had laughed, she'd
not taken offense. "You won't get it until you're older, but every
living thing comes into the world glowing with it—plants, trees,
animals, especially kittens."

Sitting in the dark and stroking the kitten's frail-but-perfect
body, Ava got a sense of what her grandma had been talking
about.

Finally figuring out how to maneuver the syringe into the kitten's mouth with minimal fuss on his part, Ava continued dripping the remaining cc's of formula onto the back of his tongue
and making sure he swallowed. Halfway through, the kitten
seemed to grow accustomed to the reward accompanying the
intrusion into his mouth and struggled less. Rolo hovered beside
them the entire time, panting and wagging his tail.

"I'd love to know what you're thinking, you know."

At the sound of her voice, Rolo pressed in and licked the side
of her jaw.

"You're the best dog, absolutely the best." She rested her head
atop his for a moment, soaking in the feel of his silky fur against

her cheek. "Don't let it go to your head, but there's something about you that melts my heart like it's made of chocolate on a hot summer day."

By the time the syringe was emptied, Ava was exhausted enough to wish she could curl on the couch with the kitten and fall back to sleep, but he was undoubtedly safer inside the cardboard box.

She was in the kitchen, holding the kitten in one hand and wetting a cotton ball with warm water from the sink faucet to stimulate him to use the bathroom when she heard one of the puppies whining from Jeremy's room.

Hearing it too, Rolo trotted off into the bedroom. By the time Ava was tucking the kitten back in the box, both Rolo and Millie were heading down the hall toward her.

"Partners in crime, huh?" she whispered. She scooped the puppy into her arms and headed back for the second one. Her brother was prancing on the edge of the bed, eyeing the jump to the floor. Ava scooped him up as well and headed for the door.

She made as quick of work as she could of letting the puppies into the backyard for a bathroom break, then getting them back in their crate. As she did, the mama doodle stirred at the opposite end of the sunroom, perking her ears, but didn't seem restless enough that Ava was compelled to give her a potty break of her own. After the kitten's next feeding, Ava would make sure to give them all one.

It was strange, she thought as she headed up the back stairs with Rolo, to make herself so comfortable in the home of someone she'd only known a week. On the other hand, Ava couldn't remember feeling as if she were right where she belonged the way she did here in a long time, maybe even since she was a kid—back before the world began pressing in.

As if in affirmation, as she headed inside, her gaze landed on the blanket and pillow on the couch Jeremy had put out for her. *Please say he gets it too.*

Ava paused by the kitten's box and sank onto the back of her bare heels, staring through the darkness until she could see the rise and fall of the kitten's ribs. Rolo took a few sniffs, then seemingly satisfied, took off down the hallway toward Jeremy's room.

After setting her alarm, Ava collapsed onto the couch and snuggled into the blanket. She loved Jeremy's cozy and down-to-earth apartment, with its almost-too-crowded blend of complementary furniture and decor. Her grandmother would approve if she ever saw it, no doubt—unlike the way she'd frowned at Ava and Wes's pristine and trendy condo when she'd come to the city last year for a ball game.

In the dim light coming in from the streetlights, Ava scanned the framed photographs of Chicago cityscapes on the walls, thinking of how earlier Jeremy had mentioned having taken a college photography class, and the assortment of knickknacks on the shelves and furniture. "I get a lot of thank-you gifts from my students when they're graduating from the program," he'd said earlier in explanation.

In the darkness, Ava could just make out the titles on the stack of books in front of her; they were a collection of psychiatry textbooks and related topics on self-healing as well as an assortment of science books. They were topped with a library-bound sci-fi title that Ava had heard reference to a few times over the years. An image of Jeremy reading here at night, Rolo cuddled next to him, warmed her, and she snuggled deeper into her pillow.

She was here for the kitten, no question. Her little crush on Jeremy had nothing to do with it, even if a part of her wished she were brave enough for another peek at his sleeping form sprawled across his bed. In her mind's eye, she blew him a kiss instead before giving in to the wave of sleep that was beckoning her.

Chapter 18

WHEN JEREMY OPENED HIS EYES TO THE EARLY-MORNING LIGHT pouring through the windows, alarm ebbed in. He'd set his phone alarm but must've slept right through it. Remembering he'd dozed off with the puppies on his bed, he jerked upward. The cuddly bundles of heat were nowhere in sight. Neither was Rolo.

Bracing himself for a mess, he got up, dragged a hand over his face and through his hair, and headed out of his room. He wondered if he had better odds of finding Ava still asleep on the couch or gone. His shoulders sank at finding the couch vacant and the blanket folded, pillow on top. *It's not like you should have expected her to stick around if she woke up.*

Steeling himself, he crossed the room and peered into the kitten's box. "What do you know…" The little guy was asleep, curled into a cozy but deliberate ball, looking much stronger than last night when he'd been limp and had hardly responded to touch.

Jeremy stroked the smoke-gray kitten's head and chuckled when the little thing stirred, meowing softly before slipping back into a doze. "Looks as if you might be out of the darkest woods, anyway."

He whistled for Rolo but got no response. Returning to his bedroom, Jeremy looked out into the backyard. He spotted his dog walking along the fence line as if on sentinel duty before a two-legged creature, and a remarkable one at that, drew Jeremy's attention.

So, she hadn't left after all.

Ava was walking the labradoodle, who from up here seemed to be hating the leash a bit less this morning than he had last night. They'd made the decision to leash him when they didn't know if the mama cat was loose in the yard.

After a quick trip to the bathroom that included brushing his teeth, he slipped on a pair of flip-flops and jogged down the back stairs.

"Morning!" he called as he stepped out onto the patio. "Who can I grab?" Cool air greeted him, void of the humidity that had begun making an appearance some days. Rolo dashed over from the east corner of the yard. Reaching him, Rolo hoisted up on his back legs and planted his paws on Jeremy's chest, licking his chin, and Jeremy buried his hands deep in Rolo's fluffy scruff for a return scratch. Since Jeremy was the only human Rolo was bonded with enough to greet this way, Jeremy had never been compelled to break his mostly well-behaved dog of the habit.

Ava had made it halfway across the joined backyards and was urging the distracted labradoodle in Jeremy's direction with gentle tugs on the leash and some clicks and kisses. From the distractions of birds flying overhead to insects in the grass adding to the dog's high energy and short attention span, Jeremy had no doubt it was no easy feat. "Morning!" she called as they neared. "The mama doodle hasn't been out yet. She was the least squirmy, so I saved her until last."

"I feel about two inches tall for not hearing my alarm last night." After so much running around and tennis-ball chasing yesterday, the labradoodle no longer seemed to have more energy than a thoroughbred about to enter a starting gate. There was hope, at least. "I'm not sure how big of a thanks I owe you for all you've done, but I suspect it's sizable."

Ava shrugged, a soft smile playing on her lips. "Everyone

needs a hand sometimes. Besides, I'll take every minute I can get with that kitten. He's eating better, by the way. No question."

In the early-morning light, she looked every bit as if she were playing the part of the earth goddess as she had last night in her sleep. With eyes that were even more of a striking arctic blue when unlined by makeup, and hair tinged with specks of gold by the morning sun, she completely uprooted him. Refocusing on the labradoodle as Rolo dropped back to all fours, Jeremy cleared his throat. "I peeked before coming down. He seems stronger, that's for sure."

"I still don't feel like I can fully exhale until Gabe gets here to look him over."

"What time did he say he's coming?"

"Seven thirty-ish."

Jeremy glanced at the eastern sky. "I forgot my phone. What's it now, a little after six?"

Ava pulled her phone from her pants pocket as they headed into the sunroom. "You're good. Six eleven."

"You'll be tired today, I'm sure. I can't say I know much about real estate, but I do know Saturdays are big days. How much sleep did you get?"

She shrugged as they stepped into the sunroom. "About four hours maybe, but I can deprive myself of sleep one night and function fine so long as there's adequate coffee. Besides, you're right about Saturdays. Starting about ten o'clock this morning, I won't have a minute to notice."

Rolo headed straight for the goldendoodle's crate and gave her a thorough sniff through the bars. "Thanks for the pillow and blanket, by the way. And that couch is pretty much a nest."

The way she pressed her lips together as soon as she was finished, it was clear they were both thinking about him moving her there. He dragged a hand over his mouth and down his beard in hopes of dissipating the whole-body ache that stirred to life at this reminder. *Get it together, man.* "Yeah, well, it wouldn't do to have you going through your day today as stiff as a board." *That's right, act like this whole thing means nothing.*

"All the same, you didn't have to." There was something in her gaze suddenly, an unapologetic directness he'd not seen before that had him reaching for the comfort of his coins, but he'd woken up fully dressed, and they were still upstairs lying atop his dresser. "Last night—once it started to seem as if he was going to keep hanging on—sitting there in the quiet darkness, listening to his soft noises, it was nothing short of magical. I got goose bumps like I did sitting in churches with my dad when I was a kid."

There was no question about it; Ava was getting under his skin. "I can imagine why."

Turning the conversation toward something he could handle better, he nodded at the dogs. The puppies were curled together in the shape of a pretzel, dozing, but the mama doodle was awake and wagging her tail. "Another day to get the routine down, and I think the older two will be fine to have the roam of this room. I hate to keep Mr. Ants in His Pants constrained, but Eleanor doesn't want any of them loose in the house until they're solidly potty trained, since everywhere else is wooden flooring."

"I can see why. For original floors, they're in great shape, but yeah, being able to roam around in here will help, I'm sure."

As Jeremy knelt beside the mama doodle, she stood to her full height in the kennel and wagged her tail expectantly. "Morning, sweet mama. This is more trust than you showed when I met you, that's for sure."

"I might as well keep Mr. Ants in His Pants out with me awhile longer," Ava said.

Jeremy smiled at the way she'd parroted back the nickname while the two dogs sniffed noses after the mama doodle stepped clear of her crate. With what could only be described as a skeptical look on his face, Rolo headed for the door.

As they headed out again, Rolo trotted over to the carriage house. "So," Jeremy said, "about that coffee you'll need to get through the day... How about a good breakfast to go along with it while we wait for Gabe to get here? I owe you more than that for taking care of everything while I was snoring away in my bedroom."

Ava laughed. "You weren't snoring, and you don't have to feel obligated to make breakfast, but I'll take a coffee."

He coughed playfully. "That comment tells me you didn't get a close enough look inside my fridge when you were grabbing the formula. The only breakfast I could offer you here would be a bowl of Frosted Mini-Wheats with oat milk. I gave up on real dairy because it expires faster than I drink it. There's a breakfast place not far away that I mentioned earlier. The coffee's good, and they're known for their breakfast burritos wrapped in tortillas they make in-house."

"The Griddle and Grind, you mean? I keep hearing about the place, but I've not been by yet."

He cocked an eyebrow. "If you're game, we could attempt walking these two down there to pick something up. It'll be some impromptu socialization on their part."

"Heck yeah. You're speaking my language. Coffee and breakfast burritos." She waggled her eyebrows. "And I'm always up for a walk in this neighborhood. But what about Rolo? Won't he be sad not to go?"

"He'd be dejected, all right. He'll be fine tagging along," he said as Rolo turned to look their way at the sound of his name being spoken. "I probably shouldn't admit this, but he knows the routine. I get coffee there four or five days a week and burritos at least twice, and he always comes along."

"And you eat Frosted Mini-Wheats on days you don't." She laughed, gathering her hair into one hand. It was a habit he'd picked up on, just like how she brushed her fingers over his shoulder when she wanted his input on something. Realizing that in less than a week, he'd spent enough time with her that he was picking up on her habits had him reaching into his empty pocket again out of habit.

"Do you mind watching both dogs a minute?" she asked, offering him the labradoodle's leash. "If we're heading into a public space, I shouldn't walk in looking like I slept on a couch and haven't since looked in a mirror."

"You look phenomenal." It was out before he even felt it on his tongue, and he could tell by the abrupt way she looked at him that his words ungrounded her as much as they did him. He was beginning to accept that no matter how many times he reminded himself she was here to teach his kids yoga, his body was going to be in competition for something else entirely. "I've got these two," he added before too much of a delay had slipped in. "I'll meet you out front when you're ready. Take your time."

"Sounds good."

As she headed for the house, he asked her to grab the waste bags and Rolo's leash from the coat closet while she was inside.

"Rolo on a leash…that'll be a sight, but sure, I'll grab them."

"As you noticed, most of the time I don't even put it on anymore, but there's a chance he'll behave differently with these two in the mix." Just before Ava stepped inside, he added, "Oh, and my wallet, it's on my dresser. Will you grab it too?"

"Sure thing, but that means I'm buying the next one."

The next one. Surprisingly, all his conflicted parts seemed to be unanimously okay with this easily stated promise of the future.

Jeremy led the dogs around to the side of the neighboring garage, wondering if the mother cat was inside. The bowl of food

they'd put out was empty, but that could be credited to a raccoon or possum who'd wandered into the yard to pilfer from the
garden as they sometimes did. Not wanting to linger in case the
cat was watching through the window from the safety of her box,
he circled the garden before heading to the front gate.

The mama doodle took her time sniffing certain peaks and
mounds as Jeremy urged her forward with one hand while bracing against the labradoodle's sporadic pulling on the other. The
excited dog kept forgetting he was tethered to a person and
attempting to take off to investigate anything that interested him,
most especially when he spotted a bumblebee buzzing between
the clover buds.

"You're better off leaving bees alone, big guy." At the sound
of Jeremy's voice, Rolo stopped walking and looked over, ears
pricked. "It's all good, buddy." Jeremy opened the front gate and
let Rolo out ahead of the other two.

When Ava joined them a few minutes later, she passed him his
wallet but draped Rolo's leash across her shoulder. "My grandpa's
dogs are never on leashes, but he farms several hundred acres, so
it's not the same. Rolo has a thousand times more distractions."

"It works in my favor that he's compelled to stay in my line
of sight."

As they started down the sidewalk, Ava relieved Jeremy of the
mama doodle without feeling the need to clarify it, and they fell
into step as easily as they'd fallen into the routine of washing the
dogs last Saturday, which Jeremy figured was another way his
body was reminding him how they'd be great together.

"Did you ever find out anything about Rolo's history before
he was surrendered?"

Dog talk—here was something that came easily to both of
them and filled the space of all the things his mind wanted to toss
around that they could do in the space of a twenty-minute walk,

given they had the inclination and a bit of privacy. "A little, and it wasn't great. He and a handful of other dogs and one cat were brought in as part of a drug bust. Wherever it was he lived, they weren't just selling, they were cooking too."

Ava grimaced. "Meth?"

"Unfortunately. But the animals were kept outside, so they were spared a bit of the toxicity they could've been exposed to."

Ava's lower lip turned down in a pout. "People can really mess up, can't they?"

"That they can."

Rolo was keeping just ahead of the two leashed dogs on the narrow sidewalk, the same as if a leash were around his neck as well. As if sensing he was the center of attention, he glanced back and whined.

"I swear, everything about your dog makes me want to engulf him in a hug and give him a thousand kisses."

For a split second, Jeremy envisioned being the recipient of that kind of affection from her, and his body responded with a strong enough "hell yes" that he needed to shift the labradoodle's leash from one hand to the other in an attempt to refocus. "I can honestly say he doesn't seem any the worse for wear now with the exception of hating being left alone."

"Are you giving any thought to adopting one of the foster dogs—to help with that?"

"It's crossed my mind, but when it comes time, I suspect I'll have more kids vying to adopt them than dogs. Besides, I honestly think if Rolo had any say in the matter, his choice of a domestic companion would be of the feline variety."

"I don't think I'll ever forget him finding that kitten—twice," Ava said with a sigh.

"Why do I see myself ending up with a feral mama cat as a pet who dislikes people as much as Rolo dislikes being alone?"

"They'd be a pair, that's for sure." As they continued on, she brushed the tips of her fingers over his arm, nodding toward an incredibly put-together Victorian mansion they were passing. "Isn't that one breathtaking?" She clicked her tongue in appreciation.

Jeremy agreed before pausing to redirect the labradoodle who nearly backflipped in excitement when a pair of old beagles passed on the opposite sidewalk. As they began walking again, Ava nudged Jeremy gently with her elbow. "Mind if I ask what happened in your marriage?" Her shoulders raised a touch as she said it, like a part of her was bracing for a "That's none of your business" reply.

Her question stirred up the image that frequented his nightmares of Kristin's car smashing into the median in the early-morning hours after a night spent clubbing on the outskirts of Chicago. They'd been doing party drugs and drinking. Jeremy remembered bits and pieces of an argument that had taken place not long beforehand: him wanting to sleep it off in the parking lot; her insisting she was okay to drive. He'd come to shortly after; Kristin had been passed out at the wheel, her forehead a bloody mess.

He worked to pull himself up from the drowning sensation that went hand in hand with the memory of those few seconds before he lost consciousness again. The way he'd been struggling for breath, he might as well have been underwater. "Addiction." Knowing Ava deserved more than a one-word explanation, he added, "To drugs and alcohol—the both of us. A drunk-driving accident was the breaking straw for me. I wasn't behind the wheel, but I didn't stop her from driving either. In the aftermath, I was ready to get sober; she wasn't."

Ava closed her hand over the back of his arm. "That kind of difference would make it hard in even the best of marriages."

"True."

As they walked, Rolo mostly kept a few feet ahead but trotted back for attention from Ava as often as he sought it from Jeremy. Tentative as the mama doodle was, she walked along relatively easily, sniffing tree trunks and the cracks between uneven slabs of the sidewalk. She jumped at a few loud noises, stepping closer to Ava as she did. The labradoodle was unfazed by the noises and cars, though he was more high maintenance, attempting to put half of what he came across in his mouth.

"You know," Jeremy said, circling back to their conversation after having to wrestle a discarded candy wrapper out of the labradoodle's mouth before he swallowed it. "I'm a believer in the fact that life presents us with the experiences we can most learn from. I hope hers came when she was ready to receive it. For me, it happened after the accident. I was in the hospital overnight, and if I put my recovery to any one thing, I'd put it to a conversation I had with a fourteen-year-old who was there visiting his father."

Ava looked his way expectantly after pausing to nudge along the mama doodle.

"The kid's dad had nearly killed himself in an overdose and was too out of it to even know he was there. This kid, he went through things no kid should have to go through, but he still looked at the world like it was half-full, not half-empty. That conversation we had was what motivated me to change majors and to focus on teens, for that matter."

She shook her head. "And look what you created."

"I won't pretend getting sober didn't take considerable effort—that first year, especially. But thank you." He never talked about this stuff. The truth was, it was easier with Ava. He couldn't pretend otherwise.

"Are you still in touch with her?"

Jeremy thought back to the last time he'd seen Kristin after he'd finished hauling the last few boxes of his stuff out of their apartment—Kristin, whose parents had had an ugly divorce when she was thirteen and who hated being alone and who was in the throes of addiction but not ready to admit it. "I hope you drive headfirst into a semi, Jeremy Walker!" she'd screamed down from the second-story window.

"I reached out once during my first year of being sober, as part of my steps, but I think she was in a different place. We haven't talked since the papers were signed eight years ago."

"The circumstances are different, but I suspect it'll be the same with me and Wes." Ava stepped around a puddle on the sidewalk from a lawn that had been watered and brushed against his arm in the process. "Like we're really done, you know? Not at all like with family. You can leave them behind, but they're still your family, and the bond… It's there just like always whenever it really counts. You know what I mean?"

Jeremy cleared his throat. He didn't want to agree with her. He wanted to say you could leave your family behind the same way, but a part of him knew it would be a lie. "Yeah, I do."

They reached the coffee shop in about twice the time it normally took. Like the center, the independently owned restaurant filled the first floor of another converted century-and-a-half-year-old brick home. Most customers took their purchases to go, but there were a handful of picnic tables outside as well as a small dining room inside.

Tail wagging expectantly, Rolo led them around the side of the building where the staff took walk-up orders through a modified double-wide window. The girl working the window waved as she spotted them stepping into line while waiting to take the order of an older couple who was discussing the merits of two different seasonal coffees. She pointed at the two leashed dogs and gave Jeremy a thumbs-up.

"Rolo, stay," Jeremy said, seeing that Rolo was ready to side-step the couple in front for the day-old bagel treat he was certain to get.

Ava laughed at the exaggerated whine Rolo let out. "I see you weren't kidding about you two being regulars here."

Unsure of their new surroundings, the leashed dogs glanced around, tails tucked as they sniffed the air. Spotting the girl on the other side of the window, the labradoodle began to bark wildly, while the mama doodle began shaking lightly. Jeremy offered them both encouraging pats before pointing out to Ava the chalk-board menu next to the window under the awning.

"I wouldn't be surprised if you can hear my belly rumbling," she said as she studied the menu. "I'm so hungry, and everything sounds great. As much as I'm trying to end my love affair with sweets, those salted caramel croissants sound like heaven."

"They're pretty close. How about I order a couple to go with breakfast? Edith and Eleanor won't eat them, but Gabe'll finish off whatever we don't, no doubt."

Ava raised an eyebrow. "Sounds good to me."

"What are you thinking as far as something heartier?"

"The burritos all sound great. Something vegetarian though. I've never been able to stomach anything with meat in it before dinner."

Jeremy suggested two of his favorites, an egg burrito with black bean and avocado and an egg white with spinach, avocado, and feta. When they got to the window, and the girl at the counter had bagel bites ready for all three dogs, Ava ended up choosing the latter and a hazelnut coffee with cream but no sugar.

After swiping his credit card, Jeremy closed a hand over Ava's shoulder before realizing he was doing it. This touching thing—he needed to stop it before it gained momentum.

Thankfully, Rolo was around to draw some attention his way.

He'd sucked his bagel down in two chomps even though his piece had been the largest of the three. The mama doodle was holding onto hers rather than chewing it, and a slim line of drool was escaping from the corner of her mouth. The labradoodle, on the other hand, had turned his back on everyone and was chowing down, tail tucked.

"Aww." Ava's lower lip turned down in a pout. "I'm guessing they aren't used to treats like this." She glanced around. "I'll take mama over in the grass by herself so she can relax long enough to eat hers."

"Rolo, stay," Jeremy repeated when Rolo started to trot after them. Reluctantly, Rolo sank to his haunches, looking like a toddler who'd had his lollipop taken away. His dejection lifted when the girl working the window slipped him another bite a few minutes later.

When the coffees and food were ready, Jeremy and Ava met up again, and Ava nodded toward the open picnic table farthest from the commotion. "I think that one is out of the way enough, don't you?"

After taking turns running inside to wash their hands, they wound up on the same side of the bench in order to allow the dogs ample space from the commotion around them. Ava's leg brushed against Jeremy's calf as she wound the mama's leash into a half-hitch knot and secured it to one leg of the bench. Cashing in on his freedom, Rolo sank down directly behind Jeremy and Ava where he could be the first to claim any crumbs that fell.

After unwrapping the waxed paper, Ava took a bite of her burrito and made a little groan that warmed Jeremy's blood, and she gave him a thumbs-up while finishing up her bite.

He grinned. "You can trust me when it comes to food."

She dipped her head to the side, studying him. "I believe you, but that kind of goes without saying. There's something about

you that exudes trust right off the bat, food or no food." She
dabbed at the corners of her mouth with a napkin. "Like you're
the guy who gets asked to get people's mail and take care of pets
and store an extra copy of passwords, and such."

He scoffed. "Not that long ago, not too many people would
have agreed with you. Very few, actually."

"But things are different now. That's what's important."

Her eyes were so damn blue, and her mouth proved to be no
less tempting whenever his gaze dropped to it. *You're no better
than Rolo salivating over a piece of string cheese.* He cleared his
throat. "True."

"What you said last night about your dad... I wish no kids had
to go through anything like that. I thought I had it rough when I
was little, but looking back, I can't say I did. I was grounded a
dozen times before I was ten and sent to bed without dinner even
more often. But no one ever hit me. Not even once." She shook
her head and her shoulders raised just a touch again. "Your dad...
Was it bad?"

Jeremy had just taken a bite of his burrito and used the time to
consider his response. He'd told very few people over the years
about the concussions, cuts, and broken bones that hadn't only
come about because of him being a rough-and-tumble kid. And
he wasn't going to break tradition and tell her. Not a chance in
hell.

While waiting for him to respond, she surprised him by
brushing her fingertip over the hairline scar that ran along his
eyebrow—the one he'd gotten when his dad had backhanded him
with the blunt end of a longneck bottle of Coors. Ava's innocent
touch was enough to make him want to jog over a few blocks to
Randall's for a bottle of Jack and down it before common sense
kicked in. Instead, he excused himself and headed to the window
for a short pile of napkins they didn't need. Rolo followed,

eyeing him with his notoriously sharp curiosity. By the time they got back to the table, Jeremy could see on Ava's face that she regretted asking the question.

"It was survivable," he said as he sank down onto the bench again. Sometimes a day late and a dollar short was the best that could be expected.

After eyeing him for a few seconds that called out his bullshit answer better than words, she smiled sympathetically. "You know, from the outside looking in, you've done more than survive. The way you've turned it around, getting clean, helping those kids, you've thrived."

He huffed before he could stop himself, then shook his head. "I've never been good at compliments, but thanks."

"I know friends can be as close as family, but I hope you have some family somewhere you can count on too."

"My uncle is pretty much it. We're pretty close though." After a pause, he added. "That's not true. There's my mom. We aren't as close, but we text. Sometimes we talk on the phone. I see her about once a month, though I often find myself putting her off."

Ava nodded, giving him space to say more. When he stayed quiet, she said, "In yoga, we call it collective trauma, the stuff our parents inherit and pass on mostly without meaning to."

Jeremy thought of his father, wasted and vengefully angry, shoving him against a wall hard enough to break the drywall. How old had Jeremy been? Nine or ten maybe. And another time, cracking him over the head with a dinner plate hard enough to knock him out. He'd been eleven and in fifth grade that time. His mother had begged him not to tell anyone at school or his father would be locked up again.

A lot of good his silence had done.

Proving she picked up on more than his words, Ava closed her hand over the back of his shoulder. "Sorry. We can switch topics."

"Thanks, though, yeah, I know what you're talking about." Then, before he knew he was going to say it, he added, "Your ex must be a real bonehead."

Ava smiled. "I've certainly started thinking so. Why?"

He was halfway there; he might as well finish. "Because he parted ways with you."

Her eyes opened a fraction wider before she began to fiddle with the corner of her wrapper.

He was searching for a safe way to defuse his words when Rolo shoved his face in between them, eyeing burritos that had been ignored for too long, and it no longer felt right.

Besides, as astute as she was, she'd know it was a cop-out anyway.

Chapter 19

BY THE TIME THEY MADE IT BACK, GABE AND OLIVIA WERE WAITING out front. Rolo reached them first, happy to be doused in a fresh round of pats and praises.

"I came along too," Olivia said as they neared, "because who doesn't have a thing for kittens? And we're carpooling. Gabe's dropping me off at the shelter before he heads to work."

"I'm glad you're here." After maneuvering around the tired mama doodle, Ava gave her sister a hug and offered the bag containing the second salted-caramel croissant. She and Jeremy had made short work of the first one after the burritos. Good as everything had been, Ava was as stuffed as a Thanksgiving turkey. "You're going to love that croissant. Trust me."

After glancing inside, Olivia raised the bag to her nose for a whiff. "Wow, talk about instant salivary gland activation." She showed it to Gabe. "Thanks, Sis. We'll devour this, for sure."

"The thanks goes to Jeremy."

He smiled. "A good breakfast was the least I could offer, with as little sleep as she had."

Picking up on the pointed look her sister directed her way, Ava did her best to stay focused on Gabe, who was dressed in scrubs for a half day at the office, as he unleashed a short slew of questions to get up to speed again.

As they headed inside to kennel the dogs, she and Olivia fell behind, and at her sister's deathly glare, Ava mouthed, "I'll explain later."

Gabe continued talking as he followed Jeremy into the

sunroom. "If the mother cat's eating the food you put out for her and sticking around to nurse the rest of the litter, I'm disinclined to do much at this point—assuming you're okay letting them be. I'm sure you've got your hands full with the foster dogs."

Jeremy shrugged. "We'll gladly make it work, so long as it's what's best for the cats."

"I'd like to get a look at the mother, but I'm betting it is." Gabe motioned to Olivia. "We brought a can of tuna to tempt her out, but if it doesn't work, I'm apt to leave it be. Unless the mama's really not in good shape, an empty garage is a considerably safer place than where many feral cats get their start—storm drains, discarded trash cans, you name it. Once the kittens are ready to be weaned, we'll want to bring them in. The shelter will adopt them out, but taking them in now could create enough stress for mama that her milk dries up."

"I was worried about that," Ava and Jeremy said in unison, at which point Olivia's hazel eyes widened a touch. Ava knew just what her sister was thinking. Olivia had been a fan of jinxing ever since the second grade. Thankfully, she had the decency to refrain this morning.

"Based on how protective she was last night, my bet is that she's doing well enough to care for them," Ava added.

"I agree," Jeremy backed her up.

After Jeremy and Ava had rekenneled the worn-out mama doodle and the considerably more relaxed labradoodle, Gabe opened the back door and stepped out onto the patio. "Edith and Eleanor are still sleeping, I take it?"

Jeremy chuckled. "For another hour or two, at least."

Ava felt a peculiar stab of jealousy witnessing Gabe's familiarity with the place.

Gabe gave Rolo a second scratch behind the ears as they headed to the patio. "How's this guy doing with all this change?"

"Good," Jeremy said. "A bit of mild jealousy, but nothing I'm worried about. Though he's not that interested in bonding with the new arrivals either."

"Give him time. I bet he comes around." With a glance at his watch, Gabe added, "We've got about twenty minutes before I need to take off. Once we set out the tuna, we can hang out on the patio and see if she comes out. Where's the kitten? Upstairs?"

"Yeah, but we can bring him down here. We've got him in a box." Jeremy looked at Ava and raised his eyebrows as if offering her a choice of tasks.

"Oh, I'll go with her to get him," Olivia answered on Ava's behalf as she fished a mostly empty paper lunch bag from her purse and handed it to Gabe. "Kittens trump tuna baiting any day."

Ava shrugged. "We'll be right down."

Even before the back door of the house was closed, Olivia prodded her sister in the back of the shoulder. "Oh my gosh, Ava. You're killing me. Spill it. *Everything*."

Ava shot her a look as they filed up the back stairs. "Keep your voice down, will you? Sound carries, you know. Besides, there's nothing to tell. Last night was all kitten care."

"Not buying it," Olivia replied, her voice a decibel or two lower. "I saw how close you two were walking before you spotted us. That was couple intimacy, if I ever saw it." Olivia started poking her rapid-fire with the tips of both pointer fingers as they rounded the top of the steps, making Ava laugh.

"That was a tired goldendoodle who's spent the majority of her life confined so far." As they stepped inside Jeremy's apartment, Ava closed the door behind them. "The class went great, by the way. The kids didn't stone me…or even call me names."

"I figured you'd rock it." Olivia blinked dramatically. "Spill, please."

Ava turned up her hands. "Nothing happened. Really. I spotted the cat—as you know. The rest of night revolved around the kitten."

Olivia groaned. "Nope, still not buying it, but you'll tell me when you're ready."

With a roll of her eyes, Ava pointed to the box in the living room. "Want to check him out while I get his next feeding ready?"

"No, not at all," Olivia quipped, heading straight over. Her exclamations of adoration that filled the room a few seconds later made it clear she wasn't serious. She lifted him out gently and cradled him to her cheek. "Aww, he's so tiny," she whispered. "You didn't say he was this tiny."

Ava grinned, soaking in her sister's enthusiasm. "He's perfect, isn't he?"

"That's a nicely defining adjective for him. Look at that little face and those little paws. What are you naming him?" Olivia let out a little gasp as a frail meow traveled across the room.

Ava opened the fridge, this time taking a closer look. Jeremy wasn't kidding about the lack of selection. Aside from a bag of apples, a loaf of artisan bread, lunch meat, cheese, oat milk, and the usual assortment of condiments, it really was almost barren. "We haven't talked about names. I've just wanted Gabe here so he could work a miracle, but it's looking more and more promising that the little guy is working his own."

Olivia kissed the top of the kitten's silver-coated head right between his ears. "One of you two is going to end up keeping him. How could you not?"

"If anyone does, it's only fair that it be Jeremy, for Rolo's sake. I mean, that dog saved his life."

"You have a point, assuming Jeremy wants a cat. Sooo…you really don't have anything to share?"

With the syringe of formula warming inside a damp paper

towel, Ava headed into the living room. Why was it that crushes went hand in hand with insecurities? She sank onto the couch, remembering that cared-for feeling she'd experienced waking up with the cozy blanket he'd laid over her. She'd spent the night in his apartment, and he'd bought her breakfast. And she'd caught something in his gaze more than once, yet he'd seemed to shut himself down as soon as he noticed it too. "He's really nice." Ava shrugged. "I don't have a clue what he's in the market for, though—not that I was looking for something either."

"Maybe not, but you do have eyes, right? I've been thinking you two really could be good together. Heck, you even *look* good together."

"Between me and you, I'm interested, really interested, it's just... I kind of have a feeling he's chock-full of scars that he doesn't want to show the world." She folded in half and buried her head in her hands. "And the thing is, I can't escape this feeling that I won't be enough."

"Won't be enough for *whom*? You know as well as I do that until we're enough for ourselves, we can never be enough for anyone else."

"Touché, little sis." Ava settled back and closed her eyes. "I know that. I do. But some concepts are easier to grasp than to embrace."

"Just don't forget, you deserve the kind of nice that sticks."

That was her sister. She could pick up on Ava's emotions like they were carried on dust particles floating through the air. The girl inside her who'd been doing her darnedest to show up as her best, most polished version of herself for so long suddenly wanted to curl into the most comfortable couch she'd been on in ages and have a good cry. Not only had she not yet chosen for herself that kind of nice, but she also had a failed marriage to show for it. "Thanks. I know that, but it's nice to hear it."

Still cradling the kitten in one hand, Olivia sank onto the couch next to her and pulled her into a half hug. "Maybe take it slow, be friends, and see where it goes. There's no rush."

"I know. My mind knows, anyway; my heart wants to jump into the deep end."

"My advice—give him time. Some people can be standing in front of the most amazing sunset of the year and still take a while to notice it."

At her sister's words, Ava remembered being on the farm at twelve or thirteen and walking through the west cotton field at sunset when the sun was a big, red globe about to fall below the endless, flat earth, and the cotton puffing up from the cotton bolls seemed to be on fire. "I'm just hoping he hasn't become one of those people who's no longer willing to notice one at all."

Chapter 20

IT WASN'T UNTIL AVA SWITCHED GEARS FROM AGENTING TO AN HOUR of yoga instruction that she reconnected with the calm she'd experienced while nurturing the tiny kitten. There was nothing like an hour on the mat to work small miracles. It was a close second to those silky-soft rounded ears, pink nose, and sweet little mouth, not to mention those deep-blue eyes the few times they'd been opened.

She ached to see him again. *Sweet little Louie*. It had all happened so fast this morning, Ava couldn't quite remember who'd suggested the name first, but perhaps it was her sister. It was short for St. Louis, everyone had thought it was perfect, and so Louie was named.

She rolled up her mat after subbing for a friend who taught a Saturday-afternoon flow class in Maplewood. Over the course of the last hour, while guiding the dozen people who'd attended, Ava had worked out all the tension in her shoulders and calves that had set in while racing through open houses and new-to-market listings.

After the last of the yogis headed out, Ava spent a few minutes in quiet, soaking in the soft afternoon light in the empty studio as she packed away the last of the blankets, blocks, and supplies. She took a few centering breaths before pulling her phone from her purse, suspecting the craziness from earlier in the day would no doubt be waiting for her.

Activating her screen, she spotted a text from Jeremy nestled between a slew of client texts, and a warm glow filled her.

How are you this afternoon? Catch any rest?

Last week at this time, she'd been washing dogs with him after having just been introduced. A soft smile spread across her lips. Maybe her sister was right. Maybe he just needed time to trust himself and to trust her.

Feeling restored thanks to my flow class just now. :)
HBU? Service project w/ the kids go well?

She didn't need to wait long for a reply.

It was a good but short day because of Louie and the dogs at home. Two benches installed at High Grove. Going back tomorrow. Will send pics.

Two photos of the hillside behind where they'd been washing the dogs last weekend followed his text a second or two later. Two sturdy benches, one facing each play area, had been set in concrete and looked every bit as good as the professional benches at city parks.

Well done! Great job. I bet it was rewarding for the kids. How's little Louie? I've been thinking of him all day.

"And you too," she muttered.

It was, and Louie's eating well, sleeping comfortably, and meowing louder and louder when he's hungry.

That makes me so happy. Please kiss that tiny little forehead of his for me, will you?

Her blood warmed as she envisioned those lips of his brushing against Louie's forehead.

> *Will do. Sleep well, and thanks again for all your help yesterday and last night.*

Standing in the quiet studio, she forced herself to contemplate her response over the space of several breaths before throwing out an offer.

> It really was my pleasure. Speaking of which, so long as I'm not intruding, I'd love to run by later for a quick Louie fix before I crash early tonight.

She breathed through three or four additional breaths before he responded. Her feelings for Jeremy aside, she really did want to see Louie.

> *Sure thing.*

Sure thing. It wasn't a declaration of love, but considering the fear of vulnerability she suspected he was warring with, she'd take it.

> Great. When's his next feeding? I can help with the dogs too.

> *He just ate, so not until 7. Come hungry. When E & E spy you, you'll be expected to join for dinner.*

Ava laughed.

That I can do. :) CU then.

She slipped her phone back into her purse; she'd tackle the rest of her texts and emails once she'd grabbed a bite of food and reached the office where a mountain of paperwork waited for her.

Another evening with Jeremy. Add Rolo, Louie, and today's remarkable weather to the mix, and things were close to perfect.

She walked along the busy strip of Maplewood storefronts to her Jeep, taking in the shop windows with what felt like a perpetual smile on her face. When one of the storefronts happened to be a garden store and her gaze landed on the items on display, she stopped in her tracks. There in front of her was the cutest ladybug house she'd ever seen. It would be perfect for Edith and Eleanor's garden, and why not get it for them? They were the most consummate of hosts.

"Maybe getting clear about what you want really is half the battle." With a smile lighting her face, she headed inside.

―⁓―

After Louie finished his bottle, Ava settled back into the chaise lounge and stretched out her legs. Stifling a yawn, she gazed out into the night-darkened backyard as she stroked the kitten's soft fur with the tip of her thumb. Louie's big blue eyes blinked closed at the beginning of each stroke and opened again at the finish of it.

"I know it's not possible, but he seems twice as big as he did twenty-four hours ago."

"Considering how stunted and dehydrated he was, that might not be as impossible as you'd think." Jeremy was stoking a newly started fire in the fire pit just off the wide patio. While she was getting Louie's bottle ready after dinner with Edith and Eleanor, he'd asked if she was in the mood for a fire. Even him adding that he wanted to let the dogs roam the yard in hopes they'd sleep through the night hadn't been enough to quell the blissful feeling radiating from her center into her limbs at the extended invitation.

It wasn't only this crush thing that had her happy to soak up every hour she was offered here. For the last several months, Ava had been a compass without a north. She didn't feel that here. Not even close. Even bone-tired as she was from a long week and those missed hours of sleep, she couldn't think of any place she'd rather be.

"He's taming up so fast too." She offered a playful smile. "In case you've been thinking of a feline for that dog of yours to cuddle with that isn't stuffed and floppy in the center."

Jeremy laughed but put a finger to his lips. In the soft firelight, his teeth gleamed. "Shh. Please don't give him any ideas." Strung along the edges of the pergola above her, the soft glow from the Edison-bulb string lights made the surrounding yard seem even darker. "The truth is, I'd convinced myself that Rolo enjoyed it being just him and me as much as I did."

"With a dog like him, it's easy to see why you were so content."

"He's a good dog, that's for sure."

Belly full, the kitten was beginning to doze off. He was snuggled into the valley between Ava's breasts, and his eyes were staying closed longer and longer between strokes. She had no objection to his getting comfortable; her sister spent Saturday nights with Gabe and wasn't waiting on her to get home.

Rolo got up from the stone floor and came over to sniff the kitten again, resting his chin on Ava's boob in the process and making her chuckle. The curious puppies, who seemed to understand that Rolo was the king of their little pack, trailed after him, chasing his tail, Mortimer more determinedly than his sister.

Ava couldn't be more in agreement with the names Jeremy's kids had settled on via their online poll. Mortimer suited the boy goldendoodle puppy perfectly. His sister was officially Millie, making it perfectly acceptable for the kids to keep calling them "the M & Ms." The most fitting name of the bunch as far as Ava was concerned was the one they'd given the high-energy labradoodle: Dash. Even tonight, Ava suspected he'd still be tearing across the yard if he wasn't confined by a tether so that the mama cat could have the freedom of darkness to do whatever it was she might feel inclined to do now that she had an unlimited supply of food and water nearby. Mellow or young as the other three new arrivals were, they were content to mill about the patio and nearby yard now that darkness had set in.

The tentative mama doodle, who'd been named Luna, had planted herself on the cool stone floor not far from Ava and was watching the commotion and eyeing the occasional lightning bugs and moths that flew overhead.

Fighting another yawn, Ava shifted in her chaise. "It's been entirely too long since I've enjoyed a fire that wasn't in a gas fireplace. That crackle, you can't replicate it."

"You can't, can you? It's one of my favorite sounds in the world, I guess because it goes hand in hand with peace and contentment." Jeremy rested the poker at the edge of the pit and stood. He walked over to where Luna was curled up and scratched the top of her head. She licked timidly but thumped her tail.

"I never thought of that before, but you're right. When you're sitting around a fire, everything else falls away."

Millie got up from playing with her brother and wandered to the edge of the patio, staring out in the darkness, occasionally growling into the sights and sounds indiscernible to Jeremy and Ava. A handful of moths fluttered from one dimly glowing light on the pergola to the next while a nighthawk flew high overhead, its peenty cry piercing the night.

After looking at Ava for a beat or two longer than normal, Jeremy dragged a hand through his hair. "I should've asked earlier, but can I grab you something to drink? Hot chocolate, tea, wine... Name it. Edith and Eleanor have a selection of Perrier too."

"Mmm, hot chocolate's tempting, but how about a cup of hot herbal tea, if you have it? I know it's May, but it's almost chilly out here."

"I think I have chamomile, but if I don't, Edith and Eleanor will."

Ava nodded toward the dozing kitten. "I'd offer to help, but it would be close to tragic to disturb him. Hey, Louie's purring really softly. I thought so earlier, but this time, I'm sure. Before you go, want to see if you can feel it?" Rolo had settled down next to Ava on the other side of the chaise from Jeremy, and Luna was gently mouthing the puppies in play.

It wasn't until Ava's offer was out there and Jeremy was pausing next to her that she remembered how the kitten was snuggled smack-dab in the center of her chest. When Jeremy paused with his hand halfway extended, Ava suspected he was noticing it too. After a second or two, he pressed his middle and pointer fingers to the side of the kitten's neck as if checking for a pulse. He was close enough that Ava could feel the warmth of his arm radiating against her cheek. She was nearly bowled over with the desire to brush her lips against it to experience the soft hairs along his forearm, especially where they circled above his wrist bone. And then there were his hands, sculpted and strong. "You're right. I can feel it."

She wondered what it would be like to entwine her fingers in his. She imagined doing so might help stabilize that spinning-compass feeling she'd been experiencing and quiet the storminess inside her.

Frustration welled out of nowhere. The friendly wall of professionalism that was forming between them was all wrong. Ava wanted to knock it down in hopes of reaching something she was certain they both needed more. She'd heard about monarch butterflies born into one phase of a complicated three-chain migration. How they knew where to go was a mystery, but they *knew*. Ava didn't need to be able to read ancient hieroglyphs to know what her body was telling her either. She and Jeremy would be good together. Great even.

When Jeremy lingered next to her longer than necessary and didn't pull his fingers off the kitten, an electric field made the fine hairs on her arms rise. She met his gaze, and her cheeks warmed from wanting him and not knowing what to do about it.

The kitten lifted his head to sneeze, the sound soft and frail, then burrowed back into a ball. Jeremy stepped back half a foot. "I'll grab that tea."

Disappointment sank into her toes at the missed opportunity as he headed into the house. She did her best to cool her blood with breathing tips she'd learned. After three rounds, she was calmer but didn't want Jeremy any less, and her body wasn't letting her forget it.

As she finished the third round and opened her eyes, she caught a movement in the darkness in the neighboring yard near the carriage house and bet it was the mama cat. Soon, she spotted several small bundles in the grass near the open door. The kittens! Louie's healthier littermates were already venturing out into the night. Gabe had said to expect it anytime, though he'd promised they wouldn't go far as young as they were.

After scanning the area a bit more, Ava realized they were venturing out without their mother. "Look at that, Louie. Your brothers and sisters are exploring."

Chuckling to herself, she watched as the kittens hung near the garage, occasionally venturing farther into the grass to pounce on something before skittering back toward the safety of the propped-open door. Ava was willing to bet that they were completely unaware that fifty feet away, humans and dogs were enjoying time outside as well.

While Rolo was certainly no danger to them, Ava was thankful Dash was tethered on the opposite side of the patio. While the young dog didn't seem to have a territorial bone in his body, the few squirrels who'd come in the yard while he was free earlier proved he enjoyed a good chase.

In the quiet of the night, the kittens seemed to be playing a game of dare, inching farther and farther from the safety of the door when Luna barked loudly in their direction. They scattered at once, dashing for the safety of the carriage house as Luna surprised Ava by hopping to her feet and racing across the yard after them. "No, Luna!" Hurriedly returning the kitten to his box, Ava ran after her.

Thankfully, Luna skidded to a halt in front of the door, barking excitedly and wagging her tail.

Even though she sprinted her fastest, Rolo beat Ava across the yard by a longshot. He shoved himself in front of Luna, giving her a single baritone warning bark that sent her backing up several feet before he turned to sniff the ground around the door.

"Good boy, Rolo! You teach these dogs how to behave around cats." Breathing hard from the sprint, Ava locked her hand around Luna's collar and urged her the other direction. "Come on, back to the patio with you." On her second step, something sharp pierced the ball of her left foot. "Ow!"

Pulling Luna along by the collar, Ava hobbled across the yard. Rolo trotted behind her, keeping Luna moving and showing the herding-dog blood that ran through his veins. Mortimer and

Millie had scattered underneath the safety of one of the chaises at the commotion, while Dash was pacing at the edge of his tether and whining up a storm, wanting in the mix.

Jeremy stepped out of the house empty-handed as Ava neared the patio. "Hey, what'd I miss? You okay?"

"I'm fine; it's just a splinter. The kittens were out!"

"Oh yeah? Awesome."

"Luna's got more spunk in her than we realized. Rolo—no surprise—saved the day. This dog could seriously find fame as a cat herder if you ever need to supplement your income."

Laughing, Jeremy retrieved the nearest leash and hooked it onto Luna's collar while Luna craned her neck to get a better look at the carriage house again. "I know Gabe said to expect it, but I wouldn't have bet they'd venture out this soon. Not compared to how helpless Louie is."

"That's for sure." Free of the dogs, Ava hobbled to the nearest lounge chair and inspected her foot under the warm glow of the lights overhead. "Dang. Do you have tweezers?" The tip of a thorn was embedded in the ball of her foot.

"I do. I'll go ahead and get her and Dash crated and grab them. The water's on still too."

"Sure, no rush. Now that I'm not stepping on it, I can't even feel it."

Rolo stretched out against the far edge of the patio, blocking the route to the cats. "I hate to break it to you, but considering we're down to two puppies who are afraid of the dark, I figure you're not going to have very challenging guard duty."

"Did you have any idea Rolo had such a thing for cats?" Ava asked when Jeremy returned a few minutes later with two mugs of steaming tea.

"Honestly, no, not in the slightest."

With his chin resting on the stone floor ten feet away, Rolo looked back and forth between them, ears perked, as if discerning whether he was the subject of their attention.

Jeremy set the mugs onto a wrought-iron table next to Ava's chaise, then pulled a second chair alongside her. He reached into his pocket and handed Ava a pair of tweezers and a tube of antibiotic ointment. Their fingers brushed together, making Ava yearn for the full experience of his hand locked around hers.

She sat up and crossed her legs, tucking her left foot on top of her right thigh, struggling to see in the dim light. She slipped her phone from the side pocket of her linen pants and shined the flashlight on her foot.

"Want some help?"

"If you're good with splinters, be my guest."

"I can give it a try. I'm pretty decent at getting them out."

Before she realized it, Jeremy was taking a seat at the bottom of the chaise and sucking all the air from her lungs.

"How about you hold the light?" He relieved her of the tweezers and moved her foot onto his thigh with a confidence that surprised her.

Thank the Lord for that pedicure last week. Aware that looking at him would unground her even more, Ava did her best to stay focused on keeping her phone light steady.

"Tell me if it hurts."

They'd been this close together while washing the dogs last weekend, but at the shelter, there'd been all that commotion. Out here in the darkness, the night was suddenly still and quiet. He smelled perfect, a subtle, clean, masculine scent that hinted of a blend of deodorant mixed with the smell in Edith's dinner— savory tomato soup and a traditional cheese pudding—and smoke from the fire.

She wanted to lean close, shut her eyes, and inhale deeply, the same way she wanted to brush her fingers over the hairs on his forearms and memorize the shape of his hands and fingers. As he worked, she soaked in as many details as she could, like the smoothness of his neck, the strength in his jawline, and his thick brows and lashes. The fingertips of her free hand itched for the experience of his skin. So much so, she dug her nails deep into her palm.

"Almost there." Jeremy picked at the punctured skin another few seconds, then Ava felt a sharp prick right before he pulled the splinter free. "There. Got it." He offered it her way.

Ava leaned in for a closer look, conscious of the fact that her foot was still resting on his thigh. The skin where he'd held her steady felt naked without his hand there any longer. She wanted those hands on her in a dozen places, and she'd be in no hurry for him to let go. The same way she wouldn't be in any hurry to stop exploring all the places on him that had been beckoning her all week.

"Oh wow." The words were hers, but she was hardly focusing on the splinter. *You haven't initiated a first kiss since high school. Go for it, and you'll be rejected. You know you will.*

She proved too drawn in by those lips of his to listen to warning. Besides, if he didn't want her the same way she wanted him, why was he suddenly staring at her mouth?

Feeling a bit disconnected from her body, Ava slipped her free hand around the back of his arm. The solid strength of his triceps was enough of a surprise that she nearly chickened out. Instead, she leaned in more, brushing her lips against his.

This close, his taste and smell were intoxicating. When he didn't pull away, she opened her mouth, savoring the sensation of his lips, firm and soft at the same time, tasting of the tea he'd brought them. After dropping her phone, she closed her other hand on the side of his jaw, sliding it along his jawline until her fingertips disappeared into his hair. She pressed harder against his mouth, terrified he'd reject her but craving him too much to bow to the fear.

How many seconds passed, she had no idea. All she knew was that she was kissing him, and he was neither reciprocating nor rejecting her. The hairs of his beard pressed into her lips and chin, somehow heightening her desire to never pull away.

Then there was a soft clink of the tweezers hitting the pavement as his mouth opened and his hands locked on either side of her head, knotting in her hair. A mixture of bliss, relief, and arousal swirled through her like a Spirograph. She wanted to laugh and cry with relief and unbutton his pants all at once.

His tongue brushed against hers, and Ava's hands locked against the sides of his face again. She was inhaling his exhale and still yearning to be closer. She swung one leg over him and straddled his lap. His hands locked around her back, drawing her tighter against him.

As happy as she was to be connecting in this way, her body had needs of its own. She ground her hips against his lap and tasted his murmur of appreciation on her tongue. His hands slid down her back, cupping her ass and drawing her even tighter against him. She parted from his kiss to explore the skin of his neck and ear.

She could tell he would be a good lover—a great lover—by the confidence in his grip and in his kiss. As much as she'd wanted him before now, this wasn't the Jeremy she'd been getting to know—the one who was kind, calmly spoken, and grounded. This part of him was something else entirely. Something wilder. Something intoxicating. Something bordering on addictive.

As he slid his hands over her breasts, Ava dropped her head back and arched her spine. She exhaled until her lungs were empty, savoring the sensation of being wanted by him. After one of his hands locked around the side of her neck for a few seconds, he pulled one side of her silky top over her shoulder and down her arm, warring a bit with its tightness before the mound of her breast was free. She buried her fingers in his hair as his mouth closed over her, driving her wild with increased want.

His bulge pressed harder against her, enticing her to grind against it as tears stung her closed lids. Her body, mind, and heart all wanted parts of him. She'd never wanted anyone like this; it was a want so big it made her feel as if she might slip away into the clouds and cease to be herself altogether.

He lowered her against the bottom of the chaise without ceasing his exploration. Ava was locking her legs around his hips, wishing there wasn't such a thing as clothes, when Rolo pressed in, planting his front paws on the frame of the chaise and panting in their ears.

When they didn't acknowledge him, Rolo let out a single bark, and Jeremy went still. Too still. Not my-dog-is-annoying-but-cute still, and Ava knew what it meant even before Jeremy unwrapped himself from her and began pacing the patio. He exhaled in a burst and dragged his hands through his hair, making a wilder mess of it than she had.

Even before he spoke, her heart was cracking like the dry earth of late summer. *No, no, please don't do this. It'll all be over, and I don't want it to end*.

"I'm sorry, Ava. Sorrier than I can ever explain. But that doesn't change the fact that we can't do this. I want to, but that doesn't make it right."

She took a second or two to collect herself. "I don't understand what makes it wrong."

"*I'll* make it wrong—worse than wrong. At least the addict in me who'll never fully go away will. I can't handle you." He cleared his throat. "I don't expect you to understand how I know, but I'd ruin it."

Looking between them, Rolo barked and wagged his tail. Still snuggled together underneath the other chaise as they playfully gnawed on each other, one of the puppies yipped in response.

The pain was so sharp, Ava could taste bile in the back of her mouth. "You're right. I don't understand. I don't know how you could know that even before we try. We're consenting adults. We can work through it. We can be careful." Humiliated, she yanked her top up over her shoulder, covering up a part of her that thirty seconds ago made her feel like a goddess by being exposed.

Perhaps stirred up by the barking, Louie was meowing. She walked over on shaky legs and scooped him out of the box, pressing him against her cheek. A wild fear rushed through her that this was the last time she'd ever see him. Or any of them—Rolo, the foster dogs, Edith and Eleanor, the kids. Jeremy. A voice inside her insisted that it didn't have to be over completely; up until now, they'd been navigating this as friends. It would be awkward, but they could go back to that.

You can't do that. Not when you feel like this.

Spying the kitten out of his box, Mortimer galloped over with that sideways puppy gallop of his and whined up at her, his full attention on the kitten.

Jeremy had stopped pacing and was watching her.

Was it right to fight for something that was only just on the cusp of beginning? "As much faith as you have in the kids and in these dogs," she heard herself saying, "you don't seem like the type to commit to something failing even before it begins."

Fifteen feet separated them, and Rolo had planted himself smack-dab in the middle, looking back and forth between them, reading their energy and the tone of their voices. He whined anxiously. Ava wanted to comfort him, but she didn't dare step any closer to Jeremy. She was already on the verge of losing it and holding back tears that burned like poison.

"I know as well as I know that the sun will rise tomorrow that I'd lose myself with you, Ava. Nothing good would come of it. I'd fail myself and hurt you."

"*Nothing good?* How can you know that?"

"The ways I'm broken… I'll never be whole. The kids, my work, Edith and Eleanor… I built this life because I can handle it. I'm alone for a reason. If I hadn't walked away from my marriage when I did, I'd be dead or in jail right now. You wouldn't mean to, but you'd bring things to the surface that need to stay buried."

"You're sure then? You won't give us a chance?"

His shoulders dropped. "If I thought there was the slimmest chance I could handle you, I'd have you right here on that chaise, Ava. But I can't. I'm sorry. I really am."

Ava closed her eyes as something sharper and more painful than a thorn stabbed at her. She walked with the kitten to the edge of the patio, looking out onto the garden. Louie was a package of warmth and softness in her hands, and he was purring loud enough that she could hear him, which only made her hurt more.

She pressed back a silo full of tears that were threatening to overflow. How many times had her grandpa told her not to let anyone see her cry? "Most certainly not anyone who matters," he'd added a dozen times under his breath.

She pulled in a single shaky breath and released it. Maybe she'd stop at Ted Drewes to order a large concrete and drown out the pain the best way she knew how. Swallowing back the mountain that was pressing in, Ava tucked the kitten back in the box and gave his little head a few more strokes with her thumb. *Little Louie, I'd bring you with me if I could.* "I should go."

"Ava, I'm sorry. I wish things were different. I can't tell you how much I mean that."

She'd left her purse on the seat of a chair at the wrought-iron dining table and headed over to get it. "The thing is, I've seen what you're capable of, Jeremy." She motioned around her. "All this, the program, your life. It's extraordinary. Whatever happened to you, I know it was bad, and what you said about your dad, nothing like that should ever happen to anyone. But I'd put everything I own on you being stronger than you think you are."

Without waiting for a reply, Ava headed through the darkened yard to the gate in the neighboring property. Her lungs were burning as if they were on fire and her nose was dripping like a sieve, but she refused to shed a single one of the lake of tears damming up behind the surface of her lids.

The gate latch was stuck, and she fiddled with it aggressively in the darkness. By the time it was freed, she heard a whine behind her. She turned to see that Rolo had followed her. He was a foot away, watching her in the darkness, his head cocked.

She bent over and enveloped him in a fierce hug, burying her forehead in his bushy fur and savoring the comfort-giving scent of a well-cared-for dog. "I don't want to go either," she mumbled into his fur. "But something tells me you'll forget me long before I forget you."

Chapter 21

IT WAS POINTLESS TO ASK HIMSELF WHAT HE SHOULD'VE DONE differently, especially when he knew the answer. There was *so much* he could've done differently. That stricken look on Ava's face... Jeremy might as well have stabbed her through the heart.

All week, at every step, he'd found himself pulling her in deeper, regardless. Showing up at her yoga class and taking her to dinner. Inviting her to meals with Edith and Eleanor. Spending an entire night together caring for the kitten. Building a fire when he'd not wanted a remarkable night to end.

The gremlins of shame and regret gnawed away at him as he paced the yard under the black sky after he'd kenneled the rest of the foster dogs. The naked truth was that he'd wanted Ava as much as it seemed she'd wanted him. He should've been clear up front when he'd realized right from the start that he couldn't handle her.

He remembered counseling a hoarder during his internship out of grad school. It had been one thing to hear the woman's account of her unhealthy addiction, and another thing entirely when she'd pulled out her phone to show him the photos a family member had taken. In a similar vein, he could try his darnedest to tell Ava that no matter what work he'd done to leave his childhood and adolescence behind, it was still there, crowded behind doors he was doing his best to bolt shut, but she'd never really get it until she saw it for herself. By then, it would be too late. She'd be too pulled in by this unpredictable emotion called love, and she'd ride it with him until she was the worse for wear.

When his coins and reciting the Serenity Prayer didn't help, Jeremy texted his sponsor, asking if she was up for a midnight call, something he'd not needed to do in over a year. She called in the space of a minute, her steady, familiar tone an immediate comfort. As he knew she'd be, Janice was attentive as he rambled on about the way he felt about Ava and the choice he'd made. "It would never have worked," he said as he finished up. "I know my demons."

Jeremy kept pacing the backyard as he spoke. It was just him, Rolo, the stars, and a few glimpses of a stray cat who wasn't used to human company at this time of night and was sticking to the darkest shadows.

Janice had been in bed reading when he texted but had gotten up and was doing dishes that must've originally been left for morning. The distant but familiar sounds against his ear of running water and the scrubbing of dishes served as an unexpected comfort. She'd been mostly quiet as he talked, asking a question here and there, knowing that listening was as much a part of the support she offered as her advice.

The water shut off before it was her time to reply. "All that training of yours, you know those demons better than anyone I've met, and you've locked them down better too. You know it, and I know it. You did the steps. With most of them, you rolled up your sleeves and did the work admirably. And you know where you were doing the motions but not the work."

Knowing where she was going, resistance filled him, making his skin tight and itchy and filling him with the energy to pound something into oblivion. "How do you forgive a man who beats a nine-year-old badly enough he pisses his pants, then kicks him in the stomach because he did? How do you forgive the woman who wasn't strong enough to stop it?"

She was quiet for several beats. "The way I see it, it's like what you tell your kids, Jeremy. You can know something in your head, but until you do the work, the pain is still there in your body. It's not about absolving your parents of the abuse they racked up on you. It's about living forward in recovery and about letting go." She must've paused to collect herself because when she restarted, her words came slower. "You were beaten. You became an addict and an alcoholic. Because of the unhealthy relationship you fell into, sex became a pathway to feeding those addictions. But you aren't that man any longer. That isn't who you are now. If you step into all that fear and face it head on, you'll know it too."

He stopped pacing and stood still, taking in her words. A visceral fear welled inside him, bigger than his body, stretching out higher than the hundred-and-fifty-year-old sycamore at the back of the yard. "You're saying you think I should try it? A relationship with Ava?"

"What I'm saying is it's my job to remind you of the difference between the uncertainty that goes hand in hand with growing compared to the misery of *not* growing, Jeremy. I think what you need to answer is whether you're ready to trade safe and lonely for scary and all the risk and possibility that comes with it."

He closed his eyes, taking several beats to collect himself, the chirping of crickets and a soft sigh of Rolo the only sounds in the quiet night. "How come you always know what to say?"

They talked a little more, and he went to bed knowing the coming hours would be broken by more than the need to feed the kitten. By the time the silvery light of morning lightened the eastern sky, he'd had even less sleep than the night before. While noticing how the tasks of feeding the kitten and taking care of the dogs were so much more barren in the absence of Ava's vivaciousness, Jeremy brooded over Janice's words.

By quarter to eight when he was finished with the animals, he found himself loading Rolo into his van without really admitting to himself where he was going.

After crossing over the river bordering St. Louis's east side and entering Illinois, Jeremy drove past parceled-up farmlands and aging silos until he reached the unadorned single-story buildings speckled throughout his hometown. The various storefronts mostly dated back to the 1950s and '60s when St. Louis's businesses and the bridges across the Mississippi had built up enough that Cahokia become an overflow for the city's white- and blue-collar workers. Since then, urban sprawl had swept people out even farther out, leaving Cahokia an impoverished mid-twentieth-century boom-and-bust town, so much so, it had recently been swept up with neighboring towns into a newly formed city in hopes of revitalization, but so far, Jeremy hadn't noticed any big changes.

Jeremy slowed the van to a crawl as he passed the run-down quickie mart where he and his childhood buddies had bought slushies, day-old doughnuts, and eventually under-the-table cigarettes and booze whenever they could scrap up the cash. Eddie, one of his best friends from those days, still lived here the last Jeremy had heard, scraping out a living as a mechanic. Tom died from a meth overdose five years ago. Paul had worked on one of the riverboat casinos for years before taking off for Vegas.

The closer Jeremy got to the slab ranch home where he'd spent his youth, the more a thousand memories rushed in. "Those scars you came with, Rolo? Well, this is where I got mine."

Either as a result of the drop in speed or Jeremy's tone, Rolo whined from his spot on the middle-row bucket seat.

"Don't worry. We aren't getting out." Wishing he'd brought a bottle of water, Jeremy attempted to swallow down the dryness snaking up his throat. "Those nights I wake up covered in sweat, this is why. Not *this*, really. I'm betting most of the people here don't make their kids wear long sleeves in May to cover up their bruises."

Rolo whined again in answer.

Jeremy turned into his old neighborhood, a stark contrast from the polished and renovated two- and three-story historic redbrick homes in Lafayette Square. Here, where land was cheap, houses were farther apart and sided in wood or vinyl rather than brick. He drove past an unassuming row of houses with sparse landscaping and a few dilapidated cars parked out front of a handful of them.

As the van rolled to a stop in front of his old house, Jeremy's palms were sweating enough that he needed to wipe them on his jeans.

A year and a half after Jeremy left for Chicago, his father received a twelve-year jail sentence when his drunk driving resulted in the death of a thirtysomething-year-old man in an oncoming car. A few months afterward, the house went into foreclosure, and his mother moved in with a friend she'd been cutting hair with most of her adult life.

"This is it, Rolo. Where I grew up. Forgive me for not showing you around."

There were blinds on Jeremy's old bedroom window, the corner one, but as a kid, he'd had a single-panel curtain that didn't quite span the width of the window. He'd fallen to sleep most nights staring through the open six inches at the side, locating the planets and constellations he'd been able to identify and watching the swaying branches of the mimosa tree out front.

Those nights…those had been the good nights. On the bad nights, he'd either been hiding out in his closet or crammed underneath his bed in case his father barged into his room looking for him while on one of his rages. As he'd gotten older, he'd stopped hiding and started climbing out his window at the threat of a bad night, making sure not to come home until well after dawn. Getting home when his dad was still drunk and awake never got Jeremy anything but a new set of bruises to hide from his teachers.

Whoever owned the house now had spruced it up. It was a ranch with a carport, three bedrooms, yellow vinyl siding that was no longer mildewed across the north-facing side, and a newish-looking swing set out back. In addition to the blinds, there were bushes and flowers in the strip of landscaping in front of the house and a lawn that had been mowed instead of having gone to seed. Jeremy wondered if the new owners had any idea of the residue of old energy undoubtedly still clinging to the walls and hiding in the crevices.

Rolo barked once. When Jeremy looked his way, he wagged his tail. "We aren't getting out, buddy."

As he turned around in the cul-de-sac, a girl of about ten ran out of the house. She had dark-brown skin and hair in a ponytail and was wearing bright-yellow shorts and a pink top. She headed straight for the mimosa tree and hauled herself up into the low branch that veered off at a ninety-degree angle and created the perfect lounging spot. She pulled a few small toys from a draw-string bag slung around her shoulder, her face a picture of the oblivious contentment of a child absorbed in play. Jeremy was surprised by the wash of memories of the hours he'd spent in that tree as well.

Not all his childhood was bad, not even close.

His fingers itched to pick up his phone and call his mother. As wrong as she'd been in covering up her husband's disease, she'd been there for Jeremy in a hundred other ways, from setting aside her tip money to making sure he walked into his first day of school each year in a new pair of shoes to always stocking the canister at the back of the pantry with Ding Dongs, a childhood favorite for him. She'd also been the one to make homemade finger paint with him and to ice his bruises after his father's rampages.

It was Sunday morning; she'd be off, and she'd never been one to go to church. She'd pass the day in front of the TV, waiting for Monday when her week started over again.

What good is calling her going to do? It won't change a damn thing.

He paused at the end of the street, debating whether to dial her number, and he found himself turning the fan for the AC up another notch or two. He was still at war with himself when he punched in her cell number. It rang three times, and he ended the call before it went to voicemail.

"I didn't have anything to say anyway."

When he first moved back to St. Louis, he'd hoped to use the window of his father's time in prison to help his mom see life from a different lens. He'd even penciled out Tuesday evenings to go with her to Al-Anon meetings. He'd been optimistic that hearing other people's struggles and stories of healing would help. The meetings had seemed to be making a difference, at least until she mentioned them to his father on a visiting day. Considering she backed out of going to any more after that, Jeremy could only guess what his response had been.

Jeremy had all but washed his hands of her then. If she spent the next several years waiting for his father to come home and start drinking again—which Jeremy had no doubt he'd do—that was her decision.

He was headed back to Route 3 when he glimpsed someone in the Aldi parking lot who made him tap the brakes abruptly, remembering how his mom liked to shop first thing on Sundays to avoid a slew of weekend shoppers. Sure enough, he spotted her in the nearly empty lot, loading her bags into the trunk of her seen-better-days Chevy Cruze.

Perhaps catching his braking out of the corner of her eye, she glanced over, checking out the van but likely not recognizing him from a hundred or so feet away.

From this far away, she looked older and harder than was warranted by her years—a gently sloped back and rounded shoulders, faded jeans, worn tennis shoes, and thin, curly hair swept up in a bulky salon-style hair clip. There was a cigarette between her lips that no doubt she'd lit as soon as she'd stepped out of the store.

Rolo whined as Jeremy debated whether to keep driving. "I guess we're doing this." He turned into the side entrance of the parking lot and circled around, pulling into the open space next to her and stepping out after lowering the windows for Rolo, who popped his head out and woofed once in her direction. His mother had never been much for dogs, and the two had never really bonded.

"Hey there."

She gave him a nod. "Thought that was your van. Wondered if you'd stop." She paused the loading of her bags to puff on her cigarette. They'd fallen out of the habit of hugging each other years ago.

The lines around her mouth and eyes—eyes that were the same hazel-green hue she'd passed on to him—were deeper in the morning light than he pictured them. There wasn't a gray hair on her head, but then again, she'd been coloring it ever since he could remember, rotating between different shades of blond, brunette, and auburn within any one year.

"I, uh, was in the area." He couldn't attempt to explain to her why he'd driven here because he didn't know himself. "I called you."

"Oh yeah? My phone's at home. It hasn't been holding a charge. Well, it's good to see your face anyway, rare as it is on this side of the river."

The fine hairs on the back of his neck pricked at the pointedness in her tone. "The last time I checked, it was possible to drive across that bridge in both directions." *All that work you've done, and you didn't even make it ten seconds without getting pissed?*

She took a puff of her cigarette. "You know I've never been comfortable in that neighborhood of yours. All those uppity millennials in their tight jeans and man buns and Harry Potter glasses."

A part of him wanted to laugh, but he held it back. "It's called a comfort zone, Mom. Sometimes it's healthy to step out of it."

Her left eyebrow nearly disappeared into her hairline, an expression she'd mastered decades ago. "Or to leave it behind entirely?"

Jeremy massaged his right temple with his thumb and cleared his throat. From the back seat, Rolo panted but didn't beg to get out and greet her as he would nearly any other human on earth save one or two.

"Want to come by Mary's?" his mom asked into his silence. "I bought a tube of frozen lemonade I can fix up. We've got coffee, too, and I just bought some cinnamon bread I can toast up as well. You used to like it."

"I would, but I'm tight on time. Thanks though. How are things? How's business?"

"Same as ever. Hair's still growing and turning gray. How about them kids of yours? You still turning them out?"

"Yeah, business has been good. Lots of referrals. Lots of good kids."

She took another puff of her cigarette and blew the smoke out the side of her mouth. "Where would we be if we didn't have the ills given us by our parents to gripe about?"

"Healthier, quite possibly."

She huffed as she loaded the last two bags into her trunk and shut it. "You grew up in tough times, Jer. Your brothers had it better. I wish you would've known your father before those lay-offs got the best of him."

If his brothers had had it much better, Jeremy suspected they wouldn't have taken off the first chance they got. He took a slow breath. "I survived, and I'm committed to not passing it on. That's what matters."

She walked closer to the window and Rolo let out a single bark, proving beyond a doubt how well he read Jeremy's energy. "What is it that's got you out this way so early?" She surprised Jeremy by letting Rolo sniff her hand and then giving him a quick pat on the forehead.

Jeremy gave a light shake of his head as he fidgeted with the rubber edge of his windshield-wiper blade. "Not much. Just taking a drive."

"Your father used to do that, to collect his thoughts."

How'd that work out for him? was on the tip of Jeremy's tongue, but he held it back. "Reminding me what we have in common isn't going to get you the reaction you're hoping for, Mom."

She finished her cigarette and lit another one immediately. "You might think I talk all day, cutting hair, but I have plenty of time to think. Lately, I've been doing a lot of that. There's a lot I'd do differently if I could go back. But I can't. And you can't. And he can't."

"That's true."

"But we can make better decisions moving forward. If he drinks again when he gets out, I'll leave him. This time for good." After another puff, she added, "Those meetings you and I were going to? I've been thinking about going again. It would be good to get into the routine before your father gets out."

Surprise washed over him. "I agree completely. If you need company, I can go with you."

"I'd like that," she said before coughing into her elbow. "You know, Jer, I'd like to get together sometime and not talk about your father. Not even once. Maybe you could come by the salon and I could cut your hair. We could sit out back after and have some Ding Dongs and milk like we used to."

Jeremy took a breath before responding. "Yeah, maybe. Sometime. That'd be nice." He wasn't quite convinced it *would* be nice, but she looked old and frail enough today that his answer carried a ring of nostalgia.

"Well, don't be shy about it. You know how time gets away, and things don't happen the way we mean for them to."

A woman pulled into the space next to his mother's Cruze and went to the back seat to get her child out of a car seat. The young girl was whining, and the mother was snapping.

Jeremy dragged a hand over his mouth and down his cropped beard. "I'll text you, Mom. For now, I'd better get going. I'm taking a group of kids back to the shelter this afternoon."

"Well, I won't keep you."

Likely surprising her as much as him, he stepped forward and hugged her. She was thin and smelled of cigarettes and hair spray along with a hint of the off-brand lemon dish soap she'd used when he was little.

She reached her arms around him and patted his back. "You're looking good, Jer. Handsome as your dad was when we met."

Back when you were sixteen, and he was almost twenty-six, he thought but didn't say.

As he got back in the van, a hesitance to part from her surprised him. "I'll text you about coming over."

"I'd like that." She gave him the single, swift nod he remembered seeing a thousand times.

He drove off, the experience settling over him more fully. He'd made it another mile and was headed onto the Interstate 55 on-ramp before he realized his windows were still down, and he rolled them up, much to Rolo's disappointment. Ahead of him in the distance, the St. Louis Arch gleamed in the morning sun. It hit him with a clarity he'd not experienced before how short of a distance there was between his childhood home and the one where he'd rebuilt his life. A handful of miles, a big river, and a bridge were all that separated them.

That and the walls he'd built inside himself, walls to keep the pain of his childhood at bay. Walls to keep his father and anyone like him out. Walls that were keeping Ava out the same way.

He thought back to Janice's words last night. She was right. The question he needed to answer was whether he was ready to carve out a door in those walls inside him. This, he realized, was one of the most frightening questions he'd been faced with yet.

Chapter 22

JEREMY DID HIS BEST TO KEEP FOCUSED ON THE KIDS WHO'D JOINED him today for the second half of this weekend's service hours, which, considering they were working in the High Grove storage room checking expiration dates, reorganizing the stock system, and labeling cat and dog chow for allergy content, required attention to detail. Considering the complex new shelving system that Patrick had designed, it required a considerable attention to detail at that.

The playful banter and questions of the three kids as they worked helped keep him present. Still, no matter what Jeremy did, every time he wasn't forcing himself to stay focused, his thoughts circled back to Ava and how she'd looked as she'd tucked Louie back into his box and crossed the yard, mustering an almost regal dignity even though she'd been on the verge of tears.

He also kept remembering the way his dog had skulked back to the patio after she'd gone, looking as dejected as he had the few times he'd gotten in trouble over the years.

"You wouldn't understand," he'd said defensively, to which Rolo had whined softly. If Rolo had been doubting Jeremy's actions last night, he seemed calm and happy again this afternoon. He was stretched out in the hallway, watching the activity with interest.

Jeremy had been itching to text Ava all day but hadn't yet found the right words. It didn't help that he was as sleep-deprived as he was busy.

As they were wrapping up, Patrick came into the doorway of the small room to check out the kids' work. "It smells as if you've been exerting yourselves." His tone was as matter-of-fact as ever, which made it clear he wasn't making a joke.

Hailey's eyes grew wide, and she turned to Jeremy. "Are you gonna tell me I'm not supposed to take that as an insult?" One of Hailey's goals in moving through Jeremy's program was to become less reactive when someone or something triggered her.

When Patrick answered for him, all Jeremy had to do was cock an eyebrow. "Exertion is effort. Effort is commendable. I meant it as a compliment."

After considering Patrick's words a few seconds, Hailey shrugged. "Uh, thanks, I guess."

Next to her, Adam sniffed his pits before fanning his nose. "Effort must trump antiperspirant because my pits stink."

This started a round of who smelled worse than whom. When he was able to get a word in, Jeremy said, "We're almost finished up in here, Patrick. We still have a little over half an hour before the kids are picked up if you need anything else today."

"Something *with* dogs," Adam grumbled.

Patrick took a second, processing Adam's comment. "Tess and Fidel are in the fenced training areas on the back hill with some of the dogs who were brought in from the puppy mill confiscation. They're doing some basic training now that the dogs are out of quarantine. In only two training sessions, they're progressing more rapidly than one might expect after such neglect." He looked at the kids. "If you help bring the dogs to them from their kennels, Tess and Fidel will be able to get to more dogs."

The kids erupted into a chorus of yesses. They endured projects like this but far preferred dog walking over anything else.

Jeremy couldn't blame them. "These guys are never going to turn down one-on-one time with the dogs."

Patrick headed out, and Jeremy and the kids relocated the last twenty or so bags of dog food to their new spots on the shelves according to expiration dates and possible allergens. While doing so, Jeremy fought back another urge to text Ava.

Finish this, get your thoughts together, and give her a call. After last night, you owe her more than a text. Hell, you owe her more than a phone call, too, and you know it.

"You know, Sis, I hate to break it to you, but I think your memory of my artistic ability may be tainted by your bubbly view of—well—everything."

Olivia was hovering over her, hands on her hips and head cocked sideways as she examined the dog and cat caricatures Ava had spent the last three hours painting on the wall of the new veterinary office that Gabe was about to open with Yun. Alongside the life-size cat and dog Ava had painted were items like a bowl of kibble, a ball, a stuffed mouse, and a bone with end nubs and a shaft that, no question about it, bore cartoon-penis qualities.

"They're cute. Really cute." Olivia nodded as she spoke, as if agreeing with herself. There was a splattering of buttery-yellow paint in Olivia's hair from roller brushing one of the exam rooms while Ava had been up front creating the playful dog-and-cat scene.

"What about getting Mia over here to polish this up? You know her, right? She's the volunteer who painted the mural next door." While her sister had been the one to pull her into volunteering recently, Ava had been a supporter of High Grove ever since she'd attended a gala a few years back, and she'd enjoyed watching the mural come together on their social media posts.

"Yeah, I know her. Mia's great. But this is just like I envisioned. I'm sure Gabe and Yun will love it."

"I guess we'll know soon enough." Ava wiped what she was able to of the colorful acrylic paint smears off her hands. Gabe and Yun were outside working on the footbridge at the side of the property that would connect the new veterinary office with the High Grove Animal Shelter next door.

It was Ava's first time here since the building's closing sale, something she'd overseen, and even though she'd woken up feeling like something the cat dragged in and certainly hadn't felt creative enough to do this paint job the justice it deserved, she forced herself to crawl out of bed midmorning and join her sister here. It helped that she'd been eager to see the construction changes Olivia had been raving about, especially since she'd been the one to introduce Gabe and Yun to the property.

In the weeks since the closing, the property had been converted from a tired jewelry store with a dated look to a trendy new veterinary office whose business was sure to boom. Located next door to High Grove, it seemed impossible that it wouldn't, especially considering that Gabe had recently taken on the role of the shelter's primary vet.

The grand opening was in another four weeks, and by then the footbridge would be finished. The shelter would be participating in the opening celebration with a summer open house of their own. Olivia had signed up for the shelter's planning committee, and she'd been filling Ava in on all the fun activities being planned for both dogs and people.

Before last night, Ava had begun hoping she might attend with Jeremy, his kids, and the foster dogs. *That won't be happening now, that's for sure.*

Blinking heavily even though she definitely wasn't fighting back a fresh well of tears, Ava got up from her seat on the floor and crossed the lobby to study her work from afar. Thankfully, further away, the cartoon animals were a bit more forgiving. With perky ears, big eyes, round faces, and big paws, they were upbeat and happy, if nothing else.

At least one wall in each room of the front portion of the building had been painted in bright colors: canary yellow, cardinal red, and indigo-bunting blue. Neutral coordinating walls in each room softened the colors and, thanks to a talented staff member who worked part-time as a pet photographer, were about to be decorated with large-scale, colorfully framed prints of former shelter animals who'd been treated by Gabe, Yun, or the previous practice owner, Dr. Washington.

Ava had been asked to paint the cartoon images along the portion of the waiting room that was being turned into a kid play zone. While she hadn't drawn in years, she'd drawn and painted cartoon dogs and cats as a kid, and her sister had been her biggest fan. Ava had done a handful of practice sketches in the last few days while waiting on clients and such and had figured painting would be like riding a bike after a several-year absence. *With the skill of a returning tricyclist maybe.*

After waking up this morning with legs and arms that seemed to be filled with sand and a splitting headache to boot—no doubt thanks to the abundant tears she'd shed when her Terramizzou concrete hadn't dulled her sorrows—she was beginning to feel like herself again, even if there was an unceasing dull ache in her belly.

If she could turn back time, she'd force herself not to kiss Jeremy. As exceptional as those fleeting moments had been, she couldn't see around the fact that those few minutes would likely stop a budding friendship and a long list of other great things along with it.

Although her sister had noticed her puffy lids when they'd met up here this morning, she'd seemed to buy Ava's excuse that her allergies were kicking in. Tonight, when they were home,

Ava would curl up around a mountain of pillows and confide the whole thing to her. Here, she was determined to keep herself together. Gabe and Yun could walk in at any moment, and Ava wasn't about to fall apart in front of them.

Olivia gave Ava's painting job one last nod. "They really look great, Ava. I'm so happy it worked out that you could take the afternoon off and join us, even though I can only guess what you had to turn down to do it."

Ava was on her knees closing the tubes of paint. She didn't need to admit it right now, but after a lot of debate about taking weekend hours off two weekends in a row, she'd asked an agent friend to host an open house for her this afternoon. "Considering how I've been giving more and more thought to scaling back, it was something I wanted to do." She shrugged. "I want hours that are mine without feeling like I'm cheating to get them."

Olivia cocked her head. "You know me. I'm all about you giving yourself permission to do that. A nice house and a nest egg will be there when you're ready for it, but you can't get these years back if you work straight through them."

"Well said, Baby Sis."

Olivia pulled her into a hug, no doubt passing along a few dots of canary yellow to complement the drips of acrylic paints Ava had already gotten on herself. "Did you hear that just now? That was me not commenting on the 'baby' part and focusing on how much I love you."

With only a year separating them, Olivia hated being referred to as the baby sister, though nothing seemed like it could dull her sister's positive outlook today. No doubt she was riding on a love bubble. Ava had a suspicion Gabe was close to proposing.

"Thanks again for coming today. It's more fun with you here."

"If you asked me to peddle newspapers in morning traffic, I'd do it."

Olivia laughed. "I have zero doubt you would. You're one of the most giving people I know."

Ava's thoughts flashed back to the ladybugs hopefully taking up residence in Edith and Eleanor's garden thanks to the ladybug house and the fresh supply of ladybugs she'd brought Edith and Eleanor at dinner last night, along with the toys she'd brought for the dogs. She'd been throwing herself at Jeremy all week. Her cheeks flushed hot with embarrassment. *Not true. You'd have done the same thing regardless of any crush. You know it, and it doesn't matter if he doesn't.*

"Do you think there's something wrong with me?" The question was out before she knew she was going to ask it.

Olivia frowned. "Absolutely not. What's up? And don't say 'nothing' because I know when you're lying."

"I'm fine." When she could see by the look on her sister's face that she wasn't buying it, Ava added, "Let's talk tonight, please."

"Yeah, okay. For sure. For what it's worth, I've been thinking a lot lately about how we grew up in a house where nobody talks about their feelings and the kind of damage that does. Before I started dating Gabe, I never gave our family's lack of affection much thought. Around him, it's just so apparent. He never hangs up from his parents without telling them he loves them. Or his grandparents either. And they say it back. Heck, they *initiate* it most of the time."

Ava let out a low whistle. "Can you imagine Gramps telling Dad he loves him? Or even us for that matter."

"I can't. Stoicism that strong goes back generations, no doubt. Nobody ever told him, either, most likely."

"Yeah, it's a cycle. Only how'd it skip Dad? He's a lover, that one."

"It's got to go hand in hand with that artistic side of his."

"I bet it does." Ava gathered up the various brushes she'd

used. "I should wash these out with a hose. Wanna walk out back with me?"

"Yeah, sure. We can see if they've made any progress on the footbridge while we're outside."

They headed out the back through a room that was going to be the overnight kennels and post-surgery recovery area and would be staff access only. No bright colors in here, but muted, soft ones and dimmable lights.

As soon as they stepped out the door, Ava realized what a great day they'd been missing. With low humidity, temps in the low eighties, a light breeze, and azure-blue skies, it was a perfect summer Sunday, the kind that called for picnics and watermelon and badminton.

"How goes it?" Olivia called out as they headed around to the spigot on the side of the building. Gabe and Yun were twenty-five feet away at the edge of the lot.

A series of thick posts had previously been set in concrete, and today they were beginning to connect the base. With the dry creek only about six feet deep and twelve feet wide in the spot they were building the bridge, it would be a big project but not an overly daunting one.

"It's going," Gabe said. "Knock on wood, pretty smoothly too. How about with you two?"

"The mini-mural looks great! You're going to love it."

Ava jabbed her lightly with her elbow. "Ah, no one told me you were calling that a mural, mini or not. That adds an entirely different level of pressure regarding anticipated quality." She bit her tongue before she discredited her work any further. One of the things she'd always admired most about her dad was the way he'd always been so happy with the stained-glass windows he'd designed himself. He never stood back to look at them and pick apart their flaws. Instead, he focused on what he liked most.

"I can't wait to see it," Yun said. Wearing work boots and a Red Birds baseball cap and an oversize tool belt around her slim waist, she looked quite different than the other times Ava had seen her. Most days, Yun rocked a pair of traditional blue scrubs that made Ava debate whether to call her "doctor."

"Yun's wearing me out. We'll head up in a minute."

"Yeah, whatever, Mr. I Can Carry Ten Foot Posts with No Help."

Ava laughed. "You two and your quips." She'd grown accustomed to their banter when she'd been showing them property. She loved that Gabe's best friend was a woman and that this didn't create an ounce of worry for her sister.

Perhaps it was no surprise that this made her thoughts circle to Jeremy again and to how, had she been lucky enough to enter into a relationship with him, she suspected she'd have been fine with whoever he chose for a friend.

The crushing sensation in her middle stirred to life again. Just thinking of Jeremy had the deep, baritone barks from next door sounding like Rolo instead of the generic dogs they most certainly were. *As if you were even around Rolo enough to know his bark.*

Rubbing the palm of her hand over her sternum in an attempt at self-comfort, Ava looked through the scrubby trees over at the shelter. No surprise for a Sunday afternoon, the front parking lot was crowded.

She'd just spotted a familiar van in the parking lot when Gabe said, "Uh-oh, looks like they have an escapee…"

Ava strained to see through the thicker trees toward the back of the lot. A lone black-and-tan dog was rushing away from the rear of the shelter. Hearing a loud, piercing whistle coming from the direction of the fenced training pens behind the building, she realized she'd been right. "Rolo!"

Barking excitedly, Rolo loped along the side of the shelter and dove into the narrow strip of woods dividing the two properties, scaling the small ravine with surprising ease.

It still seemed as if Ava's processing skills were in slow motion when Rolo bounded up their side of the ravine and continued to run straight for her. "Hey, boy!" She'd hardly gotten the words out when he jumped up, planting his paws squarely on her chest. Big as he was, she needed to adjust her footing to keep standing. One of her flip-flops caught on the uneven pavement, and Ava went flailing backward. She landed hard enough on her backside for the shock to ricochet through her body. Oblivious, Rolo eagerly licked her face as Ava struggled to suck in air.

"Are you okay, Ava? You went down hard!" Olivia was kneeling beside her and gently pushing Rolo back a few inches. Gabe and Yun were scrambling up from their spot halfway down the ravine and staring at her in concern.

Ava nodded, wishing she'd managed to keep her balance. "I'm fine." She was fine, aside from the fact that it felt as if someone had taken a bat to her spine, and a sharp pain was snaking from her left wrist into her hand and up her arm. She moved her hand cautiously, and a bolt of searing pain shot up her arm. "Ouch!"

"Your wrist?" Gabe asked.

"I think so." When he whined anxiously, Ava patted Rolo reassuringly with her other hand. "It's okay, boy. And I'm happy to see you too."

Oblivious to the other three people hovering around them, Rolo swiped his tongue over the tip of Ava's nose. He was panting and wagging his tail, ears perked forward.

Just as it occurred to her that this would undoubtedly mean coming face-to-face with Jeremy, Ava heard his voice coming up the hillside. Seconds later, he rounded the top of the dry creek. By then, Gabe was kneeling beside her and giving her a reason not to look Jeremy's way. "Mind if I check that pain out?"

"Sure." Ava braced herself for the sharp, stabbing pain to repeat.

Gabe started with her elbow, which she was able to bend with no discomfort, and moved to her wrist. "Want to try to rotate that wrist for me?"

She gave his request a shot but grimaced as pain stabbed through her arm, sharply enough to make her queasy. "It hurts really bad. So much so, I might throw up if you make me move it again."

Gabe frowned. "Can you point to where the pain is strongest?"

Ava pointed to the outside of her arm right below her wrist. "Right here."

"It could be a bad sprain, but I'm more worried about a fracture of the ulna. We could ice it and see how you feel in an hour. But considering where that pain is centered, I'd recommend going in for an X-ray now. Better to know if it's a break and get it stabilized."

As if picking up on the tension floating around, Rolo sank into a fully prone position and rolled onto his back, whining. Ava buried the fingers of her right hand into his fur and scratched his belly. "It's okay, boy."

"I've still got one last student here, Ava, and she's getting picked up any second. I'll take you," Jeremy said.

Bracing herself for a different sort of pain, Ava looked his way. No surprise, his expression was one of deep concern. The adrenaline already coursing through her body got a different sort of boost. In addition to that look of his, Jeremy had an outdoorsy vibe today—thanks to his faded camo pants, snug gray T-shirt, and work boots—that to her surprise one hundred percent did it for her.

She was about to say that her sister would take her when Olivia blurted out something else entirely.

"Oh, would you mind, Jeremy? Broken bones drop my blood sugar into the danger zone, and I'm not even kidding. Just looking at the pain my sister's in makes me want to vomit."

Ava's mouth fell open an inch. Her own flesh and blood had palmed her off on Jeremy without her consent. "You could stay in the car, you know. Jeremy's got Rolo here anyway."

Hearing his name, Rolo clambered back up onto all fours and gave an all-body shake. A handful of dog hair floated away, caught by the breeze. *He must have smelled me*, Ava realized. *And he came running. For me.* It was the one saving grace in all this. Rolo was as crazy about her as she was about him.

"Eleanor can swing by and get him." Jeremy's hazel-green eyes bore into her. "My ill-behaved dog may have broken your bone. There's no way I'm not going with you."

Ava swallowed hard, and not from the pain in her wrist. "He's not ill-behaved. I tripped on my flip-flop."

"He did full-body pummel you, just saying." Olivia gave Rolo an affectionate pat as if to show she meant no offense. With a shrug, she added, "Not that I don't have an ill-behaved dog of my own at home to contend with."

"We can start a support group exactly for this sort of thing," Gabe suggested, laughing away any tension lingering in the air. "We'll call it Dogs Behaving Badly Unleashed."

"Morgs hasn't even graduated to off-leash freedom yet," Olivia said. "And if we do start it, you and Samson wouldn't be invited unless Samson's the mascot or something. I've never seen that dog be anything but perfectly behaved, off leash or on."

Ava was having a hard time processing all the jesting. She met Jeremy's gaze for a second or two, then dropped it like a hot potato. No one else here aside from him had any idea that this may well be the second part of her to break in less than twenty-four hours, and the first was going to take more than a brace to heal.

Fortunately, Yun stepped in. "Before you two start writing rules for your hypothetical support group, why don't you help her to her feet, and I'll run down to the shelter and grab some ice, since our fridge hasn't been delivered yet."

As much as Ava didn't want to admit it, there was no denying that her wrist and hand were already swelling. This was going to be a major setback to her yoga classes right as they were beginning to take off, a disappointment she wasn't ready to fully process yet.

"Ava, once Sammy is picked up, I'll grab the van and drive it over." The concern on his face threatened to melt Ava into a river of magma. "I shouldn't be more than a couple minutes."

She didn't know what else to do but agree. Suspecting any words voiced to him would come out in a squeak, she did nothing more than nod.

"Rolo, come, boy," Jeremy said as he turned toward the ravine.

Not budging from Ava's side, Rolo dropped to his haunches and barked while wagging his tail, causing Jeremy to pause mid-step. Rolo always came at Jeremy's command.

"He can hang out with us," Gabe said. "I'll drop Rolo by your house on my way home."

So, there it was. Ava's wrist hurt badly enough that she'd be crying right now if she hadn't shed ten years' worth of tears last night. Everything was being decided for her the same as if she were a child. Or at best a teenager. Then there was the setback this would be to her burgeoning yoga career. To top it all off, she was going to be alone with Jeremy less than twenty-four hours after the most painful rejection of her life. And Rolo wasn't even going to be there for emotional support those first awkward minutes in the van.

What was it her grandmother had always said? "When you find yourself in a hole, the first thing to do is to stop digging."

Ava wasn't sure who to hand it to, but she was ready to surrender her shovel.

Chapter 23

THE THING ABOUT JEREMY, AVA WAS FINDING, WAS THAT IT WAS impossible to hold a grudge against him—a grudge that had nothing to do with his dog breaking her wrist and everything to do with him breaking her heart. But as tempting as it might be to her bruised ego to let the grudge holding commence, it wasn't going to happen. He was too darn sweet. And who was she to really understand what he was ready to let go of and what he truly needed to get him through?

Besides, grudges couldn't be held while the room was spinning so strongly.

Stifling a giant yawn, Ava curled onto her side atop the patient bed at the comprehensive urgent care center that Gabe had suggested might be less crowded than an ER but still had the capability of setting bones if her wrist was indeed broken.

Gabe had been right about the lack of a crowd. After only two or three minutes in the waiting room, Ava and Jeremy had been led into a private room where they'd spent all but a handful of minutes the last hour alone. While waiting for her X-rays to be read, Ava tugged the sterile blanket higher, her left arm rested on top, her wrist cradled in a temporary splint.

"Are you still cold?" Jeremy's voice was soft and layered with gentle concern, making Ava imagine what he'd be like if they were a real couple.

"A little. More than that, I'm dizzy."

"That would be the acetaminophen with codeine they gave you."

"It must be kicking in. All I feel is a dull throbbing now." She forced her eyes open to take in his profile. He was on a chair next to the bed, twirling a tongue depressor in between his fingers with surprising dexterity. She'd noticed before now that he was frequently fidgeting with something—a pen, a leaf or blade of grass, a fork or knife, sunglasses, or even the silky fold of Rolo's ear. "How many years did you smoke?"

He cocked an eyebrow. "From about twelve to twenty-six. It was the last thing I gave up, almost three full years after I got sober."

"My mom used to smoke. She quit when I was a kid. She fidgets too."

He smiled. "Fidgeting helps."

"If it wasn't for the fidgeting, I'd never believe you were once a smoker."

He shifted in his chair and let out a breath. "Would you believe before turning eighteen, I completed nearly a hundred hours of required community service and spent three months in juvie?"

Even having had a sense that he'd had a rough childhood, surprise washed over her. "Considering the person you are now, no, definitely not. But I guess that explains the way you are with the kids."

He raised an eyebrow. "I don't talk about it to anyone really, but I've been sitting here thinking i'm ready to tell you. In hopes it'll help explain last night better than I was able to."

Ava resisted the childish urge to pull the blanket over her head and pretend she couldn't hear him. She suspected whatever he had to say was going to feel as if he were picking at a splinter in her heart instead of her foot. "Okay."

"You're getting to know the kids in the program. Hopefully enough to trust me when I tell you no kids get put in juvie because they're born bad. Some kids are more impulsive and have a bigger challenge getting control of that reptilian part of the human brain than others. But most of the kids I've worked with are products of the environments they were raised in. They've taken on anger and shame and borne the brunt of neglect or abuse."

"Is that what happened to you?"

"My story's not much different from theirs. My father's an alcoholic and a rager. My mother never had the self-esteem to believe any of us deserved any better."

Ava shifted on the bed and a muted pain shot through her wrist. "I'm sorry." When he stayed quiet, she added, "I used to think I had it rough growing up, but it's a matter of perspective. When I was in middle school, a friend of mine had a father who was an alcoholic. She was afraid of everything. She'd gnaw her nails to the quick until they bled, and loud noises made her jump. What you went through... I have zero doubt it must've been unbelievably hard."

"It was, but not all of the time." He dragged his hand over his mouth, drawing Ava's attention to his lips. "When my father was drunk, he was mean. Verbally and emotionally abusive, if you're looking for labels. When he was drunk *and* angry, he got physical."

"I'm sorry." She'd said that already, but something about this bedside confession hadn't left her with the right words in her arsenal to do any better at the moment.

He shook his head. "The thing is, Ava, you deserve someone who never wakes up from a dream wanting to throw his mattress across the room. Someone whose scars aren't so thick they'll never heal." He fell quiet for a second and cleared his throat. "Someone whose father never made him stand in front of a dart board while his drunk friends took shots at him for a bet."

Suppressing a sharp inhale, Ava pushed herself to a sitting position, no longer cold or dizzy or tired. Now that the pain medicine had kicked in, the throbbing in her arm had dropped a few decibels. "Jeremy... I don't know what to say."

"I'm not looking for your sympathy, Ava, or your compassion. Though I know how naturally it comes to you to offer it. What I'm trying to get across is that I've recovered enough to know I'm too broken to be the man you deserve. As much as I'd like it to, that isn't going to change."

As his words settled in, a defiant anger filled her. "Well, I never would have guessed you were so presumptuous."

Jeremy stopped fidgeting with the tongue depressor and looked at her, his eyes widening in mild surprise.

"To know what I deserve after meeting me for the first time a week ago," she added.

The muscles in his jaw tightened. "I know myself, Ava. It's enough."

"Is it?"

He looked down at the floor, a scowl lining his forehead.

"Because another possibility is that maybe you're locking yourself in a box because you're afraid of what might come next."

He fell quiet for close to a minute. She needed to smash her tongue against the roof of her mouth to give him space to respond.

"I heard pretty much that same thing from my sponsor last night after you left."

"In the words of one of the world's greatest writers ever, 'A truth universally acknowledged...'"

He huffed. "Why does it not surprise me that you're quoting Jane Austen?"

"Why does it surprise me that you knew who I was quoting? Are you an Austen fan?"

"No." He laughed. "Not even close. I don't do romance novels, no matter when they were written."

"You're forgiven." With a smile, she added, "You know,

I may not have a master's in social work, but I know locking ourselves down so that we don't pass on our trauma isn't the answer."

"I suppose you're going to tell me what you think the answer is?" he asked after a handful of seconds passed.

"I was hoping you'd ask that." She swung her legs over the table, placed the flat of her right hand against his shoulder, and began to push against him, slowly but steadily, applying enough force that he needed to lock his muscles to keep from falling off the chair. "We're meant to bump up against each other, Jeremy, and push each other out of our comfort zones. It's how we grow."

"I don't—"

It was all he got out before the door flew open and the nurse practitioner who'd taken Ava back for X-rays stepped through the doorway. If he wondered why Ava was attempting to shove Jeremy off his chair, he didn't comment. "The verdict's in. It's a break, an oblique fracture of the ulna, but it's clean." He was wheeling in a cart loaded with materials to make a cast.

Ava sat back on the bed and felt her shoulders sag. There went the hope that it was only a sprain, and she'd be on the mend in no time. "How long do you think I'll be in a cast?"

"Six weeks typically, for this type of break."

After digesting this a few seconds, she shot Jeremy a pointed look. She might have to find substitutes when it came to her other classes, but not with Jeremy's. "Looks like you get to be my yoga assistant the next six weeks. Those kids of yours have started this journey; we can't leave them hanging."

He held up a finger. "Didn't you notice my lack of flexibility Friday night?"

"Uh, weren't we just talking about exactly that?" she asked with a waggle of her eyebrows.

He shook his head, a half smile revealing a hint of white teeth.

"Yoga, huh?" the nurse practitioner said, pulling a rolling stool chair up to the other side of Ava's bed and drawing the cart alongside him. "My little sister's always trying to get me to go to classes with her. I keep telling her I'm not meant to bend like that."

"You should consider giving it a try. Odds are you did all sorts of yoga poses naturally when you were a toddler. The good news is your body will remember." She flashed Jeremy a pointed but playful glance. "Assuming you're willing to step out of the box and give it a try. Men typically need to break through a bit of resistance and inflexibility that they've built up over the years. Teenage boys tell themselves a pretty convincing story about what they're supposed to be and 'flexible' is rarely a part of that dialogue."

"Or vulnerable, right?" the nurse practitioner asked with a laugh.

Jeremy shook his head. "I'd swear you could hear us through that door."

He held up his hands. "Not a word. But, bro, if a woman like this wants you to be her yoga assistant, take my advice and start adding namaste pillowcases and stretchy pants to your online cart tonight."

Dragging a hand through his hair, Jeremy looked between them. "When you put it like that... Though I'm gonna take a pass on the pants."

As she held out her arm for the nurse practitioner to remove the temporary splint, Ava gave Jeremy's calf a gentle nudge with her bare toe. "Deal. You pick the pants. I'll pick the poses."

Jeremy's answering gaze seemed to hold a promise even before his words reiterated one. "Then it seems it's a date."

Chapter 24

AVA WAS SPRAWLED ACROSS HER SISTER'S COUCH LATE MONDAY afternoon, a few pillows mounded underneath her throbbing arm and her kitty camped out on her lap, when Jeremy texted to see how she was feeling. A bubble of happiness swelled up to spy his name on her phone screen, though she made herself wait a full three minutes before responding, not to look too acquiescing. *It's not like he has no clue you're interested or anything.*

> Pretty good here. It's hurting a bit more, but I took the day off, and my sister's here now. We're bingeing on movies and popcorn like when we were kids.

Unlike her, he didn't wait any length of time to respond.

> *It's good you're taking it easy. Rolo is quite sorry. He wrote you an apology the length of a dissertation. Then he ate it. Instead, he sends this.*

Smiling, Ava stared at her phone screen in anticipation. A few seconds later, a photo popped up, a close-up of Rolo's face that was utterly frameable. He was in a muted patch of sunlight, his warm-brown eyes looked like chocolate syrup, and his head was cocked just enough to appear as if he were begging.

> Please tell him he's 100% forgiven for me tripping on

my flip-flop. How ru? Doing any practice poses today to get ready for co-teaching with me Friday night?

Yeah…about that. Will u be too sore? Not that I'm trying to get out of this or anything.

Nope. We've got this. ☺

Okay, but I choose to remain a skeptic. Willing to let you prove me wrong.

Ava was debating how to answer when a second text popped up.

So, Edith and Eleanor heard about your arm, and Edith made a pot of her signature chicken poop. Okay if I bring some over?

Ava snorted. "I'm hoping he meant 'soup.'" She looked at Olivia, who was grading a math test her eighth graders had taken while the two of them watched *Ten Things I Hate About You* for the first time together since before Ava left home at eighteen. Morgan was sprawled at Olivia's feet, dozing. Every so often his feet would pulse as if he was dreaming of loping across a field. "Jeremy wants to bring over some chicken soup."

Olivia glanced up from her papers. "Want me to leave? I'm headed to Gabe's for a late dinner in a few hours anyway."

"No, stay please. With the whole 'let's start from friends and move slow' thing we settled on last night, it's too weird to be alone with him right now. Considering the snogfest I initiated Saturday night."

Ava had caught her sister up to speed last night, which included telling her about the talk they'd had after her cast was on and he was driving her here, a talk that ended in Jeremy committing to doing his best to keep the weight of his past in check and requesting they ease into whatever was developing between them as friends first and then take it from there.

Ava had wanted to ask if this meant they'd be keeping their attraction for each other one hundred percent in check and for how long, but she'd been too nauseous from the pain medicine and hadn't been ready to tackle the weighty topic just yet.

"Sure, Sis. Whatever helps."

Jeremy texted again.

Soup, not poop. Sorry. Voice to text.

Ava sighed. "Have I told you how cute he is?"

"Ahhh, two maybe three times since last night."

After a roll of her eyes, Ava texted him back.

I'd love some chicken soup if you don't have anything going on.

I'll be wrapping up here soon. I was thinking maybe I'd bring Louie along.

YES PLEASE. And UR welcome to binge-watch rom-coms with us. Next is 13 Going on 30.

Hmm. At the risk of sounding inflexible, I'll pass.

Ava bit her lip.

Pass granted. We won't begin to tackle flexibility, or the
lack of it, until Friday's class.

When he texted a smiley face and that he'd be there in forty-
five minutes, Ava sent a thumbs-up, then slid her phone onto the
coffee table. "It's entirely possible no one has had me this giddy
before."

When her sister's eyebrows raised, but she kept silent, Ava
added, "No smug I-told-you-so's. But I will admit I had no idea
I had a Cupid for a sister." Last night, Olivia had followed up
Ava's confession with one of her own. She and Gabe had been
talking one day, and Gabe had mentioned that he thought Jeremy
would be a great match with Ava, thus the dog-wash invitations
to both of them.

"You two ended up doing all the work. All Gabe and I did was
get you in the same place."

"Well, whatever happens, thanks for that."

"Look, I can tell he's a good guy, Ava, but I'm sure Gabe had
no real idea the kind of stuff Jeremy's dealing with. Aside from
their connection through Dr. Washington and the shelter, they
don't know each other that well. So, what I'm saying is, Jeremy
was smart to want to take it slow. In the meantime..." Olivia
shrugged. "I don't know that I'm qualified to preach, but just be
discerning."

"I will, but I've seen him with the kids and with his landlords.
He's a good man. A really good man."

"And *you're* a really good woman. Don't forget that either."

Ava closed her eyes for a moment. "Sometimes I think I'm
still trying to prove that. Leaving home like I did and following
that boy here to St. Louis, you know how the whole town talked."

Olivia moved her stack of papers from her lap to the coffee
table and twisted to face her after pausing the movie on a

particularly stoic look by Heath Ledger. "They talked. I won't pretend they didn't. But I see it now from a different lens than I did back then. You were eighteen and doing what was right for you. It wasn't any of their business." She raised her eyebrows. "If it helps, that was the year of the drought and that big heat wave that dried up everything. It didn't take long before they stopped talking about anything aside from that for months on end."

"What timing," Ava said with a laugh. "You know, I think I worked twice as hard as I might've those first several years mostly to prove I could do it."

"And you did."

With a grin, Ava motioned around the living room. "As can be seen by me living in your one-room apartment, sleeping on a couch or sharing a bed with you for the last few months."

"I've helped you with your tax returns the last couple years. I'll never believe that."

"Ha, though you have a point. The thing is, the more aware I become of how much some of that drive was to prove myself to others, the less motivated I am to keep going at that pace."

Olivia squeezed her knee. "That's because you're figuring out who you are, not who you want people to see."

Her sister's words rang true. Ava wouldn't deny that. It wasn't until this afternoon, halfway through a lazier day than she could remember in eons, one that hadn't started out with a double-digit to-do list but had consisted of lying around with her cat on her lap and her sister—and best friend—nearby this afternoon, Ava felt confident that maybe, just maybe, she was finally ready to be the person who seemed to have been here all along, patiently waiting for her to reach the point that she was ready to embrace her.

Chapter 25

THIS WASN'T THE TIME FOR AVA TO THINK ABOUT JEREMY'S BODY
parts—any of them—or how there was hardly a single inch of
his body she didn't want to explore. From the smooth skin of
his neck to the dip in his sternum to his strong, lean thighs and
the toned patch of skin above his groin visible when his T-shirt
shifted, these spots and a dozen others competed for her attention
just the same.

Nope, not cool. When Jeremy was stretched across the mat
next to her at the side of the garden, helping teach an audience of
nine impressionable teens and two older women, Ava would need
to keep her mind on yoga. She'd chosen ten poses to introduce
tonight and was attempting to do so in a way that would be easy
for the kids to grasp.

With her arm in a cast and throbbing a little anytime it dropped
lower than heart level, it would've been considerably easier to
have an assistant on the mat next to her who was familiar with
today's poses. As the sun sank in the sky, lighting the yard and
garden in a warm glow, Jeremy did his best to move through the
poses as she instructed, but she still needed to guide him into
Warrior I pose with nearly the same instruction as she would the
kids.

Of course, had she thought about it more, she should have
expected nothing different. Yoga wasn't a one-and-done exercise; yoga skills were built over months and years rather than
days or weeks. On the bright side, it would be good for Jeremy's
kids to see the vulnerability that came with exploring new poses.

Her goal with today's class was to get Jeremy to move through and hold poses in demonstration as she circled the group, offering ways for the kids to experience yoga postures that would help relax their minds, release some tension from their bodies, and help them understand that not every body, or even every day with their bodies, was the same.

Because putting her hands on Jeremy to guide him into position threw off Ava's concentration enough that she lost track of the sequence of some of the longer poses, she switched tactics halfway through class. At this point, she began demonstrating with her own form and posture to guide him through the poses.

"Like this," she said when he dropped into the lunge of Warrior I without his hips aligned correctly. She planted herself at the top of his mat and swiveled her hips from the forty-five-degree angle he was holding to a front-facing one.

"Got it." He shifted his hips and torso, owning the pose in a way that was both masculine and vulnerable at the same time and made Ava's hormones rev into overdrive. Really, there was no debating it; he was close to perfect.

"Nice." Suspecting she'd been gawking at the tightness in his front thigh, she stepped away to circle the mats and help the kids move into the pose.

After Warrior I, they made their way down to their seats, and Ava worked with Jeremy to lead them through a few final poses, ending in savasana again. The ladybugs she'd brought for Edith and Eleanor were active the whole class, landing on Ava, Jeremy, and several of the kids, some of whom seemed to consider it a stroke of luck while others squirmed and shooed them away.

The growing kittens made a few appearances during the class as well, distracting the kids a couple times by dashing in and out of the open doorway of the carriage house with their tails fluffed, getting braver as the sun sank lower. Once he spotted them, Rolo, the only dog allowed out on the mats during tonight's session, split his time between the yogis and the kittens, where he stretched out in the grass next to the carriage house door, proving he was as gentle with these kittens as he was with Louie.

Before class, it had become clear that tonight's group of kids seemed split on what they were more interested in adopting: the kittens or the foster dogs. From what Ava gathered earlier from their boasting, two or three of them had claimed their parents were giving their adoption hopes serious consideration. Ava couldn't think of anything better than knowing all the dogs and kittens could possibly end up finding their forever homes with the kids in Jeremy's program. She might not know them well yet, but she had no doubt as to their being a great group of kids who'd be loving pet owners.

When savasana ended, and Ava guided the group back into easy pose amid a chorus of yawns and stretches, Jeremy winked at her. Ava didn't have to wonder what the wink meant; the kids had been attentive and vulnerable the entire class, which was as much as they could ask for. For certain, they'd both be checking it off as a success.

"You guys did great. Each one of you."

"You did," Jeremy agreed.

Ava picked up the book she'd brought, and even though she didn't need it for tonight's quote, she flipped to the page she'd bookmarked. "I'll leave you something every practice. Tonight, it's this quote from the Bhagavad Gita: 'Yoga is the journey of the self, through the self, to the self.' It's my sincere hope that you caught a glimpse of yourself tonight that you've either not seen in a while, or you've not been wanting to acknowledge. As always, it was my honor to share this practice with you tonight."

Nolan grinned. "I saw myself when we were doing the downward dog."

"Are you always sarcastic?" Hailey shot back.

Ava didn't mind their grouchy banter. The kids had taken off their armor in class, but now parents were lining up at the side of the yard, and it was time to put it back on.

"Let's remember to roll up our mats and take them inside," Jeremy said. "And whoever wants to and can stay, you're welcome to stick around to get the dogs out for a short run."

"I'll stand guard in case the kittens decide they want to come back outside," Ava offered as she rolled up her mat and began to bag her teaching materials. Even when the carriage house door was closed, the kittens were beginning to clamber in and out of the open window.

"That'd be great. I won't be long."

"And while I'm standing there, I'll count Dash's laps around the yard. Maybe he'll break his own record tonight."

The energetic labradoodle wasn't showing many signs of calming down after more than a week of extended freedom. Luna and the puppies typically ran after him now when they were first let free, but they quickly dropped off and explored the yard at a more leisurely pace.

The foster dogs had settled in well in the span of a week, and Luna and Dash were no longer being shut in their crates during the day. Instead, the sunroom was closed off from the rest of the house with a stair gate, allowing them to roam the room and still access their cozy beds inside their crates for naps. Jeremy and the program kids must have been getting them outside enough throughout the day because even the puppies hadn't had a single accident in two days.

Leaving her things beside the garden, Ava headed for the carriage house, where Rolo was still camped out next to the door. She sank onto her heels and stroked his soft fur, keeping her casted arm up and to the side to minimize the throbbing that had increased over the course of the day. Rolo licked his jowls and thumped his tail as he soaked up the affection, the picture of contentment.

"I missed you yesterday," she said. She'd not seen him since Wednesday when Jeremy had dropped off another dinner for her and Olivia. He'd hung around for an hour making small talk with Olivia while she fed Louie and Rolo outcompeted Morgan for space on the couch, which wasn't hard to do since Morgan hadn't yet gotten comfortable on furniture, something likely accredited to his pre-adoption years spent alone locked in a dog pen.

Rolo thumped his tail harder as he sniffed Ava's cast.

"I don't know if you'll appreciate this as much as I do, but I looked up your name. It's a variant of a name that means 'famous wolf,' which is pretty darn cool, especially since you're going to be featured in the shelter's alumni column in their next newsletter about how you rescued Louie. Your dad texted me the picture they're going to use. That face of yours is going to melt more hearts than mine."

Soaking up the affection, Rolo flipped onto his back, his legs flailing in the air. Ava gave his belly a hearty pat before standing up and heading inside the carriage house. She paused in the doorway. "In or out?"

Rolo hopped to his feet with a grunt and followed her in. Ava shut the door behind them, knowing that any minute, the dogs would be tearing about the yard. Still barefoot, she walked across the part-concrete, part-dirt floor to the shelves. Two of the kittens were camped out on one of the high shelves, one boy and one girl, both a blend of white and marble, staring down at Ava and Rolo with big eyes. The other two, both girls, were dozing inside their nesting box.

The fading sun was shining through the dusty old windows, spreading a warm glow across the exposed brick walls. Ava smiled as she looked around the building. She couldn't think of a single abandoned structure she'd ever been in—and she'd been in more than most people—that was more inviting.

Hearing a hiss, Ava spied the mama cat across the open room, watching from the top step of the open stairs leading to the small loft above. "Hello, Mama. We won't bother you. Or your kittens."

Spying her as well, Rolo trotted over and stretched across the four lowest steps to sniff the air. Considering how thin and steep the steps were, Ava wasn't sure if she should stop him if he attempted to climb them and was relieved when he did nothing more than wag his tail and whine. After watching him for a minute, the mama blinked at Rolo in the trusting way that cats did.

A brush of envy swept over Ava at the thought of the mama and her babies tucked away in here. What a serene place to raise a litter of kittens. With the outer frames of the old horse stalls still intact on the far side of the building, it almost seemed as if time had stood still in here, as if by listening hard enough, she'd hear murmurs of its past inhabitants—horses and footmen and who knew who else.

Ava had been in real estate long enough to believe wholeheartedly that buildings carried their own energy. Sometimes the simplest of houses could be the most welcoming, and sometimes the most exquisite ones could turn out to be uninviting or even unnerving. And as time-saving as it would be in her line of work if she could get a feel for a place from its photos, it took stepping inside a place to get an accurate sense of it.

Ava walked over to join Rolo at the bottom of the steps and peered up at the mama cat.

"Look at you, pretty girl. You look stronger already after eating the food we've been putting out for you. And I don't know if you've picked up his scent on us, but thanks to this dog here, Louie's alive and doing great. I'm hoping you can be reintroduced soon."

The mama cat's tail flicked and the hair along her spine stood up at Ava's words, but she didn't run off and she didn't hiss again, both of which Ava took as positive signs.

Ava twisted in place to peer at the loft above. If it wasn't for the cat blocking the way, she'd head up and take a closer look. If this place were ever turned into a studio apartment, a modest bedroom and small bathroom would fit well up there without closing off the entire main floor.

She stepped back on instinct when an insect flew past her face and landed on the banister next to her. A ladybug, she realized as it folded in its wings and began making its way upward. A smile spread across Ava's face as she watched it climb.

Closing her eyes, Ava said a prayer of thanks for all of it: for Jeremy, even undefined as their relationship was; for Rolo; Edith and Eleanor; the kids; and the kittens. All of it together had Ava feeling as if she belonged here more than she'd belonged anywhere in a very long time. And even though she'd been the one to introduce the ladybugs to the garden, witnessing them make their way around the grounds somehow brought it all together.

She was finishing her prayer when the door pushed open. Ava turned to see Jeremy in the doorway, staring at her a bit hesitantly. Her cheeks warmed at being caught with her eyes closed in prayer; it was one thing to feel thanks for a relationship that was incredibly undefined and another to acknowledge aloud that she was doing so.

The mama cat and her two roaming kittens dashed into the shadows as another human visitor intruded into their home.

Ava joined Jeremy at the door as he stepped inside, leaving it partly open next to him. The foster dogs were being unleashed and beginning to run around the yard like mad. A couple of the kids ran after them, making about as much noise as the dogs and puppies were making with their excited barks.

"You were great tonight," Jeremy said. "For a blended group of kids like we had to give it such an earnest shot—that's not easily accomplished."

"Thanks. I have to admit, the classes have gone a lot better than I first feared." She grinned. "Though the first few minutes of each one, I've had my doubts."

He smiled. "If you want the truth, I did, too, but you gave them what they needed to succeed. I'm sure you know the buzz words—vulnerability, authenticity, genuineness. I've learned over the years that if you're not willing to put yourself out there, they won't be either."

Ava's cheeks warmed from the praise. "Thanks. I guess I'm getting better and better at putting myself out there when I really want something." Her blush deepened, but she shoved the words out anyway. "I'm guessing you figured that out last week."

Jeremy huffed and a smile pulled at his lips. Dusk was settling in heavily, fading the brilliant colors of the day, but not enough to keep Ava from being mesmerized by those eyes of his. "Considering all that I expect from these at-risk teens, I wish I could say it was easier for me do that too."

"Yeah, well, once they're on, suits of armor aren't so easy to shed."

"True." Jeremy unexpectedly brushed the tips of his middle and pointer fingers across the hollow of her neck and along her collarbone.

Ava froze, a thousand pinpricks of sensation igniting as his fingertips trailed over her skin. Not that she had any objection, but friends didn't touch each other like this. And they didn't look at each other like this either. She was acutely aware of the breath entering and leaving her lungs, of her bare feet planted on the earth, and of the cooler evening air enveloping her skin.

"I was going to save this discussion for later, but the thing is, that armor... You make me want to shed it."

Don't faint, Ava. "That's a good thing, right?"

His finger paused at the bridge of her collarbone. "What if it isn't? For you, anyway."

"How about you worry about you, and I worry about me?"

He cocked his head. "Before I met you, I didn't have a single complaint about my life. I'd been sitting in the shadows for so long, I'd forgotten what it was like to savor the sun. And then you walked in and caught me off guard, and I wanted to pull down the shades even tighter. You're the sun, Ava. I know I don't always act like it, but I *want* to keep the shades open. Can you please remember that when I'm being defensive and resistant and stubborn? Assuming you even want to. I can't promise it's going to be easy."

Ava swallowed. The only thing keeping her upright was the feel of the dry, smooth earth underneath her feet, reminding her of one hot, dry summer when she was in elementary school. She'd been walking through the cotton fields with her grandma, scanning the western horizon for the clouds the local meteorologists had promised were coming. Ava had been consumed and saddened by a classmate's birthday party invitation she'd not received and had been pouting all afternoon.

"See these withered plants," her grandma said, no doubt tired of her sulking. "Every one of them has an ache inside as big as yours. It don't make your ache any less important to you, but it's a lesson we could all use remembering from time to time. Each living thing is aching for something. Whenever I forget it, Mother Nature has a way of reminding me."

Ava had been so busy working and trying to build a perfect

life that she'd forgotten a hundred pieces of wisdom her grand-parents had doled out over the years. But something about this experience with Jeremy and the kids was bringing those memories back.

"I can remember it," she replied, closing her hand lightly around his arm. "How could I not when that's the most beautiful, real, and raw thing any guy has ever said to me?" She dug her top teeth into her lower lip. She wanted to kiss him, but this time, she didn't want to be the one to initiate it. "Jeremy, I want you the way that garden out there wants rain in a dry August, and I want to be here for you in every way you need me. But I also want it to be right for you. Actually, I'll bet a gazillion dollars it *will* be. I'm just hoping you trust yourself enough to let me in."

A loud bark pierced the air, making Ava jump. Rolo had abandoned the cat and joined them at the door. He was less than two feet away and staring at them intently, his ears perked forward and his tail wagging.

Jeremy's face pulled into a mock scowl. "What, bud? You want me to kiss her or something? Things aren't always so simple in the people world. Not even close."

Rolo barked again.

"You know," Ava said, "I'm all right going for hard and complicated. All the really good things are worth fighting for."

"When you put it that way…" Jeremy's lips had connected with hers—creating an instant chorus of ews and yucks from the surrounding yard and alerting them that they had an audience—when the half-open door thwacked heavily enough against him that Jeremy and Ava's teeth mashed together. Dash stood on the other side, his head cocked as he checked them out for a few seconds before dashing off to run another lap of the yard.

Ava ran her tongue over her front teeth. "Ow! Judging by that hit, we're getting to the hard part already."

"No kidding. You okay?"

"Yeah, I'm fine. You?"

"Really fine." Jeremy reached out to gently pull something from Ava's hair. "Ladybug." He opened his fingers and let it fly away.

Ava watched as the ladybug flew right for the ceiling. To her surprise, there were a dozen more congregated in a small group in the corner of the ceiling. "Looks like they like it in here."

"I'm glad they're sticking around." Jeremy gave Ava a lop-sided grin that melted her into a puddle. "So, uh, what do you say we get these kids out of here and pick that kiss back up in half an hour? Assuming you don't have a fat lip, that is."

Ava was about to utter an emphatic yes when Rolo's shrill single bark pierced the air. Instead, she jutted her head in the dog's direction. "Yeah, what he said."

Chapter 26

THERE WAS NO WAY AROUND IT. THE MEETING OF PARENTS—AND grandparents—constituted a big "next step" in his relationship with Ava. Jeremy would be the last to deny he was proving to be a myriad of contradictions, from first telling her he couldn't be with her to requesting they tread slowly as friends, then, more recently, to not being able to keep his hands off her. In his defense, those yoga postures she'd demonstrated in class right next to him along with those innocent touches had set him on fire.

Now, nearly two full weeks into "officially dating," he was driving down to meet her family—with an entourage in tow. His entire new group of kids were joining them, as were the dogs who could be trusted off leash: Mortimer, Millie, Luna, and Rolo. Dash was spending the weekend with Hussein, one of Jeremy's students, and had been picked up last night. It had been strange not having the high-energy dog around afterward, and a quieter, calmer air had taken over the house and yard.

Olivia and Gabe would be joining them later in the day, and they'd be bringing Morgan and Samson as well. Jeremy suspected this would be more dogs than had ever congregated at Ava's grandparents' farm at once. Ava promised her family was excited to welcome the big group of teens and dogs, and Jeremy hoped she was right. It was no small intrusion on their weekend.

To add to the chaos that was almost certain to come, the whole group would be camping overnight and heading back to St. Louis tomorrow morning. Four of the kids were riding down with him, and three were in Ava's Jeep. With the kids, camping gear, dogs, and food, both vehicles were jam-packed.

From the back row of the van, Nolan yawned loud enough to project over the other kids' conversation. "Man, I haven't gotten up so early on a Saturday in my life. My stomach's telling me it's time for lunch, and it ain't even ten o'clock."

Jeremy chuckled and flipped on his right blinker as, in the Jeep ahead of him, Ava merged into the right lane. Jeremy's GPS showed they had only another mile or two on the highway and just twenty minutes until they were at their destination. He wondered if she was battling her own set of nerves the closer they got.

"You were quiet for over a half hour there," Jeremy answered Nolan. "I thought maybe you'd fallen asleep." They'd been aiming to leave before seven and had managed to pull out of Edith and Eleanor's at seven thirty, so not a bad start. Today, the kids would be getting their service hours in on a working farm.

"I might've," Nolan said. "It'd explain why I'm so hungry. I always wake up hungry."

Sammy, who was complying with today's work-boot requirement by donning a brand-new pair of Converse work boots, had taken on the role of doling out food from the middle row of seats. She sifted through the two reusable totes that had been loaded with snacks for the ride down and back. "Want an apple or a banana?"

"You got any hamburgers in there? Double cheese with extra pickle preferably."

"I wish. How about trail mix or the Goldfish?"

"There's string cheese in the top of the cooler," Jeremy offered.

"Man, I've only known you a few weeks, and I'm already calling you on that string cheese and chocolate milk bullcrap." To Sammy, Nolan said, "Toss me the Goldfish, will you?"

Jeremy laughed. "I have no idea what you're talking about."

"As soon as things get heavy, you offer a stick of string cheese or a carton of chocolate milk."

"I didn't notice that," Sammy said, a touch of defensiveness in her tone.

"Even if he does, which I didn't notice, either, those *are* throwbacks to easy times," Adam interjected. "Just saying."

"Nolan, are things feeling stressful for you now?" Jeremy asked, still chuckling.

Nolan's response to his harder-than-average young life so far had been to coat everything in humor, and then, after he'd held in so much that he burst, had been to swallow a near-lethal dose of his aunt's pain medicine for the chemo she was undergoing.

"Ain't nothing stressful for me, man."

"I bet you have some stress. We all do."

"If any of us is stressed right now, I bet it's you, 'bout to meet your girlfriend's parents for the first time."

Jeremy shrugged one shoulder. "I'm not going to hide it. My palms are sweating."

"They should be, man. Meeting the parents is one step away from a proposal for most chicks."

"You're so full of it, Nolan," Sammy said. "Jeremy knows that stuff better than you."

"Considering I've only known Ava about as long as you guys, I don't think she'll expect a proposal anytime soon."

"Just so we're clear, you should totally propose." In the passenger seat next to him, William, the smallest of the group but not the youngest, wagged his eyebrows. "*Está muy caliente.*"

Jeremy huffed. "How about giving *me* a piece of string cheese, Sammy?"

As she popped open the cooler, all four kids laughed hard enough to wake Rolo from a nap where he was splayed in the middle of the floor since all the seats were taken.

Tethered in as he was, Rolo couldn't get close enough to Jeremy as he unwrapped the plastic encasing the cheese to make it obvious he was waiting for his usual bit off the end, so he whined instead.

Jeremy reached back to offer him the end piece after they had pulled off the highway and were heading out into farmland.

"We're getting close. You guys ready to get to work?"

As they headed away from the small strip of stores near the interstate, farmlands stretched as far as they could see. Jeremy's phone rang with Ava's number and he pressed accept on his dashboard. "You're on speaker."

"Works for me. How's it going in there?" As her voice filled the van's interior, Rolo whined and perked his ears, proving how bonded with her he'd become.

"Other than the voracious hunger of teens, great."

"Ha. Well, we can dive in to our sandwiches early if they want to. Oh, and do you all see that field to the right? Those are cotton plants."

Earlier, as they were loading up the supplies and dogs, and Ava was prepping the group for what was ahead, most of the kids had said they'd never seen a cotton field. Jeremy couldn't say he had, either, that he knew of anyway. Most fields in and around St. Louis and up past Chicago were planted with corn, wheat, or soy.

"I don't see any cotton," Nolan said.

Even though he was in the back, he said it loud enough that Ava heard him. "It hasn't bloomed yet. It won't until later this summer."

"Huh," William mumbled. "I thought cotton plants were brown."

"They will be. This time of year, they're green and lush. Maybe we can do another trip back here in fall to see it harvested."

Jeremy wasn't sure if his palms started sweating again out of fear or excitement to hear Ava talking long-term.

Ava entered a dip in the road first, and the connection was lost. Jeremy wasn't sure if she heard the kids' easy agreement or not. He'd remember to tell her later.

"Bet you two are engaged by then," Nolan said before asking Sammy to toss him a piece of string cheese as well.

"You know what they say, Nolan. Time is the ultimate teller of truth."

"Yeah, well, maybe, but so are those stupid looks you give each other. You two are in deep."

It occurred to Jeremy that what Nolan likely needed more than anything was a male role model in his life who wasn't afraid of a bit of vulnerability. And even if Jeremy was battling his own inner discomfort about admitting how much Ava meant to him, he bit back his fear.

"The truth is, Nolan, I can't speak for Ava, but I am. As deep as it gets."

Suddenly William was jabbing his elbow and pointing at Jeremy's infotainment system that was somehow showing Ava's number again and a live call. His fingers tightened instinctively around the wheel.

"I thought we lost you there," she said, her voice still patchy. "Nolan, I can't say I heard all that, but me too. As deep as it gets."

As the kids in both vehicles erupted into a chorus of groans and laughter, Jeremy figured he could think of worse ways to start a conversation that needed to be started.

Chapter 27

AVA WOULD BE LYING TO PRETEND THAT ON THE DRIVE DOWN HERE she hadn't had moments of complete reservation. What had made her confident seven at-risk kids from the city would love a day on a working farm in rural southern Missouri, she didn't know.

Thankfully, she'd been right. She was good at reading people; not perfect, but she had a solid B+ track record. What she hadn't been one hundred percent convinced about was how her set-in-their-ways grandparents would embrace teens so different in style, attitude, and for some, ethnicity as compared to most of the teens they'd been exposed to. As it turned out, they'd been more than congenial from the start, even if her gramps had gotten big-eyed at Hailey's recently dyed pink-and-purple hair and numerous earrings, William's oversize tattoo of the number 4 emblazoned large on his upper arm representing the four languages he was fluent in, and Sammy's easily spoken declaration over lunch about how she'd known she was attracted to girls since she was in kindergarten. "Huh," had been Gramps's only response at hearing that.

Ava didn't blame him for not understanding them; the world was changing and fast—at a much faster pace even than when she'd grown up. He'd carved out his entire life here, where satellite television was likely several years away from being replaced by streaming, landlines were still preferred over cell phones with their unreliable service, and cotton was king. How could he, at his age, grasp how the world was moving at a different pace elsewhere?

She'd been confident her parents would enjoy the teens' company, but she'd known going in that they wouldn't have the same amount of interaction with them, busy as their days were elsewhere. While her parents were pulled in to help with certain tasks several times a year, for the most part, they had their own careers, and farm operations were left to Ava's seventysomething-year-old grandparents, her uncle, and a few seasonally hired farmhands.

Belly rumbling after an exhausting but rewarding day of labor in the warm sun, Ava stepped out the back door of her childhood home carrying two cans of the off-brand soda her grandparents kept stocked in the spare fridge. She headed across the yard to the towering basswood tree that had shaded the backyard since long before she'd been born.

Sliding into the empty seat next to her grandfather at one of two eight-foot folding tables where her loaded plate was waiting, she handed him the orange soda and kept the root beer for herself. He gave her knee a double pat in thanks—which in terms of affection was as much as he could ever be counted on doling out.

Jeremy was at the second table, sandwiched between Hailey and Nolan. Having gone through the line first, everyone at Jeremy's table had started eating. Jeremy met Ava's gaze and gave her a wink that sent a wash of happiness over her. They'd hardly had a minute alone today, but today hadn't been about them, and she had no complaints.

Besides, Ava had received the best possible confirmation she could've asked for that his feelings mirrored her own, thanks to the cell phone service around here. *He's in as deep as it gets.* Really, could she ask for anything better than that? She didn't think so.

"Think you got enough food?" Her grandpa winked, eyeing her loaded plate.

"We'll see." Ava refused to be goaded. "I haven't been this hungry in forever. Grams, this looks delicious. I've been craving your potato salad for months."

"It was hardly any trouble, and well worth it besides, as helpful as these kids have been today," her grandma said. Across the table, Ava's grandma waggled a finger at her grandfather. "With as much work as you won't have to do tomorrow, Walter, we can drive into town and tackle that rainy-day shopping list I've been adding to the last two months."

"Ava, tell your grandma she's best off not holding her breath," her grandpa said with a chuckle.

"No thank you, I know better than to get in the middle of that." Ava gave her loaded plate a quarter turn as she picked up a fork, her mouth watering in anticipation.

"Save a little room for pie, everybody," Ava's mom said from three seats down. "I brought home three whole pies with me from the diner: strawberry rhubarb, coconut cream, and apple."

The kids grunted their excitement through mouthfuls of food they were practically inhaling. Her grandparents had insisted it was no trouble, but Ava was still glad they'd agreed to accept Jeremy's offer to pay for the cost of the food after they'd learned he had a grant to cover outing costs, including the kids' food. The giant bowls of potato salad and coleslaw, bulging foil pan of baked beans, fresh-from-the-garden green beans and tomatoes, dinner rolls, and the mountain of barbeque chicken drummies and fried catfish had almost certainly cost more than a full week's groceries for the two of them.

A year or so after Ava moved out, Ava's parents had saved up enough money to build an A-frame home on the rear of the property, accessible only by a private dirt road that went past the rear barn. As far as Ava knew, her parents and grandparents only had dinner together about once a week anymore. There was no question in Ava's mind that all six Grahams under one roof for all those years had caused a strain in their relationship, along with her dad's choice of career. Having a son who was a full-time stained-glass artist had never been something her grandfather could get his head around.

Earlier, when she'd been working with Lily and William to clean out the feed room in the front barn, helping the best she was able with one hand still in a cast, it hit home that she'd been away for nearly a third of her life now.

For so many years before she left, she'd dreamed of escaping. No doubt that had at least in part been due to the power she'd given the friendly jabs from her peers about the fact that her parents couldn't afford a home of their own. If she saw any of those kids again, she'd have no qualms letting them know how thankful she now was to have been raised in a multigenerational family.

Today, as the kids scrubbed water troughs, mended fences, stacked hay, and learned more about cotton than they'd ever imagined there was to learn, it had occurred to Ava that she'd forgiven her family for the strained years after she'd left and the pressure they'd put on her to come home. They'd not been ready or willing to accept that she'd needed to find her way on her own. And honestly, for that matter, she'd done a terrible job of explaining herself. How could she when she hadn't yet known that it was in going away that she'd finally connect with all this place had meant to her?

The fact was, they'd only ever wanted the best for her.

As he deboned a hunk of catfish, her grandpa said, "Got yourself a nice fellow there, seems like."

There was enough jabber all around that it was unlikely anyone heard him but her. She nodded in agreement, still savoring the crisp, salty coating of fried catfish she'd just bitten into.

"Thanks, Gramps. I think so too," she said after washing the fish down with a drink of root beer.

"I've found that you can tell the way a man's going to treat his wife and children by the way he treats his dog. Which, in his case, is with considerable care."

"I remember hearing you say that over the years, and I guess it finally sank in," Ava said. "The first time we met, we were at a dog wash. And that was one of the biggest things that pulled me in, the way he treated not only Rolo but the rescued dogs too."

Rolo had just finished circling the tables and planted himself behind her, no doubt hoping for a bite of scraps once the meal was over. Rather than sitting up on his haunches to beg, he stretched out on the ground, clearly worn out from the hours he'd spent circling the small flock of sheep and the cows and hanging out with her grandma's big yellow tomcat, all the while ignoring the other dogs. Now that everyone was eating, the rest of the dogs were settling down as well, after spending most of the day alternating between savoring the ability to run freely and cooling off in the shade after overdoing it.

Her grandpa smiled, calling her attention to the deep crevices lining his blue eyes from a lifetime of working in the elements. "Well, I'm glad I could teach you a few things."

"You and Grams taught me a lot. I'm still figuring out how much, actually. I know I'm overdue in saying this, but I wouldn't trade my childhood years for anything."

He took a swig of orange soda before replying. "If it makes a difference, I wouldn't either."

Ava had taken another bite of catfish and squeezed his shoulder instead of answering. Knowing her grandpa, this bit of sentiment was as much as he'd want to dole out anyway.

"Thanks again for thinking of all the projects for the kids," she added when she finished her bite.

"You can't say it wasn't in my favor to do so." After eating a forkful of green beans, her grandpa added, "Those service hours the kids were talking about, are they required for community service?"

"They're part of Jeremy's program," Ava said.

"And they get me out of being grounded for the next year," Christopher chimed in from the other side of the table with a sheepish smile.

After a look of surprise passed over his face, her grandpa simply nodded. "Makes sense."

Adam's face lit in surprise. "What're you grounded for?"

Christopher shrugged a shoulder nonchalantly. "Being a dumbass… Sorry," he said with a glance at Ava's grandpa. "A series of unfortunate events. Let's leave it at that."

Her grandpa wiped his mouth with his napkin, and a small piece of it tore off and stuck to the bristly daily growth of beard on the side of his chin. Ava swiped at it with one finger.

"Sowing your oats in the wrong field is a part of growing up, is all," he said, directing his words to Christopher. "I sowed a few wrong fields in my time too. Often ends up being one of the fastest ways to realize there's something better out there for you."

Her grandpa gave her knee another quick pat, which made Ava suspect his message was meant for her as much as it was Christopher. She draped an arm over Gramps's back and shoulders, which she realized was more affection than she'd offered him in a long time as well. Maybe it was up to her to break that tradition her family had of being cautiously reserved. "You're a smart man, Gramps. And a good one too."

"Yeah, well, I suspect those smarts passed down to you came from your grandma's side. You can give me credit for your ease at diving into hard work, young lady," he said with a chuckle.

Ava glanced down the length of the table. Her mom was

laughing at something Gabe had said, and her father was at the end, deep in conversation with Lily. From the way he was sweeping one flattened hand in the air, it was safe to assume they were talking about some aspect of art. In addition to gardening, Lily was a budding artist, and she'd loved seeing Ava's dad's workshop in the far barn.

Confident her parents wouldn't hear only this snippet and misunderstand, Ava said, "You and Grandma, I'm realizing how much better off Olivia and I will always be because we had you two in our lives every day when we were growing up." She motioned past the fenced-in yard toward the fields that stretched out into the far tree line in all directions. A hundred aspects of this farm, like its loamy smell in summer and the way the earth itself seemed to burst into bloom this time of year, had soaked into her like fine grains of pollen into the ground. "This place too."

Her grandpa stabbed at another hunk of catfish that he'd cut off the flank with the side of his fork. "That door swings both ways, you know."

On the other side of the table, Adam and Christopher smirked at hearing an expression that had a different meaning nowadays than her grandpa would ever guess.

"Thanks, Gramps." To keep from smiling in response to the looks the boys exchanged, she took another bite of potato salad. Thanks in part to her grandma's secret of adding the vinegar to the potatoes while they were still steaming warm, it was easy to understand why it had been voted the best in the county at least three different times at the county fair over the years.

As she reached for her root beer, Ava glanced down the length of the tables and met Jeremy's gaze again. His smile was subtle and private and full of the promise of more wonderful things to come, and she returned it with the feeling that her cup was most assuredly overflowing. It seemed next to impossible that in one day's time, she had so many new awarenesses to share with the man who was very quickly becoming one of the most important people on the planet to her.

Time and awareness, Ava; trust that you've got them both in spades.

Chapter 28

THE HARD GROUND UNDER AVA'S BODY HAD HER DREAMING OF the fairy tale about the princess and the pea. After hearing the tale as a kid, she'd worried about being feminine and finely bred enough to feel a pea under all those mattresses. Now, it was obvious no one could. Lying here on the ground, half-dozing, half-awake, she could, however, appreciate the comfort afforded by a fine mattress—which for her was still in a pod, waiting for her to decide her next big step in life. The couch and even the well-worn mattress she shared with Olivia whenever she couldn't take another night on the couch weren't exactly a stay at the Ritz, but after the long night she'd had, she had a newfound appreciation for them.

There was Jeremy's bed now too. Sort of. Ava didn't know what it felt like to actually sleep on it yet, but she suspected she would soon. They'd had "the talk," no diseases either of them, and she was on the pill. The only time she'd been on his bed so far, she'd been too aroused to notice if his mattress was even slightly more comfortable than a marble floor.

They'd had a handful of intense make-out sessions elsewhere, too, and she was becoming familiar with his body, his touch, and the sounds of his breathing and soft murmurs when he was aroused. But they hadn't spent the night together, and they hadn't fully consummated their relationship.

While he was wary of demons stirring to life, he'd also moved her deeply with the wish to take things slow. "You're different, Ava, and as far as I'm concerned, we're in a marathon here, not a hundred-yard dash. I want to savor every layer of you along the way."

Ava couldn't be more in agreement, especially with him putting it like that.

Stifling a yawn, she wiggled in her sleeping bag and turned onto her side as quietly as she could. The three girls in her tent were all sleeping soundly after talking late into the night. She didn't have her phone nearby, but Ava didn't think it was her imagination that the darkness surrounding the tent seemed to be lessening, and the sounds of the summer night were quieting as night prepared to ease into day. Ava's best guess was that it was still in the four o'clock hour but closing in on five.

She had little doubt that if she clambered out of the tent now to relieve her full bladder, she'd be too awake to fall back to sleep. She was doing her best to drift off again when she heard the tent zipper open from the guys' tent fifteen feet away. Jeremy's voice, saying "Come, Rolo," was just audible.

Not wanting to disturb the girls or her other tentmates, Luna and the puppies, Ava wriggled out of her sleeping bag and padded over to the entrance of the tent as quietly as possible. Unzipping it just enough to slip out, she wormed her way out and zipped it behind her, grabbing the pair of flip-flops she'd left by the door.

Outside, the considerably cooler night air raised goose bumps on the bare skin of Ava's arms. Locking her arms over her chest, she scanned the darkness until she spotted two familiar silhouettes on the far side of the yard against the fence line. Though duller now than when she'd gone to sleep, thousands of stars still studded the cloudless sky.

After slipping on her flip-flops, she crossed the yard. Rolo spotted her first and trotted over, burrowing his head underneath her closest hand, which happened to be the casted one. She scratched his ear before waving to Jeremy.

"Hey," he said as he reached her, his voice low and intimate.

"Could you not sleep?" he asked before leaning in to give her a kiss, tickling her lips with his beard.

"I slept enough." She kept her voice down to a whisper. "I was half-awake and attempting to doze off again, but I heard you come out and my bladder wanted to join you. Unlike you two," she added with a glance over at the dark house across the expansive backyard, "I'm happy with my long-standing relationship with toilet paper and prefer to make use of the bathroom inside the mudroom." Her grandparents had left the back door unlocked so the campers would have use of the half bath.

Jeremy smiled, a strip of his teeth gleaming in the dim light. "I guess we have it easier that way. We'll walk you over there if you'd like some company."

"You won't be getting any complaints from me by offering your company. Ever." Their hands found each other as they started walking. Rolo flanked Ava's side, shoving his head under her other hand again.

"The boys sleeping okay? The girls were all breathing deeply when I stepped out."

"They're out like lights. I've got zero doubt we'll have to wake them up for breakfast when it's time to pack up."

Ava's grandpa's Lab, Jack, came trotting around the house, no doubt from the fluffy bed where he spent his nights on the front porch. He and Rolo sniffed noses briefly, and he circled them once before trotting back around the side of the house.

"Do you need a light?" Jeremy asked.

Ava squeezed his hand before letting go. "Nope, but thanks. I can find my way around here in less light than this. Be right back."

Ava let herself in through the sliding door, made her way through to the bathroom, and headed back outside again without flipping a single light switch. Before stepping out, she grabbed two bottles of water from the spare fridge in the mudroom.

"Thirsty?" She offered one his way.

"I am, thanks." He opened his and took a long drink. After recapping it and dragging his hand across his mouth, he said, "Ava, you were great with the kids yesterday. It means a lot."

Thanks to her cast, Ava was struggling with her cap when Jeremy stepped in close to help. The chilled water hit the spot after yesterday's long day in the sun. "Well, thank you, but trust me when I tell you it was my pleasure. I had no idea how healing it would be to come back and have my family welcome this eclectic group of kids, but it absolutely was."

After both set their bottles on the patio table, she stepped in for a hug. It was still too dark to make out colors, but the darkness only heightened her sense of touch as her cheek brushed against Jeremy's stubbly one. She stood there in no rush to step away, soaking in the feel of his strong, solid body against hers.

Eventually, his hands closed over her sides, and she savored the way a few of his fingertips brushed the bare skin where her T-shirt had lifted.

He must have appreciated it, too, because he slid both hands underneath her shirt and caressed the sides of her body. Their lips met, and Ava became intensely aware of the fact that she wasn't wearing a bra and how close his hands were to figuring that out.

"You feel good," he murmured. "Really good."

Ava moved in closer, burying her fingers in his hair, careful not to bump her casted wrist against his head. "You feel even better." She brushed her lips over his earlobe and tasted his skin with the tip of her tongue.

This trip hadn't been about them, and she'd not expected anything much in the way of stolen kisses. They'd have their time back in St. Louis, but that didn't mean she wasn't going to savor this one.

As their mouths met again, his hands moved higher. He

murmured a muted groan before his mouth left hers to explore her body. Ava's head fell back, and she soaked in the sensation, her blood pooling between her legs.

"Remind me when we get back to St. Louis that I'm more than happy to jump past any final remaining hurdles between what we've done and what we haven't, so long as you are," he mumbled against her ear, his voice low and husky. "Actually, what am I saying? You aren't going to have to remind me."

Ava laughed quietly and grabbed his hand, leading him around the side of the house in the dim light. "Indulge me a minute, will you?"

"How so?"

"These white pines at the side of the house... As you were kissing me, I was thinking about how, when I was a hormonal teen, I daydreamed about climbing out my window and down the biggest pine at the end to a boy who was waiting. We'd make out like you and I just were, only it never happened. Not here anyway. I doubt any boys around here wanted to risk taking on my grandpa and my dad at the same time. And really, by that, I just mean my grandpa."

"I don't doubt you there."

Ava led him along the outside of the three pines until they were midway between the two that were closest to the front of the house. The pines were even bigger now, but there was still the perfect nook between them like she remembered.

Having neared the front porch, Rolo smelled her grandpa's Lab and trotted off to check him out again. The sky was clearly beginning to lighten, because Ava could just make out through the sparser branches at the side that Jack was standing squarely at the top of the porch steps, looking out onto the long driveway, a perfectly posed sentinel.

"Olivia's and my shared room was on this end of the house.

You can't see 'em from here, but the two windows over the top of this side of the porch open to it."

"So, you dreamed of climbing out your window and risking life and limb to scale this tree to make out with a boy?"

"Well, not just *any* boy. That was back when I believed in knights in shining armor."

He stepped in and brushed his lips against her forehead. "And what do you believe in now?"

Ava closed her eyes and pulled in a slow breath. "Jeremys and Avas and doing your best and making mistakes but being mature enough to get past them."

"I could believe in that, and you don't even have to risk breaking your other arm climbing down a tree."

Ava met him in the middle for a short kiss. "I'm actually hoping for the whole package." She kicked off her shoes and wormed her way toward the back of the tree.

Even in the dim light, she could spy his amusement. "What exactly do you mean by 'the whole package'?"

While she'd never met a boy at the bottom, she'd gotten to be an expert of climbing out her window onto the porch awning and into the pine tree. The scariest part had always been the trust fall down half a foot to one of the big, sparsely needled branches facing the side of the house, but from there down, the stair-step branches of the tree had been a cakewalk, and the way back up had been a breeze as well.

After kicking off her flip-flops, she started to climb. As her bare feet brushed against the rough bark, Ava realized she'd learned a lot about climbing since the last time she'd scaled this tree, thanks to a series of rock-climbing lessons she'd taken a while back. Using her casted arm for nothing more than balance, she relied on the strength in her legs to propel her upward.

"How high are you going?" Jeremy asked when her feet were level with his head.

"It's not much farther," she said, testing each branch for a smooth spot to place her feet before finding her footing on it. "Want to check out my room?"

"Won't the window be locked?"

"Not likely. All I've ever had to do was jiggle it. The security latch was broken, and I'm betting it hasn't been fixed."

"The practical part of me who talks kids off ledges feels I should remind you the back door is unlocked."

Ava swept her hair to the side and grinned down at him in the silvery predawn light. "Trust me, I've got this, but if you want to come up, I'd love to show you my room. Chances are the front door is unlocked, too, if you want to come in that way. Just take a left at the top of the stairs; my grandparents' room is on the opposite side. They won't hear a thing. I'll meet you in there."

"I'll meet you up there," he said, "but please be careful."

Ava started climbing again. She was just a few branches from the edge of the porch awning, which she thoroughly tested with her weight before letting go of the branch above her. Feeling like she was at the top of a roller coaster and a second or two from descending, she grabbed onto the gutter and took a practiced step of faith onto the awning.

This, Ava, this is the leaping-before-you-look stuff you're always berating yourself for afterward.

When her bout of nerves settled, she grabbed onto her window ledge and hauled herself up to it, a feat that was considerably more challenging with one wrist in a cast. With the roof tiles digging into her knees, Ava shimmied the window open like she had a dozen times as a kid. Olivia was going to faint when she heard she'd done this for old time's sake.

Just as she was about to crawl in, she saw movement in the tree. Jeremy was climbing up instead of taking the stairs.

"Hey, Jeremy, you definitely don't have to do this."

The branches shook, and his head appeared over the edge of the awning as he climbed. "I was heading for the door, but I figured I've been treading the straight and narrow for a while now. What I'm *not* about to do is test the strength of that awning with both of us on it at once."

"Well said." Ava climbed in through the window, a task that was considerably harder than she remembered. Once inside, she turned around and stuck her head out. Down below, Jack barked several times, unhappy with the commotion overhead; Rolo, who must've been hanging out next to him, barked once as well. "For the record, this is one of those things I only need to relive once."

Jeremy chuckled from where he was standing on the branch just below the awning. "I'm good with that. So," he said, "grab the gutter and just go for it?"

"Ah, test the awning with your weight first before you let go of the tree, will you? You're a little heavier than me."

Ava held her breath as Jeremy tested the roof of the porch and took the leap of faith from the tree onto it. Unlike her, he remained standing and walked the few steps at a sharp angle over to her window. She backed up as he began to crawl inside.

Halfway through, he twisted around and entered with his back facing into the room which seemed a little more fluid than her entrance. "Making it through the window is the hardest part." She kept her voice at a low whisper even though her grandparents wouldn't hear, and her grandma's shih tzu was almost completely deaf.

"You actually did this…a lot?" He kept his voice low as he swept his hand through his hair to catch a handful of stray needles.

Ava shrugged. "The window part was easier when I was smaller, but from about twelve on, yeah. Sometimes once a night in summer just to do it. Or we'd sit on the porch awning and look out at the stars and daydream about what we were going to do when we grew up. Only sometimes was I actually breaking curfew." She stepped close and gave him a ferocious hug. "You have no idea how sweet it is that you indulged me in this."

He pressed his lips against her forehead, then her temple, and hugged her more tightly to him. "That works both ways, you know. You make me feel alive in a way I haven't been in a long time." He locked a hand over her hip. "And thank you for not minding my setting the pace as I fully step into this, Ava."

She blinked her eyes a bit overdramatically. "It's not like it hasn't been fun…a lot of fun. And for the record, you aren't the person you used to be, Jeremy. Nor am I. Coming home proved that so clearly for me. The unhappy girl who left here had a back-pack full of blame on her shoulders when it came to all the imperfect things in her life. That's a coping mechanism I don't need any longer. And I know our childhood experiences weren't even close to the same, but if you ask me, with all the work you've done, I hope you don't allow your past to define you. I've been around you know enough to know you aren't that broken guy still physically reeling from a mountain of abuse no child should ever have to experience." She brushed her lips against his as his hands locked over her back. "Jeremy, this man you've become—"

Her throat locked up and she swallowed hard, on the verge of tears she'd taught herself never to shed. Since she was letting go of habits and judgments, maybe she didn't have to be that person who didn't shed a tear anymore. "This man you are now rocks my world, and that's a little bit terrifying because it'll hurt really bad if you walk away." She took a shaky breath, steadying herself. "But it's a risk I'm willing to take."

He kissed her hard before pulling away to press his forehead against hers and run both thumbs along the sides of her chin. "I'm usually the one with all the words, a side effect of the trade and all—but what you said."

Smiling, Ava brushed her lips against his before stepping away to walk the length of her room, the worn-carpeted floor creaking softly underfoot. The matching quilts that her grandma had used to replace the brightly colored, flower-filled ones of her youth after she left stood out as an oddity in this still intimately familiar room. She crossed over to the door, shut it quietly, and flipped the lock. "Were you serious outside about skipping those last few layers when we get home?"

His eyebrows lifted. "Ahh…" The sky had brightened enough that she could read the expression on his face from several feet away. "As serious as a heart attack—wait no, I don't want to say that. What's serious but not depressing? Words are suddenly escaping me."

Ava laughed softly and crossed over to the bed nearest the windows. "This one was mine." She pulled down the quilt and straightened the pillow. "And I'd love it if you were interested in joining me on it for a bit." Before giving him time to answer, she pulled off her T-shirt and slid out of her shorts and underwear, and even before taking in the look of stunned appreciation on his face, feeling free and beautiful and not at all like the girl who stood in front of a mirror picking apart her curves and imperfections.

"You know," he said, "I grew up believing I'd never be anything but down on my luck. I haven't thought that for a while, but right now, I'm pretty damn sure I'm the luckiest man on the planet."

She'd already begun to memorize the feel of him against her, but it was even better with no layers of clothing between them. As their bodies joined, tears slipped endlessly from Ava's lids.

Jeremy brushed them away with his lips, following their trail. "You sure you're okay?"

She nodded and pulled him closer. "I was thinking about the first time I saw you that day at the shelter. I got this feeling that I couldn't explain. Not until now." Before her lips met his, she added, "Somehow I knew being with you was going to feel like coming home."

Chapter 29

"Do you think it's time to bag it and pop more?" Lily was eyeing the still-warm kettle corn in the giant kettle with a discerning eye.

Jeremy peered inside to find it was approximately one-third full.

"We have four more big bags and three small ones left up here," William called out from over at the sales table.

Jeremy eyed the crowds split between the new vet center and the shelter. "I bet we can go another ten or fifteen minutes if two of you want to take one of the dogs around again. It's your turn for a break."

It was the first Saturday of July, and with the Fourth on Monday, the start of a long weekend. Jeremy and his students had signed up to work the drink and kettle corn tents at today's grand opening event. The day-long festivities included more than a dozen activities for people and their canine companions, both inside the new vet center and outside on the grounds of both facilities.

Rolo had spent a half hour with him and Ava, doing the rounds before the crowds of people started arriving. No surprise, Jeremy's chillaxed dog hadn't had much interest in the agility run, but he had soaked up the Maze of Summer Scents—hay bales lined up to form a maze that had been enhanced with a variety of enticing scents—enticing for dogs, at least. A few bales had labels marking invisible scents like "stinky trash bin" that made Jeremy shudder to think of sniffing but had Rolo drooling in pleasure. After that, they visited the sprinkler station, and

Jeremy's water-loving dog had gotten happily soaked. They'd ended with a stop at the "pupsicle" station.

Now, Rolo was hanging out by Ava on the opposite side of the rear parking lot of the vet center at the face-painting tent. With her cast removed last week, she was excited to have full use of both hands to put her artistic skills to use. Jeremy had gotten to know Ava's cartoon sketches well enough that he was able to spot her work from those painted by the other two volunteers working with her when kids came by to sample and buy kettle corn.

Inside the shelter, a special adoption event was taking place that included three of the kittens from Jeremy's backyard. Now that they were well over eight weeks old, they were weaned and at the perfect age to bond with whoever adopted them. The fourth kitten, a girl, had already been adopted by Lily after getting her shots and a checkup.

Turtle, the kittens' young tortoiseshelled mother, was inside the shelter as well. She hadn't been as easy to catch as her kittens, but earlier this week, after cornering her in the carriage house, Ava had been able to wrap her in a blanket and slip her into the kennel with her babies to bring her here. Now, Turtle was in the shelter's private quarantine room. Her tests had come back proving she was healthy, she was getting a complete round of shots, and she was recovering from yesterday's spaying. She might not have another litter of kittens, but with any luck, the remainder of her life would prove to be a good deal easier than her first year had been.

Back in May, Jeremy had begun the foster-dog program tossing around the thought that he might adopt one of the dogs permanently. Life, however, had taken a different turn. His cat-loving dog had taken to Louie more than any of the dogs he'd been sharing his home with the last six weeks. Instead of adopting a dog, Jeremy and Ava were keeping Louie, who was quickly becoming as cuddly as he was playful. This had worked out for the best because the foster dogs had all been offered forever homes by families of kids in Jeremy's program. In fact, the foster-dog project had gone over so well that Jeremy intended to do it again with the next group of kids entering the program.

As Jeremy hung near the front of the tent in the event Sammy needed help covering sales, he spotted Edith and Eleanor crossing the footbridge after checking out the festivities over at the shelter. They waved in his direction before stepping into the short line of kids waiting to have their faces painted. It was one of the things Jeremy loved most about them; they never thought of themselves as too old to savor the small things.

His mind had been whirling all morning with the news they'd shared with him over coffee earlier. "We want to spend more time traveling," Eleanor had said in explanation of their unexpected proposal to sell him the house—at a bargain price—and temporarily rent the smaller apartment from him while he moved in to their considerably larger one.

"And we'll be completely out of your hair within the year, I bet," Edith had added. "That retirement community we've been looking at has been calling to us more and more. Facing those stairs every time we want to go outside is a pain—those are ten-foot ceilings on the lower level, you know. Then, you can have the whole top floor. Surely by then you two'll want to knock down that wall between the apartments and make room for babies."

"You do remember we've only been dating two months, right?" he'd said with a smile.

When Eleanor had commented that when right was right, time didn't have the same appeal, he'd fallen silent. There was no arguing with Eleanor, especially when her argument was valid.

Jeremy hadn't stopped thinking about the offer since. Even though he'd wanted to accept the second they'd brought it up, he'd asked for the weekend to think about it. When the craziness of today was over, he planned to talk it through with Ava, and he really hoped she'd be on board. Maybe they had only been dating for two months, but Eleanor knew what she was talking about. That newness didn't invalidate the staying power all of them sensed this relationship had, Jeremy and Ava included.

And he hoped like hell Ava would like their idea.

For someone who'd been in as many houses as Ava had, she genuinely seemed to love it there. There was that glow about her after doing yoga in the garden and the relaxed state she fell into when they lounged around on the patio at night, listening to music when it was too warm for a fire.

As Sammy sold two of the small bags of kettle corn to a family with four kids in tow, Jeremy noticed Ava pausing in her face painting to look abruptly in his direction. She'd been chatting with Edith and Eleanor, who were next in line, and Jeremy suspected he knew just what they were talking about.

So much for being the one to propose the sale to her.

"Hey, Sammy, yell if you need me, will you? I'll be right back."

As he headed over, Ava seemed to be doing her best to refocus on the child in front of her, a boy of about six or seven years old, but her face was alive with a bewildered excitement.

"How's it going over here?"

Edith and Eleanor, who'd been perusing the available options from a poster on the table, looked up at the same time.

"Jeremy, are you getting your face painted?" Edith asked. "Eleanor's settling for the row of paw prints along her cheek, but I'm thinking the whole-face kitten." She blinked playfully. "Quite apropos, don't you think?"

Jeremy chuckled. "You'll rock a kitten face, Edith. As for me, I'll wait until things settle down." Turning his attention to Ava, he cocked an eyebrow.

"Hey," she said as she added a nose and freckles to the dog on the boy's cheek. "Let me finish this up, and I'll step away a sec."

"Yeah, sure."

Rolo stood from where he'd been sprawled under the table and headed over to greet Jeremy, which was as far as his leash would allow. Jeremy had begun leashing him here whenever it was too hectic to keep close track of him. Likely because Rolo tended to stick right next to his people, the easygoing dog hadn't seemed to notice his loss of freedom.

After showing the boy his puppy in a handheld mirror and sending him on his way, Ava motioned Edith into the open seat. "I'll just be a sec."

"No rush. I can wait, especially now that I have a better sense of all that you two still have to talk about," she said, her expression dramatically sheepish.

Jeremy chuckled as Ava freed Rolo's leash from under the leg of her chair and grabbed her purse.

"You know, earlier, as things were starting to get crazy and I asked where you want to go to dinner tonight?" he said as they headed to the edge of the narrow strip of woods splitting the two properties.

"Yeah…" Ava said with a laugh.

"Well, there was something I wanted to run by you, but from the look on your face a minute ago, I suspect it won't come as a surprise any longer."

"You aren't kidding about that." Rather than looking at him, Ava was digging through her purse.

"Everything okay?"

"Yeah, I just wanted to give you this." Ava pulled out her business card and passed it his way with a touch of dramatic flair.

Jeremy gave a light shake of his head as he studied it. Instead of it being the real-estate-agent card he'd anticipated, it was the one she'd had made up for her yoga instruction. "Nice card." He cocked an eyebrow. "How much for an hour of private instruction? I could get into that."

"I bet you could, and so could I." She planted a soft kiss on his lips. "But this is business. As an aspiring new homeowner of a split residential and commercial property, how would you feel about living next door to a newly rehabbed upscale yoga studio? No big crowds, classes of eight or ten tops."

"The carriage house, you mean? You remember Edith and Eleanor don't own that lot, right?"

"I remember, but it doesn't mean we can't get the owner to sell it. Just because he wouldn't a few years ago doesn't mean he won't now. I'm pretty persuasive when I want to be."

He cocked an eyebrow. "You, persuasive? I had no idea."

"I'm serious, Jeremy. Your buying that house from Edith and Eleanor, it's meant to be. And so is my buying that property next door. The first time I stepped inside that carriage house... I don't know how to explain it, but I had this feeling that it was meant for me. I've been wanting to talk to you about it, but I didn't want to come across like the overzealous new girlfriend. But if you're buying that house..."

"You want to be my neighbor?"

She laughed and brushed her lips against his again. "Says one fellow proprietor to another."

Doing his best to adopt a mock-serious expression, Jeremy dragged his hand over his mouth and along his chin. "Hmm..."

As if sensing Jeremy was toying with his new special person, Rolo barked up at him determinedly.

"All right, all right." Jeremy locked his hands over her arms. "Ava, I can't think of anyone in the world I'd rather share a property line with than you."

A delighted grin lit her face, and her eyes were as radiantly blue as he'd ever seen them. "The garden'll stay as is, of course. We'll make walkways on both sides to get from the street to the studio. And the kids will have a great space to practice yoga when it's too cold or rainy to practice in the yard."

"Think your dad will come up and work on those windows? Because I really want to see you sitting on that floor in easy pose with sprays of color hitting your body."

She locked her arms around him and hugged him as tightly as she could. "I love that you remember that. You're the best man I've ever met, you know that? One hundred percent the best. You have no idea how much I love you."

Love. Until this moment, that complicated four-letter word had only been spoken in the bedroom when things were heated or immediately afterward. "I love you, too, Ava Graham. More than I thought possible."

Tears brimmed in her eyes and she grinned. "Yay."

"Yay," he parroted back with a chuckle as he lifted her off her feet, making Rolo want to get in on the action. He barked and wagged his tail, then rubbed up against them.

Jeremy was still holding her off the ground a few inches when across the parking lot two of the kids yelled his name, waving him over, yelling something about not being able to find the new tub of oil. He cleared his throat, nearly swept away by how completely his world had changed in such a short time.

"It seems that duty calls." He brushed his lips against hers.

Rolo barked as Jeremy started off across the lot. Looking between them, he wagged his tail and whined loudly enough to be comical.

Ava offered the leash his way. "I think he wants you."

Jeremy jogged back to take the leash from Ava and patted Rolo on the head. "Neither of us is going anywhere, bud. That's a promise." To Ava he said, "You know, I think he'd agree with me that before we met you, neither of us thought we were missing a thing."

Ava stepped in to brush her lips over his. "That's okay. Sometimes you just don't know what you're missing until you've found it."

Epilogue

AFTER A LONG, SWELTERING SUMMER SPENT LYING OVER THE air-conditioning vents and munching ice cubes that Jeremy passed his way, the air was finally chilly enough to delight Rolo's nostrils and tongue as it passed across them. The breeze carried the rich, musty scent of the wilted leaves falling from the big shade tree and the withering plants in the garden. As far as Rolo was concerned, the only time better than this was when the snows came. Nothing was ever more fun than when he and Jeremy romped in the snow.

Life was changing in other ways too. Rolo spent his nights in a new part of the house now, the space where the two women had slept, and they had taken up Jeremy's and his old space. The dogs that had been here had gone away, though sometimes they came back with the young people who'd taken over their care.

Rolo didn't mind that they'd left. He had Jeremy, and Jeremy had him. And they both had Ava now too. Rolo sensed she was here to stay. And almost as good as that, Rolo had gotten to keep the kitten. Louie was as much fun as the deepest of snows. The once-sleepy kitten pounced and batted and chased Rolo's heels and tail wherever he went. Louie also liked to climb things, sometimes to the displeasure of Jeremy and Ava. "Down, Louie!" could be heard at least once every day, sometimes much more so. Rolo's two favorite humans didn't seem to understand that cats weren't as quick to pick up commands as dogs were.

Louie's mother, Turtle as they'd begun calling her, was back again, too, but she was too wild to want to play, and Louie was too playful to want to be wild. Rolo doubted Turtle would learn to trust humans the way Louie trusted them. After a long stretch of time in which Turtle hid under the beds until the house fell dark and silent, then stared out the window in the dark, her tail twitching, Jeremy and Ava began to allow her back into the yard. By then, she'd grown accustomed to life indoors enough that she stayed out all night but showed up at the back door each morning, ready to eat and to find a quiet place to sleep away the day.

Rolo wondered if she avoided the abandoned place where she'd had her kittens because of the men who smelled of sweat and wood who showed up most days to work inside it. One day, after the men had gone for the day, Jeremy brought Rolo in there with him. One of Jeremy's pockets was bulging with treats, and the other held a tiny box that fit into the palm of his hand.

Inside the building, many of the old, familiar smells had been replaced by new ones that Rolo wanted to further explore, but Jeremy kept Rolo's attention by teaching him a new game they'd never played before. Jeremy hid the tiny box behind a small cabinet door high on one wall and tied a rope to the door handle. It took Rolo a bit to understand that Jeremy wanted him to tug on the string with his mouth to open the door. Once he did, Jeremy gave him as much praise as he did treats.

Later, when Ava had returned from wherever it was that she went, Jeremy brought Rolo there again, and this time Ava was with them. Rolo bounded with excitement, eager to delight Ava the same way he'd delighted Jeremy.

All the changes inside the building made Ava very happy. She circled it, a long string of praise leaving her lips.

Rolo wagged his tail to smell the treats in Jeremy's pocket but waited for his owner's signal before tugging open the door with the rope. Sure enough, Jeremy rewarded him with a handful of treats.

Salty-smelling tears rolled down Ava's cheeks, and Rolo whined in distress until he realized they were tied to happiness. Taking the box, Jeremy sank to the floor and pulled out something small and round and shiny that didn't smell enticing at all to Rolo but made Ava gasp with joy and leap into Jeremy's arms once he stood again.

Wanting to share in the excitement, Rolo jumped up and planted both paws against them, trying to lick their faces as they pulled him into the embrace too. Rolo didn't understand what they were so happy about, but he was certain by the energy in the air that it was one of the best things to happen yet.

If you love swoony happily ever afters and animals with personality, read on for a taste of *Warm Nights in Magnolia Bay*

Book 1 in the Welcome to Magnolia Bay series from author and animal communicator Babette de Jongh

Available now from Sourcebooks Casablanca

Chapter 1

"I HATE PEOPLE." ABBY CURTIS WADDED UP THE HEM OF HER YELLOW bathrobe and dropped to her knees in the ditch. A pair of green eyes stared at her from the middle of the culvert. "Here, kitty, kitty," she called.

The eyes blinked, but the kitten stayed put. Another stray dumped in front of Aunt Reva's house, and it wasn't going to trust humans again anytime soon. For a nanosecond, Abby thought about running back to the house to get Reva, but something told her the kitten would skedaddle the moment Abby turned her back.

Reva's dog, Georgia, a Jack Russell terrier/cattle dog mix, peered through the other side of the culvert and whined. The kitten spun around to face the dog and hissed.

"Georgia." Abby snapped her fingers. "Stay."

The frightened kitten puffed up and growled at Georgia. Abby didn't have Reva's way with animals. But with the little dog's expert help, she might be able to catch the kitten without bothering her aunt, who was in the house packing for a long-postponed trip.

Georgia whined again and the kitten backed up farther, her full attention on the dog.

Thankful the ditch had been mowed and recently treated for fire ants, Abby eased forward onto her belly in the damp grass. She reached into the culvert, ignoring the cool, muddy water that seeped through her robe and soaked her T-shirt and panties. Shutting out images of snakes and spiders, she scooted closer and stretched out farther.

Just a little bit more…

Georgia seemed to know exactly what to do. She fake-lunged toward the kitten, who spat and hopped backward into Abby's outstretched hand. "Gotcha!" Abby grabbed the kitten's scruff.

The kitten whirled and spun and scratched, but Abby held on, even when it sank needle-like teeth into Abby's hand.

"Shh. Shh." Abby got to her knees and stroked the kitten's dark tortoiseshell fur. A girl, then. Like calicos, tortoiseshell cats were almost always female. "You're okay, little girl. You're all right."

Abby's robe had come open in the front, and the kitten pedaled all four feet with claws extended, scratching gouges in Abby's exposed skin. She held on to the scruff of the kitten's neck, crooning and humming. "You're okay, baby."

Georgia leaped with excitement, begging to see the kitten, who continued to struggle and scratch and bite.

"No, Georgia." Abby wrapped the kitten in the folds of her robe and held it close. It calmed, but Abby could feel its body heaving with every desperate breath. "Not yet. She's too scared."

If this catch didn't stick, Abby wouldn't get another chance. Abby's fingers touched a raw, bloody patch on the kitten's back: road rash from being thrown out of a moving vehicle.

God, Abby hated people. No wonder Aunt Reva had all but turned into a hermit, living out here in the boondocks alongside the kind of people who would do this. But then, Abby had learned that evil lived everywhere—north and south, city and country. She cuddled the kitten close, even while it tried to flay her skin with its desperate claws.

"Nobody's going to hurt you, I promise. Nobody's going to hurt you, not ever again." She could make that promise, because she knew Reva would keep the kitten or find it an even better home. All strays were welcome at Bayside Barn.

Abby herself was proof of that.

Disgusted with all of humanity, Abby struggled up out of the ditch, her mud-caked barn boots slipping on the dew-wet grass. She had just scrambled onto solid ground when a Harley blasted past, turned in at the drive next door, and stopped just past the ditch.

Uncomfortably aware that her bathrobe gaped open indecently and her hair hadn't seen a hairbrush since yesterday afternoon, Abby hid behind the tall hedge between Aunt Reva's place and the abandoned estate next door. Georgia clawed Abby's legs in a "Help, pick me up" gesture.

"Lord, Georgia, I can't hold both of you."

Determined, Georgia scrabbled at Abby's legs. One-handed, Abby scooped up all thirty pounds of the scaredy-cat dog. "It's only a motorcycle."

The sound of garbage trucks in the distance promised an even more terrifying situation if she didn't get the kitten into the house soon. She held Georgia in one hand and clutched the covered-up kitten with the other, jiggling both of them in a hopefully soothing motion. "You're okay. You're both okay."

The loud motorbike idled near the estate's rusted-out mailbox. The rider put both booted feet down on the gravel drive. Tall, broad-shouldered, he wore motorcycle leathers and a black helmet with a tinted visor.

Georgia licked Abby's chin, a plea to hurry back to the house before the garbage trucks ravaging the next block over ushered in the apocalypse.

"Shh. I want to go home, too, but..." If she fled from her hiding place, the motorcycle dude would notice a flash of movement when Abby's yellow robe flapped behind her like a flag. What was this guy doing before 8:00 a.m. parking his motorcycle in a lonely driveway on this dead-end country road?

The rider got off the motorcycle and removed his helmet. His light-brown hair stood on end, then feathered down to cover his jacket collar.

His hair was the only soft thing about him. From his tanned skin to his angular face to his rigid jaw, from his wide shoulders to his bulging thighs to his scuffed black boots, the guy looked hard.

He waded through the tall weeds to the center of the easement and pulled up the moldy For Sale sign that had stood there for years. He tossed the sign into the weed-filled ditch and stalked back to his motorcycle. The beast roared down the potholed driveway to the old abandoned house, scattering gravel.

—◦◦◦—

Quinn Lockhart sped down the long drive, a list of obstacles spinning through his head:

1. Cracked brick facade: possible foundation problems.
2. Swimming pool: green with algae and full of tadpoles, frogs—probably snakes, too.
3. Overgrown acreage: ten acres of out-of-control shrubs choked with vines and weeds.

He'd seen all this on his first and only inspection; he knew what he was getting into. Though he had never attempted to renovate and flip a long-abandoned house before, he knew he possessed the necessary skills to do it successfully. Hell. Even JP—his ex-business-partner and ex-friend he'd known since high school—had made a fricking fortune flipping houses. If all-talk, no-action JP could do it, Quinn could roll up his sleeves and do it ten times better. The sale of this polished-up diamond would provide the seed money he needed to start his own construction business in Magnolia Bay and, maybe even more important, prove his talent to future clients.

When his lowball offer was accepted, he hadn't known whether to whoop or moan. The hidden gem of this dilapidated estate could only go up in value. Located on a remote back road several miles outside Magnolia Bay and an easy hour to New Orleans, the place was a rare find he wouldn't have known about if he hadn't been dating the local real-estate agent who helped him find an apartment here after his divorce. But the next-to-nothing price and a small stash of cash for renovations had consumed every penny of the equity he'd received in the divorce. And he still hadn't quite convinced himself that leaving New Orleans to follow his ex and their son to her hometown was the best decision he'd ever made.

He reminded himself that moving to Magnolia Bay was the only way he could spend enough time with his teenage son. After years of working more than he should and leaving Sean's raising to Melissa, Quinn knew this was his last chance to rebuild the relationship between him and his son. Quinn was hoping they'd bond over the renovation, if he could convince Sean that helping out would be fun. So it wasn't just a business decision; it was a last-ditch effort to be the kind of father Sean deserved.

When Delia Simmons—his real estate agent—showed him this estate, a thrill of excitement and hope had skittered through him. This old place had good bones. Putting it back together again would be the first step toward putting his life back together again.

And when she told him the rumor she'd heard around town that the adjacent acreage between this road and the bay might soon become available as well… Maybe it wasn't a sign from God, exactly, but it sure lit a fire under his butt. With the right timing, he could use the money from the sale of this place to buy the strip of Magnolia Bay waterfront land that ran behind all five estates on this dead-end road.

He could subdivide the bayside marshland along the existing estates' property lines, then sell each parcel to its adjoining
estate. If he had enough money, he could build nice elevated
walkways from each estate to the marsh-edged bay; maybe even
haul in enough sand to make a community beach complete with
boat docks and shaded pavilions.

Maybe he was dreaming too big. But he couldn't stop thinking
that with perfect timing on the sale of the estate and the availabil-
ity of the waterfront land, he could make an easy-peasy fortune
for not too much work. And—dreaming big again—the ongo-
ing maintenance for five private boat docks would give him a
steady stream of income doing seasonal repair work that he could
depend on from here on out.

Quinn parked his bike on the cracked patio around back of the
sprawling bungalow-style house and killed the engine. Expecting
silence, he was assaulted by a loud racket of braying, mooing,
and barking.

"Are you kidding me?" He walked to the hedge separating his
property from the annoying clamor. When he'd toured the property with Delia, it had been as peaceful as a church. She hadn't
warned him it cozied up to Old McDonald's farm.

Or, maybe more accurately, Old Ms. McDonald's farm. He'd
glimpsed the crazy-looking woman hiding in the shrubbery with
her wild mane of honey-brown hair, ratty bathrobe, and cowboy
boots. How the hell would he get top dollar for a house with an
eccentric animal-hoarding neighbor next door? He stalked to the
overgrown hedge between the properties and bellowed at the animals. "Shut. Up."

The noise level escalated exponentially. "Fork it," Quinn said,
forgetting that without Sean here, he could've used the more satisfying expletive.

The multispecies chorus ramped it up. Parrots screeched loud enough to make the donkeys sound like amateurs. Parrots? "What next? Lions, tigers, and bears?"

Fine. He would work inside today. Quinn planned to get the pool house fit for habitation in time for Sean's scheduled visit next weekend—unless the kid canceled again, claiming homework, football practice, school projects, whatever.

All great excuses, but was that all they were? Excuses?

Did his son really hate him so much that he never wanted to see him again?

The thought hit Quinn in the solar plexus with the force of a fist. If it had been a woman treating him that way, he'd have gotten the message and moved on. But this was his *son*. His heart. The kid was fifteen now, so Quinn had only three years of court-mandated visitation to compel Sean to keep coming around.

Three years suddenly seemed like a very short time, given all the inattention and absence Quinn had to make up for. And yet, it had to be possible for him to retrace his steps and rebuild the bridge between him and his son.

Quinn was a carpenter, after all. He knew how to build anything, even a rickety, falling-apart bridge. And he would rebuild this one, no matter what it took. The fight for Sean's time and attention generated its own list of obstacles, but Quinn had ordered the first round of obstacle-climbing tools online:

1. Cool guy furniture.
2. Flat-screen TV.
3. Premium cable and internet.
4. Xbox game system.
5. Paddleboards (secondhand).

Quinn knew of only one way to close the distance between

him and Sean that compounded daily—worse than credit-card debt—because of his ex-wife Melissa's subtle sabotage.

He must become the best weekend dad he could afford to be.

—⁓—

"Got you another one," Abby announced above the sound of the screen door slapping shut behind her. "Saw her run into the culvert when I took the trash up to the road."

Reva came into the kitchen, dressed in Birkenstocks and a tie-dyed hippie dress, her prematurely silver hair secured with an enormous jeweled barrette. "Oh my Lord." She set her suitcase by the sliding glass doors and reached for the kitten. "Just this one? No stragglers?"

"She's the only one I saw, but I'll keep a lookout in case there are others."

Reva held the kitten like a curled-up hedgehog between her palms. Her magic touch calmed the kitten, who immediately started purring. Reva closed her eyes, a slight frown line between her arched brows. "She's the only one." Reva opened her hazel-green eyes, her gaze soft-focused. "But kitten season has begun, and folks'll start dropping off puppies next. Are you sure you can handle this place by yourself all summer?"

No, not at all. Abby had only recently mastered the art of getting out of bed every morning. But Reva deserved this break, this chance to follow her dreams after years of helping everyone but herself. "Yes, of course I can handle it." She glanced at the kitchen clock. "Don't you need to leave soon?"

"No hurry. My friend Heather will pick me up after she drops her kids off at school, so rush hour will be over by the time we get into the city. And the New Orleans airport is small enough that I can get there thirty minutes before departure and still have plenty of time. It's all good."

Abby gave Reva a sideways look, but didn't say anything. Abby knew her aunt was excited about her upcoming adventure, but equally afraid of reaching for a long-postponed dream she wasn't sure she'd be able to achieve. She might be stalling, just a little.

"What can I do to help you and your suitcase get out the door?"

"Would you get a big wire crate from storage and set it up for this baby?"

"Sure."

Cradling the purring kitten, Reva followed Abby through the laundry room to the storage closet. "Litter box is in the bottom cabinet, cubby for her to hide in is on the top shelf."

Abby hefted the folded wire crate. "Where should I put it?"

Reva closed her eyes again, doing her animal communication thing. "Not a big fan of dogs—or other cats, either. Wants to be an only cat." Reva smiled and stroked the kitten's head. "You may have to adjust your expectations, little one, just like everyone else in the world."

Not exactly an answer, but Abby knew Reva would get around to it, and she did. "She'll need a quiet place away from the crowd for the first few days. Let's put the crate on top of the laundry room table."

While Abby set up the crate, Reva gave instructions. "Take her to the vet ASAP; she's wormy and needs antibiotics for this road rash. You can use one of the small travel crates for that. But other than the vet visit, keep her in here until next week, Wednesday at the earliest. Then you can move her crate to my worktable in the den. That'll get her used to all the activity around here. When she's had all her kitten shots, you can let her out into the general population."

Abby put a soothing hand on her aunt's arm. "I'll remember." She knew that Reva secretly thought no one else could manage the farm adequately—with good reason. This place was a writhing octopus of responsibilities. Critters to feed, stalls to clean, and two more weeks of school field trips to host before summer break. Even in summer, there would be random birthday parties and scout groups every now and then. No wonder Reva was having a hard time letting go; hence all the detailed instructions on how to handle the newest addition to the farm's family. "I promise I'll take good care of everything."

Reva gave a yes-but nod and a thanks-for-trying smile. "I'll text you a reminder about the kitten, just in case."

Of course you will. Reva had already printed a novel-length set of instructions on everything from animal-feeding to tour-hosting to house-and-barn maintenance. Smiling at Reva's obvious difficulty in releasing the need to control everything in her universe, Abby filled a water bowl from the mop sink and placed it inside the crate next to the food dish. "All set."

"Call me before you make that decision."

"What decision?" Reva had returned to a previous train of thought that had long since left the station in Abby's mind.

"About when to let the kitten out. She might be more squir-relly than she looks. Let me check in with her and make sure she's ready. Don't want to have her hiding under the couch or escaping into the woods through the dog door." Reva paused with a just-thought-of-something look on her face. "But I'd totally trust you to ask this kitten if she's ready to join the herd. This summer at the farm will be a good opportunity for you to practice your animal communication skills."

Right, well. Abby didn't trust herself, even though Reva had been tutoring her since Abby first started spending summers here as a child. "I'll call first. I'd like to keep the training wheels on a little longer if you don't mind."

Reva laughed. "Training wheels are not necessary. You just think you need them. You're a natural at animal communication."

Abby didn't feel like a natural at much of anything these days. The fact that Reva trusted her to run the farm all summer attested more to Reva's high motivation to get her license to care for injured wildlife than to Abby's competency. Three months of an internship at a wild animal refuge in south Florida would give Reva everything she needed to make that long-deferred dream a reality. Abby was determined to help out, even though the responsibility terrified her. It was the least she could do.

Reva tipped her chin toward the open shelves above the dryer. "Put one of those folded towels on the lid of the litter box so she can sit on top of it."

Abby obeyed, and Georgia started barking from outside. "That's probably your ride, Aunt Reva. I've got this, I promise. You don't have to worry." She held out her hands for the kitten.

Reva transferred the purring kitten gently into Abby's cupped palms. The kitten stopped purring, but settled quickly when Abby snuggled it close. "About time for you to go, right?"

Reva gave a distracted nod. "Don't forget to make the vet appointment today. You want to go ahead and get on their schedule for tomorrow, because they close at noon on Saturdays. But call before you go. I don't know why, but everyone at Mack's office has been really disorganized lately. The last time I went in, they had double-booked, and I had to wait over an hour."

"I will make the appointment today, and I'll call before I go."

"Oh, and don't forget to drop that check off at the water department when you're out tomorrow. Those effers don't give you a moment's grace before cutting off the water." A car horn blasted outside.

"I won't forget." Abby put the kitten in the crate and shooed her aunt out the door. "I'd hug you, but I'm all muddy."

"I know I'm forgetting something." Reva glanced around the room one last time. "Oh well. I'll text you if I remember." She leaned in and kissed Abby's cheek. "Bless you for doing this for me."

"I'm glad we can help each other. Don't worry about a thing." As if Reva wasn't the one doing Abby a big favor by giving her a place to stay when even her own parents refused, for Abby's own good. They were completely right when they pointed out that by the age of thirty-three, she should have gotten her shit together. After all, they'd had good jobs, a solid (if unhappy) marriage, a kid, and a mortgage by that time of their lives.

It wouldn't have helped to argue that up until the moment she didn't, she'd also had a good job (dental office manager), an unhappy relationship (with the philandering dentist), and a kid (the dentist's five-year-old daughter). Okay, so she didn't have a mortgage. Points to mom and dad for being bigger adults at thirty-three. Whoopee. It was a different economy back then.

After Reva left, Abby showered and dressed to meet her first big challenge as the sole custodian of Bayside Barn—ushering in three school buses that pulled through the gates just after 9:00 a.m.

When the deep throb of the buses' motors vibrated the soles of her barn boots, Abby tamped down the familiar flood of anxiety that rose up her gut like heartburn. The feeling of impending disaster arose often, sometimes appearing out of nowhere for no particular reason. Only one of the reasons she'd come to stay at Aunt Reva's for a while. This time, though, she had reason to feel anxious. These three buses held a total of ninety boisterous kindergartners, enough to strike fear into the stoutest of hearts.

Abby hadn't forgotten Reva's warning about the timing of her tenure as acting director of Bayside Barn. Two weeks remained of the school year, and those last two weeks were always the worst; not only did schools schedule more trips then, but the kids would be more excitable and the teachers' tempers would be more frayed.

Abby hurried to get Freddy, the scarlet macaw, from his aviary enclosure. "You can do this," she muttered to herself, remembering the Bayside Barn mission statement that Reva made all the volunteers memorize: *Bayside Barn will save the world, one happy ending at a time, by giving a home to abandoned animals whose unconditional love and understanding will teach people to value all creatures and the planet we share.*

If that wasn't a reason to get over herself and get on with it, nothing was.

Acknowledgments

Age seven was an important year for me; it was when I learned my parents' desires superseded Santa's ability to grant my Christmas wishes. More than anything, I wanted a dog badly enough that my daydreams were filled with thoughts of a canine companion. While my dad was open to the possibility, my mother wasn't. At some point, sensing my wish was doomed, I began asking for a cat instead. While there was no feline under the tree that year, soon afterward my parents adopted a cat, and our home was petless no more.

Having ample experience now with both cats and dogs, it was so fun to write about a cat-loving dog. Rolo's exuberant nature was inspired by my own cat-loving canine, Nala. She's one of those dogs who wholeheartedly loves her family, from the people, other dog, and two cats who are part of it. She sinks to the floor to play with the youngest cat and cuddles with the other. On walks, she recognizes that outdoor cats aren't to be chased like rabbits and squirrels, though few of them have ever been drawn in by her wagging tail for a nose-to-nose greeting.

One of my favorite things about writing this series has been the inspirational and heartwarming stories that dedicated Rescue Me series readers have shared with me about their dogs. Dogs make their way into our hearts in a way few living things can. Thank you, readers, for embracing the series as you have.

As always, I want to thank the amazing team at Sourcebooks Casablanca—including Deb Werksman, my editor—for their guidance, support, and creativity at all stages of the publication process. You are the greatest group to work with, and I know these stories wouldn't be the same without you. The same goes to my agent, Jess Watterson, who at various times has been an invaluable advocate, a shoulder to cry on, and a wealth of creativity and knowledge for brainstorming new story ideas. Much thanks goes to my go-to beta readers Theresa Schmidt and Sandy Thal as well.

Last but never least, I'd like to thank my family and friends for their steadfast support during the completion of this book, which proved to be more of a challenge than most as it coincided with my mom having a severe stroke. As she began her road to recovery, my creative bucket was filled again thanks in part to some very cherished downtime with both my parents and my kids, Emily and Ryan, who are rapidly emerging into adults, to countless long walks with Laura and Susie, and to so many fun times with Scott. While it can be tempting to live in words and stories, it is through connection with all of you that my spirit blossoms.

About the Author

Debbie Burns is the bestselling author of heartwarming women's fiction and love stories featuring both two- and four-legged stars. While her books have earned many awards and commendations, her favorite praise is from readers who've been inspired to adopt a pet in need from their local shelter.

Debbie lives in St. Louis with her family, two thoroughly spoiled rescue dogs, and a ridiculously grumpy Maine coon cat who everyone loves anyway. Her hobbies include hiking in the Missouri woods, attempting to grow the perfect tomato, and day-dreaming, which of course always leads to new story ideas.

You can also find her on Instagram (@_debbieburns) and on Facebook and Pinterest (@authordebbieburns).

Also by Debbie Burns

Summer by the River

RESCUE ME
A New Leash on Love
Sit, Stay, Love
My Forever Home
Love at First Bark
Head Over Paws